Colter, sometimes you can be a first-rate ass, Josh thought to himself.

"Aw, hell, Alex..." His guard slipped. He dragged out a chair and straddled it, keeping the back like a barricade between them. "I didn't mean..." Josh slapped his hat down on the table and raked one hand through his hair. "I'm sorry. Sorry this happened. I feel like—"

"Like saying I told you so?" She made a small sound in the back of her throat that could have been a chuckle.

"Never," he lied, having thought that exactly. She looked so pitiful. It was all he could do not to reach out and pull her into his arms, to hold her until the fear went away.

Don't even think about it. She's trouble. She's the one woman in the world you can't have.

Yeah, he knew that. So how come she was the one woman he wanted so much?

Dear Reader,

Josh Colter is a rancher on a trail of revenge. Alexandria Gibson is on a journey to find her brother. Both are looking for the same man in Susan Amarillas's new Western, *Wyoming Renegade*. Susan's last two books have won her 5★ ratings from *Affaire de Coeur* and many new fans who've been eagerly awaiting this tale of two people who must choose between family, and love and honor. Don't miss this exciting story.

Catherine Archer's *Lady Thorn* is the story of a Victorian heiress who falls in love with a sea captain who promises her protection in exchange for her help in locating his son. We hope you'll find this gifted author's story—in the words of the reviewer from *Affaire de Coeur*— "impossible to put down."

USA Today bestselling and multiaward-winning author Ruth Langan's new series, THE JEWELS OF TEXAS, moves into full swing with this month's *Jade,* the story of a small-town preacher who surrenders his soul to the town madam. And in Kate Kingsley's new Western, *The Scout's Bride,* a determined young widow decides to accept the help of a rugged army scout who has made himself her unwanted protector.

Whatever your taste in reading, we hope you'll keep an eye out for all four titles wherever Harlequin Historicals are sold.

Sincerely,

Tracy Farrell
Senior Editor

Please address questions and book requests to:
Harlequin Reader Service
U.S.: 3010 Walden Ave., P.O. Box 1325, Buffalo, NY 14269
Canadian: P.O. Box 609, Fort Erie, Ont. L2A 5X3

SUSAN AMARILLAS
WYOMING RENEGADE

Harlequin Books

TORONTO • NEW YORK • LONDON
AMSTERDAM • PARIS • SYDNEY • HAMBURG
STOCKHOLM • ATHENS • TOKYO • MILAN
MADRID • WARSAW • BUDAPEST • AUCKLAND

ISBN 0-373-28951-0

WYOMING RENEGADE

Copyright © 1997 by Karen L. Amarillas

This edition published by arrangement with Harlequin Books S.A.

® and TM are trademarks of the publisher. Trademarks indicated with ® are registered in the United States Patent and Trademark Office, the Canadian Trade Marks Office and in other countries.

Printed in U.S.A.

Books by Susan Amarillas

Harlequin Historicals

Snow Angel #165
Silver and Steel #233
Scanlin's Law #283
Wyoming Renegade #351

SUSAN AMARILLAS

was born and raised in Maryland and moved to California when she married. She quickly discovered her love of the high desert country—she says it was as if she were "coming home." When she's not writing, she and her husband love to travel the back roads of the West, visiting ghost towns and little museums, and always coming home with an armload of books.

To my "big sister" Madeline Baker
There from the first, there for me still

Many thanks

Prologue

Zeke Larson was going to die. He knew it, and so did his captor.

Moonlight, white and cold, flooded the valley, casting the red rocks in black shadows. The woeful howl of a coyote and Zeke's harsh breathing were the only sounds.

He was strung up to a cottonwood tree like a damn four-pronged buck, his arms stretched painfully over his head, hemp rope cutting into his wrists. Every time he moved, the trickle of blood oozing from his side turned into a crimson rivulet.

Close by, stood his captor. A motherless gut-eating 'breed by the dark look of him. Zeke hated half-breeds and Indians and just about anyone else who wasn't what he thought of as "his kind."

"I'm telling you I ain't the one you're lookin' for," Zeke argued, not for the first time.

The man didn't answer, just pushed the cold, hard barrel of his .45 deep into Zeke's wound.

Zeke groaned against the searing pain. "Damn you, 'breed!" he spat.

"Absarokee," his captor corrected flatly. "Are you ready to tell me?" His voice was soft, almost serene, as though he hadn't been torturing Zeke for the past several hours.

Zeke knew he could end it, knew what the bastard wanted. Damn 'breed had said so plain enough at the beginning. He wanted the names of the other two who'd gunned down a group of Indians a couple of weeks back.

Zeke had denied everything, not that it had done him any good. Zeke liked to drink and he liked to brag. He had made the mistake of doing both at the local saloon. He figured that was how this coldhearted scum had gotten on his trail.

Now Zeke was trying frantically to come up with a way out of this—an excuse, an alibi, a deal. So far nothing had worked.

A sage-scented breeze rustled the leaves of the tree, but it didn't do a thing to ease the sweat that beaded on his forehead. He swiped his face on his sleeve. He was determined to outlast this bastard. No Indian was gonna get the best of him!

"Are you ready to tell me?" his captor repeated.

"I don't...know nothin'." Zeke ground out the words between clenched teeth. That bit of defiance earned him another slap in his throbbing wound.

"Son of a bitch!"

"Tell me."

Zeke wanted to stay alive, at least he did if he could get free of this. He knew the other man meant business, knew that once he told the bastard what he wanted to know, there was nothing and no one to stop his captor from killing him.

Another sudden slap against his wound and he wasn't so defiant anymore. Pain pulsed and trembled through him, searing his mind and body in a blinding red haze.

The scent of his own blood filtered into his nostrils, his sweat-soaked shirt clung to his chest.

It wasn't any kind of loyalty that kept Zeke from spilling his guts; it was spite, and the knowledge that this information was the only thing keeping him alive. Besides, there wasn't much to tell.

They'd split up right after their little "party." Cordell had said he was headed south. Hell, that could be anyplace from Colorado to Texas. And there was the kid, Gibson. They'd picked him up in Gunlock. He had been working in a bank, of all things, and when they'd said they were headed out to look for ranch work, he'd come along, eager for excitement. Well, the tenderfoot had gotten his share, and then some.

A few days out of town, they'd spotted a bunch of Indians camped by Lazy Horse Creek. Zeke didn't know one tribe from another, didn't care. Everyone knew them redskins were causin' trouble, slipping off the reservation, stealing horses and cattle. There were way too few soldiers to keep them in line, teach 'em just who this land belonged to.

It hadn't taken much talking, or much drinking, for the three of them to decide to ride on in and put the fear of God into them heathens. Why, it was a white man's patriotic duty. Hell, they were only doing what the army did. They were probably saving some rancher's life, they'd told themselves. It had seemed a mighty fine idea then.

Zeke lifted his head slightly to see that his captor had stepped directly in front of him. The breeze stirred the 'breed's shoulder-length hair and the moonlight caught on the beading of his buckskin shirt. Without a word, he put his gun barrel next to Zeke's thigh and fired, the bullet ripping through flesh and muscle.

"You bastard!" Zeke snarled, then clamped his jaw down hard to hold back the scream. He yanked at the restraining ropes, wrapped skin-tearing tight around his wrists.

His captor only smiled, a slow menacing smile. "Tell me."

Zeke remained silent. He tried to think of something, anything, but the constant pain. But no matter what he tried, the only thoughts that came were ones of them Indians. One in particular. He'd never seen such hatred in a pair of eyes, not that he'd cared. She was just some whoring squaw. He'd held her down and forced her legs apart. He'd rode her hard, ignoring her screams.

When he let her up, she'd charged at him, claws bared. He'd had to kill her—self-defense and all.

The sharp metallic click of a gun's hammer being pulled back brought reality clearly and painfully into focus an instant before the gun fired, the bullet ripping through his other leg.

This time Zeke did scream. Blood soaked his clothes and his skin. Pain was a living force inside him. There were no other senses, no other emotions, only the pain and the knowledge that this was just the beginning. A man could last like this for days if he let himself.

"Anything! I'll tell you!" he screamed.

"I'm waiting," the man said quietly.

"Cut me down, dammit. I'll tell you."

There was a moment of hopeful silence, then the sound of the gun hammer being cocked again.

Zeke sagged in defeat. He told the man everything, the names, the smallest detail of descriptions, every little bit he knew about destinations. When he was done, he said, "Kill me. Just kill me and be done with it."

"You mean quick?" his captor said, sliding his gun back into his holster. "Or do you mean slow, the way you killed my sister, you bastard?"

"Sister?" Zeke's head came up and he was eye to eye with his tormentor. Moonlight illuminated the man's face and eyes, hard eyes, black as Satan's.

He knew then his fate was sealed. Reason was lost. "Well, just so as you know, the squaw was good. Real good. The way she clawed and bucked under me—"

The scream of rage that came from the half-breed's throat bore no resemblance to human sound. It pierced the night like a war lance tearing through human flesh.

"I'll see all of you in hell," the half-breed snarled, and plunged the blade of his knife into Zeke's throat.

Chapter One

Alexandria Gibson stood in the elegant parlor of her Nob Hill home. She pushed back the curtain covering the double French doors, and the delicate white lace brushed butterfly soft against her hand. The night was ink black, the barest beginnings of fog drifted up from the bay.

"I'll be leaving in the morning." She didn't look at her father, who was seated five feet away on one of two matching love seats. She could practically feel his icy gaze boring into her. "Eddie will be here bright and early."

"What do you mean, Eddie?" her father demanded, his baritone voice seeming to fill the high-ceilinged room.

Alexandria looked at him along the line of her shoulder. Even at fifty her father was a fine figure of a man—tall and lean, his brown hair graying, but thick enough to make a younger man envious.

"New evening clothes?" she asked, ignoring his question. She didn't want to get into another long discussion. They'd been going around and around about her trip since Monday, when she'd announced her plan.

"Yes," he muttered, momentarily distracted. "I'm playing poker with Strickland later at the club." Anger sparked quicksilver bright in his blue eyes. "Never mind my clothes."

She sighed inwardly. Well, if he was intent on being stubborn, she could be equally stubborn. She was her father's daughter, after all, and that gave her more than a fair amount of hardheadedness.

"What's Eddie got to do with this?" her father grumbled.

"He's going along."

"As what, your chaperon? Ha! If I can't keep tight reins on you, then Eddie sure as hell can't."

"Don't be difficult."

"Me? I'm not the one who's being difficult." He shook his finger at her in a way that made her feel like a child, which she wasn't, not at twenty-five. That short temper of hers was moving up the scale faster than mercury on a July day.

"I need help, with the horses and such." She gritted her teeth to keep her voice calm.

Her father scowled. "This is going to give the gossips enough grist to fuel the rumor mill for months, maybe years."

"Yes, I'm sure it will. Just as I'm sure they will blithely overlook the fact that Eddie is only eighteen, my first cousin, and has enough freckles sprinkled across his face to make him look tan even in winter."

"And you don't care a whit what's said, do you?"

"No, not a whit." She'd been her own person since, well, all her life and she saw no reason to change now. "You, of all people," she told him, in what she hoped was a reassuring tone, "shouldn't worry about me."

"But I do. More than I want to, dammit." He surged to his feet and paced—marched actually—across the room, until he practically slammed into the upright grand.

He faced her, one hand braced on the top edge of the gleaming mahogany, the other curled into a fist at his side.

"It's no use, Alexandria." He had a granite-hard expression that said he wasn't going to be put off. She braced for the fight.

He continued. "Letting you go off to the Pennsylvania Academy of Fine Arts was one thing. But how the hell you ever talked me into letting you go to Paris to study that damn painting business..." He shook his head again. "But no more. Do you hear me? No more. You should be settled, married. I *want* grandchildren."

Muscles down her back tensed in reflexive response. *Not again!* If she had a dollar for every time they'd had this discussion in the past six years, she could finance her own trip back to Europe instead of having to rely on his financing.

With resignation, she steeled herself to try to explain one more time. "Papa, you are too conventional, and I'm too stubborn to be someone's submissive little wife."

It wasn't the marriage part she objected to, it was the submissive part she couldn't get past.

She dropped down onto the side chair, the pale green silk upholstery smooth and cool against her skin. A shiver prickled over her shoulders.

Her father's voice carried across the room to her.

"How do you know you couldn't be someone's wife, missy?" She heard him moving closer. "Good Lord, Alex, men have been turning up on the doorstep since you were sixteen. You've never given any of them half a chance."

Out of the corner of her eye, she saw him headed for the small walnut table on the far wall that held an array of crystal decanters with an assortment of whiskey and bourbon.

He tossed the stopper down with a clunk and snatched up a glass. He sloshed the Irish whiskey into the cut crystal. It spilled over the top and over his hand and he quickly held it away from him, letting it drip onto the carpet.

He sipped the drink down a quarter inch.

"If your mother had lived...*she* would have made certain you were settled." He took a hefty swallow.

Alex faced him, the love seat like a defensive wall between them. "Please, *please* don't worry about me. The world doesn't begin and end with marriage. I do fine on my own."

"For now, but I'm thinking of later. What about when you're forty or fifty or...?" He took another drink. "I think you're too picky, Alexandria. What about Ned?"

"Your precious Ned is only interested in himself and his blossoming career with your bank."

He regarded her through narrowed eyes. " 'My precious Ned,' as you call him, is a man with ambition. It's usually considered an attribute."

"Yes, I know about ambition, only in women it's considered a failing. I have no interest in marrying just to be Ned Hager's stepping-stone to success. He's going to have to earn that by himself. I have my own plans."

"To be an artist." His tone was skeptical. "Do you know how many successful artists there are in the world? Damn few, and even fewer women artists."

"Then there's room for one. I'm leaving tomorrow for Wyoming. My plans are made."

He glared at her.

She glared back. Finally, wanting to end this, she said, "I'm going to see Davy while I'm there. Don't you think he's been exiled long enough?"

"Your brother is not exiled. You make it sound like he's in Siberia. I simply sent him to our bank in Gunlock."

She knelt on the love seat, her fingers curving over the smooth wood trim. "Papa, please. He's learned his lesson, I'm sure."

"Well, it'll be a miracle if he has. As I recall, his habits included public drunkenness, gambling, staying out all hours...and let's not forget the women. David's only nineteen. At the rate he was going, I doubted he'd live to see twenty."

There was a hitch in his voice, a crack that expressed his feeling more accurately than his words. It was that little crack that quelled her temper. "I know," she told him softly, sincerely.

Tears threatened, and she blinked them back. "I know you love Davy. Just as I know you love me."

His chin dropped to his chest for a moment, and she wondered what he was thinking?

Drink in hand, he moved to the other love seat. They faced each other across the small expanse. Elbows on knees, he said simply, "David doesn't make loving him easy."

With a feeling of déjà vu, she leaned forward, touching his sleeve with her hand. "I know he's been difficult, but he means well."

She missed her brother terribly and loved him unconditionally. "You miss him, too, don't you?"

"I miss him."

His voice was husky, and far away—as far away as Wyoming. "It's time," she told him firmly, confidently, maybe a little more confidently than she felt. She'd failed to stand by Davy once, but never again.

"Yes," he said, and sighed. "Tell him to come home."

She let out the breath she'd been holding. "I'll make it my personal mission to take care of him until he gets settled, until I leave for Paris."

"Thanks," he said absently, his gaze still focused on the dancing flames.

"Now that that's settled, I'd better get to bed. I've got an early start in the morning."

She hadn't taken three steps when—

"Hold on there, missy. Thought you had me, didn't you?"

I was so close to making a clean getaway, she thought.

"Assumed all this talk about your brother would make me forget about that blasted contest and about your trip, didn't you?"

"I didn't think you'd forgotten. But I'm done talking."

"By that I guess you mean you can run off to Wyoming and *I'm* supposed to give my stamp of approval? *I'm* supposed to pay the bills for this fiasco."

She needed up-front money, his money. She'd used the last of her savings to pay the fee. The entry form had been mailed and accepted. Everything was in place, but it all hinged on her ability to make this trip.

"Two months," she coaxed.

"You don't need a career."

"I'm an artist."

"It was supposed to be a hobby," he retaliated from his love seat.

"It's an occupation."

"It's futile."

"It's exciting and challenging." This time she took an aggressive step in his direction. "This is not some whim, Papa. I've been working hard in Paris. It took me a long time to find my place, my style. I've already shown two paintings in an exhibit and—"

"Two paintings! In all these years!" He raked his hand through his hair. "You call that success?"

"I call that a start. It's more than I've been able to do here. I have to go back. You've said you won't support me any longer, and I accept that. This contest money will let me make it on my own. I have to go. *I have to.*"

She wanted him to understand how she felt, the urgency that drove her, the excitement that filled her every time she made a painting, captured a feeling, a bit of herself on canvas. "Two months is all I'm asking."

Uncertainty flashed in his eyes, and she gave him what she hoped was her best, most imploring smile, the one that had been letting her get her own way most of her life.

"I'll be back by August."

He shook his head, but he was vacillating, she could tell. "But all alone..."

"I won't be alone. I'll have Eddie."

That head shake was getting more adamant.

"All I'm asking is for you to trust me, to understand. I'm not asking you to do it *for* me, just don't stop me." Very softly, she entreated, "Please."

Heart pounding, she waited for the decision that would determine her future. She wondered for the first time what she would do if he refused. Would she give up painting? Would she try to find the money somewhere else? There was nowhere else to turn and there was a deadline rushing at her. Who knew when she'd have another opportunity like this?

Panic prickled along nerves already tight with anticipation. "Papa, I have to—"

"All right."

"What?" she repeated, not certain she'd heard the words she'd waited for. "What did you say?"

"I said all right. On one—"

"Thank you!" She hurled herself in his direction, threw her arms around his neck and kissed his beard-roughened cheek. "You won't regret this!"

"One condition." He tugged at her arms and set her away from him. His expression was executioner serious.

"Condition?" Dread coiled and swirled in her stomach like acid. She stepped back, her heel catching on her hem and making her more off balance than she already was.

"I'll let you go on this trip. I'll fund your expedition on the condition that when you *don't* win this contest, you will give up this art business and allow me to find a suitable husband for you."

"You can't be serious?"

"I'm very serious."

"You'd force me into a marriage?"

"Not force. Encourage."

"But I . . ."

"What's the matter, Alexandria, aren't you willing to play the long shot? I'm giving you what you wanted. Have you changed your mind? Aren't so sure you'll win?"

She pulled herself up to her full height. "It's a deal."

"I want your word, Alexandria," Jack Gibson said. "You will honor this arrangement. No arguments later. This contract is not renegotiable."

Knowing her whole future was riding on the outcome, she said, "I agree."

Chapter Two

Gunlock was a two-day journey northwest of Cheyenne. It was tucked into the notch of three hills that protected it from the wind, while a cluster of cottonwood trees guarded it from the sun. To the north, a fast-moving stream insured the town of water, an all-important fact in a place as barren as Wyoming.

There was no train in Gunlock. The Union Pacific, on its push to Promontory Point, had taken a more direct route. That fact alone should have assured the town's demise. It didn't. Ragtag Gunlock was smack dab in the middle of the Montana Trail, the route for the thousands of cattle being pushed north from Texas.

Saloons were plentiful in town, all at the eastern end of the one and only street. Covered in peeling paint and raw wood, they were a hodgepodge, everything from false fronts to two stories with balconies. A pine-plank sidewalk ran the length of the street, connecting the rowdier side of town with the respectable west end.

So, while the good folks lived and shopped a few hundred yards closer to the setting sun, cowboys, tired and thirsty and looking to blow off a little steam, crowded into the saloons.

It was late afternoon when Josh Colter reined up in front of McGuire's Saloon and dismounted, tethering his chestnut gelding to the gnarled hitching rail.

He stepped up onto the plank sidewalk, his spurs jingling as he moved. He was tired and dirty and mean, and all he wanted was to get this over with.

A woman walked past. He nodded but didn't speak. He was in no mood for polite civilities. In the nearly eight weeks since the rape and murder of his sister, Josh had tracked and killed two men. It didn't sit well with him, killing a man, but he'd done it and would do it again—perhaps today.

The thought of vengeance made his fingers flex, his palm brushed against the smooth wood handle of his Smith & Wesson. He tested its fit in the worn holster, reassured by the easy way the metal slid against the leather.

With grim determination, he dragged in a steadying breath and pushed through the double doors of the saloon. The doors banged closed behind him.

He blinked twice against the sudden darkness and stepped away from the doorway. Sunlight at his back made him an easy target, should anyone take a notion. Not that he expected trouble waiting for him. Hell no, Josh was the one bringing trouble—for one man, at least.

Skirting around an unoccupied table, he headed for the bar. His boots made scuff marks on a floor that hadn't seen the business end of a mop in years. The sharp scent of cigarette smoke and unwashed bodies burned his nostrils. He'd never hated saloons before, but in the past few weeks he'd had enough of them to last him a lifetime.

They all seemed to look the same, as though there were a regulation somewhere that predetermined the arrangement. The room was long and narrow, with the bar of unrecognizable wood taking up most of one wall. There was a poor excuse for a painting of a naked woman hanging on the wall behind the bar; a couple of bullet holes marked the spots where her nipples used to be.

Six or seven mismatched tables, round and square, were scattered around the room, paired up with an assortment of chairs. A dozen cowboys, whom he figured had trailed up the cattle herd he'd passed outside of town, had taken up residence. Some were drinking. Some were playing cards. Two near the back seemed to be arguing about who was going to go first with the one and only woman in the place. Her red-lipped smile was widening in direct proportion to the bidding.

"Whiskey," he told the slick-haired bartender as he leaned one elbow on the scarred surface.

He angled around to survey the room. His heart drummed furiously in his chest, and his fingers were funeral cold. Inside, he was determined yet scared. But he didn't let on. Instead, he let his gaze wander across the faces of the men present, pausing, searching, looking for the last of the men he sought.

They all looked young, too damned young, he thought, feeling suddenly old at thirty. He hesitated once on a tight-lipped cowboy playing cards, but then the man shoved his hat back, revealing dark brown hair. Josh let go the breath he only now realized he'd been holding. Larson had said Gibson was blond, definitely blond.

"Damn," he muttered to himself.

Well, did you expect him to be sitting here? A man can hope, can't he?

"Two bits," a man's voice said.

Josh actually flinched and jumped a little at the sound of the bartender's voice right behind him. He wheeled around, leaning more fully on the bar, holding the empty glass while the bartender poured.

It looked like whiskey but smelled like horse piss, and Josh wasn't so sure he wanted to drink it.

So he toyed with the glass, revolving it between thumb and forefinger, absently making a game out of not spilling it. A couple of men came in and took the table closest to him. He eyed them suspiciously and discounted them just as quickly.

When no one was paying much attention, he asked the bartender, "You seen Gibson around lately?" He made it sound like they were old friends, though Larson and his pal, Cordell, never got around to first names.

"Davy Gibson?" the barman replied. He was cleaning a glass with a grimy-looking towel that needed to spend a couple of hours in the company of hot water and soap.

"Yeah, Davy Gibson," Josh repeated, taking in the new information. "He around?"

The barman seemed more interested in the glass he was wiping than in conversation.

Behind Josh, a round of laughter came from a group of cowboys, and he turned with heart-slamming speed, his hand instinctively resting on his gun. It took a couple of seconds to realize the man was busy telling tall tales to his pals and totally unaware of Josh. He willed his heart rate down to something less than a stampede pace and focused on the bartender, who still hadn't answered his damn question.

"About Gibson?" he prompted, struggling to keep his anger in check. Lord, he was tired and he wanted to end this—today, if the spirits allowed. He hoped like hell they did.

The barman held up another glass toward the window as though studying it. He talked as he worked. "I know Gibson. What of it?"

"Like I said, he around?"

"How the hell should I know?" He called to a cowboy nearby. "Hey, any you boys seen Gibson from over at the bank?"

"Heard he left town," one called back.

Like air to a flame, Josh's temper flared. "Damn." He fixed the bartender with an icy stare. "You *sure* he's gone?" He couldn't keep the flinty edge out of his voice. At least it was sharp enough that the bartender stopped what he was doing.

"Well—" he put the glass down on the shelf behind the bar "—that's what the man said, didn't he, or are you deaf?" He braced both hands on the wood, arms straight, revealing a beer stain on the sleeve of his dingy white shirt.

"But you don't know for certain," Josh pressed. He didn't want maybes, he wanted answers. He wanted the bastard Gibson squared off in front of him in what would be a fair fight—fair as it could be, considering that Josh knew he was faster with a gun than most men.

"Hell, how many times I gotta say it, mister?" The bartender spoke as though he were talking to a child. "I ain't seen him around." He made a sweeping gesture. "So...I figure...he must be gone. That clear enough for you?"

Meanness was fast overtaking patience. This guy's smug attitude was grating on Josh's nerves and he was beginning to warm to the idea of rearranging the man's face.

"Well, where the hell did he go?"

"Hey, what am I, his mother? He sure as hell didn't come in here and say goodbye, if that's what you mean." He gave a cocky laugh and started to turn away.

One second Josh was thinking about his sister and the men he'd killed, the man he *would* kill, and the next second he was reaching over the bar and dragging this grimy weasel toward him.

All sound in the room ceased. Wisely no one moved.

In a voice, deadly cold and hard as a Montana winter, Josh said, "Now, you little runt, you tell me where the hell he went or so help me—" he pulled the squirming barman up a little closer "—I'll kill you right where you stand."

The man's blue eyes bulged in his head. He opened his mouth to speak but the only sound was a gurgling, like a man dangling at the end of a rope.

Josh loosened his grip a fraction, then shook the barman hard enough to make him groan. The man's beady eyes darted around the room, searching for escape or for help. Neither was an option.

"I…" He pried at Josh's hands, his dirty fingernails digging into the flesh. Josh hardly noticed. Muscles along his shoulders tensed. Tendons in his back pulled wire tight. His breath came in hard, shallow gulps of smoke-filled air.

"I…" The barman wheezed again. "I don't…know nothin'." He swallowed hard, his Adam's apple bobbing up and down in his throat. "Check at the bank."

"What bank, dammit?" His fingers were still twisted in the man's shirtfront. There was the distinct sound of cotton ripping.

"City Bank o' course." The bartender's hands pried at Josh's fingers again. "Gibson worked at the damned bank!"

Josh had what he wanted. He released the man so suddenly, he half fell, half staggered back. Wide-eyed, the barman sidestepped away and pushed his crumpled shirt back into place.

"Say, mister, you ain't got no call to do that," the barman muttered, sounding a lot less smug than a few minutes ago. He raked his hands through his thinning brown hair. "Davy owe you money or somethin'?"

"Or something." Josh tossed back the whiskey and winced. He threw a ten-dollar gold piece on the bar. "For your trouble."

No one said a word as he strode for the doors.

Outside, standing on the boardwalk, he took a deep breath, then another.

He glanced over his shoulder at the saloon. *Damn, Colter, you're losing it.*

Yeah, well, killing did funny things to a man. Lack of sleep didn't help, either. He hadn't slept in weeks, or at least it felt that way. Every time he closed his eyes, all he saw was his sister's bloodied, lifeless body. Even now, if he—

Stop it! You're doing no one any good like this!

Now there was a truth if he ever heard one.

Okay, so the bastard is gone. You'll find him.

Hand clutching the rough wood of the porch post, he stood there, letting the sun warm his body through the blue wool of his shirt.

All things in time, he told himself.

Slowly his muscles uncoiled, first in his shoulders, then his back. His heart, like his body, responded to the gentle warmth of the sun. People moved past him. Across the street, two children chased a calico cat. The sights and sounds of everyday life filled in and they, too, calmed him.

He swung down off the walk and went to where his horse was tied. Tossing up the stirrup, he made as though he were checking the cinch while he rested his head against the saddle; the sun-heated leather felt good against his forehead and cheek.

Like a gallows-bound man given a last-minute reprieve, the reality of the situation filtered into his mind. There would be no killing today. How long he stood there, he wasn't exactly sure. When he lifted his head, he knew he was in control again. He waited another minute, unconsciously rubbing his hand on his horse's neck as he did, letting the trembling in his fingers cease, taking solace from the touch of another living thing. Death and grief made a man seek out the living, if only to confirm that he, too, was alive.

Lifting his head, he glanced at the horse, which had craned his neck around to stare at his master. Josh managed a ghost of a smile. "Yes, I know. Don't look so worried."

The horse shook his head, whether in disgust or agreement, Josh wasn't sure.

"Well, boy," he mumbled, dropping the stirrup back in place, hearing the leather creak, "let's go ask a few more questions." He glanced around and spotted the bank at the end of town, and then his gaze settled on the hotel. "You know, Sundown, I think I'll get a room for the night. I haven't slept in a bed since I left the ranch."

A buckboard rattled past, a man and a young boy perched on the seat, the boy loudly asking if he could have a licorice whip at the mercantile.

It all seemed so normal, so easy, so safe. Josh smiled: for the first time in days, weeks, probably, he smiled. It felt good, human. He dragged in a deep breath and swung up onto the saddle. A sage-scented breeze ruffled his hair along his collar and he adjusted his hat more comfortably on his head.

He glanced over at the hotel again as though it were a sanctuary, and he was suddenly anxious for a refuge. Business first, though, he told himself as he reined over and headed for the bank.

An hour later, he'd learned that Gibson had quit a couple of months ago and that he had been seen around town with two men fitting the descriptions of Larson and Cordell.

Okay, so, at least he was on the right track, though the image of a mousy bank clerk as a murderer didn't fit.

Josh had asked questions at the mercantile, and at the livery when he'd stabled his horse for the night. Everywhere, he'd gotten the same answer: Gibson was gone and no one knew where. North, someone had said, and though "north" was a helluva big place, it was a start.

Josh would find him if it took a week, a month, a year. The man couldn't hide forever, and since he didn't know Josh was on his trail, odds were he wouldn't cover his tracks. It was only a matter of time, Josh promised himself. Only time. He had that.

Feeling reassured, or at least resolute, he headed for the hotel. That bed and bath were sounding better and better.

The hotel was called the Palace, like a hundred others scattered from San Francisco to St. Jo. This particular palace was two stories of white clapboard with forest green shutters. The glass panes in the double front doors were clean enough to reflect the red-orange glow of the setting sun.

Saddlebags slung over his shoulder, and carrying his rifles and shotgun, Josh walked into the lobby. It was small and clean—a good sign. The walls were covered in flowered wallpaper, red roses and green vines. Not his taste, but then, it wasn't his hotel.

A staircase led to the second floor. Off to the right he noticed a small dining room, the tables empty but set for dinner—calico tablecloths and white china. The definite scent of fresh bread baking made his mouth water. Yep, dinner in the dining room tonight. Something that hadn't been cooked over a camp fire, something he didn't have to cook himself.

He put the arsenal he was packing on the dark pine counter and, seeing no one around, he rang the small brass bell next to the desk register.

A man appeared through the door off to the left. "Afternoon," he said, his thin face wreathed in a crooked-toothed smile.

He was of medium height and medium build with medium brown hair—about as ordinary as you can get, Josh thought. His white shirt was open at the collar, and his dark blue pants were shiny from one too many pressings.

"Room, please," Josh said with confidence, his half-breed status never an issue with him. Since he was dressed in range clothes—not Indian garb—most people never inquired, and he never clarified.

The clerk flopped the book open, spun it around, then pointed to a place halfway down the page for Josh to sign. "Will you be staying long?"

"One night, I think." Josh spotted the inkwell, but there was no pen in sight. "Pen?"

"What? Oh..." Startled, the clerk glanced around the counter, lifting the register as if he thought the errant pen was hiding there. "Where the devil..." He checked the small shelf behind him and, not finding it, turned away. "If you'll just wait a minute." He was already heading back through the door.

Josh sighed. All he wanted was to get settled. He wanted to stretch out on something more forgiving than hard earth sprinkled with rocks that always ended up directly under his aching spine.

He thrummed his fingers impatiently on the gleaming counter surface and was about to go hunt up the man when a banging on the front doors made him turn.

"What the—"

One door crashed open. The glass rattled dangerously. The hinges creaked from swinging a bit too far.

A woman half stumbled, half walked through the opening. She was loaded down with two oversize carpetbags and a wicker traveling case. She was so busy trying to keep her hold on the bags she obviously didn't notice him, but he noticed her all right.

In a heartbeat he took her in. She was slender, a little too slender for his taste, but tall. He was partial to tall women. She was wearing green, the color of willow leaves. Her skirt was full, her jacket short, with a pale yellow shirtwaist underneath. She had light hair, sort of honey colored. It looked soft where it peeked out around the battered old Stetson she was wearing, though only God knows why she'd chosen to cover up such a glorious attribute.

She had her head turned so he couldn't really see her face, but he did see one carpetbag take a nosedive for the floor about the same time she said, "Oh, no!"

A couple of long strides and he was there. "Let me help you," he said, snatching up one bag and reaching to take the others from her, his hand naturally covering hers as he did so.

She angled her head up to look at him, and he found himself staring into the bluest eyes he'd ever seen, dark and luminous like a high mountain lake.

Her cheeks were flushed, her lips breathlessly parted, and her eyes, those wondrous blue eyes, were wide with excitement. She looked tousled and wild, like a woman fresh from a very lucky man's bed, he thought, his own lust stirring.

You've been too long without a woman, Colter.

For the span of two heartbeats, neither of them moved, then, as though they'd both been hit with the same bucket of ice water, they abruptly straightened, nearly banging heads in the process. Each gave an awkward chuckle.

She slipped her hand free of his, her skin velvet smooth against his palm. He kept hold of the carpetbag, though he'd rather have held on to the lady.

He did the gentlemanly thing and relieved her of the other luggage. His father had taught him good manners at an early age.

Alex turned a wary gaze on this stranger who had rushed to her rescue. Tall and dark, at first glance he looked every inch the outlaw, from his overly long hair to his dust-covered clothes, to the way a pistol hung low on his hip.

His face was all chiseled angles and smooth curves, high cheekbones and a straight nose. But it was his eyes that held her attention, midnight black with a restlessness that intrigued and frightened at the same time.

Maybe it was the artist in her that was making her stare—maybe it was simply the woman.

She sucked in a breath, straightened and cleared her throat. Somebody better say something, she figured, so she muttered her thanks, at least she thought that was what she said, she wasn't altogether sure.

She managed a smile that fell a little short of true confidence. "Thank you, Mr...."

"Josh Colter," he said with a grin that seemed to touch his lips and his eyes at the same instant. The change was startling. Those trembly nerves of hers moved up the scale to pulsing.

"Well, then, Mr. Colter, if you would accompany me to the desk?" Her voice sounded off, formal, but at least she had put a coherent sentence together.

"I'm yours to command," he replied, wicked grin firmly in place. He hefted the baggage to a more comfortable position under his arms.

"You know, Mr. Colter—" she spoke as she walked "—a man could get himself into trouble being this forward."

"Forward? Really?" His expression was all boyish innocence. "How so?"

"Oh, I don't know," she mused, coming to a halt at the front desk. "A husband, for example, might take exception to a man flirting with his wife."

His smile faltered, but he recovered so quickly she probably wouldn't have noticed if she hadn't been looking right at him. She saw his gaze flick to her left hand, which was covered with a leather glove. This time she did keep her smile in check.

"And is there a husband I should be concerned about?" His tone indicated absolutely no misgiving at all. And, judging by the arsenal displayed on the counter, he was a man who could take care of himself in any situation, including going toe-to-toe with an irate husband.

Still there was a certain mischievous thrill about intimidating a man who looked so formidable. The fact that she was in a public place with help, she hoped, within earshot, bolstered her confidence. "One never knows...about husbands. They're apt to turn up at any moment."

"Ah." He put the bags on the floor between them, one carpetbag sagging against her skirt. He lounged casually against the counter. "So I should be prepared to be called out?"

"Could be," she replied, and hoped he didn't notice the glint of amusement in her eyes.

She couldn't miss the spark in his eyes, and it wasn't amusement, that was for darned sure. No, that look was hotter than August in New Orleans and just as sultry. Her experience with men might be limited, but even a girl of fourteen would recognize the look.

She tore her gaze away, focused on a spot of chipped paint on the wall behind the desk and said, "Now, where's that desk clerk? Never one around when you need—"

A man came careening around the doorway, speaking as he moved. "I found the pens I was looking for," He waved a couple of pens and lurched to a halt when he spotted her.

"Are you speaking to me?" A bit confused, she glanced from the clerk to Josh and back again.

"No, ma'am. Sorry," the clerk said. "I was looking for a pen for Mr...."

"Colter," Josh supplied for the second time.

There was a moment of awkward silence, then Josh said, "Please." He made a small gesture toward the register with his hand. "After you." He took the pen from the clerk and offered it to her like a chevalier offering his sword.

"Thank you."

She scribbled her name and Eddie's, whom she'd sent on to the livery with the horses and wagon. He'd join her later for dinner.

"How long will you be staying?" The desk clerk asked the standard question.

"One night, I think. Maybe two. I'm not exactly certain."

She'd thought she'd be here longer, maybe spend a few days in the area making sketches and, of course, visiting with her favorite brother. But, no, leave it to Davy to complicate matters. How could he have quit like that and then taken off for parts unknown? Now she not only had to complete her sketches for the competition but she had to find her brother, hopefully before her father got the news of Davy's latest exploits.

Please don't let Davy be in trouble.

She dropped the pen into the holder. "I'll need two rooms. One room for me and one for my traveling companion. He'll be along soon." She added that traveling companion part deliberately. She enjoyed a bit of mystery, a bit of being...a touch risqué. Too long in Paris, she supposed.

"Yes, ma'am," the clerk said casually, and she was disappointed at his lack of shock. Evidently things were more relaxed on the frontier.

He removed two keys from the brass hooks behind the desk. "Rooms 5 and 6. I'll bring up the bags as soon as I finish with Mr. Colter."

"Anytime is fine."

"The rooms are connecting, if you—"

"Thank you." She cut him off, seeing no need to explain herself or her traveling arrangements to anyone, particularly a tall, dark man who was taking this all in with undisguised interest.

"So, there is a husband, after all," Josh said softly, his expression suddenly serious.

"And if there were?"

"I'd be disappointed. Of course, if you were my wife—" he let his gaze travel blatantly down the length of her and back again "—I would never ask for *two* rooms."

Heat moved up her neck and skidded to a halt on her cheeks. She knew about sexual banter from her encounters with men in Paris, but she was getting in over her head here, and much as she hated to retreat, there was a time to fall back and regroup. This was definitely one of those times.

"If you'll excuse me." She kept exactly the right amount of aloofness in her voice.

She had one foot on the bottom stair when his voice stopped her.

"Then I'll see you for dinner?"

"I think not."

"Well, I have to eat and you have to eat and there is only one dining room, so unless you're planning to eat in the saloon . . ." He arched one brow in question.

"Besides, I'm looking forward to meeting your husband. He's a lucky man."

How could she not smile. "Good evening, Mr. Colter."

Josh watched her go. The woman was something: beautiful, tempting and fun. Yes, fun, he realized with a start. He didn't believe for a minute there was a husband, or, at least, he was hoping like hell there was no husband. He was banking on what he'd said earlier. No man who had her for a wife would willingly sleep alone. So who was the other room for? He didn't know—sister, mother, brother—and he didn't care. These past few minutes with her, he'd felt more like himself, more like the old Josh, than he had in weeks. A grin lingered on his lips when he turned back to register.

"You're in Room 2, Mr. Colter," the clerk prompted.

"What? Oh, thanks." He reached for the pen when her whiskey-rich voice stopped him.

"Excuse me."

Both men looked up. She was poised on the staircase, looking quite regal, he thought, even with that damn hat.

"I understand David Gibson had a room here. Is that right?"

Her words sliced through him like a lightning bolt. He must have heard her wrong. He went very still. Wariness coiled in the pit of his stomach. His gaze was riveted on the woman at the top of the stairs.

"Yes," the clerk said. "Mr. Gibson did stay here, but he left some time ago. I can look it up if you want to know exactly."

What the hell was going on? Josh wanted to ask, but didn't, couldn't, all things considered. He had no choice but to clamp his jaw down—hard, so hard his back teeth hurt.

She continued. "I was wondering if you knew where Davy...Mr. Gibson went?" Her brows were pulled down, her sensuous mouth curved in a thoughtful frown.

Davy, huh? Josh's fingers closed into a fist.

The desk clerk said, "Mr. Gibson didn't say anything. Just packed up and left."

"Ah," she muttered, looking disappointed.

The clerk spoke up. "Well, there was..."

"What?" She came down a step.

"Mr. Gibson came in with two other men and, as they were leaving, I heard him tell the others that he knew someone who might give them work...cowboying, I think he said." He rubbed his chin. "I'm trying to think where..." He made a clicking sound in the back of his throat. He shook his head, signifying his failure to remember.

That noose knot in Josh's stomach drew in tighter. This was going from bad to worse.

Then something sparked in her face, her eyes—recognition, understanding perhaps. "You did say cowboying, didn't you?" she prompted, her head cocked to one side. "Not something else, like gambling or—"

"Cowboying. I'm certain."

"Cowboying? You're *absolutely* sure?"

"Yes. I told you." Impatience tinged his voice. "Somewhere up north, I think."

She grinned. "Thank you very much. You've been a big help."

She spared Josh some of that smile, then turned and practically raced up the stairs.

Josh dragged in a breath that didn't do a thing to quell the frantic beating of his heart. What the hell kind of cryptic conversation was that? Whatever it was, two things were clear. The woman was somehow involved with Gibson, and she knew, or thought she knew, where he'd gone. That was all Josh needed to know. He was nearly to the stairs when the clerk called to him.

"Mr. Colter, you didn't register."

Who the hell cared about registering now! But he figured it was faster to go along than to argue. He grabbed the pen and dragged the register closer to him. Halfway through writing his name, he paused to read the signature above his—her signature. It was then he realized she'd never introduced herself. It was then his world took a sudden tip to the left as he read and re-read the name written there.

A. J. Gibson.

Chapter Three

Josh paced the length of the hotel room. Eight by ten, it was either three long steps or four short ones from the gingham-covered window to the walnut bureau on the opposite wall. He'd been pacing ever since he slammed in here about an hour ago.

A dozen times he'd started out the door, bent on going to her room, demanding to know what she knew, demanding to know where the hell Gibson had gone.

He'd stopped every single time, because there was no way, no easy way, no *certain* way, to get the information he wanted.

It hardly seemed likely he could go there, bang on the door and say, "Pardon me, but would you mind telling me where David Gibson is? Why? Oh, so I can kill him, of course."

Yeah, that was a surefire way to get what he wanted, what he desperately needed to fulfill his debt of honor, to finish this bloody business and go home.

He sank down onto the bed, the coiled springs creaking in protest. His fingers absently traced the threads on the brightly colored patches of the quilt.

Feet on the floor, knees bent, he fell back on the bed. His eyes slammed shut. In the next motion, he surged to his feet, unable to remain still. He paced over to the window, his boots making a hollow thud on the pine floor, his spurs adding to the scarred surface.

Leaning one shoulder against the white wood framing, he stood very still, thinking about the men who'd murdered his sister.

In a heartbeat, the scene flashed in his mind. He could see Mourning Dove's lifeless body, broken, contorted, while blood pooled under her. Rage had filled him, turning him hard and cold. Someone would pay for this atrocity. He would see justice served. No white man's court would ever bring a white man to trial for killing an Indian, for killing three Indians, he corrected. There were others dead that day besides his sister.

But there'd been survivors, enough to tell him the descriptions of the men who'd done this, enough to start him on the path to revenge. That day, as they'd buried the dead, he'd pledged to the others that he would not rest until justice was served.

He was nearly done, finished with his grisly task. For Josh Colter was not a murderer, not a man who resorted easily to violence. He was a man who believed in honor and family—a man willing to do whatever it took to preserve both.

Now he had no family. Mourning Dove had been the last. He had the extended family of the Crow, but it was not the same. His family, his mother and father were gone years ago, and now so was his sister.

He felt alone, bone-chilling alone. Maybe it was that feeling of being alone that drove him, as much as the death of his sister, for he, too, had been robbed, robbed of family, robbed of someone to care about him and for him to care about.

He stared out the window, over the rooftops to the vast grassland beyond, grass greening with the promise of summer sun and gentle rain. Fifty years ago there would have been herds of buffalo roaming those hills, now there was cattle.

Things had changed, and for the Indian they had changed for the worse. Confined to reservations, their days of being lords of the plains were over. The government said it was for their own good. For the government's good was more like it. No blankets, no supplies, no dignity. Only lies and empty promises from corrupt Indian agents.

It was no wonder that small groups of Indians from all the tribes were slipping off reservations, returning to the hills or fleeing over the border to Canada. That's what Mourning Dove and her husband, Blue Crow, had been doing that day they'd stopped to camp on Josh's land. He wished they'd been together all the time, but Mourning Dove had been born later to Josh's mother and her new husband. She knew only the Indian world.

He'd welcomed their small band of twenty. He'd given them food and supplies and tried to convince them to stay permanently with him. It wasn't the first time he'd offered, but like all the other times, they'd refused. He knew they saw it as charity, and it was not what they wanted. A man had his pride, Josh knew that well.

He straightened and paced over to the stove, cold and lifeless, waiting for someone to kindle the fire and bring it to life again.

He wished he could bring his younger sister back to life as easily. That rage was pulling in tighter, threatening to choke the breath out of him. Arms braced on the wall, he let his chin drop to his chest. *Breathe. Slow.*

Again. Again. Again. The rage receded to a more manageable level.

He stood like that for a long time, head down, arms braced, fingers digging into the cool white plaster walls while that last day played itself over in his mind as though he could find some answer.

Guilt and regret rolled and spiraled inside him until he could no longer separate the two. He should never have left them that night, but no, he had had a business meeting early the next morning. He had needed to do some paperwork, get things in order before he went into town.

You had no way of knowing, the voice of reason entreated for what must have been the millionth time, and it was true. He knew it was true. Yet somewhere deep inside, where logic didn't reach, somewhere close to the heart and soul of him, he felt he should have known, should have guessed. Dammit, he should have been there. They had been on his land. He'd promised them food and safety and he'd failed. His sister was dead because of it.

Beautiful little Mourning Dove, she had been only eighteen. Newly married, she had been looking forward to having a family—to making Josh an uncle, which to the Crow was the same as being a father.

Father, yeah, Josh would have liked that.

But there'd be no children now.

Josh was alone in the world.

It seemed, sometimes, as though he'd always been alone. It hadn't been easy living in two worlds, speaking two languages, being a half-breed.

His parents had lived together on the ranch until he was nine, then his mother had chosen to return to her people. Her request hadn't come as a surprise to Hank

Colter. Looking back on it, Josh figured his father must have seen it coming for a long time.

She hadn't been happy in the white man's world. She loved them both but could not stay, it was that simple.

It was the only time Josh had ever seen his father cry, that day when he'd given his mother her freedom to go. He had loved her enough to let her go. In some ways, perhaps, it was the greatest love of all.

They had explained it all carefully to Josh. He would stay with his father, be educated in the white man's world, take his place in that society.

Some had made comments about old Hank Colter's half-breed son not being up to the job of running one of the largest ranches in Montana. Josh had proved them wrong. He'd worked hard, damned hard, and had earned his place in the community. To do less would be to let his parents down and that he wouldn't do. Family was everything.

So that brought him full circle. He'd taken an oath, a pledge. His vow would be complete when he found and killed David Gibson.

His gaze drifted toward the closed door to his room. Two doors away a woman had the answers he was seeking.

"Okay, Colter, what now?" He spoke to the empty room.

There weren't many options—asking, begging, threatening. None of those sat well with him. Then another idea flashed in his mind. It was an idea as old as time.

Speaking of time . . . he checked his pocket watch. Seven forty-five. He closed the lid with a snap.

Scooping up several handfuls of water, he splashed his face, relishing the cool cleansing of the chilled water as it cascaded down his face, saturating his collar. He made a quick job of shaving and running a brush through his hair. He stripped off his shirt and retrieved the last clean one from his saddlebags.

He did up the buttons and was still tucking the shirt into the waistband of his trousers as he went out the door.

One way or another, he was going to get what he wanted. Judging by the way the lady had responded to him this afternoon, he thought he knew just what to do.

Josh paused in the doorway of the hotel dining room. Heads turned in his direction. All talking ceased, followed by the low murmur of voices. Men looked stern. He was used to that. Several women offered discreet smiles. He was used to that, too.

But tonight he wasn't interested in women, only one woman. His gaze swept over the ten or so people scattered at the eight round tables. Kerosene lamps flickered and reflected off the dark paneled walls. White china was in stark contrast to the bright calico tablecloths.

He spotted her immediately, as though his gaze were instinctively drawn to her. How could he not? Dressed in blue linen the color of her luminous eyes, she was clearly the most beautiful woman there.

The light caught in her glorious mane of blond hair, hair the color of sunshine. Then she turned toward him as though knowing he was there, watching. She favored him with a half smile.

His body quickened.

Careful, Colter, this isn't a woman to get involved with. This is business.

Yes, he knew that, had confirmed it not five minutes ago when he'd decided on his plan of action. He chose to ignore his reaction to her this afternoon. Then and now it was lust, pure and simple. He'd been a long time without a woman, after all, and a man had needs, didn't he?

Alex and Eddie had both turned to see what was the cause of the sudden silence in the room. Somehow Alex wasn't all that surprised to see Josh Colter standing in the double wide doorway.

He was dressed in a green shirt and black wool trousers, dark colors that only seemed to intensify his commanding presence. The gun he wore hardly seemed necessary to the powerful image he presented.

So he had come after all, was her first fleeting thought. She had to admit, to herself, that she'd wondered if perhaps he'd changed his mind, made other plans. Why was it she suddenly felt relieved, exhilarated at the sight of him?

His smile was faster than lightning and twice as hot. It pinned her to the spot.

His boots were silent on the well-worn fabric of the braided rug that filled the center of the room. The jingle of his spurs blended with the renewed conversations.

He angled between two tables and headed straight for her. There was a predatory gleam in his eyes that made her feel as skittish as a rabbit. She stiffened, resisting the feeling.

That lasted about ten seconds, which was the exact amount of time it took for him to stop directly in front of her.

She extended her hand in greeting. "Good evening, Mr. Colter." She was pleased her voice sounded much calmer than she felt. She was anxious enough as it was, what with the contest deadline and now Davy taking off. And she did not need some sable-eyed stranger complicating her life, not now.

Her small hand was enfolded in his larger one. His thumb swept across the back of her hand in a sensuous gesture that made her stomach do funny flip-flops.

She blinked once against the sensation, resisted the impulse to groan. What the devil was wrong with her?

Evidently she wasn't as focused as she'd thought, because she'd thought about *him* all afternoon. Yes, shameful as it was, she'd just lain on her bed and thought about the tall, dark stranger who'd sent her pulse racing in the hotel lobby with a few words and a long, sultry look.

Discreetly she took a deep breath and let it out slowly. She forced her smile up a peg or two and looked from Josh—correction, Mr. Colter—to Eddie and back again.

"Good evening," he returned. His eyes never leaving hers, he took her hand and lifted it toward his mouth. The air around them charged as though in anticipation of a coming storm. Lightly, oh so lightly, his mouth touched her knuckles. His lips were moist and warm.

Well, you could have heard a pin drop in that dining room. She gazed up at him through her lashes and the heat that sparked in his ebony eyes was hot enough to melt granite. Lord knows it was melting her.

Still, in what was left of the rational part of her mind, she understood this was a game, more complicated than before, but a game nonetheless. Pretending a confidence she didn't feel, she determined to play along, not wanting to end it and so give the victory to him.

"Won't you join us?" she asked demurely, sliding her hand free of his warm grasp.

"I was hoping you'd ask." His voice was husky, sensual. He dragged out the chair next to hers. "I never like to keep a beautiful woman . . . waiting."

"I'll take that as a compliment," she said, keeping up her end of the game, though an unfamiliar heat was stirring inside her at his nearness, at the soft tone of his voice. Where was that woman of control, of purpose?

Fortunately Eddie was not so affected. His chair scraped back, snagging on the rug. He stood, his narrow face drawn into a frown. "Alex? Who's this?" He still held his calico dinner napkin in his left hand, which rested lightly on the tabletop.

Alex saw Josh look up at Eddie, eyes widening as though seeing him for the first time. In less than an instant, his gaze returned to her, one black brow arched in utter disbelief. "Don't tell me this is the husband I'm going to have to kill?" he inquired, craning around as though searching the room for someone else, someone more appropriate, to his way of thinking at least.

She knew he was kidding, knew it was more of their game. "Well, if you feel you must." She gave a one-shoulder shrug and kept her pose nonchalant. "But would you mind doing it outside? I'm trying to decide on dinner here, and fights are so distracting, don't you agree?" She focused her attention on the chalkboard near the kitchen door where the four daily specials were listed.

Eddie's brown eyes got saucer big. "What do you mean, kill? What's he mean, Alex?" Eddie's voice was half concerned, half youthful bravado. He puffed out his chest, straining the buttons of his brown tweed jacket.

"Well, then, this is it, I suppose," Josh said with feigned gravity as he braced one hand on the table and made to stand. Eddie's gaze was riveted to the gun tied to Josh's leg.

"Now, wait! Now just a minute. What's he talking about, a husband?" Eddie's voice moved up both in volume and pitch.

"Why, Eddie, darling, you mean you aren't willing to die for me?" Her cousin was always so easy to rile. She'd been teasing him since he was five.

"Well, sure—what! No!" Eddie tugged at his collar. "What the devil are you talking about?" He dropped down in his chair. "Now, see here, Alex," Eddie sputtered, "I am most empathetically *not* your husband, and you know it!"

Alex chuckled. "A little louder, Eddie, darling, I don't think the folks at the table near the window quite heard you."

"We heard everything just fine," the man called loudly, and gave them a wave.

Eddie looked mortified.

Josh burst out laughing.

Alex tried to looked indignant but failed miserably.

Soon the whole restaurant was laughing.

"Well—" Josh started, his voice rich with laughter "—am I still invited for dinner?"

"By all means," Alex confirmed, warming to the game and the man, especially the man. One minute he looked savage enough to carry out his threat of killing, the next he was full of roguish charm. He was a mystery, an intriguing mystery to be sure, but one she didn't have time to solve, not unless it could be accomplished over dinner.

Josh angled around to face Eddie. "I'm sorry about that. It seems we started this little...game this afternoon. It was unfair of us not to let you in on it."

Eddie dragged in a breath and let it out slowly. He tugged on his collar again. "Jeez, Alex, give a man apoplexy, why don't you?"

Alex was still smiling when she reached across the table toward him, her hand not quite reaching his. "Sorry, Eddie. Really. Besides, what would make you think Mr. Colter would kill you?"

"Maybe because the man looks as hard as a whetstone and—" Eddie broke off, instantly apologetic. "I'm sorry, sir, I didn't mean—"

"It's all right...Eddie, is it?"

"Yes, sir. Edward Story."

Well, Josh thought, at least this one wasn't a Gibson. "Don't worry about it, Eddie. I've been called worse, much worse, believe me. Besides, I suspect it's true. This country out here tends to harden a man."

Eddie offered his hand, and Josh accepted. "I really am sorry. It's just that this is all a little new to me and seeing you with the gun and the talk about killing..."

Josh sobered. "You have every right to be angry. Killing is something a man shouldn't joke about. My apologies if I frightened you."

Apology flashed in Alex's eyes.

Josh lounged back in his chair, feeling the wooden curve press into his back. "Since I know young Eddie here isn't your husband, a fact for which I'm eternally grateful—" his smile was lush "—then he's..."

"I'm her cousin—on her mother's side," Eddie said, a grin replacing his earlier frown.

"Ah," Josh acknowledged. He toyed with the fork next to his plate. *So far, so good. Keep it friendly. So, she's here with her cousin, but why?*

"Is your visit to Gunlock business or pleasure?"

"Both," Alex replied.

Just then the waitress, a buxom woman in her forties, ambled over to take their orders. Josh ordered steak, well-done. Eddie followed suit. Alex ordered the fried chicken. Coffee for everyone was understood, and the waitress brought that first.

There was a minute of awkward silence. The ping of silverware on china, the murmur of voices filtered around them.

Josh sipped his coffee. It was strong enough to float a horseshoe and black as the bottom of a mine shaft. Just the way he liked it. Ignoring the saucer, he put the cup on the tablecloth, holding it lightly between his fingers. "You know, we were never properly introduced this afternoon. I confess I looked on the register. Is it Miss or Mrs.?"

She chuckled. "It's Miss Gibson."

So she wasn't married to the bastard, that was something anyway, he thought, strangely relieved. Why? Why should he care if she was married? He didn't, he told himself emphatically. This was business, brutal business. She had information that he wanted, and he was willing to do whatever he had to get it.

"So, what brings you to Gunlock?" Absently he traced the curve of the cup handle, the china smooth to the touch.

"Alex is an artist," Eddie piped up, pride obvious in his voice. "She's going to be famous after she wins the competition."

"An artist?" He shifted in the chair, the wood creaking in response. "You're kidding?" If she'd said she was the queen of the Nile, he couldn't have been any more surprised.

There was something in the way he said "artist" that pricked Alex's temper. It was a tone, the barest skepticism, that she'd heard before. It was a sure-you-are tone, as though she couldn't possibly be competent. "Yes," she said flatly. "I *am* an artist."

He leaned in, resting his forearms on the table edge. "What kind of artist?"

About that time the waitress banged through the kitchen door, loaded down with three plates, and headed straight for their table. She served the meals with all the grace of someone slinging rocks in a pond, although she did stop long enough to refill the coffee.

Josh smiled his thanks, then to Alex, said, "You were saying you're an artist. What do you paint? Portraits?"

"Occasionally." Her tone was guarded. "I prefer landscapes."

Josh put the napkin on his lap and started to cut his steak. "Have I seen any of your work?"

Alex paused, her fork resting on the mound of fried potatoes on her plate. "I doubt that you would. I've been working in Europe until recently."

"What medium do you prefer, oils or watercolors?" Josh took a bite of steak.

"Oils mostly."

"In the classical or impressionist style?"

"You are familiar with the impressionists?"

Josh chuckled. "I've been known to wander into a museum from time to time."

"You must have wandered a long way, because as far as I know, the closest museum showing impressionists is the Metropolitan in New York."

"That's right." He lifted a forkful of potatoes to his mouth.

"You'll excuse me if I'm a little surprised."

"Why?"

"Well, you hardly seem the type. I mean...I thought..."

He chuckled again. "I'm a rancher. From time to time I have to go to New York on business. I've also been known to go to Chicago, and even all the way to San Francisco. I've been known to drop by a theater, and on rare occasions, a library."

"Touché," she replied with a ghost of a smile. "It isn't often I meet men with an appreciation for art."

"Why, thank you, ma'am," he said. "This time I'm the one who will take it as a compliment." He smiled a slow, easy smile that lit up his face like sunshine after a storm. "You, I mean Eddie here, mentioned something about a competition?"

She sliced into her chicken. "There's a national competition for the most original sketch or painting that best depicts the culmination America's Manifest Destiny."

He sipped his coffee. "And you hope to find that in Gunlock?"

"Not in Gunlock but here in the West." She put her fork down. "The western expansion typifies what's best in America today. Pioneers taming a savage land. It shows the ultimate in character, strength, courage—"

"Patronization, condescension and forced assimilation," Josh muttered.

"What?"

"Oh, I was only thinking about the Indians all those pioneers murdered in order to conquer the wilderness."

"Murdered seems rather a harsh choice of words, don't you think, Mr. Colter?"

"I call it like I see it." He didn't try to keep the sharpness from his voice. How could he when murder was so fresh in his mind?

If she noticed his sudden change of tone, she didn't show it. Instead, she seemed to consider his remarks, then said simply, "I'd call it progress."

"I see." He thought of the high price the Indians had paid for this progress, knowing hers was the prevailing attitude. "I guess this means you won't be making sketches of Indians then."

"Indians?" Eddie spoke around cheeks pouched out with steak. He swallowed hard and cleared his throat. "Good Lord, are there still Indians running around?" He fixed Alex with a hard stare. "You didn't say anything about savages, Alex."

There was that word again. Why the hell did all whites think all Indians were savages? When whites massacred Indians, it was a great victory. When Indians retaliated, it was a great slaughter.

For a moment he wondered what these good people would think if they knew he was half Indian?

"Don't worry, Eddie," Josh reassured him. "With only a few exceptions, all those savages, as you call them, are on the reservations."

"Whew." Eddie heaved a sigh of relief, and Josh didn't resent him for it. He was a boy. How could he know the truth? He wished they could see what it was like, how the Indians lived, then perhaps . . .

Eddie leaned in. "I was worried there for a minute, Mr. Colter. I mean, I agreed to come along to help Alex, you know, with the wagon and such, but I wasn't counting on any trouble. Of course, I mean to protect her."

Josh gave the boy the once-over. "And just who is it you are protecting her from?" By the look of him, he couldn't protect a baby in a bathtub, let alone anything the frontier would throw at them. "I don't want to worry you, but Indians are the least of your problems. San Francisco and New York might be civilized, but out here the James Boys are still holding up banks, not to mention several other gangs running loose between here and the Canadian border."

"Outlaws?" Eddie repeated in a hushed whisper, as though he thought such men were lurking behind the potted palm.

"This is a wide-open country, you know," Josh told them. "There isn't a policeman or a sheriff on every corner. Hell, there aren't even very many corners."

Eddie turned a worried gaze on his cousin. "Alex, maybe this isn't such a good idea. Montana is awfully far."

Alex stiffened. "Mr. Colter, please don't frighten Eddie." Then to Eddie, she said, "Don't worry so, we'll be fine. The mere fact that it *is* such a wide, open country means the chances of us running into some such group as the James Gang is highly unlikely."

Eddie dragged in a breath. "Are you sure?"

"Sure," Alex confirmed, not liking this turn of conversation. She had to finish this trip. She couldn't do it alone, and she didn't appreciate Mr. Colter scaring Eddie to death.

But all this talk about outlaws brought caution to the fore. She'd heard about men who pretended friendship to unsuspecting travelers, only to be scouting for some group who would later waylay them and rob them. She was a woman alone, well, nearly alone.

The caution bell in her head sounded.

It went to the level of a six-alarm fire when Josh Colter said, "I'm leaving tomorrow myself. Perhaps if you told me where, exactly, you are going, I could give you directions, tell you what to look out for and such. I believe you said something about Montana?"

"That's right," Eddie began, "there's a friend of Alex's who has a ranch—"

"You know," Alex interrupted, "it occurs to me, Mr. Colter, that I don't know you very well. And if what you say is true, then it would be unwise for me to discuss my plans...with anyone." She gave him her sweetest smile in an effort to soften her words.

Smart girl, he thought grudgingly. Too smart. "I applaud your caution. It's just that I'm heading north myself and thought I could ride along, give you a hand."

"Yes, Alex," Eddie entreated, "wouldn't that be a good idea?"

Alex's expression was blank. "It's very kind of you to offer, Mr. Colter. However, I think we'll be fine by ourselves. We are well-armed, should the need arise. I am an excellent shot," she added deliberately.

Josh made a derisive sound in his throat. "What do you shoot? Targets?"

"Why, yes."

"It's a lot different when you're about to blow a hole in a man."

The silence was long and discomforting. Alex pushed her plate away and folded and replaced her napkin on the table. "I'm quite finished with dinner. How about you, Eddie?" She stood.

"Well, no." Eddie glanced between the two. "Oh, yes, I'm finished." He stood. "Nice meeting you, Mr. Colter." They shook hands again.

She didn't extend her hand this time. "Good evening, Mr. Colter. It was nice to have met you."

With that, she turned and strode from the dining room with Eddie following close behind.

Josh sat there for a long time, his dinner forgotten.

Lady, you and I are a long way from finished.

Chapter Four

The team had been hitched for the past thirty minutes. The remaining supplies had been loaded and all was ready. Alex was sleepy but excited as they pulled away from Frankel's livery stable at daybreak.

The wagon creaked and groaned like the old-timer it was. The canvas covering was dirty white and looked a little thin where it curved over the front bow. It flapped and fluttered with the movement and with the early morning breeze.

Not a soul stirred as they rolled out of town. Too early even for the dogs, she thought, stifling a yawn with the back of her gloved hand.

She shifted on the seat, grateful that Eddie had put a folded blanket over the rough wood. She could tell, already, this seat was hard as granite and it was going to get a lot harder as the day wore on—and her behind wore down.

Eddie was engrossed in trying to get a little speed out of the team, moving about as fast as ice freezing.

"Git up!" Eddie ordered with another slap of the thick leather reins. If the horses were at all impressed or concerned, they gave no indication of it.

"This is war," Eddie grumbled to the team, and Alex chuckled.

Well, war or not, for better or worse, they were off. As they rolled away from the town, she had a minute or two of second thoughts. After all, she'd put her whole future on this undertaking. Her father had called it a wager, and that was true, but there was more than just money on the line, there was her happiness. For all her bravado, she had her doubts. Oh, she knew she was a good artist, better than most, not as good as others—not yet anyway. But still, that didn't mean she could win a national contest, this one specific contest. She was an unknown in America. And she painted in a style that many were only lukewarm about—impressionism.

It was all or nothing now. She was determined to have it all.

About a mile out of town, they rolled through a stream, the crystal clear water churning around their moving wheels.

The road turned north and so did they. The sky was brighter now, nearly white at the horizon, darker shades of gray the farther west she looked.

The persistent breeze fluttered the hair at Alex's neck where it was tucked up under her battered old Stetson. Goose bumps skittered over her arms. Instinctively she tugged her coat closed in front, overlapping the edges without doing up the half-dozen black bone buttons. "Brr. It's cold, isn't it?" Not cold enough to frost her breath, but darned close, and she rubbed her hands together again to ward off the chill.

Eddie didn't comment.

"What are you scowling about?" She nudged him in the ribs with her elbow.

"Jeez, Alex, it's practically the middle of the night. How can you be so cheerful?" His youthful face was screwed up tighter than a mason jar.

She chuckled. "Mornings. I love mornings."

"Yeah, well, I don't, so give a guy a break, will ya? I need the sun to be up, I mean really up, for a couple of hours, *then* I can put words together."

"Okay. Okay." She held up her hands in surrender. "I get the idea. I promise not to talk to you for a while, how's that?" Instead, she focused on the surrounding countryside.

The sunrise had turned into a glorious display of pink and red and lavender, the sun inching up like a golden ball rising from some sorcerer's magic box. It was, in a word, breathtaking

Overhead, a pair of red-tailed hawks appeared in the sky, circling, gliding, hardly flapping their wings at all, just soaring effortlessly on the warming air.

Around them the world was quiet. As far as she could see, there was nothing but rolling hills and grass and sagebrush. Way in the west there was the shadowy blue shape of mountains, but between here and there, just prairie: no trees, no houses and no people.

Amazing. Having lived her whole life in one large city or another, it was startling. Just miles and miles of nothing but miles and miles. It might have been intimidating; instead, in a way that was unexpected, she felt not overwhelmed but calm, free. It was as though she'd come back to a place that was familiar, which was absurd, but she felt it all the same.

They rode along in companionable silence for the next hour or more. And though there wasn't much to sketch, she felt as though something were missing if she didn't have her sketch pad in her hand, so she climbed over the seat to retrieve it.

The back of the wagon was filled with boxes and crates and bags of supplies. She reflected that maybe she did overbuy on the supplies: canned food including milk and fruit, dried food, grain for the horses, just in case. Yes, the livery man had told her it wasn't necessary, but suppose the horses didn't like eating grass? She'd had a colt once who wouldn't eat anything but hay from a certain farm. She wasn't taking any chances.

There were two trunks of her clothes and a couple of carpetbags and the wicker traveling case, and then Eddie had a couple of carpetbags, though how in the world he'd manage with so little was beyond her.

Her sketch pad—actually there were a dozen of them—was tucked in the red wooden trunk with all her other art supplies: oils, palette, thinner, brushes and the rest. She pushed aside the several precut pieces of canvas already rolled up, and some precut pieces of wood for making frames to hold the canvas.

Pulling out one sketch pad, she let the lid slam shut. Feet braced, she staggered up to the front again.

In an unladylike flurry of petticoats and legs, she rejoined Eddie on the seat, grateful he was her cousin, whom she'd known all her life.

"Lunch in a couple of hours, okay?" Eddie muttered as she settled beside him.

"Okay." Neither of them was much for breakfast.

The road, two ruts in the loamy brown soil, stretched straight in front of them, dipping like a dragon's back as it disappeared over each small hill only to reappear again on the next rise.

The sun shone summer bright, warming her face and arms, drying her skin. She was fair, and prone to sunburn, so she rolled her sleeves down.

Thank goodness she'd had the good sense to bring her Stetson. Okay, it wasn't her hat exactly, it was Davy's. He'd worn it that summer they'd traveled to Santa Fe. Her father had bought Davy the hat at a shop in the square. Davy had been so proud. Wearing it made her feel close to her brother. Lord love him, Davy had always had an adventurous nature. She couldn't wait to see him again.

With warm thoughts of her brother on her mind, she settled back, her sketch pad on her lap, a pencil in her hand, only to surge to her feet. "Look! There! It's antelope." Eyes wide, she pointed in another direction. "Look, Eddie! There. Aren't they beautiful?" Spread out on the hillside, bold as you please, were antelope, hundreds of antelope. Their tan-and-white coloring had made them almost impossible to see until one of them had moved.

"Stop the wagon!" Heart racing, she didn't wait, just started over the side. *Antelope. Just look at them.*

"Whoa!" Eddie pulled back on the reins and slammed the brake into place with a clunk. The horses neighed and shook their heads in objection to the sudden command. "Whoa!" The wagon rocked forward and back.

Alex managed to find footing somewhere. All she knew was there were antelope and she was going to sketch them. She plopped down right there, her skirt ballooning out around her.

Eddie slid across the seat and spoke to her from above. "Jeez, Alex, what's the matter with you?"

"I can't draw in a moving wagon."

"Well, you can't draw if you're crushed under a wheel, either."

"Yes, yes." She gave a dismissive wave of her hand, already focused on the animals. "Look at them. Aren't they beautiful?" She arched her hand and arm to a new angle. She was only half talking to him, mostly she was talking to herself.

Fast as she could, she made her sketch, squinting against the sunlight. "This is wonderful," she muttered, her hand flying over the paper.

"Come on, Alex, between you and these lumbering excuses for horses, we'll never get there if we have to keep stopping. Besides, I have the feeling we're going to see a lot of antelope before this trip is finished."

"Wait."

Fifteen minutes later, Eddie prompted her again. "Come on."

"Okay. Okay." Putting the finishing touches on her sketch, she scrambled to her feet. She knew he was right, they probably would be seeing a lot of antelope and buffalo and elk and about a dozen other animals this trip; it was just that this was the first.

Brushing off her skirt, she handed her drawing pad up to Eddie then, unaided, climbed up.

From then on, she kept the pad on her lap, her hand lightly caressing the rough paper. Paper and pencil, canvas and paints depicted who she was as accurately as a sketch depicted what she saw. She'd been like this ever since that first visit to the Louvre, when she had been twelve and they had been on a family vacation to the Continent.

She could remember how her parents had coaxed and threatened to get her to go along. She'd wanted to visit a certain carousel that was near the cathedral. She wasn't interested in paintings by dead men, for heaven's sakes.

But her parents had won out, as parents had a way of doing. It would be good for her, they'd promised in a way that she'd known meant she was going to be bored silly. She'd given in and gone along so they'd get it over with, and she could visit the carousel.

The museum was large, a converted palace, with huge corridors stretching this way and that. She remembered how loud her footsteps had sounded on the marble floors and she'd had this tendency to want to tiptoe and whisper.

But from the first painting, she had been enthralled.

It had seemed so easy then. She'd learn to draw and paint and have her paintings hanging in museums. Ha! It was, without a doubt, the hardest thing she'd ever done. For all the hard work, for all the gnashing of teeth and pounding of fists, she'd stayed with it, because every time she walked away, she couldn't escape. Scenes, paintings were everywhere she looked. Ideas seemed to haunt her, to materialize right in front of her. She had to paint, that's all there was to it.

Mama had been her champion until she died. Alex missed her terribly. True to her mother's faith in her, she'd continued, returning to Paris to finish her studies. Then, just when things were breaking for her, her father had wired for her to return home. He'd cited recent changes in certain European governments; a fear of trouble brewing was his cryptic comment. She had been shocked, disappointed. She had wired back, asked for extensions but she hadn't been able to delay the inevitable.

That had been almost a year ago. She had asked to return to France. Her father always had excuses, reasons, most of which had something to do with her darling baby brother.

Yes, Davy was always in trouble, but it was always innocent. Who could stay angry at him when he smiled? He had a smile that would melt a witch's heart.

Davy and Alex. Alex and Davy. Over the years, they'd been a team. When they'd been little, she'd been the brains and he'd been the brawn. In other words, she thought up the mischief and he carried it out.

Her ears were still ringing with the lecture. She was convinced Papa had it written down somewhere—either that or he'd memorized the darn thing because, every time, it was the same, word for word. They must conform. Good boys and girls didn't behave in such a manner. *They* had a reputation to uphold. *He* had a reputation to uphold as San Francisco's leading banker.

She and Davy had tried to take it seriously. They'd tried to conform. Mostly they'd tried not to recite the speech along with him.

Mama had encouraged them both to follow their dreams. Alex had pursued her art but Davy, being the only son, had been expected to come into the family business and so his dream of writing the great American novel was never realized. Perhaps that was why they were so close, why they'd always supported each other...until that day six months ago. The day of Davy's banishment.

Those first few days she couldn't have felt any more guilty if they'd sold their favorite puppy to wandering gypsies.

Yes, Davy had gotten out of hand. Yes, his gambling debts far exceeded any income he could earn, which he didn't. Yes, he had been spending an inordinate amount of time at a certain saloon on the Barbary Coast and the rumor was there was a woman.

Her father had convinced her that they must send Davy away for his own good.

His own good. She'd said those words like a litany for days before and weeks after. Now, having seen Gunlock...

She shook her head. No wonder Davy had taken off. There were no stores, no theaters, nothing to occupy a young man's idle time. It was a miracle he'd lasted as long as he had. Cowboying must have sounded very exciting to Davy.

Cowboys were the stuff of dime novels, of adventure, of romance, of men like Josh Colter—dark, powerful, dangerous with warm sable eyes that seemed to look right through her and into her soul. A delicious warmth curled in her stomach and moved out through bone and flesh. She swallowed hard.

Never mind him. Get your mind back on business.

Yes, business. She stiffened and snatched back any further thoughts of the tempting Mr. Colter. Up ahead, a dust devil whirled across their path and disappeared in the grassland. She dragged in a calming breath, the tangy scent of sage sharp and refreshing. The sun continued to warm her face, adding to the heat that had stirred inside her.

Spring, the time for things new and bright and fresh, and sometimes for infatuation. Ah, of course, that was probably why she was feeling all this...this attraction.

Chapter Five

About an hour before sunset, Eddie veered off the trail and headed for a grove of cottonwoods near a stream. They'd put in a long day. Judging by her stiff back, it was more than long enough. Besides, this was the only shade for miles.

"I'll take care of the horses," he told her, jumping down from the wagon seat. His hat fell off. He snatched it up and slapped it on his thigh a couple of times. "See if you can find some firewood." He tossed the hat up onto the seat.

Alex climbed down without help. She was getting used to this wagon business.

She peered at him over the edge of the wagon box. "Firewood?"

"Down by the stream," Eddie added, with a chuckle at her uncertain expression.

"Of course." *Come on, Alex, where else would you find wood except down by the trees.* "How much wood?"

"An armful will get us started. Try to find some different sizes, not all big ones, okay?"

"Okay."

Walking felt good. The muscles in her bottom were tight as a well-stretched canvas and moving, flexing, really helped. What she needed was a feather pillow, the one thing she'd forgotten.

Camping wasn't going to be easy, she could tell that right now. Thank goodness, she had Eddie to take care of the horses and cook.

She reminded herself that she'd better get the firewood or there wouldn't be any dinner, and she was hungry. The cold meat and crackers they'd had for lunch wasn't exactly sticking to her ribs.

At the top of the embankment, she hesitated, sizing up the slope. There was only one way down.

She hitched up her skirt, yards of green linen and more yards of white petticoats, and looped it all over one arm like a cape. The other she kept free to use for balance. Good thing, because two steps down her foot sank and twisted. She lost her balance and ran the last three steps to keep from falling.

"Well, that was graceful," she spoke out loud.

Tucking her hair back behind both ears, she took another second or two to collect herself. The stream bubbled along in front of her, pooling in a particularly deep spot on the opposite side. The soft soil was rich and dark and the air was moist. Ferns, green and lush, sprouted around a large rock at the edge of the pool. Overhead, a songbird chirped its cheerful song. Now this was more like it.

Her grumbling stomach was an urgent reminder that she needed to get moving. Ten minutes later she had an armful of wood and, going up the embankment, she was careful to sidestep slowly. She made it with no trouble.

She spotted Eddie near the wagon, where he'd tied the team to the rear wheel. He had a horse's hoof balanced on his bent knee.

She shifted the wood to the other arm, unmindful of the dirt smudging the front of her shirtwaist. "Is he okay?"

"I think so." Hanging on to the hoof, Eddie positioned himself around to get a better view in the fading light. "There's a stone caught in the hoof and I want to make sure there's no damage. Can't have the horse coming up lame. Would you mind starting the fire?"

"Uh, sure. You need anything?"

"Nope." He was feeling the soft center of the hoof. "I'll be along in a couple of minutes."

She went to the other side of the wagon, away from the horses, and tossed the wood down with a small crash.

"You okay?" Eddie called.

"Yes."

She found a bare spot, stacked the wood, and when it failed to light after three tries, she did what anyone would do. She poured on a pint of coal oil.

Alex struck a match, tossed it and whoosh! The sky lit up like a second sunset. The flames towered above her like a fiery giant. The wood snapped and cracked and sparks flew upward, higher and higher, chased by flames that could be seen for miles, she supposed.

Heart racing, Alex circled the fire, back and forth, like a drover circling a herd, trying to make certain the flames didn't escape her own special corral.

"Alex, what the devil was that?" Eddie hollered.

"Just getting the fire going. Don't worry." Lord, it was amazing how calm she could sound when she was terrified. Then, as suddenly as it had flared, it receded.

Fast as you could snap your fingers, the flames sank down like someone had turned off a gas jet.

Thank goodness, she thought with a chest-heaving sigh. That was close. She pulled her hair forward, half expecting to see the ends singed. All safe.

Well, she knew how to start a fire now, that was for sure. Better yet, she did it herself without asking for help.

The rich scent of burning wood filled the night air. The flames seemed friendly now, warm and welcoming. She held her hands out to the fire, feeling the heat on her palms and her face. "Eddie, aren't we ever going to have dinner?"

"Be right there," he called over his shoulder.

Hunger was a great motivator, so she figured she'd better help out if she was going to expedite things. Muscles straining, she dragged the food locker across the wagon bed and out onto the tailgate, the chains stretched tight as a clothesline.

The crate was light pine and rough enough to make splinters. She pried the lid off. Her stomach growled in anticipation. Salted ham sounded good. Forget the beans, they took too long. Ah, yes, canned tomatoes should work, oh, and canned peaches for dessert. Perfect.

About that time Eddie joined her.

"What do you think?" She felt rather pleased with herself since this was a first for her.

Eddie appraised the campsite, the fire, the food display with the aplomb of a general reviewing the troops. "Fire going, food out...nice job." He grinned and gave her shoulder an affectionate hug. "Thanks."

Eddie rolled up his sleeves and went to work carving the ham, putting the slices in the skillet.

She watched him work for a minute, grateful that Eddie and Uncle John went camping every summer in Yosemite. "Is that going to take awhile?"

He arched one red brow. "Ten minutes or so to get it ready and another ten or so to cook. Why? Hungry?"

"I'm starved, but I was wondering if you'd mind if I washed up a bit before dinner?"

"Sure. Go ahead. I'll do the same thing after we eat." He pushed his hair back with the curve of his elbow, his fingers sticky with tomato juice.

It only took a minute to fetch her towel and soap from the trunk. She managed the embankment in a little more ladylike fashion this time. The fact that it was getting darker didn't help much. The first stars of the night, the brightest ones, could already be seen in the sky. A full moon hung low over the horizon.

Hurrying up the stream, she found the pool she'd seen earlier. There was a chill in the night air and she decided not to undress completely. No, a nice sponge bath would do fine.

It was like being in her own private world. The sound of the water was melodic, soothing, relaxing. The rustle of the leaves in the breeze added to the night song.

Even in the chill, she felt muscles relax, felt the tension ease in her shoulders and back. Eyes open again, she glanced around. Yes, this was a lovely spot.

Seated on the rock, she hurried to wash, the scent of frying ham wafting down to her. There was nothing like a little washing and a good meal to set the world right.

Eager to get to that meal, she eyed the stream again. It was going to be cold. She summoned an inner grit and splashed handfuls of water against her face.

Alex groaned and shuddered as her skin turned icy. It was as refreshing as lemonade in July and just as welcome.

She made quick work of rinsing her arms and legs. Water clung to her face and eyelashes and she swiped at them with the backs of her hand.

Still blinking against the water, she grabbed up her towel and dried her skin, rubbing to get the blood moving.

She slipped on her skirt and reached for her blouse. If she was lucky, Eddie would have dinner ready by the time she got back to the camp fire. Blouse done up except for the top two buttons, she gathered her towel and soap and turned.

Two men were blocking her path.

Fear shot through her. Instinctively she stepped back, clutching the towel to her chest like armor.

Both men were cast in shadow, and she wondered how they could have gotten so close to her without her hearing them. Probably her distraction and the sound of the stream.

How long had they been standing there? Had they been watching her bathe?

Calm. Stay calm. This is the West and there could be a rational explanation for this. Stay calm.

The voice of reason preached calm, the voice of caution screamed to run for her life. Still they hadn't made a move in her direction, hadn't said anything threatening, so perhaps she was overreacting.

It took a couple of tries to get her voice to work. "Good evening," she finally said with all the bravado she could muster, which wasn't a whole heck of a lot. The night suddenly seemed much colder and much darker. She didn't move. Neither did they. "We're about to have dinner,'' she continued, though she wasn't sure they could hear her over the pounding of her heart. "Would you care to join us?"

For what seemed like an eternity, they stood there staring at her in a way that made her feel naked, even though she was dressed. Self-protection was overtaking all other emotions. Her fingers curled into tight fists, although she knew, deep down, she was helpless against two men.

She took another step back, her heel sinking into the soft earth at the edge of the stream, throwing her off balance, and she reached out to steady herself. One of the men said, in a voice cold and ominous, "You and the kid out here all alone?"

The man on the left spoke, his voice snake-oil smooth and equally slimy. From what she could make out, he was dressed all in dark colors—blue pants, brown shirt. A gun was tied to his left leg; *that* she could see with stark clarity. His hat was black and settled low so she couldn't see his face. He was tall and thinner than his companion.

He took a menacing stride in her direction. "I asked you a question, lady." His voice sent a shiver up her spine. "Is it just you and the kid out here?"

In a heartbeat she realized two things—first, they'd seen Eddie, and second, she and Eddie were going to die.

Chapter Six

Moonlight cast the glade in ghostly white and gray. Her first thought was to escape, to run and not look back. The voice of self-protection screamed louder than a banshee. But she couldn't. Eddie was there, somewhere, in the camp. She couldn't leave him, abandon him to these men.

Panic was like a living thing inside her, eating her up. Her whole body shook with a force that threatened to knock her over.

Think, Alex. Think fast.

Stall them. She had to stall them until she could find a way out of this for her and Eddie.

"If it's money you want..."

"Money," the shorter one repeated in a sinister tone that said he had all the cards. "Sure we'll take your money, honey, and *anything* else we want, if ya know what I mean."

God help her, she knew exactly what he meant.

Think, Alex, think.

She tried to think. She couldn't. Her breath came in shallow gasps. Her heart threatened to explode in her chest. Dear God, this couldn't be happening. It couldn't. It was.

Think.

Eddie. They had asked if it was just her and Eddie. They didn't know how many they were.

She had to clench her jaw to keep her chattering teeth from giving her away. Her fingers dug into the coarse cotton of the towel she still clutched. Somewhere in one of the trees, a night owl hooted softly.

"If you don't want dinner, then you are not welcome here. The *men*—" she emphasized the word "—will be back any minute. I suggest you be gone by that time." She waited, holding her breath.

The tall one stood there, arms at his side, his hand dangerously close to his gun. "And just where have these men—" his voice dripped with skepticism "—gone?"

"Hunting...for dinner," she added, trying to find some plausible explanation. "So, unless you want trouble, I suggest you leave."

For a full five seconds they didn't move, didn't make a sound, and then they laughed. Both of them laughed, a cruel, hard sound that sent dread snaking up her spine.

"Oh! Oh!" the second man whined in a high, mocking voice. "I'm shakin' in my boots."

They both laughed again.

"Sorry to disappoint you," the tall one said, "but the kid up there said as how it was just the two of you right before he *invited* us to share a little grub." He straightened. "Course, that was our intention anyways."

There was more laughter. "Alls a man needs to survive out here is a good horse, food and—" he took another step in Alex's direction "—a woman. Come on, honey, what say you and me..."

Terror overcame reason. "Go to hell!"

He grabbed her, his fingers digging into the flesh of her upper arm through her blouse. Alex lashed out with everything she had, fists, feet, and finally she raked his face with her nails. She dug in hard, feeling the wetness of his blood on her fingertips.

"Damn you, bitch!" He released her, pushing her away as he did. Alex staggered back, her foot sinking ankle deep in the muddy streambed. Grabbing nothing but air, she fell backward into the water.

Her skirt soaked up water like a sponge, and in no time it seemed to be anchor heavy.

Someone laughed, she wasn't certain if it was one man or both. Muscles in her back and legs strained against the weight of the skirt. Her wet hair was plastered to her face. She wiped it back. Water gurgled and swirled around her.

Like an animal, she managed to get to all fours, the rocks of the stream sharp against her tender palms. She pushed hard, determined to get up, to turn and face her attacker.

She never saw the blow coming, only felt something on her back an instant before she slammed face first into the water again.

Breathing was impossible. Icy water rushed into her nose and mouth. There was no sound. She tried to rise. Something or someone held her down.

Fingers digging into the streambed, she strained up, twisting, frantic for air. She couldn't move.

Her lungs ached in her chest. Blood pounded in her ears. Cold. She was mind-numbingly cold. It was so dark. Random thoughts of her father and brother and mother flashed like fireflies in her mind and were gone. She knew she was going to die and there was nothing she could do about it.

Air slipped from her lungs and darkness threatened.

Suddenly she was hauled up. Rough hands held her by the shoulders. She was slammed back against a man's chest. The skin around her eyes pulled tight as she was held by the hair.

Air rushed into her lungs. Blessed air. Nothing else mattered. Choking, coughing up water, she was too weak to do more than sag against her captor.

Water poured off her in rivulets. Her skin was colder than January snow.

The man's face pressed against hers; cheek to cheek, he held her. His stubbled face scraped her skin, his putrid breath smelled of whiskey and tobacco.

"Not so feisty now, are you, lady?" he sneered, his lips moving against the side of her face. She shivered, this time not from the cold. Her stomach heaved and bitter bile rose in her throat.

With more strength than she ever thought she possessed, she slammed her elbow hard into his ribs. It didn't hurt him, but it shocked him enough that he released her.

Legs too cold and stiff, she couldn't run, but she did manage to face her enemy. She might die here tonight, but she wouldn't surrender.

He grabbed her wrist and twisted. Pain shot up her arm. "Why you—"

"Cut it out, Lyle," the tall man commanded from his place on the bank.

Moonlight cut across her attacker's scarred face. He hesitated. "The hell I will. The damn bitch clawed me." He twisted her arm harder. She had to bend to keep her arm from breaking.

The man on the bank said, "I thought you liked it rough." Dimly she saw him lift up in the stirrups.

"You've had your fun, now bring her. I'm hungry. We'll see who goes first with her after I get some grub in my gut. Besides, Fred'll want in on this."

Her attacker, the one called Lyle, stared at her with ferretlike eyes and she thought he wouldn't obey his comrade, then he surprised her and said, "Come on, you."

The man half dragged her from the stream. The water-drenched skirt pulled her down. The muscles in her legs cramped and she fell. Mud oozed up between her fingers, smeared her face and clothes.

"Get the hell up." He yanked her by the hair. Her neck snapped back. Tears pooled in her eyes and slid down her face, blending with the water that cascaded from her matted hair.

A night wind skimmed the tops of the cottonwoods. The leaves fluttered and rattled together. The gurgling of the stream faded as she crawled up the embankment. Her teeth chattered. She shook so hard, she thought she'd shake apart from the force of it. All she knew was that she was alive. For a little while, another minute, she was alive.

Think. Find a way out, a way to survive.

Twenty feet away, she could see the fire she'd started a short while ago. Bright red flames tinged with blue danced and played among the wood she'd stacked there. She remembered the flames shooting into the night sky and wondered if that was how these scum had found them.

She staggered into the camp, her dress dragging behind her like a royal train. Eddie was seated by the fire, his back to her. They both were alive—but for how long?

Across from Eddie was a third man. He had thin-ning blond hair and a scraggly beard of the same dingy color. His plaid shirt was pulled button-straining tight over his fat belly. A rifle was balanced on his knees, his hand caressing the metal like a lover touches his mate. He didn't speak, just watched her in a way that made her skin crawl.

"Look see what we found, Fred."

The one by the fire nodded. Eddie glanced around and his gaze found hers. His face was pale, all the brightness gone from his eyes. His red hair fell across his forehead, and it took a moment in the dim light for her to see the ugly gash above his left eye. Blood trick-led down his face and pooled at his earlobe before dripping onto his blue shirt collar.

"You bastards!" she cried, and tried to twist free. "Eddie!" She twisted again, the man's fingers digging into her arm, tearing the tender flesh.

The one called Fred watched for a moment, then of-fered a yellow-toothed smile that made her stomach roll over again. "Well, now, looks like you boys done found us a real hellcat." His grin got bigger. "Just bring her right on over here to me. Ol' Fred knows how to treat a woman." He rubbed his crotch for emphasis.

Every muscle in her body drew in, wire tight. Terror, as pure and raw as anything she'd ever known, shot out along all the nerves in her body.

"Let me go!" she commanded, and punctuated her demand by applying her booted foot to her captor's leg with all the strength she had.

"Ouch!" he yelped, and loosened his grip enough that she got free. She heard the distinctive sound of a rifle being cocked. She didn't care. She was going to die anyway, and in the distant recesses of her mind she thought she preferred being shot to the other options.

Her dress tangled around her legs, and she fell. She crawled the last couple of feet to Eddie's side.

The men laughed. "Ain't that a sight?"

"Always did like a woman to come crawlin'."

They laughed again.

Alex ignored them. "Are you all right?" She touched his wound and he winced in response. Blood stained the ends of her fingers. "Oh, Eddie, I'm so sorry." She tore off a piece of her wet petticoat and dabbed at his wound.

He managed the barest of smiles, a grimace really, but his eyes never left their attackers. "Are you all right? Did they—"

"No." She covered his hand with hers.

Behind them, the fire snapped and popped, red flames against a black velvet sky.

Lyle tossed another stick into the flames, sending a cascade of brightly colored sparks fluttering into the night. The tall one lounged against the wagon wheel, shoveling in the food that Eddie had cooked.

The man at the camp fire spoke up. "Well now, aren't you two a pair." He served up a plate of food for himself. They'd obviously opened several of the cans she'd brought.

"She yours?" Fred gestured with his fork. He shoveled more ham into an already full mouth. He sloshed in a drink of whiskey from a bottle he produced from his pocket. The dark brown liquid dribbled out of the corners of his mouth and down his chin, staining an already stained beard. "Well, boy, I asked if she was yours."

"Yes."

"No."

Eddie and Alex spoke in unison. The man paused then laughed, a hard nasal sound. "Well, sonny, which is it?"

Eddie stiffened, pulling Alex into the curve of his arm. "She's mine, as you put it."

The man regarded them thoughtfully. "Wife?"

"Yes."

"Ha!" the man by the wheel sneered.

"She's my wife." Eddie's tone was adamant. He stood, pulling Alex up with him. She didn't know what was happening but she went along.

"How come she doesn't seem to think so?" the tall man asked with a sneer.

"She's confused. Being held at gunpoint will do that to a person." Now it was Eddie's turn to sneer. He inched back, nudging Alex with him.

The man at the camp fire stopped eating, his hand sliding around the trigger of the rifle still balanced on his lap. "Where you goin', boy?" His tone was menacing.

"You're welcome to the food and to whatever is in the wagon." Eddie took a brazen step back, this time shoving Alex fully behind him as he did.

The man who was eating scraped the last of the food from the metal plate and tossed it down with a clink. He dragged his sleeve along his mouth, leaving more stains on the cloth.

"We were gonna do that anyway...boy." He hefted his rifle in the curve of one arm. "Frank." The man nearest the wheel straightened. "Take a look-see in the wagon, seein' as how this young fella's been so kind as to offer it."

Frank followed orders and disappeared around the side of the wagon. Alex saw the wagon sway slightly as the man climbed inside.

"The woman, Fred?" Lyle asked eagerly, licking his lips as he did. "What about the woman? I mean, we ain't been with no white women in a month o' Sundays and I'm getting tired of them redskin bitches."

Alex felt her skin crawl. She wanted to scream. She wanted this all to be some terrible nightmare.

"Hey," a voice called from the back of the wagon. "Ain't nothing in here but clothes and food and some kinda paints...."

Eddie took another step back, pulling Alex along with him. Firelight flashed on the barrel of gun being pointed in their direction. The hole in the barrel suddenly seemed enormous. "Don't be leavin' us, boy. Why, the party's just about to get going."

"Hot damn!" Alex's attacker, the one called Lyle, surged to his feet and strode for her. "Me first." He licked his lips and wiped them on his sleeve again. Alex clung to Eddie, her hand gripping his arm for support, for strength.

"No," she barely whispered. Inside she was screaming, but outside she was paralyzed.

With clear intent, the man advanced on them. Eddie stepped between Alex and the man. The man hesitated for about two seconds. "Git outta my way, boy." He took another step. "I'll kill you where you stand." He produced a gun from the waistband of his pants.

"Eddie, don't," Alex whispered.

"Yeah, Eddie," the gun-wheeling man sneered. "Don't."

"Stay away from her," Eddie pronounced, refusing to back down. He kept inching away, pulling Alex with him. "We told you to take whatever you wanted, just leave us alone."

"Trouble is, boy," the man near the fire said, "you have what we want."

"Hey," Frank called from the wagon again. "Found some money. Looks like...maybe...nearly a thousand."

Both men halted, their attention drawn to their companion and his announcement.

Eddie kept moving back. In a low voice he whispered, "As soon as you're in the shadows, run." He kept inching while the men gathered around to count their loot. The shadows were close, a couple more yards. A few more steps and—

"Dammit, boy," was the only thing Alex heard, then a shot.

Eddie yelled in pain. He fell to his knees, his eyes wide with disbelief. As though in slow motion, he lifted his hand away from his side. Blood, bright red, pooled in his palm and dripped between his fingers onto the ground.

"Eddie!" Her voice sliced through the night like a razor's edge. "Eddie!"

Eddie didn't answer, just looked at her, then his eyes fluttered closed and he fell the rest of the way to the ground.

Chapter Seven

"No! Eddie! No!" Alex made a lunge for him but she was caught up short. Lyle grabbed her by the elbow and jerked her toward him. She slammed into his chest. His hairy arms snaked around her ribs, holding her to him. Cheek to cheek, his rancid breath burned her nostrils.

"Let me go!" She struggled, pushed and twisted against him, frantic to get to Eddie. "Let me go!" she ordered again. She had to help her cousin. She had to!

All three men laughed, harsh sounds with no trace of warmth or compassion.

Disbelief and rage blurred together inside her. She fought hard. "Eddie!" she screamed, desperate for some answer, some sign that he was still alive. Nothing. Not a sound. Not a movement.

The crimson stain on his side was growing larger with every second. Oh, God, why was this happening?

"Let me go, you bastard! I have to help him!" She fought and flailed, her feet kicking out uselessly into the air. Her head whipped back and forth. Her wet hair slashed across her face like tiny whips stinging her flesh and eyes.

The man's grip tightened, his hands clamped viselike around her upper arm and waist, her back against his chest.

"That's it, honey," he sneered. "I like it when you wiggle on me."

All the fury she possessed welled up in her. Muscles pulled noose-tight, blood pounded like thunder in her brain. All she could see was Eddie, bleeding to death. She kicked and squirmed and clawed the backs of his hands, making the same deep furrows she'd made on his face earlier.

"Son of a bitch!" he snarled, and released her so suddenly she careened forward, sprawling face first into the dirt. Breathless, tears streaming down her cheeks, she scrambled to Eddie.

Gasping for breath, she shoved the hair out of her face again and gently nestled his head in her lap.

"Eddie, can you hear me?" She stroked his cheek, relieved that his skin was warm. He was alive, but for how long? "Eddie..." She kept repeating his name. "Please speak to me. Don't—"

Hard hands grabbed her shoulders and snatched her up, her feet leaving the ground. She spun around to face her attacker, ferocity her only weapon. "No! You bastard! I'll kill you for this!"

"We'll see who does the killing." Lyle pulled back his gnarled fist and—

A shot rang out in the darkness, the bullet slammed into the man's head, shattering his skull. Brains and blood splattered on the wagon canvas. The outlaw fell like a giant sequoia.

The sound of the shot, the reality of a dead man lying at her feet was more than she could bear. She kept staring at the blood and gore, unable to move, unable to close her eyes to it.

A scream bubbled in her throat but no sound came out.

The other two men seemed as stunned, but they recovered quickly.

Frank grabbed her and pulled her in front of him like a shield, his gun pressed hard into her side. "What the hell's going on?" he demanded of Fred, who'd dived for cover under the wagon. Eyes straining, the two men scanned the surrounding darkness, searching for the source of the shot.

Reality slowly dawned on Alex. Someone was out there. Someone who would help her?

Please, God, let it be so. Don't let it be another of these animals come to prey on us.

Hopeful, terrified, Alex, too, scanned the area around their camp. The moonlight was bright. She saw no one, nothing moved, yet she knew someone was out there, lurking like a wolf in the shadows.

The light from the camp fire was low, only the barest glimmer of flame flickered on the remains of the firewood.

There was no sound except the heavy, frightened breathing of the man who held her. The canvas covering the wagon fluttered in a sudden gust of wind. The man holding her jumped at the sound, slamming back into the wagon as he did. The wood creaked, the canvas top snapped.

Finally Fred, concealed under the wagon, called in a loud whisper, "Did you see where it came from?"

"No," his partner replied, his dirty fingers bruising her arms through the cotton fabric of her blouse. He smelled like whiskey and sweat. His hot breath brushed across her ear making her shudder in revulsion.

Desperate for help, any kind of help, she sought to take advantage of the situation.

"I told you the *men* were hunting and they'd be back." She tried to keep her voice calm, her tone level and confident.

Out of the darkness, a hard male voice cut sharp through the night like an arrow. "Let go of the woman!"

Alex's heart took off faster than butterfly wings, and her stomach was clenched in a hard knot. Someone was going to help her, really help her! They were saved. Her spirits soared.

The coward holding her shifted anxiously back and forth, always careful to keep Alex positioned in front of him, his boots treading on the sagging hem of her skirt, grinding it into the dirt.

"We'll kill the woman," Frank shouted back. He shoved the gun under her chin as proof of his intention, the metal hard against her jaw, the barrel pushing her head up and back into his shoulder.

The voice in the darkness answered. "Hurt her and I'll kill you, too. You know I mean what I say." The unmistakable double click of a rifle being cocked emphasized the statement. The man lying dead a few feet in front of them was proof that whoever it was out there was not above cold-blooded killing.

The man hesitated. She felt the rapid rise and fall of her captor's chest against her back. The one hiding under the wagon angled around. The two men exchanged glances, clearly worried glances, if the look on Frank's face was any indication; sweat beaded prominently on his forehead. They were cornered, trapped like the rats they were.

Good. She was glad. Her hands curled into tight fists. Whoever the hell was out there, she hoped he killed both men. They deserved to die for what they'd done to Eddie.

"Let the woman go," the voice called out again. "Do it now or die!"

Her captor inched toward his cohort. He dragged Alex with him, making her sidestep, her shoes leaving small furrows in the dirt. When he reached the wheel, he looked down and said, "What do ya think?"

Alex looked down to see the partner peer out, his eyes wide with terror. His gun hand trembled slightly and he switched hands long enough to wipe his sweaty palm on his denim-clad leg. "You wanna hang in, I'll play along for a while. Maybe he wants to share, is all."

Frank nodded. "Come out. We'll be glad to share the woman."

"No!" the voice answered emphatically. "Release her."

"Money! We've got money here. We can split!"

A shot zinged past them, slamming into the wagon inches from where they stood. Wood shattered. She turned her face quickly to avoid the flying splinters.

Frank made a growling sound deep in his throat. "I still have the woman. Come out or I'll shoot her and it won't be pretty." He grabbed her hand, and, in plain sight, shoved the gun barrel against it. Obviously Frank had realized that if he killed her he'd have no protection. "Show yourself."

Five seconds passed, and Alex realized what he was going to do. Shocked, terrified, she tried to break free, pulling down on her hand. Using her whole body like a weight, she sagged to the ground.

Another shot rang out, this time it smashed into Frank's outstretched elbow. He screamed in pain and released her. His arm sagged to his side and he fell to his knees, cupping his bloodied elbow.

Alex pulled away and ran for her cousin, picking up the outlaw's gun as she did.

"Help me," moaned the wounded outlaw to his partner.

"No," whined the other man.

"Dammit, you're my brother." His thin face was contorted in pain. "You get out here or so help me, I'll shoot you myself first chance."

The man slunk out of hiding like a cur, gun in hand, his eyes darting back and forth as he tried to scan the darkness.

Frank writhed on the ground, moaning, groaning, rocking back and forth. He yanked his dirty red bandanna from around his neck and, using his hand and his teeth, tied it around his arm. His brother helped him.

Alex wasn't concerned about them. Somewhere in her mind she knew her rescuer would protect her. She skidded to a halt at Eddie's side. Hand shaking, afraid of what she'd find, she touched his face. Warm. *Thank you, God.* The flow of blood had slowed, or at least it appeared so, but she wasn't a doctor. She ripped off another piece of petticoat and wadded it against his side. Eddie moaned as she pushed too hard. She was thrilled by the sound, the sweetest sound she'd ever heard.

His eyes fluttered but didn't open. He was alive— barely. These men, these animals had done this. Eddie, sweet, innocent Eddie, he'd offered them everything, he'd tried to protect her and this was what they'd done.

Hatred, raw and blinding, surged through her with the power of a flash flood. "I'll kill you for this!" Using one hand, she levered the gun upward, moonlight glinting on the smooth barrel.

Her arm shook with exhaustion and fear and anger, mostly anger. Tears blotted her vision. She swiped at her face with the crook of her elbow, the mud-caked cotton rough against her skin. Quickly she repositioned the gun, pointing it straight at the two men. She'd never shot a man before, but now she thought she could. More than that, now she wanted to. She wavered, moving the barrel back and forth between the men, trying to decide which one she hated more, which one deserved to die first.

Adrenaline rushed through her veins. Hatred left a bitter taste in her mouth. "Now it's your turn to die."

Frank staggered to his feet, one hand braced on his knee for support. "Wait," he pleaded, blood trickling down his arm and onto the leg of his brown trousers. "We didn't mean no harm, did we, Fred?"

Fred was already lifting his gun.

"Don't even think about it," a hard male voice said, very close behind her. "Put it on the ground."

Fred did as he was ordered.

But Alex wasn't concerned with who was armed and who wasn't. Rage overcame all other emotions. She still held the makeshift bandage against Eddie's side. It was his blood that was oozing warm between her fingers. She was helpless to stop it, but she wasn't helpless to stop these men. They'd pay for what they'd done.

With resolute determination, she hooked her thumb on the hammer and pulled back. The metal made a sharp click, the cylinder rolled over one notch.

The two men stared at her in wide-eyed terror. Then that same male voice said, "Let me have the gun."

"No!" she screamed, shaking her head in emphatic denial.

"Dammit, woman, give me the gun. I don't have time to argue." His voice was hard and flat and held all the warmth of a blizzard.

Her breath came in shallow gulps. Those damn tears kept blurring her vision. She craned her neck around to see her rescuer standing there. Dressed all in black, looking more fierce than Satan, was Josh Colter.

His rifle was aimed at the outlaws who were groveling in the dirt about ten feet in front of them. His hat was settled low on his forehead so she couldn't tell exactly who he was looking at. She didn't care. He looked hard as granite. He looked wonderful.

His hand touched her on the shoulder. "Alex, you don't want to do this. Believe me."

"But—"

Faster than she could react, he wrenched the gun from her shaking hand. "See about the kid," he ordered, tucking the gun into the waistband of his trousers.

Rage dissolved into exhaustion. She was safe. Josh was here.

Heart still racing, she did as he ordered. "Don't worry, Eddie. Josh is here. Josh is here now. You're going to be all right," she babbled. Her fingers shook as she stroked his face, brushed the hair back from his forehead, her fingers lightly touching the gash above his eye.

She tore more petticoat and replaced the bandage she'd made just minutes ago.

Josh stepped more fully into the light.

"What's your stake in this, mister?" the wounded man muttered between clenched teeth. "We're just having a little fun is all."

"Fun!" Alex raged. "They held us captive, stole my money, shot Eddie and were going to...to..."

"I know," he said flatly, never turning his head. "Are you hurt?"

"Of course I'm hurt."

"No. I mean did they..." He took a menacing step in the direction of the men. "Did they touch you? Did they *hurt* you?"

It took her a minute to understand his meaning. His deadly intention was startlingly clear. "No," she said simply.

He didn't answer for so long she thought perhaps he hadn't heard her. "I said—"

"I heard." To the men, he said, "You're lucky. Really lucky. Toss the other gun over here. Careful."

Fred did as ordered.

"Now the money."

Again Fred obliged, the packet landing silently near the toe of Josh's boot.

"We ain't hurt her none," the wounded man whined. He stood up straight, the tourniquet around his arm having stopped the blood but clearly not the pain, judging by the way he shuddered and the thin white lines around his mouth. "We just gave her a little scare is all. A woman likes a man who's rough, makes her want it even more."

"Shut the hell up before I blow your brains out where you stand." He might just do it anyway. The only thing that was keeping his rage in control was knowing they hadn't raped her.

Josh motioned with his head toward Eddie. "Is he alive?"

"Yes," she answered, her voice a thready whisper. "Please, we have to do something. You have to help me."

Josh nodded his understanding, then surprised everyone present when he turned to the outlaws and said, "Get on your horses and ride out of here. If you come back, make no mistake, I *will* kill you."

The two men rushed for their horses.

"And take your dead friend with you," he added, nudging the body with his foot.

They did.

Alex stared in disbelief. He was letting them go!

"You can't do that," she ranted at him.

"Lady, I can do any damn thing I want."

The moon was full and Josh watched as the men forded the stream and headed out across the plains. It was chancy letting them go, but he'd figured with one wounded and one dead the other would be less inclined to come back. Besides, he had very little choice.

The kid was hurt and unless Josh wanted to kill the two remaining outlaws, and it was a very tempting thought, he'd have to take them in, which was more trouble and more dangerous than if he let them go.

His fingers curled and uncurled around the smooth metal of the trigger guard, the rifle held at the ready. He watched for several minutes, until he was certain they were gone. Immediately he turned and strode to where Alex was kneeling on the ground next to Eddie. "Is he breathing?" he asked.

Josh was angry, damn angry. She'd walked right into this mess. If she'd listened to him . . .

That I-told-you-so wasn't making him feel a whole lot better. It was almost as though his saying it had made it happen. He'd have been here sooner, except his horse had pulled up lame a couple of hours back and he'd had to take it slow, too slow. When he'd seen that bastard almost hit Alex, something fierce and hot and protective had exploded in him.

Looking at her now, all wet and muddy and bruised, that protectiveness welled up in him again. His fingers actually trembled with wanting to touch her, to push the wet, matted hair back from her cheek, to hold her and—

Stop it. Remember who she is and what you're doing.

He remembered all right, with gut-wrenching clarity. It wasn't her fault, he knew that. But he also knew he had to keep his distance. Besides, he reasoned, sort of like grasping at straws in the wind, if she was okay enough to rail at him, she wasn't all that hurt. But then why was he asking, "Lady, you need some help?"

"I'm fine. It's Eddie I'm worried about."

She looked like a whipped dog or a drowned kitten or some such and this damn ugly business kept getting uglier by the minute.

One thing for sure, she was in better shape than the kid. It was like tearing flesh to pull his gaze away from her, but he did. "So, how's he doing?"

"He's alive. That's about all I can say for sure."

"Well, no thanks to you, Miss Gibson," he snapped, holding on to his unreasonable anger. He reached out and felt the man's head and cheek. Cool.

Alex turned on him, her mouth drawn in a hard line. "What the hell are you talking about? Those men nearly killed us both, nearly—"

Tears clogged her throat. She'd thought she'd done enough crying for a while. She rubbed her eyes with the heels of her hand then wiped her runny nose along her sleeve. Lord, she was angry, and Josh Colter was as good as anyone to take it out on.

"Just what are you doing here anyway, *Mr.* Colter?"

"I'm following you, what the hell do you think I'm doing?"

"Why, so you can rob us, too?" she accused. She knew it was absurd, since he'd just saved their lives, but she said it anyway, needing to lash out at someone.

"Lady, if I wanted to rob you, you'd be robbed by now, believe me. You're damn lucky I was following you. Greenhorns—" he said it like an epithet "—acting like you're out on some summer picnic. Stupid." He glared right back at her.

"Now look, Colter—"

"Are we gonna take care of this man or are we gonna argue all night?"

Defiance flashed in her eyes and was quickly gone. "We're going to take care of Eddie. I'll deal with you later."

It didn't take a surgeon to realize the kid was hurt bad. She'd managed to get a bandage pressed to the wound and that was good; the amount of blood staining his shirt and the ground wasn't so good.

Josh covered her small hand with his, her flesh cold to the touch. She flinched as though she'd been struck. "I need to see the wound."

Wordlessly she released her hold on the bandage, her eyes never leaving his. For a second their gazes locked and lingered, hers wild and scared, his compelling and gentle, despite his harsh words.

Josh hesitated a second then lifted the white cotton cloth, careful not to pull off any clotting. The sickly sweet smell of blood wafted up to his nostrils, making his stomach churn.

Behind them the fire crackled in a last desperate gasp for life—like the kid. "Put some wood on the fire, will you?" He figured if she was busy she'd have less time to think, to remember.

"But—"

"Just do it, sweetheart."

Once she was gone, Josh lifted the bandage again. The wound was ugly, a jagged hole in the kid's chest near the bottom of his ribs. There was an awful lot that could go wrong in that spot—kidneys, liver, to mention a few. Josh sagged back. What the hell was he going to do now? He wasn't a doctor. Oh, he could make a stitch or two to close a small wound—a little soap and water, pour on some whiskey and that was that. He'd even set a broken arm once, but this was different.

He heard Alex moving around behind him, heard the clatter of wood being tossed onto the fire, felt the heat as the flames roared to life.

"What do you think?" she asked, coming to stand behind him.

"Well, the bullet must have missed his heart or he'd be dead. He seems to be breathing pretty good, so I'm guessing his lungs are okay, too."

He touched him again. "No fever so far."

"That's good."

"Yeah."

He snatched off his hat and slapped it down resolutely next to his rifle. "Okay, first we have to know if
the bullet's still in there or not."

Sliding both hands under Eddie, Josh lifted him as
gently as possible. The kid sucked in a sharp breath and
his fingers curled into tight fists, but he didn't make
another sound. Josh twisted around, trying to see in the
shadowy firelight. He ducked his head, straining to get
a better view, then lowered Eddie back to the ground.

"Damn." Josh braced his hands on his thighs.

"What?" Alex mirrored his pose on the other side of
Eddie, her eyes fearful as a cornered doe.

"The bullet is still in there. There's no exit hole."

Alex didn't speak for a moment. Then softly, in a
voice that was calm and a little too controlled, she said,
"That's bad, isn't it?"

"Yes." He wasn't going to lie to her. She needed to
know what they were facing.

"Can you—"

"Take it out?" Josh finished, guessing her line of
thought. "No. If I did it wrong then . . ." He let the implication stretch out.

"What are we going to do?" There was an urgency
in her voice that touched his heart. This was a mess, and
all he could do was try to pick up the pieces.

"Okay, we have a couple of choices—stay here and
try to nurse him ourselves with no medicine and less
skill, or move him back to town to a doctor but risk
opening the wound again. It's a helluva choice."

She stared at her cousin. Finally she said, "We have
to try to move him." Her voice was hoarse, barely above
a whisper. "We can't let him die. No matter what happens, he can't die. Do you understand me? He *can't*
die."

Tears glistened in her eyes.

"I'll do my best, but—"

She cut him off with a sharp look, a look filled with pain and fierce determination.

He was helpless to say much more than, "I'll try."

"What now?"

He scanned the area, evaluating the wagon and team. "There's enough of a moon and I think we can make it."

"Eddie," she whispered, as though trying to wake him from a gentle slumber. Miraculously, his eyes opened.

"Alex?" He gulped in a breath and seemed to be waiting for the pain to ease.

"Hi, there." She was relieved, overjoyed. She grinned like a kid on the last day of school. "Look, Josh is here. We're going to get you into town . . . to a doctor. You'll be right as rain in no time." She kept brushing his hair back with her hand even though it didn't need it. Somehow, as long as she was touching him, she knew he was alive, knew he wouldn't die.

"You stay with him. Keep the pressure on the bandage." She nodded. "I'll get the team hitched and make a place for him in the wagon."

Less than five minutes later, he was finished.

"All set?" he called around the side of the wagon.

"We're ready," Alex answered. She was still kneeling in the dirt when Josh walked over.

"Okay," he said, "first we're going to make a better bandage. Have you got any towels or sheets in there?"

"Yes, in the box marked Linens."

Josh found them quickly and returned with several, which he tore into wide strips. "Now we're going to have to move you, Eddie." He spoke to the young man even though he wasn't entirely certain Eddie was awake. In a way he hoped the kid had passed out, because moving him was gonna hurt like hell.

Alex and Josh worked together and slipped the bandage around Eddie's middle, more towels packed hard against the wound. Alex never hesitated, never faltered, though Josh knew she had to be exhausted, terrified from the ordeal and of the trip ahead.

Circling around, he dropped down to one knee. "Eddie, can you hear me?"

Eddie looked at Josh but made no sound.

"I've got to get you into the wagon. Do you understand?"

Eddie gave a small nod.

"I'm gonna pick you up and it's gonna hurt. There's not a damned thing I can do about it."

Eddie's face was pale. His lips pulled into a thin line against the pain he felt and what was to come. "Do it." His voice was thready. He slid his right arm around Josh's shoulder while Josh grabbed him around the waist and stood.

"Oh," Eddie groaned. "Damn." Sweat beaded on Eddie's forehead and his upper lip. A muscle flexed back and forth in his cheek, but he made no other sound.

Once Eddie was settled inside the wagon, Josh helped Alex up. "Okay. This ride could get rough."

"I understand."

"If it gets too rough, give a holler." He grabbed hold of the tailgate, preparing to lift it into place. "We've got to make time."

"I'll take care of Eddie. You just get us there."

Josh slammed home the tailgate and shoved the metal bolts into place. He tied his horse to the back of the wagon, then sprang up into the driver's seat.

"Git-up!" He slapped the reins on the horses just enough that they broke into a trot.

The moonlight was a gift from the spirits, the trail clear and bright. Josh kept up the pace, urging the horses faster whenever he could manage. Always he kept glancing back, checking on Alex and on the boy. He hoped like hell the kid could hang on.

Occasionally, when the wagon took a particularly big bump, he'd hear the boy moan and know that he was still alive.

"Give him all the water he wants," Josh called over his shoulder. "How's the bleeding?"

"So far so good," Alex replied.

At the speed they were traveling, Josh figured it would take until morning to get to town. The horses seemed to have reached their maximum and no matter what he did, he couldn't get them beyond a trot. Every time they tried to slow, he'd snap the whip near their ears and they'd perk up again. It was going to be a long night.

The wagon kept moving. Overhead the sky was littered with stars like diamonds on velvet. Periodically he turned around to ask, "Everything all right?"

"All right" would be the answer from the woman who was far from all right. If Josh hadn't gotten there when he did...aw, hell, he should've been there sooner, but he'd hesitated in town, not certain he was even going to follow them—not entirely liking his deceit. When he'd made up his mind, he'd been a few hours out when his horse had pulled up lame with a damn stone bruise that slowed him to a walk. He'd almost turned around and gone back, but something, some inner voice had told him to keep going, it was important to keep going. Glancing back at the woman, he realized it had been more important than he'd ever thought.

Alex sat stiff on the floor of the wagon. One hand pressed firmly against her cousin's chest. Her arm ached from the effort. Her whole body ached from the sheer terror of the past few hours. Tears welled in her eyes and she blinked them back. She wouldn't cry. She wouldn't. Not now.

She caressed Eddie's forehead with the back of her hand. His skin was warm but clammy to the touch, and perspiration glistened in the moonlight. He was so still. His breathing was slow and labored, each breath a gasp. She wanted to peek at the wound in his side, but she didn't. She was afraid. Eddie was alive. He was breathing, and she didn't want to touch or change anything.

Tears threatened again, this time clinging to her eyelashes. She swiped at them with the heel of her hand. "Don't worry," she said softly to Eddie, who hadn't moved in the past half hour. "You're going to be just fine. You'll see. Just fine."

Hurry, Josh. Please hurry.

This was all her fault. If Eddie died ... She was the one who asked, pleaded with him to come with her. She should have known, somehow, been prepared. It wasn't as though she hadn't been warned. She glanced around at the man driving the team. Yes, Josh had warned her, told her point-blank that there could be trouble. But had she listened? No.

"How much longer?" she shouted up to him, feeling the anxiety, wanting to do something more than sit idly by.

"What? Oh . . . another hour, I think." He wasn't really certain. It was hard to judge with the horses' slow speed. He was tempted to stop, to mount his horse and ride into town and bring the doctor back, but he figured that round trip would take the same amount of time as this one-way, so he kept at it. Besides, he wouldn't leave her alone again.

Gunlock appeared as a flickering light, a dark shadow against a darker sky. At the sight of the town, Josh whipped the team forward.

Alex grabbed hold on the wagon side as they bounced frantically down the hill and into town.

Josh drove straight to the doctor's office, praying the man lived there, also. If not, he was willing to wake up every soul in this town if that's what it took.

Tossing the reins down, he leapt from the seat and pounded on the doctor's door. Blessedly a light appeared. "Hurry, Doc!" he commanded. "Hurry up! We've got a dying man out here!"

Chapter Eight

The door swung open and a short, portly man of about sixty appeared, bleary-eyed. He was dressed in a blue-striped nightshirt that barely reached his chubby knees. He held a kerosene lamp in his hand.

"What's going on?" he asked, rubbing his face with the palm of his free hand, covering his mouth when he yawned. "I was asleep and—"

"Come on, Doc," Josh ordered, taking the man by the shoulders and propelling him in the direction of the wagon. He needed help and he needed it now.

"What's the—"

"I got hurt people here, Doc."

At the mention of injured people, the doctor seemed suddenly wide-awake. He took off fast, his slippered feet making scuffing sounds on the wooden sidewalk. The town was quiet, no one about. A rooster crowed at the dawn.

Josh reached the wagon a second before the doctor. He let the tailgate down with a hard thud that rattled wood and metal.

"What happened?" the doctor asked, sizing up the situation. He spared Alex a glance, then reached for Eddie. Blood stained what was once white bandage.

"He's bleeding again," Alex told them fearfully. "You've got to help him."

"It's a gunshot wound," Josh offered, trying to expedite things.

"Got it." The doctor glanced up at Alex. "What about you, little lady? You all right?"

"Don't worry about me, just save him!" She was already scrambling out of the wagon. The chill of the morning wasn't nearly as cold as she felt inside.

"Let's get him into the office." The doctor cast a questioning glance at Josh. "Can you carry him?"

"Right behind you, Doc."

The doctor took off hotfooting it the few steps back to his office.

Muscles straining in his back and legs, Josh carried Eddie inside to the one and only examination table. His boots made heavy thudding sounds and his spurs jingled as he moved. The only other sound was a small, pathetic groan from Eddie when Josh settled him on the table.

"Sorry," Josh muttered, gently giving the kid a pat on the shoulder. "You're gonna be all right now," he said, even though he didn't fully believe it. It was one of those stupid things people say, trying in some valiant way to make the other person believe it, too.

The doctor bustled around, lighting two more lamps besides the one he'd been carrying. That one he put on the shelf at the end of the examination table.

"Unbutton his shirt," he ordered shortly, all the while removing medical instruments that looked like something out of a medieval torture chamber and putting them on a white porcelain tray.

Josh finished undoing the last button.

When the doctor joined him at the table, he had a pair of spectacles perched on the end of his nose.

Alex was taking this all in from her place in the doorway. The doctor's office was small, the size of a horse stall and about as square, or at least it looked that way to her. It sure wasn't big enough for all of them to squeeze in there. The walls were painted white and looked clean. There was the distinct odor of alcohol and something else, iodine, she thought but wasn't sure.

She watched every move like a mother bear with an injured cub. She didn't know the first thing about country doctors. She was praying this one was a graduate of Johns Hopkins.

Josh had himself trapped between the table and the window and if he backed up about six inches he figured he'd go right through the glass. He was careful not to move. He kept looking at Eddie, who didn't look good, all sickly white, sweating like an icy glass in the summer heat. The kid hardly looked old enough to shave... let alone die.

"Hang in there," he encouraged, and squeezed the kid's hand. Son of a gun, if the kid didn't squeeze back.

Josh sucked in a deep breath and let it out slowly. Damn greenhorns never listened. She thought this was the civilized West, what had she said? oh, yeah, savages on reservations. Well, it damned sure wasn't savages that caused this trouble.

Alex saw the hard look Josh shot her way. Whatever his problem was he'd have to deal with it; she had enough on her mind. This waiting business was worse than the nightmare of the past few hours. Absently she kept tugging on the frayed lace cuff of her blouse. She practically unraveled the whole thing. It was hanging

down about six inches and she ran her fingers over the
fine threads as if they were some kind of worry beads.

What if he dies? What if he dies? Those four words
had been running in her head like the loop of a rope,
going around and around and around, getting tighter
each time.

"Okay, here we go," the doctor said, more to himself than anyone else, it seemed. She winced when the
doctor snipped the bandage and lifted the blood-soaked
material away from the wound.

The doctor didn't say anything for a full two minutes.

"Well?" she prompted.

Still no answer.

Then he looked at Josh, as though she weren't even
there, and said, "He's lost a lot of blood."

"We know that!" she snapped, annoyed. "What
about the bullet?"

"It's still in there." He kept speaking to Josh as
though she couldn't possibly understand.

She inched up. "Look, *Doctor.*" She emphasized the
word to get his attention, sort of like a kick in the side
will sometimes get a man's attention. Both men looked
at her. Finally. "This man is *my* cousin. I want to know
what's going on and I want to know *now.* Tell me what
you're going to do to save him."

Both brows lifted like two dark birds taking flight,
and he peered at her down his nose and over the rim of
his glasses. "Well, little lady—"

"Never mind the 'little lady.' What are you going to
do?"

In a condescending tone that irritated her, he said,
"The bullet's still in there and it's got to come out. I've
got to operate."

Her stomach clenched and her knees turned the consistency of mint jelly. She had to hang on to the table for support, but she wouldn't let these two know. "Operate?" She said the word as though she was pronouncing a death sentence.

That doctor smile was fully in place. "Now little— Now don't worry. I've done this sort of thing before. I have all the instruments and chloroform—" he gestured toward some containers in the glass case behind him "—and I can assure you—"

"Assure me he's going to live."

The doctor fell silent.

"Ah, just as I thought," she ranted. "You can't, can you? You want to operate when—"

"When there's no choice," Josh said across her words. "If he doesn't, the kid—"

"His name is Eddie," she pronounced. "Edward Story."

Josh's head came up. "If he doesn't operate, then *Edward* here is going to die anyway."

The truth of his words hit her harder than a blow to the chest. She had to gulp to get in any air. Those knees of hers were getting soupier all the time. What could she do? Josh was right. There was nothing to do except agree. The bullet had to come out. It was Eddie's life.

With a curt nod, she said, "All right. Do it." Her fingers kept working on that piece of lace.

The doctor went to gather the instruments he needed. He spoke over his shoulder. "You two clear out of here."

"I'm staying." Wild horses couldn't drag her out. She intended to watch every move.

Evidently the doctor guessed her plan, because he confronted her. "I don't need anyone breathing down my neck."

"I'll help."

He held up a can of chloroform, reading the label as he spoke. "Are you a nurse? Do you have experience in surgery?"

"No, but—"

"Look, I don't have time to argue with you. My wife is upstairs and she acts as my assistant. You're dead on your feet. I know you're worried, but there's nothing you can do here. Why don't you go over to the hotel? Have some breakfast. Get cleaned up. See if any of those cuts and scrapes need tending."

The doctor shot Josh an exasperated look. "Get her out of here, will you?"

Josh sidestepped around the table and went to her. "Come on. Let the man do his work. Who's more important here—you, or the kid?"

She was too tired to protest further. "Okay. Let's go."

Once outside, they angled across the street, stepping up on the plank sidewalk by Olsen's butcher shop. The hotel was a couple of doors up the street and that was obviously where he was headed.

Alex shoved the hair back from her face. Her fingers brushed her cheek, and she winced at the tenderness there. Bruise, probably, all things considered. The hem of her tattered skirt dragged in the dirt like a beggar's cloak. Her clothes were caked with mud and her scalp itched where it was plastered to her head—from dirt, mud, or—she didn't want to know.

As they turned into the hotel lobby, the first pink streaks of dawn illuminated its interior. Of course, it didn't take much to see that it was empty.

"You want a room?" Josh asked, his tone rather terse.

"Later, after I know about Eddie."

"Then I want coffee." With that, he left her and strode for the dining room.

Alex followed, not because he was such charming company, which he wasn't, but because she didn't know what else to do. Being with Josh was better than being alone right now, and she felt terribly alone, soul-wrenchingly alone.

Josh disappeared through what she remembered was the kitchen door. She was two steps behind him. Her knees were more wobbly than a day-old foal and so she dragged out the nearest chair. The wooden dowels in the back creaked a little as she sank down.

She was only half aware of the room—large, rectangular and white. A scarred pine table and eight chairs at this end, the other three walls filled with cupboards and counter. The lingering smell of yeast from years of bread-making seemed to permeate the room.

The stove was cool, the coals banked for the night. Josh stirred them to life, added a couple of sticks from the wood box near the door. She braced her feet on the rung of a chair, dragging it closer with the toe of her muddy boot.

As she watched, Josh started going through the cupboards, one by one, opening and closing the doors with enough force to wake anyone unlucky enough to be sleeping in rooms above them.

"Where the hell is the damned coffee?" He banged another cupboard door closed, then another and another.

"Maybe it's in the pantry," she said rather sharply, and motioned with her head toward the two double doors near the end of the counter.

He shot her an I-don't-need-any-help look that she blithely ignored. Sure enough he found the coffee.

"Told you," she couldn't resist adding.

"Yes, you did," he confirmed in a completely ungracious voice. She watched him measure coffee by the handful, then a couple of sharp motions with the pump handle and water filled the gray metal pot. He slammed that down on the stove, too.

"Do you always make yourself at home in someone else's kitchen?"

"I want coffee."

She understood that part; what she didn't understand was why he was so angry. "Will you stop all that banging?" Her head hurt as though she had a vise clamped temple to temple. She rubbed the spots, which made it worse not better. "What the devil's wrong with you? *I'm* the one who was almost killed out there."

Josh turned on her, his black eyes obsidian hard, his square jaw set. The wooden counter pressed hard against his hips. His fingers curled over the smooth edge and dug into the soft pine. "And *I'm* the one who just blew a man's head off to keep that from happening."

The silence stretched between them tight as a barbed wire and just as sharp. The pump dripped into the metal sink, each drop gunshot loud. The metal of the stove snapped and popped as the fire warmed the cool iron.

Alex met his gaze directly. Unwanted, the events of the past few hours played in her brain. The terror, the fear, the shock and the relief, the joy of looking up and seeing his face, of seeing him standing there. And slowly she also realized that he had paid a high price to protect her. A man was dead, a vile, vicious man, but he was dead nonetheless, and Josh Colter had killed him to save her.

"Look, lady, I tried to tell you. If you'd taken some help—"

"You're right."

"What?"

"You're right, and I'm sorry." For the first time since it all began she let herself relax. Muscles seemed to collapse like a starched shirt dipped in water. Her heart fluttered in her chest. Endless tears welled and spilled down her cheeks. "Thank you. I never said thank you for saving my life." She stared down into her lap, her fingers tracing a muddy stain.

When she spoke again, her voice was quiet. "I was scared, you know." Her voice cracked and she gulped down the tears. "Really scared. I thought we were going to die out there."

She looked at him, her blue eyes filled with so much sadness, so much defeat, it tore at his gut.

Colter, sometimes you can be a first-rate ass.

"Aw, hell, Alex . . ." His guard slipped. He dragged out a chair and straddled it, keeping the back like a barricade between them. "I didn't mean..." He slapped his hat down on the table and raked one hand through his hair. "I'm sorry. Sorry this happened. I feel like..."

"Like saying I told you so?" She made a small sound in the back of her throat that could have been a chuckle.

"Never," he lied, having said that exactly. She looked so pitiful. It was all he could do not to reach out and pull her into his arms, to hold her until the fear went away.

Don't even think about it. She's trouble. She's the one woman in the world you can't have.

He knew that; so how come she was the one woman he wanted?

"Thank you...Josh."

Josh. She called him Josh. It was the first time. He liked it, liked the way she said his name. The moment lingered between them, soft and warm as ten-dollar whiskey.

His mouth curved up in a slow, easy smile that touched his eyes and her heart at the same time.

"What say we see about getting you cleaned up?" He surged from his chair and went back to the cupboards.

His smile was infectious, and she responded in kind, though where she got the strength she wasn't sure. Maybe it was simply that she needed to smile at something, someone.

He spent the next few minutes banging through the cupboards again. He found a basin, some soap and a couple of soft cloths, and exclaimed, "What do you know, a bottle of whiskey tucked behind the canned milk in the pantry."

He deposited the things on the table, poured them both a cup of the coffee he'd brewed and then settled in opposite her. The knees of his black wool trousers pressed against her knees under her worn and tattered skirt.

"Come on now, drink some coffee," he encouraged while tearing one of the cloths in two for easy handling. "It'll warm you up. Here." He poured a little whiskey in her cup. "This'll really warm you up, or make you sleepy—both of which are good."

"I'm not sure I'll ever sleep again," she answered, as the terror of her ordeal coiled deep within her.

"You've been through a helluva lot," he told her sincerely. "You've survived. You *are* a survivor. It's gonna take time but you'll be all right."

She searched his face as though to verify the truthfulness of his words. He waited patiently. When she seemed content, he went back to work.

He splashed a big slug of whiskey into the basin of water and made a mental note to leave money in repayment. A little mixing with his fingers before he dipped in the cloth. "This is gonna sting."

"Go ahead."

He touched the cut on her jaw. She cringed but didn't make much of a sound. Tough lady, he thought with admiration, not for the first time. A lot of women would have fallen apart, given up. But her, well, she never backed down from outlaws, or from him, he added.

Tired and battered as she was, she'd yelled at him. Actually, *he'd* yelled at her. *Aw, Colter, the woman's vulnerable as a three-day-old pup.*

Yes, he knew that. A man would have to be blind not to see, not to feel. It was the feeling part that had him on edge, and somewhere in the recesses of his mind, he'd figured that if he had to feel something, anger seemed like a nice, safe emotion.

Because sitting here, looking at her, having her so close, was making the blood heat in his veins, making his fingers tremble. The woman was more tempting than sin, and he was not immune ... to sin or the lady.

But he had pledged an oath of honor to avenge his sister's death, and she was involved, whether she knew it or not. It would be crazy, totally and completely insane, to get close to her, lust or no lust.

Trouble was, lust had a way of drowning out conscience, especially when the subject of that lust was so
close and so alluring.

He tried like hell to keep his mind on other things
while he cleansed the bruise on her cheek. He tried not
to notice how her skin was velvet soft against his fingers. He tried not to notice the way her eyes never left
his. He wiped the dirt from her forehead and the perfect arch of her eyebrows. His hand lingered near her
mouth, and he tried not to notice the seductive way her
lips parted, the warmth of her breath on the backs of his
fingers.

He tried not to notice all of that, but like a sinner on
the road to damnation, he failed miserably. He was
aware of every curve and every breath. His own
breathing was getting a bit ragged. He watched his
thumb skim the surface of her lower lip again, feeling
the delicate smoothness. His heart rate took off like a
stampede. He was in trouble, blue-eyed trouble, and
there wasn't a thing he could do to stop it or himself.

Alex let her eyes flutter closed beneath Josh's minis-
trations. His touch was so gentle, so soothing. It felt
good to have him close, to have him touch her. It
seemed natural, right, safe, an odd thought, since
they'd been fighting since, well, practically since he'd
walked into the camp.

He was a strange man. One minute he was hard and
fierce, willing to kill if necessary, the next, he was here,
caring for her in a way that made her want to cry with
the tenderness of it, of him.

Slowly she opened her eyes, very aware of the man
sitting in front of her. His perfectly sculpted face filled
her line of vision. His black hair curled over his collar
and around his face. Funny little shivers prickled the

fine hair at the back of her neck. She rubbed the spot and felt the stringy mat of her hair on the back of her hand.

"I must be a sight."

"Honey," he said, his voice husky and rich. "You are beautiful." His face moved closer, and his gaze locked with hers. Soft sable eyes held her as surely as if he were touching her. Her heart slammed against her chest, this time not out of fear, but from tingling excitement, and without realizing it, she leaned in to meet him. His breath mingled with hers. He was going to kiss her, she knew, and her body hummed with that knowledge when suddenly—

Footsteps like a drumroll sounded on the bare wood floor of the dining room. The kitchen door burst open with the force of a cavalry charge, and a tall thin woman dressed in faded gray barreled into the room.

Josh surged from his chair like a kid caught behind the barn.

Alex sat up ramrod straight with the not-me look she had perfected in grade school.

The woman skidded to a halt, holding the door open with her outstretched hand. "What's going on here?" she demanded in the no-nonsense tone of a Sunday school teacher.

Josh never missed a beat, which was not bad considering it took him a full ten seconds to remember where he was and why. He explained the situation, about the attack, about Eddie being in surgery and how they'd needed someplace to wait.

The Colter charm had the woman immediately solicitous and understanding. There were many concerned murmurs of "poor thing" and "poor dear," and Alex and the cook, whose name turned out to be Molly, were instantly fast friends.

Molly insisted on making them breakfast even though the restaurant wasn't open officially until eight, another hour.

So while Molly cooked and kept Alex company, Josh slipped out to the front desk and arranged for a couple of rooms. He carried in the trunk and his saddlebags, then stabled the team and wagon.

Breakfast was waiting when he got back—eggs, bacon, ham, potatoes—enough food to feed a crew of lumberjacks. What really surprised him, though, was Alex. He hadn't stepped two feet inside the door when she said, "I thought perhaps you'd left."

His brows drew down. "You mean, left you?"

She nodded. "It crossed my mind."

He gave her his best smile, the one he reserved for very special people, like women he couldn't stop thinking about. "I'm not going anywhere without you."

Chapter Nine

They were back in the doctor's office at quarter past eight.

A smiling doctor greeted them. Sometime since they'd left, the doctor had donned his clothes—white shirt, brown trousers, vest to match the trousers. His spectacles were still balanced dangerously on the tip of his nose.

"Everything's fine," he pronounced. "The bullet's out, and he should make a full recovery."

Alex grinned. Eddie was going to be all right! She threw her arms around the stuffy old doctor and gave him a hug, which took him off guard.

He cleared his throat sharply and she released him, grinning from ear to ear like a cat with a box full of canaries.

"Thank you, Doctor." She couldn't stop smiling, first at the doctor then at Josh, then at the doctor again. She wanted to jump. She wanted to race through the streets, telling the world the good news. She settled for asking, "Can I see him?"

"Later, when he's awake and feeling a little stronger."

"But you're sure he's all right?"

"Sure as I can be."

"I understand." It was hard to contain the sudden burst of energy. She kept lifting up on her toes and settling down again.

"Come on," Josh said. "I'll walk you back to the hotel."

Josh was quiet on their walk across the street. He was thinking about that kiss. Okay, that almost kiss they'd almost had in the kitchen. What the hell had he been thinking? He hadn't been thinking, at least, not with any rational part of his anatomy.

He wasn't some lovesick kid looking for his first woman. He was here on business—grim, ugly, deadly business—and the sooner he remembered that and got on with it, the better for all concerned.

Inside her room, he handed her the key, dropped it, really, into her hand. It had been touching that got him in trouble the last time. Standing this close to her wasn't making things any easier. "Well, I put your trunk in the room." Her lips were parted in a seductive way and she was looking up at him with eyes that were lover soft.

He had to clear his throat to get his voice to work, though other parts of him were working overtime. "Try to get some sleep. I'm going over to the sheriff's office to report things, but I don't hold much hope anything will come of it, the time and distance involved, you know."

"Thank you," she murmured in a voice that teased the nerves on the surface of his skin.

"I'll see you later." He had to get the hell out of here now. He had one hand on the door when she stopped him.

"Are you leaving?"

"Well, yeah."

"Oh."

She looked around the room as if she'd been orphaned.

"Look, you're safe here. I'm down the hall if you need anything. Number eight. Lock your door."

"Eight," she repeated absently, running her hand over the pale yellow-and-white quilt that covered the bed. She moved over to the window and looked out on the street below.

"What's the matter?"

"I don't know," she told him truthfully.

"Try to get some sleep."

"So much has happened, it seems not right to just go to sleep as though nothing has changed."

"Nothing *has* changed," he countered, thinking of their scene in the kitchen, their near kiss. He opened the door a few inches.

She looked at him along the line of her shoulder.

"Everything has changed," she said very softly.

He knew she was right.

In the time since Josh had left her, she'd tried to sleep but couldn't, or wouldn't. There was a voice in her head that kept telling her she wasn't allowed to sleep; she hadn't earned it, didn't deserve it. Yes, it was crazy, but it was there, and she was feeling more than a little crazy anyway.

She'd gotten hot water sent up from the kitchen and taken a sponge bath. Nothing like getting clean to make a person feel better, physically anyway.

Rummaging around in her trunk, she'd found a dress that didn't seem too wrinkled. It was gray and plain and fit her mood. That skirt and blouse she'd been wearing when . . . She didn't want to think about that, and wadded up the now-offensive clothes for the trash.

She'd tried putting her hair up, but her arms didn't seem to have much strength, and after a couple of failed attempts, she gave up and simply tied it back with a pink ribbon.

With a deep breath and a smile that was more show than sincerity, she gave her cheeks a couple of pinches and marched over to the doctor's office.

Eddie, she discovered, had been moved upstairs to a small cheery room in the front that the doctor kept for guests or patients, as the need arose. There was a bed, a mahogany wardrobe and a matching bureau, complete with white doily and lamp. There was also a tray of half-eaten food discarded on the window seat.

"You'll never get better if you don't eat," she chided affectionately as she walked into the room.

Eddie was propped up in the bed. He was wearing a nightshirt, with black stripes, that she guessed had been supplied by the doctor.

"Alex." The collar brushed his cheek as he turned, and he folded it down.

"I'm glad to see you." She gave him a sisterly kiss on the cheek.

"Sit down." He gingerly gestured toward the side chair and winced from the movement.

"Be careful," she ordered, dragging the chair close to the bed. "Well, you look better than the last time I saw you."

Sunlight filtered in through the partially drawn shade, casting the room in milky white light. "You've got a little color in those cheeks again. No wait, I'm confusing that with freckles." She winked. Lord, it was good to see him.

"Never mind . . . the freckle . . . jokes." His expression turned serious. "Alex. Thanks."

"What for?" She pretended to be adjusting her skirt, feeling embarrassed at his sudden sincerity.

"You know. If it hadn't been for you and Mr. Colter and, of course, the doctor I'd—"

"Never. I wouldn't let anything happen to my chief cook." Amusement glinted in her eyes.

As if on cue, the doctor came around the doorway, stethoscope in his hand. "Well, how's the patient?"

"Pretty good, Doctor." Eddie smoothed down the white sheet and blanket over his hips, outlining his long legs beneath.

The doctor put the stethoscope in his ears. "I'll just give a listen." He made the usual doctor sounds. "Hmm." A nod. Another nod.

He looked up, a touch to the forehead, a check of the pulse. "No fever. Pulse good. I think you're gonna be all right."

There was an unmistakable bit of pride in his voice and in his grin, and Alex figured he deserved a little recognition. "You did a wonderful job."

"All in a day's work." He shrugged, but that grin of his got a touch bigger and Alex knew he was enjoying the praise. "What about you, little lady? You want me to take a look at those bruises?"

She let the "little lady" slide this time. "I'm all right. But thank you."

"Suit yourself."

"Doctor, if you'll let me know what your fee is . . ."

"Later." He made a dismissing gesture with his hand. "After he's up and around in a few weeks."

"A few weeks?" A few weeks? Her pulse took a crazy jump. She didn't have a few extra weeks. Everything was on a tight schedule.

Eddie almost died and you're worried about deadlines?

She was being selfish and she knew it, but wasn't a person entitled to a little self-pity? One look at Eddie and she could see the doctor was right, of course. Her cousin looked as wilted as a sunflower in the shade.

Bless his heart, he'd risked his life for her. He deserved nothing but her best and, dammit, that was what he was going to get.

She pushed her smile up a notch, determined to hang on even if the muscles in her face did ache. Eddie was alive and that was enough. How come she felt so devastated?

The doctor was busy completing his examination. "Let's take a look under that bandage."

His back purposely to Alex, he blocked her view. Wouldn't want the "little lady" to see something untoward, she thought, her sudden temper fueled by disappointment and exhaustion and the terrifying ordeal of the past twenty-four hours.

She snatched back her selfish thoughts and focused on the doctor, who was making those unintelligible doctor sounds again." He craned his head back and forth, his gray hair falling over his face as he did. "Looks good."

"Thanks, Doctor."

"Yes, Doctor," Alex chimed in. "We can't thank you enough for what you've done. If anything had happened to Eddie. I mean, if he'd—" She broke off and swallowed hard, wrapping her hand around her cousin's. Resolutely she said, "Now, when can I take him home?"

"Home?" Eddie piped up as if he'd just been jabbed with a needle. "What...do you mean 'home'?"

"I'll wire your father, let him know you're hurt but all right. As soon as the doctor says you can travel, I'll take you home." It was the right thing to do. It was the only thing to do.

The doctor was busy rubbing his clean-shaven chin in thought. "I'd say figure on about three or four weeks to be on the safe side. I wouldn't move him around too much before then, bleeding and such." He tossed his stethoscope onto the bureau and glanced at Eddie. "Do you play cribbage?"

"Huh, yes, but—"

"Good." He gave Eddie a pat on the shoulder. "I'll be keeping him for a while. Then, when it's safe for him to walk, we'll move him to the hotel. You can work out some arrangement with Sam over there, discount by the week. Tell him I sent you. He gives my patients extra special rates. Well, gotta go, Mrs. Stout's baby's due any time now." With that, he disappeared out the door.

Eddie's gaze was riveted on Alex. He shifted, trying to brace up on one elbow. "Ouch. What's this about taking me home? What about the contest?"

"It's not important." Amazing how she said that so calmly, as though he'd just asked her for the time.

"What...do you mean, not important?" His voice moved up half an octave in volume and tenor.

"Taking care of you is important. Getting you home safe and sound is important." This got easier with every word. Amazing. Eddie, she realized, was glaring at her.

"But—"

"But nothing. What do you think, I'm going to leave you?"

Eddie sighed. "Look, Alex. I appreciate what you're doing, but it isn't necessary. I'm going to be fine. The doctor said so." He fussed with the bed sheets again. "What are you going to do, stay around and watch me play cribbage with the doctor?"

"Yes." She paced away. "I'm responsible for this. If you hadn't come out here with me—"

"Dammit!" Eddie raised up again, this time using both elbows. The bed frame creaked. "Those three men are responsible for what happened, and if it hadn't have been for Mr. Colter, well…" He grabbed his pillows and adjusted them so he could sit up more. She helped him. "Mr. Colter was by here this morning. I told him the same thing. I'm eternally grateful. I mean that, but there's nothing anyone can do for me. So you go, win that contest, and by the time you return, I'll be ready to leave."

"And if something should happen?"

"Nothing's going to happen, and if it does, the doctor is right here. But *nothing* is going to happen."

Was she hearing him right? She rubbed her head and her eyes. Was he saying, telling her, to go without him? Could that be right?

"You think I'm going to come all this way, *get shot*, and *not* have you win that contest?"

Hope flickered like a fragile flame. He was telling her to go. She couldn't believe it. No. No, she couldn't. Could she? "You're terrific, Eddie, but even if I wanted to go—" and she desperately did "—I couldn't. I mean, I need help and with you injured—"

"Ask Mr. Colter. He's going anyway, he said so the other day. All things considered, I think you can trust him. Don't you?"

"Well, yes." She knew that whatever her concerns were, Josh Colter had saved their lives at the risk of his own. A sudden image of a man's bloody, lifeless body flashed in her mind. A shiver passed through her.

"You have to go." He gave her hand a squeeze, his grip so weak it wouldn't have gotten juice from an orange.

The flame of hope flared brighter. "Are you sure, Eddie?"

"Sure."

He was giving her permission. He was right, there was nothing for her to do. He was well taken care of and he seemed to be recovering. All those arguments made sense.

"I guess I could..."

"I want you to go."

The flame of hope turned into a bonfire. "Okay. Okay, I will!" She gave him a kiss on the cheek.

"I'm moving up in the world," he teased.

By dinnertime, Josh was feeling stronger, well, calmer anyway. That was probably because he'd scrupulously avoided *her* all day.

He hadn't seen hide nor hair of her since he'd deposited her in her room. *Deposited* was the right word; he'd been as cold as a banker putting money in the vault.

After that near kiss, ah, miss, in the kitchen, he needed distance to get his thoughts together.

He'd spent a couple of hours in his room. Stretched out on the bed, fully clothed, he'd tried to sleep. Should have been no problem. He hadn't slept for nearly twenty-four hours and he had figured he'd be dead to the world the instant his head hit the pillow. He was wrong.

All he'd done was lie there and stare at the ceiling, which was covered in white wallpaper with exactly 437 tiny blue flowers, no more, no less. He was sure, because he'd counted them twice, that was, when he hadn't been thinking about her.

Finally he'd given up and gotten up. He'd changed his shirt, washed his face in the basin and shaved. He'd spent another twenty minutes pacing the room and listing all the tens of hundreds of reasons why he couldn't be attracted to her. One reason stood out above all others. He had sworn to find and kill David Gibson.

He wasn't quite sure what Alex's relationship to Gibson was, but it didn't matter. They were related in some way and that was enough. Thinking about her and the bastard and the murder of his sister sent him storming from the room and in the direction of the Red Dog saloon.

First, he made a stop at the doc's office to check on the kid, who was doing fine, then he headed over to spend a couple of hours in the company of some fairly decent whiskey, which improved his spirits greatly. He wasn't drunk, a long way from it. Contrary to type, this half-breed didn't get drunk after one drink or even one bottle. No, Josh had inherited his Irish father's tolerance for alcohol.

While he sat there, he kept running his options over in his mind. He needed to find Gibson, get this business finished and get home to his ranch. Home. It seemed as though he'd been gone forever instead of just a couple of months. The question now was what to do? He'd thought to get the information from Alex, but

dinner that first night had failed and now so had subterfuge. Instead, the subterfuge part had nearly gotten
her killed.

Anyway, he hadn't counted on this attraction to her.
From the moment he first saw her in the lobby, he had
been attracted. It was lust, pure and undiluted. Man.
Woman. Lust. Very simple. The trouble was, he also
liked her.

Hell, he'd killed for her.

And now he had to get away from her.

So along about his fourth or fifth drink, he realized
he was going to have to get on his horse and ride out of
here. He'd go to Montana and start looking. Okay, so
it would take him months—maybe a year. If it had to
be, it had to be.

One thing was for sure. He was leaving, and he was
leaving alone.

Along about five, he realized he was hungry. He
hadn't eaten since that lumberjack breakfast and then,
what with one thing and another, he'd been kind of
distracted, so he hadn't eaten much.

The only decent place to eat in town was the hotel.

She was at the hotel.

Well, so what? He'd made his decision. He was leaving in the morning. He'd say his goodbyes and be gone.

He was feeling a bit hesitant when he walked into the
dining room. Fortunately, he was early, and the room
was pretty near empty, except for a drummer type sitting at the table next to the window, his black leather
sample case lodged in the opposite chair.

Josh took the table farthest in the back. He was not
hiding! He simply wanted quiet.

He ordered fried steak and potatoes, his mainstay
when he was away from home. The waitress, who re-

membered him from before, brought water and coffee without asking.

Looking at his cup of coffee, that scene in the kitchen flashed, unwanted, in his mind. Alex looking so soft and sad and pitiful. Him slamming and banging around the room, trying to stay angry, knowing that as long as he was angry, then she'd be angry, then there wasn't any chance of...

Of what Colter? Of kissing her inviting lips?

Damn!

He shifted uncomfortably in the chair, surprised by his body's quick and heated response. Where the hell was that dinner? He wanted to eat and get out of there.

A small, delicious shiver tickled the back of his neck. He didn't have to look to know *she* was there.

"Good evening, Mr. Colter," she said in a voice that brushed his nerves like sun-warmed doeskin. She circled around in front of him.

Good manners made him stand. "Good evening."

In a heartbeat he took her in. She was dressed in gray percale. At least, he thought it was percale. The gray part he was sure of. The top was fitted, so was the waist, the skirt was full. It showed off her slender figure perfectly. She had her hair down and tied at the back. She looked bruised and tired and altogether too vulnerable.

"May I join you?" she asked when he didn't offer.

"Please." He gestured toward the opposite chair but didn't help her with it.

Polite but not interested.

Keep saying that, Colter. Let me know when you believe it.

The waitress arrived with Josh's food and another glass of water, this one for Alex, who looked momentarily nonplussed, then ordered the same, steak and potatoes.

"So," he muttered, cutting his steak. "Have you been over to see Eddie?" He motioned toward his food. "Do you mind if I eat?"

"Not at all."

He ate a piece of meat. The steak was juicy and he thought it probably tasted good, but he was too tired and too distracted to be certain.

She sipped the glass of water. "I saw Eddie this afternoon. I spent most of the afternoon with him actually."

"How's he doing?" He tried the potatoes.

"Good. Some pain, of course, but the doctor says that's to be expected." Her mouth went worry straight. "You think that's true, don't you? You don't think he's covering—"

"It's true," he told her, even though he wasn't sure.

She visibly sighed, sagging back against the chair. The kitchen door banged open and she jumped as though she'd been fired out of a cannon.

"Did you sleep for a while today?"

"What? Oh, yes." She sipped her water again, her hand shaking. She made a nervous chuckle. "I lay down anyway."

"You seem edgy." He was a fine one to talk. He hadn't had a good night's sleep in months.

"You know how it is. Too much on my mind."

"Yeah. I know how it is." It was a bond they shared, though for entirely different reasons.

They sat in uneasy silence for a while, Josh eating a meal that could have been sawdust for all he knew. The waitress brought Alex's food.

"Hmm," she said, still far too bright and cheery. "Looks delicious." She cut the meat and cut it some more, but he only saw her take one bite.

Sizing her up, he figured she was running on adrenaline, pure adrenaline. He knew the feeling.

Another couple came into the restaurant and took a table kitty-corner from them. There was the usual scraping of chairs, deciding which one would face which way and such. Josh thought they looked young, newlyweds maybe.

"Mr. Colter?"

"Yes, ma'am," he replied, slipping back into his own formality. He'd been calling her Miss Gibson as a reminder of who she was and what he was about. After all that had happened, he couldn't use the hated name.

He sipped his coffee.

"Do you remember me telling you that I am an artist?"

"I remember." Even in this light, her eyes were the most perfect shade of blue.

"I believe I may also have told you that I was here, had come to Wyoming—" she motioned with her hand "—to find a subject for a painting I'm doing for a contest?"

He arched one brow. "Contest? Wait. Oh, yes, now I remember. Something about the taming of the West, wasn't it?" He was acting; he remembered every word, every look, every smile they'd exchanged since the moment they'd met.

"The thing about the contest is, there's a deadline that's only a few weeks away." She put her fork down and pushed her nearly full plate aside. Forearms resting on the edge of the table, she leaned in a bit, the fabric of her dress rustling as she moved. "Mr. Colter,

I need your help and I wonder if your offer of a couple of days ago is still open?''

Alarm bells sounded in his head. "What offer would that be?" He took a drink of coffee, wishing it was whiskey. Where the hell was a bartender when you needed one? Of course he knew what offer she was talking about, it was the one where he'd said he'd ride along with her, them. That was before though, before he nearly kissed her. That was before he'd started to feel things he wasn't so sure about, things he didn't want to look too closely at.

She cocked her head to one side, her gaze questioning. "Did I misunderstand? You offered to help Eddie and me on our trip north. You said you were going that way yourself."

"I did?"

Think fast, Colter. Remember you're riding out of here tomorrow. Alone.

Her brow crinkled and she regarded him through narrowed eyes. "Isn't that why you were following us? Because you were going that way?"

"Well, yes." What else could he say?

"Eddie and I have been talking. The doctor says traveling for him is out of the question for several weeks. Eddie's convinced me there's nothing I can do, that he's in good hands, and I should go on without him."

"Is that so?"

Alone, Colter. Tomorrow. Alone.

"Yes, because of the deadline, you see? Only I can't go on without him, I mean without someone to help me, and I thought . . . Eddie suggested . . . you."

Well, there it was, the chance he'd been waiting for, the one he'd been angling for only a couple of days ago.

"Uh, I don't know . . ." he stammered. This was perfect. This was dangerous as hell. *She* was dangerous as hell and she didn't even know it.

What the hell's wrong with you? Are you such a coward that you're afraid of one woman? She has the information you need to know to honor your pledge. The people are counting on you. Are you going to find this bastard or not?

Yes, but . . .

No buts, just do what has to be done. You made a promise, remember?

He had two choices: either he said no, went to Montana and spent months looking for the bastard, or he said yes, spent a few weeks on the trail with her and let her lead him straight to where he wanted to go.

What about leaving alone, tomorrow?

She straightened. "I'd be willing to pay you."

If the family hadn't been counting on him, if he hadn't been so damned homesick, he'd have turned her down flat. Instead he said, "When did you want to leave?"

"Would day after tomorrow be too soon? I'd like to make sure Eddie's all right."

"Thursday. Six a.m. At the livery stable."

"I'm grateful to you, Mr. Colter."

"Don't be."

Chapter Ten

Alex was more than thankful that Eddie was getting stronger. His appetite was back full force and so was his boyish smile.

She spent nearly every waking minute with him, which was most of the day and half of the night. When she couldn't stay any later without him becoming suspicious, she would leave, feigning tiredness, but once in her room, she avoided the bed like a coffin.

She'd tried to sleep. She'd dozed a couple of times, sitting in the rickety chair by the window. But each time she closed her eyes, those same gut-wrenching images flashed in her brain—outlaws, guns, a man lying dead, blood flowing in a scarlet rivulet to a ruby red pool.

Therefore, logic said, don't sleep. No sleep. No dreams. Perfect. In time the images would fade, she'd forget the nightmare.

For the past three days, it had been working. At night she paced the floor, barefoot. Of course, so that no one would hear; particularly a certain unpredictable cowboy with hypnotic black eyes that soothed and inflamed her all at the same time.

Inflamed? Where had that come from? Not a chance. The man had been momentary infatuation. Past tense. Emphatically, past tense.

She blithely chose to ignore that encounter in the kitchen. Yes, he'd almost kissed her. Yes, she'd almost let him. Almost? Ha! Who was she trying to kid? She'd been drawn to him like steel to a magnet. A sensual shiver rippled up her spine, making her eyes slam shut, making her palms sweat.

Stop it. Stop it right now.

Josh Colter was unlike any man she'd ever known. He was too charming, when he wanted to be, and too handsome, all of the time. He was also hard and cold and more difficult to figure out than a Chinese puzzle.

She wasn't interested. She had work to do, a contest to win, a deadline to meet. Let some other woman figure him out.

All she wanted was to get to Yellowstone, make her paintings and go back to Paris. Period. As far as traveling together, well, it was business, a matter of convenience. He was going north. She needed to go north. She trusted him, and there was no one else she could ask. She either went with Josh Colter or she didn't go.

She was going.

Wednesday, Alex paid the doctor and left a deposit on the room at the Palace. She and Eddie said their goodbyes that night over a dinner of fried chicken and potatoes, which she had carried in on a tray from the hotel.

Josh stopped in to say goodbye, also, and to wish Eddie a speedy recovery. Alex gave him her polite smile, the one used on maître d's and shopkeepers. It was the one that set barriers, limits, places.

But his gaze was rich and sultry and set no limits at all. It pulled her in faster than quicksand.

Eddie's voice broke the silence. "I owe you my life, Mr. Colter." He extended his hand in gratitude. "I know I thanked you before, but somehow it doesn't seem nearly enough."

Josh tore his gaze from her. "It's enough." His smile was instantaneous and sincerely felt. He liked the kid and was glad, really glad, that Eddie was among the living.

"Mr. Colter, could I ask you one more favor?"

Eddie made a show of smoothing the bed covers in what Alex had come to realize was a nervous gesture.

"Sure." Josh stood at the foot of the bed. He was dressed in his usual dark colors, this time blue shirt, black trousers. His ever-present gun was tied on his hip, his hat held loosely in his left hand. "Just name it." He gave Eddie a playful slap on the foot with his hat.

"Take really good care of Alex. She's like the sister I never had, you know."

Josh stilled. In a voice rich with emotion, he said, "Yes, I know about sisters."

His gaze went immediately to her, to the woman he was about to spend weeks with alone, the woman who heated his blood faster than any woman he'd known. The woman he was about to deceive, to use for his own ends and then . . . A muscle flexed back and forth in his jaw.

"I'll look after her as though she was my own." He was startled to realize that he wished it were true.

Bright and early the next morning, she was at the livery stable. At least this time the sun was up and so were the birds, judging by the frantic warbling coming from the cottonwood tree behind the stable.

A shaggy black-and-white dog was sleeping peacefully in the double-wide doorway of the barn. The livery man was nowhere to be seen, but Josh was.

His back to her, he was busy hitching a team, which was good except it wasn't her team. Her team was fat and old and gray.

"Good morning," she said, stopping a few feet away. There was a chill in the air, but the sky was clear and deep blue, a good sign. The pungent odor of hay mixed with the distinct odor of horses.

He turned but didn't smile. "Mornin'."

She hesitated at his brusqueness, but decided that evidently Mr. Colter wasn't a person who liked mornings any more than Eddie.

"I hate to tell you—" she pulled on her gloves and tucked the tops under the edge of her black wool jacket sleeve "—but those aren't my horses." She adjusted her hat, the droopy-brimmed Stetson, and fussed with the gathers in her full cotton skirt. She was fidgeting. She was feeling nervous about going off with a strange man. It had seemed much more logical and reasonable yesterday in the comfort of Eddie's room or her own. Now, looking at Josh Colter, dressed in gunfighter black, with his gun tied low on his hip, it didn't seem quite so logical.

"I know the horses aren't yours," he told her flatly as he hooked the last strap of the harness in place. "I sold your horses." Matter-of-factly, he went around to check the harness on the other side. He spoke to her over the backs of the team in question. "Actually, I worked a deal for that team of yours. Them plus a little cash and some of those boxes you had in back. You owe me twenty dollars. Don't worry, you can pay me later." One gray horse pawed the ground, making little clouds of dust. Josh soothed him with a pat.

Her brows drew down in direct proportion to her escalating temper. "What do you mean *I* owe you twenty dollars? What right have you got to sell my horses or anything else without my permission?"

"I didn't need your permission to do what's right." He retrieved his hat from the wagon seat and clamped it firmly on his head. "You ready?"

"Hold on just a minute." She couldn't believe her ears. She wasn't sure what had her more upset, his demand for the money, which she was not going to pay him, or his blasted arrogance about the whole thing.

Arrogance won out.

"Since when do you spend my money without asking me first?"

He arched one brow in surprise. "Since now. You asked me to get you there. I told Eddie I'd take care of you and that's what I'm doing."

He sauntered away, pulling on the hemp ropes lashed to the side of the wagon. He went around checking the tie-downs holding the water barrel and other equipment in place. "Come on. We've got ground to cover. You drive first."

"What? I can't... Hey, wait." She recognized fancy footwork when she saw it. She wasn't about to be outmaneuvered or bullied by him. A couple of long strides and she grabbed him by the shoulder and turned him around. "Now look. Let's get something straight. I realize that you are doing me a favor by riding along with me, but this is my wagon and my horses and my supplies."

Josh never flinched. "Look, lady. That team you had was so spavined they weren't going to make it a hundred miles, let alone all the way to Montana. And while I have a horse—" he gestured to his chestnut gelding tied to the back of the wagon "—I don't fancy us having to ride double, not if you want to haul all that stuff you've got in there." He looked exasperated. "By the way, what the hell is all that stuff? I found the boxes of canned food. You were kidding with that right?"

"Kidding? Certainly not." She rushed to peer into the back of the wagon. Several crates, she wasn't certain how many, were gone. She whirled on him, hands balled at her waist. "All that *stuff*, Mr. Colter, is my stuff." Her chin came up in a gesture that was both possessive and challenging. "Where is it?"

He came right back with a demand of his own. "What was all that junk."

"Junk!"

"The store was happy to get the canned food, but the rest of it can't all be clothes and art supplies, can it?"

Her voice was clipped. "It's clothes and art materials and food and water and grain and—what the devil do you mean the store was happy to get it?"

"Just what I said, and another thing—" he lounged against the side of the wagon, the white canvas in sharp contrast to his black shirt "—what the hell was the grain for? I used it as part of the deal for the horses."

"Mr. Colter." She narrowed her eyes. "Mr. Colter, this is mine." She slapped her hand firmly on the side of the wagon. "I don't have to explain or justify any of it to you and I won't have you giving it away!"

"I didn't give it away. I sold it...or traded it. That stuff was way too heavy," he added with a dismissive wave of his hand. "We've got a long way to go. We don't need the weight."

He shook his head, whether in wonder or disgust she wasn't quite sure, didn't care. She was fuming. She couldn't remember being so angry. The nerve of the man. "Look, you—"

He strode past her and mounted his horse in what she thought was his less-than-discreet way of ending the discussion. Well, he was in for a surprise.

"I want my supplies!"

Looking down at her, in a way that made her feel discounted, he said, "I substituted some dried meat and fruit and rice and onions. The horses will have to graze. There's plenty of water this time of year and the game is good so we'll pick up some meat along the way. Anything else?" He didn't wait for an answer or an argument. "You ready?"

"No, I'm not ready!" Her temper reached volcanic proportions. The man was exasperating and arrogant, and if she'd had any other choice right at that moment she'd probably send him packing. But she didn't, and that was the biggest problem of all.

She had to bite back the scathing retort that tingled the end of her tongue like venom. She counted to ten in French and English and Latin to quell her temper, none of which helped much. Maybe there was some truth to what he'd said and done, and maybe she was better off for his help, condescending though it may be, but, ooh, the man made her angry. In a voice cold enough to freeze Niagara, she ordered, "You drive, Mr. Colter."

His horse tossed his head and pranced sideways, making the bridle clink and rattle as he did. "Why should I drive? It's *your* wagon remember?"

"Yes, Mr. Colter, it's my wagon, but..."

He leaned forward, forearms resting on the saddle horn. "You can't drive a team, can you?" There was a smugness in his voice that grated on her nerves like an off-key soprano.

When she didn't answer, he cocked his head to one side and said, "Was that a 'no'?" He cupped one ear as though listening for her words.

Between clenched teeth, she confirmed his snide suspicion. "I can't drive." It was galling. Really galling. Was it going to be like this all the way to Montana?

He dismounted. Without warning, he grabbed her around the waist and deposited her on the wagon seat as though she were so much laundry. She was still catching her breath, when he climbed up and wedged in between her and the edge of the seat, effectively sliding her aside as he did.

Knee to knee, thigh to thigh, shoulder to shoulder, the contact was intimate, pulse-poundingly intimate. She glanced at him out of the corner of her eye. His face was hard, all sharp angles and sculptured curves, his black hair lapped over his collar and fell long and straight across his cheek.

Just looking at him, she thought she could feel the warmth of his body, even through all the layers of coat and clothing. Real or not, his nearness was doing funny things to her heart, and if this team would move as fast, they'd be in Montana by nightfall.

Propriety demanded she move, and her temper helped break the spell he created sitting next to her. She squirmed and made a little space. He squirmed and filled the gap, and she thought she saw the ghost of a smile on his lips.

Well, fine. She just wanted to get on with it.

He uncoiled the reins from the brake handle and handed them to her. His elbow brushed against her breast and her gaze darted to him, but he seemed oblivious to the contact. So why wasn't she?

Tiny tingles skittered across her skin. Had the temperature suddenly shot up fifty degrees? She swallowed hard and unfastened the top two buttons of her coat, needing a little cool air.

She tried to concentrate on what he was saying.

"Okay, this is how it's done."

Pressed tight together, his hands wrapped intimately around hers, he showed her the fine points of driving. He showed her how to lace the reins lightly but firmly through her fingers and over her thumbs. He explained the how-to of guiding the horses, which didn't seem all that difficult.

"Okay, you ready now?"

"Ready," she confirmed, her teeth still clenched. Her jaw was starting to ache.

"Then, git-up!" he shouted. The horses lurched forward and the snap of the reins nearly pulled her off the seat, she was so unprepared. Josh grabbed her, pulling her against the curve of his shoulder. With his free hand, the one that wasn't dangerously close to her breast, he caught up both reins and stopped them.

She made the mistake of looking up into his face, which was only inches from hers.

For two breathless seconds, they stayed that way, then abruptly he released her and swung down, leaving her alone on the wagon seat and feeling strangely alone inside, as well.

From his place on the ground, he adjusted his hat then looked up at her. "Okay, you've got the idea. You can manage." It wasn't a question, and before she could object, he disappeared along the side of the wagon, swung up on his horse and rode out a short distance ahead of her.

She'd show him. She grabbed up the reins again. Back stiff, feet braced, she slapped them hard on the roundness of the horses' rumps. "Git-up!"

A couple of miles and she had this driving business pretty well under control—at least the going-straight-ahead part.

As they topped the hill that signaled the last view of Gunlock, it hit her exactly what she was doing. And what she was doing was riding off into the wilderness with a total stranger. Let's face it, what did she know about the man, other than the fact that he was arrogant as hell. Oh, let's not forget rude and demanding and ruthless, a man capable of killing.

So with all that, you just naturally said sure to spending the next several weeks alone in the middle of nowhere with him.

But he had saved her life...their lives, her logical mind prompted.

The wagon creaked and groaned along, occasionally banging as a wheel dropped into a particularly deep rut, usually jarring her teeth!

The sun warmed the day quickly and when the perspiration trickled down her back and neck, she knew it was time to shed her coat, which was no easy trick, what with hanging on to the reins for dear life.

All the while, she kept watching him and ruminating. What the devil had she gotten herself into? How could she have thought of going off anywhere with a man? Winning that damned contest, that was how!

By the time they pulled off the road for the noon meal, she'd worked herself into quite a state, a little late to be sure, but it was a hand-wringing state all the same.

She was insane, of course. The first in her family as far as she knew, but certifiable. She should have stayed with Eddie, gone back to San Francisco, explained things to her father and... But when was another contest like this going to come along? What had her father said? *This contract is not negotiable.*

She was sitting there staring off into the space framed by the horse's ears when—

"Well?"

His voice startled her so that she jumped and bit her tongue!

It took a second to realize that he was there, right there! One booted foot propped on the wheel spoke, his arms stretched up to her. "Are you getting down or what?"

"Down," she stammered, fumbling to get the reins tied to the brake handle. She turned to face him, and her skirt snagged on the rough wood of the seat. Now she had to fuss with getting that untangled, and still he stood there, staring up at her in a way that was making her pulse-rate double with every beat of her heart.

"Need help?"

"No, thank you." She got the muslin free. "You know, I think I can manage on my own." To prove her point, she hitched up her skirt, just to the tops of her boots, turned and, as though going down a ladder, put a tentative foot over the side, searching for the top of the wheel with the tip of her boot.

"Oh, for heaven's sakes." She heard him grumble the same instant she felt his hands around her waist. He set her firmly on the ground. Unnerved, she rounded on him before she realized he still held her, still had her trapped between the wagon and the hard length of his body.

Her hands naturally went to his chest, the cotton of his shirt warm to the touch. Their gazes locked and they stood like that, lover close, the world suddenly lost beyond the range of sight.

Josh was drowning in her summer-sky blue eyes. His fingers tightened on her narrow waist, feeling the stiff bones of the corset beneath the soft cotton of her shirtwaist. Her lips parted, in surprise or invitation, he wasn't sure. Either way, it was hard to resist.

His breathing got a touch ragged. His blood got more than a touch hot.

Pressed length to length with him, Alex's body hummed to life, nerves she didn't know she had throbbed with anticipation.

It would be so simple to slide her hands upward, over his broad shoulders and around his neck. Fleetingly she wondered if his hair was soft or coarse?

"Alex," he murmured in a voice low and rich, which sent goose bumps skittering up the backs of her legs.

She took a steadying breath, and cleared her throat. "Thank you, Mr. Colter." The man did something to her, something that intrigued and frightened her all at once. It was the frightened part that made her say, "Don't." Abruptly she stepped sideways and free of his touch.

"What's wrong?"

"Nothing." She fussed with straightening her skirt and her shirtwaist and her hair, trying to look casual, all the while putting distance between them, like a rabbit trying to outmaneuver a cougar.

"What's wrong?" he questioned again, his tone demanding. He hadn't moved from his place by the wheel, but he watched her with a predatory intensity that she was startlingly aware of.

"Nothing." What else could she say? *I'm terrified.* She couldn't give that much away. An old adage about never showing fear in the face of danger flickered in her mind—or was it fear in the face of wolves?

Looking at him, either seemed to apply.

Her hand fluttered to the base of her neck. "I just was thinking..."

"Thinking what?" Head cocked to one side, he took a half step in her direction, his spurs jingling. She nearly bolted away; as it was she kept moving, circling, her footsteps kicking up little clouds of dust as she went.

He stood very still, studying her. She saw him glance back at the spot near the wheel where he'd held her, then back to her again.

She saw the understanding flash in his eyes a second before they turned grim. Slowly he pulled himself up straighter, taller, fiercer.

"Lady," he told her in a no-nonsense voice, "if I wanted to...have my way with you—I think that's how they put it in the novels—believe me, I would have done it before I went to all the trouble of hauling you and the kid into town. You aren't the only damned woman west of the Mississippi, you know. I don't believe in force, not where a woman is concerned, anyway."

His angry gaze pierced her like an arrow, and even across the twenty or so feet that separated them she could see he was telling the truth. Logic confirmed her senses. This was *not* a man who had to force a woman. No, looking at him, more handsome than any one man had the right to be, he was a man who women would more likely throw themselves at.

"You're right, Mr. Colter. I...I'm sorry." She shook her head, the brim of her hat flopping up and down as she moved. "It's just that after what happened, I started thinking that I was—"

"Out here alone with me," he finished for her, his tone a little softer than his scowl. "Okay." He visibly relaxed. "I can understand that." He took another step in her direction as though testing her resolve. She managed to stand her ground.

In the same soft tone, he added, "Do you want me to take you back to town?"

"Would you do that?"

"Yes."

He was serious. She knew unquestionably he was serious. "You would, wouldn't you?"

"Yes."

In that moment everything changed. A bond of trust was forged between them and she took courage from that and from him. "No, Mr. Colter, I don't want you to take me back to town. I want to finish what I came out here to do."

"So do I."

He strode for his horse, opened his saddlebags and when he turned, he had a gun. He came at her purposefully.

He shoved the gun into her shaking hand. "Now, we're equal."

Chapter Eleven

By the time they made camp that night, she was feeling more confident. She'd taken the gun he'd given her and tucked it into her skirt pocket, where it was this minute.

Of course, she knew how to use a gun; her father had taught her. She'd brought one along, though having it buried in the bottom of her trunk hadn't helped when ... well, it hadn't helped. But this one—she patted her pocket, the metal sandwiched between hand and hip—this one would.

They'd exchanged weapons like two opposing generals and had reached a truce of sorts. It was a generous gesture, one he didn't have to make; one meant to reassure her, which it had. He was a strange man, this Josh Colter. A smile curved up the corners of her mouth. She thought, perhaps, that more than being attracted him, she liked him, honestly liked him. Who'd have thought?

Josh stayed on his horse all afternoon. It seemed the safer thing to do. Riding close to her on the wagon was too much to ask of him. They'd had a strained but pleasant lunch—cold smoked ham and dried fruit. He'd been braced for a complaint about the canned fruit being gone. She hadn't said a word.

All she'd done was sit there on the overturned water bucket, eat her lunch, occasionally glance at him and slowly drive him crazy. All he'd thought about was the way her body had melded to his when he'd held her, the way her hands had felt pressed against his chest, the way her seductive mouth had invited a kiss and . . .

Dammit.

He should have left bad enough alone. The woman had said she could get down off the wagon alone, and did he listen? No. And why the hell not? Because he wanted to touch her, that's why, to see if his body quickened as rapidly as it had this morning.

He had had his answer, all right. Whether he liked it was something else all together. Holding her, looking down into her luminous blue eyes, desire, hot and clear, had pounded in his blood like tribal drums.

She probably didn't have any idea what she did to him or how much he wanted her. It was as simple as Adam and Eve, and as complicated as four hundred years of conquest.

What would she do when she found out that he was the one who was going to kill . . . someone close to her? Hell, he still didn't even *know* what. Who was this Davy to her?

Whoever he was, that relationship would be terminated. His fingers curled around the reins, the leather cutting into his skin. The well-trained horse shied and pranced sideways, not understanding its master's instructions.

"Easy, Sundown," he murmured, giving the horse a calming pat on the side of his neck. Until three days ago, it had just been him and ol' Sundown here. The two of them on a mission. Then Josh had walked into that hotel lobby and something had changed. Why was Alex Gibson so important to him? Why did it matter what *she* thought?

The flutelike call of the meadowlark interrupted his thoughts, and the bird lifted from the grassland to soar into the air a few yards in front of him. He wished he could take flight as easily.

He was here now, and he would do the job he'd pledged to do. He would not forget what Gibson and the others had done and he would not forgive, not for anyone.

It was late afternoon when they reached the spot where the trouble had been. It looked so ordinary, so calm and inviting, Josh could see why Eddie had chosen the spot. No one would ever guess, to look at it, that a man had died there, another almost had, and a woman, this woman, had nearly been raped.

The cold fury he'd felt that night surged in him, as though it were there all the time, circling just out of sight. Maybe it had been, maybe that was why he had pulled the trigger without hesitation. More likely it was seeing that son of a bitch pull back to hit her. The bastard would have crushed her skull with his big ugly fist.

So Josh had killed one man and would have killed again. As he'd stood out there in the darkness, watching, waiting like some night prowler, he'd thought of Mourning Dove, of what had happened to her, of what would have happened here if he'd arrived a few minutes later.

Feeling strangely anxious, he dropped back to check on her. He didn't say anything, neither did she. Maybe she was so caught up in the driving, she didn't realize where they were. The day was getting short and he needed to find a camp before dark, but not here.

Reining over, close enough that his stirrup brushed the wheel hub, he called out, "You okay to go for another hour?"

She nodded.

No smile. No frown. Nothing but a nod. Not even a look. She had her eyes fixed on the spot between the two horses, and that was that. Evidently the lady was tougher than he'd given her credit for.

They put several more miles and another hill between them and what he was coming to think of as "the spot."

Up ahead, there was a place where the stream made a sharp bend and headed due south. A couple of cottonwoods gave a little shade and there was enough open space that he figured he could see trouble coming.

"Okay?" He motioned with his hand and she nodded her understanding of his cryptic reference to camping for the night.

He trotted in, and she did a good job of turning the team and following him. Yes, he thought, swinging down and flexing the kinks out of his back, the lady was something.

He rubbed his shoulders and rolled them, stretched and flexed again. This eight-hours-in-the-saddle business was getting old—or he was. He chuckled.

Five blackbirds perched in the cottonwood trees, cawed their protest at having their domain invaded. Too bad, he thought and set about uncinching Sundown.

He saw her moving around, stretching, holding her lower back like a farmer who'd plowed too long today. "How's the back?" he asked, pulling off his horse's saddle and carrying it a few yards away. He bent to put it down, letting it fall the last foot or so, making a thump on the ground.

"Back's fine," she answered, but she was still holding it, rubbing it, and he figured it wasn't all that fine. He'd offer to give her a back rub, but that didn't seem like a good idea ... for a lot of obvious reasons, all involving her being horizontal and him being much too close.

He coughed, swiped his open hand over his face and eyes and wisely decided not to push his luck. Grabbing up the horse's reins, he led him to the water for a drink. He repeated the procedure with the team.

About that time, he noticed she had retrieved a large paper pad from the wagon and strolled in the direction of the creek. He followed her with his gaze. She stood by the water's edge, head down, watching the water churning and bubbling over the small rocks that lined the bed. She appeared to be lost in thought, and he hesitated, wondering what she was thinking.

"Tired?" he called out as he gathered up the reins to lead all three horses over to the meadow to graze. Sunlight glinted on the water, making it flash silver and white against the dark bottom. The gurgling sound was soothing.

Alex didn't answer, just gave him a wave and a ghost of a smile, before she strolled downstream, the sketch pad tucked under her left arm. She moved slowly, gracefully, even though he knew she had to be exhausted.

He lost sight of her while he finished caring for the horses, putting on the hobbles for the night.

According to the grumbling in his stomach, it must be close to five. With a long stride and a quick step, he started back to camp. There was a surprise waiting for him.

Alex had gathered firewood and made a circle of rocks to contain the fire. Son of a gun. It was nothing more than a few sticks, but she'd done it on her own, without being asked. She was trying to help, to do her share.

"Do you mind a little help?"

"Be my guest," she told him, her voice as smooth and easy as twenty-year-old Scotch and heating him just as fast.

The slight breeze that was rustling the tops of the cottonwood trees wasn't doing a damned thing to cool him off. But he steeled himself against his dangerous line of thought and got back to the task at hand.

"Okay," he said, a little strained. With one quick move, he produced a skinning knife from his boot. The last orange-yellow rays of the sun glinted on the blade.

Terror flashed stark and clear in her eyes.

"Kindling," he said. "Haven't you ever started a fire before?"

"Once," she responded, her voice cracking like the beginning of a fissure.

"I'm gonna make a little kindling." He dropped down on one knee, the soil cushion soft. A couple of swipes with the knife and rich-scented curls of wood fell into the fire pit. He arranged them near the wood, after he'd unstacked about three-fourths of it, that is. He struck a match.

She was quiet, so quiet. And it was finally beginning to dawn on him just how hard the whole experience back there had been for her.

She stared into the flames wordlessly. Behind her the sun disappeared below the horizon. Only the brightest stars were visible this early. The fire crackled and popped. She jumped with every sharp sound.

"Alex?"

She didn't answer.

"Alex?"

She looked at him as though seeing him for the first time. She blinked a couple of times and her vision seemed to clear. "What? Oh, yes. The fire's very nice. Thank you." She hugged herself and he thought he saw her rock back and forth ever so slightly.

"Are you all right?"

"Sure." She straightened, releasing her hold as though to prove her point. Then she held her hands out to the flames. "Nice fire."

Josh shifted around, one knee propped up, the other curved under. "I thought maybe you were thinking about...you know...what happened."

She went quite still, her eyes never leaving the fire. "No. I was not."

"Don't worry," he reassured, "nothing's going to happen."

"Okay."

That "okay" had about as much enthusiasm as a kid saying sure to seconds on spinach. He couldn't get her to talk and there was no way he could convince her that they'd be safe—that he'd make sure of it—so the only thing left to do was change the subject, try to get her mind off it. "How about some dinner? I'm starved."

Rubbing his stomach, he surged to his feet, tossed a couple more sticks onto the fire and headed for the wagon and those supplies, whistling a little tune as he went. He was putting on a show of sorts for her. He didn't like to see her hurting. He wanted to make it better.

"It's kind of late, so bacon and biscuits would do me. How about you?" He had the cast-iron skillet tucked under one arm and was pulling the other things out of the box.

"Sounds fine."

Balancing the sacks of flour and such, he held out the fry pan to her. He waited and she didn't move. "Uh, if you'll get the bacon and biscuits going, I'll take care of the coffee."

She pivoted toward him, her brown cotton skirt twisting around her ankles. "Well, I guess I could manage the bacon, but the biscuits are out of my league."

"Excuse me?" Surely he hadn't heard her right. It was simple, one of the first things any child learns to do—and any man who wants to keep from starving to death.

"I'm telling you I can't cook. That was Eddie's job, though if you tell him I said so, he'll deny it, I'm sure."

The hand holding the skillet dropped to his side, the black metal rubbing the edge of his holster. "So let me get this straight. Just who were you expecting to do the cooking on this trip?"

"Well, I thought you would."

"And what would you do if I said I didn't cook?"

"I'd say you shouldn't have been so quick to give away all that canned food I'd bought."

She had him there. He laughed. Who could argue with logic like that? Not him. "Well, at least give me a hand with this, will you?"

"Sure."

She watched him work, asking questions, seeming to anticipate his needs and handing him things before he asked. For the first time since he could remember, he was actually enjoying cooking. If his ranch hands could see him now!

She insisted on slicing the bacon, which was a little too thick, but he wasn't going to say anything. He made the biscuits. "Learned on a trail drive," he said to her unasked question.

In no time, the biscuits were baking in the Dutch oven and the bacon was sizzling, the spicy aroma filling the air.

With a snap, Josh spread his blanket on the ground, then sat down cross-legged. Alex sat on a wooden bucket on the opposite side. Their gazes met across the glow of the fire. The night sky was filled with thousands of stars, the Milky Way looked like a streak of white paint across the heaven. The constant gurgle of the brook serenaded them.

Josh relaxed for what felt like the first time in recent memory. "It'll be ready soon. You want to wash up or anything, now's the time."

Her head came up. She snapped a quick look toward the stream, then back to him. "Later. In the morning."

Good move, Colter. Sure she wants to go down by that stream again.

She was pale as snow, her mouth drawn in a tight line. The way she had her hands tucked in the folds of her skirt, well, he'd take odds they were shaking.

So what now, Colter, you idiot?

He had to keep her talking, keep her from thinking too much. "Is there any sugar?"

"What? Oh, yes, in the brown box with the coffee beans."

He retrieved it, and when he returned he sprinkled a couple of pinches on the frying bacon. "Cuts the salt.

Makes it sweeter." He kept talking. She kept staring into the flames. "So how come you can't cook?" He was floundering for things to say, to ask.

"Never needed to, I guess."

"Well, you'd never make it as a cowboy, then," he teased.

"Okay," she muttered.

"It's not difficult, you know. Why, even I can cook most stuff—stew, bacon—" he jiggled the pan in illustration "—steak, potatoes." She was clearly not here with him, but someplace else, someplace dark and ugly. He was getting desperate. It was time to divulge his most closely guarded secret. "I can make a helluva chocolate cake."

Her head came up slowly, as though the words were penetrating her brain one at a time. "Pardon me?"

Ah, he had her now. "I said, I can make a chocolate cake. Not on the trail, of course, I do need a real oven, but yeah, Mrs. Obermeyer, on the next ranch over, asked for my recipe." He grinned.

"You're kidding?"

"Nope."

"Who taught you to make a cake?"

That's it, Alex, keep talking, honey.

"Oh, we had a housekeeper for a few years—I was away at school and my father wasn't good at remembering to do ordinary things like eat and such, so one summer I hired a housekeeper." He settled in to the conversation.

"Ah." She shifted, straightening her skirt as she did. "I believe you said you live on a ranch?"

"Yes. In Montana."

"Sheep or cattle or something else?"

"Cattle. There is nothing else...ma'am." His mouth pulled down in a mock frown.

"I see." She laughed.

He liked the sound of her laughter, as if he'd been able to induce it, as if she'd laughed and smiled just for him.

He turned the bacon, which was sizzling about as much as he was, and shimmied the pan, not wanting the meat to cook too fast and be dried out. There was nothing worse than shoe-leather-hard bacon. "Another couple of minutes. Can you wait?"

"Do I have a choice?" she teased.

"Nope." He pretended to be stern.

The silence that surrounded them was as comfortable as an old robe. After a minute or so, she asked, "So then it's just you and your father? There's no Mrs. Colter waiting impatiently at home?"

He slid the pan off the fire and onto a waiting rock. "Give me that plate, will you?" She did, and he served up the bacon, half-and-half, on the metal plates. "The answer to your question is no. No Mrs. Colter. My father died several years ago. It's just me now." He checked the biscuits, the smell was making his mouth water. Ah, yes, golden and delicious. "Ready."

She held both plates out again while he served. Putting the Dutch oven aside, he took the offered dish. "Thanks."

Balancing the blue-speckled plate on her knees, she picked at the bacon with her fingers, putting small pieces into her mouth in a way that was innocent and sensual all at once.

"What about your mother?" she asked, glancing up.

Like a kid caught looking at something he shouldn't, his gaze darted away. "What?"

"Your mother?"

"Gone."

"I'm sorry. My mother died a year ago. I sometimes think death is more painful for the living than the dead. I don't mean to—"

"I know what you mean."

Another silence. This time it was Josh who spoke up. "So were you and your mother close?" Gingerly he tore at a biscuit, the hot dough burning his fingers.

"Very. I miss her. I wish, now, that I'd been home more instead of away. But she encouraged me, you know, to study art."

"Yes," he agreed, suddenly assailed with his own sadness. "I understand."

"I agree. Never wait to do something. Take advantage of every moment. Don't let anything slip away."

"I know what you mean. If you think about it, you realize that each minute of your life comes only once, then it's gone forever."

"Exactly."

She was easy to talk to, and he didn't want the conversation to end. He cracked a stick over his knee, then tossed half of it into the fire. Silently they watched it resist the flames until, finally, it succumbed.

"So," he started, "you were telling me about being away from home. Was it Europe?"

"Paris."

He popped a piece of biscuit into his mouth and wished for butter. "Paris, huh?" He reached for more biscuits. "How long have you lived there?" He'd never known anyone who had lived outside the country, certainly not anywhere as cosmopolitan as Paris. That explained her liberated attitude about things like traveling alone with a man because, special circumstances or not, he understood she was taking a real risk with her reputation. He wondered if she was as liberated about other things?

"I've lived in Paris for, oh, about five years. I shared a room over a little restaurant on St. Germain."

She said it with that proper pronunciation, the sound seeming to come from the back of her throat, like a purr.

She tore open the biscuit, put bacon inside and closed it over, sandwich style. "Hmm, delicious." She licked her fingers, one at a time, in that sensuous way again. He watched every motion with heart-pounding closeness.

Colter you're in trouble here.

"Coffee!" he practically shouted as he stood. "I think we need coffee." *I think I need to do something to keep from thinking about you in ways I shouldn't.*

"So you were telling me about Paris." He talked as he walked, his spurs jingling with each step. The plaintive howl of a coyote carried on the breeze.

The fire flickered and danced, heat warming Alex's face and neck, the first of the evening chill penetrating the cotton of her blouse. Goose bumps prickled her arms and she rubbed them to get the warmth back. "Paris is nice. It took me a while to get all the nuances of the language but, yes, I like it there. Besides, there they don't judge your talent by your gender, but by your skill."

"I gather you feel America hasn't been fair to you, or is it, to women in general?"

She angled around. "Don't get me started on America and women. Let's just say the art community here hasn't been very interested in women artists."

"So are you going back to Paris?"

"Yes."

"Where's this contest figure in?" The coffee grinder made a crunching sound as he ground up the beans. "You know, this is a luxury on the trail, this coffee grinder. I mean, I usually have to work with whatever I can carry in my saddlebags."

He banged the contents of the mill into the speckled coffeepot, filled it with water from the barrel then rejoined her at the camp fire.

"How on earth do you manage?" She looked at his saddlebags resting beside his saddle. They looked awfully small.

"Oh, well, it's one of those things you learn to do. I cook a lot of things on a spit. I can make coffee in a skillet instead of a pot. If I have to I can do without coffee." He grimaced and she laughed.

"That bad, huh?"

"Yeah, that bad." He grinned. "So now, you were saying you were going to win a contest and...?" He was becoming intrigued, genuinely interested in the woman and her goals.

"And," she said, emphasizing the word and picking up the sentence, "the prize is enough money to keep me going for a while."

"You can't do that here?"

"No. I've started to get some recognition in Paris. Besides I promised someone I'd return."

"You promised someone, huh?" He wondered if there was a man, perhaps men. That thought didn't sit well.

"A friend."

"A man?"

"A friend."

Finally he tossed another small stick onto the fire. "What's your father think about this?"

"My father has decided I should give up my art and settle down."

"And you don't agree?"

"No. I don't agree."

"How does he feel about you being out here?" *With me,* he thought to say but didn't. He wondered if she'd told her father, wired him, perhaps?

"I neglected to tell him. He thinks I'm with Eddie, and of course, Davy."

"Ah yes, Davy." His nerves tensed at the mention of the name of the person he sought. He kept his pose and voice casual. Maybe now he'd find out what he wanted to know. "I heard you mention that name in the hotel lobby. You said you weren't married, so then who is this Davy?"

"Davy? Didn't I tell you? Davy's my brother."

Chapter Twelve

Josh stood at the edge of the stream. The tree-shadowed blackness surrounded him, but it was nothing compared to the blackness he felt inside.

"Son of a bitch," he muttered, his hands curling into bone-aching fists. The bastard was her brother, her goddamned brother. Yeah, he'd known all along the two were related somehow, they had the same last name, but, her *brother!*

The man he was going to kill was her brother.

The revelation had hit him like a fence post in the chest and he'd had to get away from her to catch his breath.

He paced up the stream a ways. The gurgling of the brook grated his nerves, like a never-ending scrape of fingernails on slate.

Why the hell was this getting worse and worse? He was doing the right thing, he was sure of that, so how come, all of a sudden, someone, he craned his head upward, was making this so tough?

"You couldn't have made little Davy some distant relative, could you?" he asked aloud. "Some twelfth cousin by marriage or something? Someone she didn't know, hadn't seen in twenty years?"

Disgusted, he kept pacing, occasionally stepping in the water, not caring a bit. He kept trying to sort this out in his mind.

It always came back to one thing. His sister was dead, murdered by three men, and the last of them was her damn brother. Josh had made a pledge of honor, given his word to Mourning Dove's spirit, that he would see justice done.

So, Colter, this is a wake-up call. The woman is not for you.

He dragged in a couple of breaths of moist, clean air. The scent of sage drifted lightly on the breeze. He rifled one hand through his hair, then rubbed his face as though to wipe away the angry thoughts and feelings that were warring in his brain.

So what are you going to do?

He'd do what he had to do, what he'd promised to do. In the meantime, it was true, this was a wake-up call. He'd been getting a little too comfortable, a little too familiar, a little too attracted. All that would stop. Now.

He'd keep his distance during the day. If she needed a rest from driving, he'd give her his horse to ride, or she could ride in the back of the wagon. They'd eat meals together and sleep . . .

No, not *sleep* together. That was out of the question, he told himself, and tried to curb the sudden throbbing in his loins.

He wheeled around and headed back the way he'd come. Starting tomorrow, he'd make a hard push for Montana. It was spring and the light was lasting longer. They'd be there in about a week, seven days . . . and nights, his surging lust prompted.

The hell with the nights.

With a heavy sigh, he steeled himself to face her and walked back into the camp.

He spotted her up on her toes, putting the last of the dishes back into the wagon. He strode for the fire and his blanket. "We ought to get some sleep." It was an order, not a suggestion.

"Are you all right? I mean you seemed—"

"I'm tired. I need some damn sleep is all."

"Look, don't snap at me. If you want sleep so badly then go ahead and sleep! Who's stopping you?" She flung the skillet into the box and let the lid fall shut with a bang. "I'm staying up."

"I want to be on the road at dawn."

"Dawn. Got it," she said curtly, not letting him intimidate her.

He glared at her, his mouth set with annoyance. "Suit yourself."

She watched him take off his spurs, adjust his saddle to use as a headrest. He tossed a couple more sticks onto the fire, pulled the blanket over his body and covered his face with his hat.

No "good night." No "see you in the morning." Damn the man.

Well, actually, now that she thought about it, maybe it was better this way. No explanations, no questions about why she wasn't tired, which, of course, she was. Her head felt as if it were filled with cotton, and there were times when her limbs didn't seem to be attached to her body, they felt so numb, but she wasn't going to go to sleep. She wasn't going to have those dreams again.

The night was getting colder and goose bumps skimmed her arms and shoulders. An owl hooted from a nearby tree. The wind rustled the leaves, making them clack together, nearly drowning out the constant hum of the stream. On the far side of the camp, she could see the horses tethered, standing motionless, heads down as though they, too, were asleep.

The flames of the fire sputtered and stretched in defiance. She slid in a little closer to the fire, which was getting smaller in direct proportion to the night getting colder.

The wind picked up. Great. That was all she needed. A blanket would help. Yes, a blanket was what she needed. Wrapped over her coat, it would be plenty warm.

Doing a careful tiptoe walk, she went to the wagon. No sense waking *him*. Groping around, she located the camelback trunk with the blankets.

She dragged out the top blanket, the wool soft and cozy. Ah, yes this was going to do it. Unfortunately, the trunk lid slipped from her grasp and fell with the speed of an executioner's ax. Short of putting her fingers on the block, there was no way to stop it. It slammed louder than a thunderclap, and she stood motionless waiting to see if *he* heard it.

Nothing.

She crawled out of the wagon, the red wool blanket tucked under her right arm. This time as she tiptoed across the campsite, the soft soil seemed to crunch like gravel under her feet.

She opened the blanket, situated herself on the bucket again and made a mental note to find a more comfortable seat tomorrow, one that fit her bottom.

Now what? If she'd gotten her pad she could make some rough sketches. Yes, of course. What a goose. She made to stand when—

"Don't."

His deep voice startled her. Her hand flew to her chest as though she could still the double-time beating of her heart. Her eyes darted to him. He never moved, never even lifted his hat.

"What?" she babbled.

"Lady, go to sleep."

"I'm sorry. I didn't mean to wake you."

"Wake me?" He lifted the hat and peered at her. "What the hell makes you think I've been to sleep, what with you climbing in and out of the wagon all night?"

"It isn't all night. I only did because you went to bed too fast."

"Excuse me?" He was still prone, holding up his hat as though to shade off the sun, although, of course, there wasn't any. "You're telling me it's my fault that you have to run around here, crashing and banging?"

Her chin came up about as fast as her temper. "That's right."

He sat up, legs stretched out in front of him. "What do you want me to do, send you a damn letter? I said I was going to bed."

"Well, you should have—"

"Fine. It's all my fault. You're a saint. Now, for the love of Pete, lie down and go to sleep."

"I'm not sleepy," she lied.

In what appeared to be one motion, he stood. "Dammit. I'm telling you to lie down and go the hell to sleep."

"You can't *make* me go to sleep, Mr. Colter." That temper of hers was fueled by a lifelong defiant streak.

He fixed her with a stern look that would make an outlaw think twice before arguing. "You wanna bet?" Before she knew what was happening, he snatched up the blanket, spread it on the **ground** and said, "Alex, you've got until I count to five to crawl into that bed, because on six, I'm gonna put you there. One.''

"Who do you think you're talking to? You can't order me around." She shoved her fists at her waist, the wool rough on the backs of her fingers.

"Two."

"No one tells me what to do, Mr. Colter."

"Three."

His gaze was obsidian hard. A muscle flexed back and forth in his jaw, which was rigid. His hair fell around his face and chin in a way that made him look fierce, almost savage.

"Four."

She faced off with him. It would have been a better face-off if he hadn't towered six inches above her. He glowered at her. She glared right back.

"Five," he finished in a tone that was menacingly quiet.

Five seconds ticked past.

Alex Gibson never backed down.

There was an ominous gleam in his eyes an instant before he scooped her up and deposited her, with a teeth-jarring thud, on the blanket.

"Why you...!" All arms and legs, she scampered to get up.

"Don't even think about it," he warned. "I intend to get some sleep tonight. Now either stay put or I swear I'll tie you in the wagon."

Angry as she was, she didn't doubt him for a minute. With a theatrical sigh and a flounce of skirt and blanket, she turned her back on him.

Fine. She'd just lie there and when he went to sleep, as he was so intent on doing, then she'd get up.

He tossed more wood onto the fire, before slipping back into his bedroll. The orange and red of the flames hypnotized her. The delicious warmth soaked through the blanket and her coat, warming her skin, making her relaxed and snug.

It was so nice and warm...

The dream came slowly, peacefully. There was a castle, nestled next to a slow-moving river. She was dressed all in white, and from her window she looked down onto the courtyard where Eddie was feeding the perfectly matched team of carriage horses. All was calm, quiet.

Like an eclipse, the world went dark, and out of the darkness emerged men, big ugly men like the most hideous gargoyles. They advanced on her.

With lightning speed that belied their size, they captured her, their huge gnarled hands digging painfully into her flesh.

The darkness turned to red, wet and acrid like only blood could be.

Blood covered the castle, the earth, the sun. It was seeping up her dress, turning the white fabric to red. She pushed at it, but it would not be stopped. And she knew that she would drown in the blood if she didn't get away.

"No!" she screamed. She fought. She clawed but they never let go. Escape.

A voice called to her, "Alex."

The voice was far away. The gargoyles were laughing.

"Alex," the voice called a little louder. "Alex. I'm here."

Hands were holding her shoulders, shaking her. The distant voice kept calling, "Alex, look at me! Open your eyes!"

Heart thundering in her chest, she forced her eyes open, afraid of what she'd see.

She saw Josh Colter's handsome face. He had her wrapped in his protective embrace, hard and strong.

"You're all right." His calming voice brushed against her ear.

Around them, the night wind whispered across the open prairie. The horses neighed and pawed the earth as though sensing the sudden anxiety.

The fear and horror of the dream, of the attack, threatened to swallow her up like a person going down for the third and last time. Tears clogged her throat and filled her eyes. "I thought I...I thought the men..."

Tears cascaded down her cheeks. Sobs racked her body and she shook with the force of them. Like any desperate person, she clung to him, to Josh Colter, needing his strength, taking solace from the steady beating of his heart.

"I couldn't run. I was so afraid...." The sobs would not be contained. Embarrassed, exhausted, she buried her face against the side of his neck. Her hands drifted up his arms. He smelled like leather and sunshine. He felt like salvation.

In a voice achingly tender, he said, "I know. It's all right. It's all right. I'm here." Seated on the blanket, he held her close and rocked her as though she were a frightened child. "Shh...shh...I'll take care of you. I'll never let anything hurt you. Shh."

One hand cradled her head, holding it lightly against his shoulder, the other rubbed up and down her back. He kissed her hair and held her to him.

They stayed like that for several minutes, him giving strength and comfort, her gratefully accepting. When the tears slowed, she lifted away and looked into his face. Her hands curved over his shoulders, feeling the hard muscle and bone through the cotton of his shirt.

The flames of the fire reflected in his bottomless black eyes, held her prisoner. With his thumbs, he wiped the tears from her cheeks. She smiled tentatively, knowing she should pull away but unwilling to do so.

"Alex," he whispered, a kiss away from her. Her skin tingled, and warmth surged through her as though she'd been touched by a flame. "You're very beautiful, you know." He traced her lower lip with the tip of his thumb, teasing, exciting.

This time when she shivered, it was not from the cold. Her breath came in shallow gasps. He looked into her eyes as though questioning her or himself. He hesitated. His mouth curved up in a sensuous smile that sent her pulse-rate soaring. He lowered his head.

The touch of his lips on hers was soft, tentative, inviting. He lifted away, his mouth hovering just out of reach. An unfamiliar longing stirred inside her, aching, seeking, hot. Her body responded with the knowledge of the ages. She threaded her fingers through his hair, silk against her flesh, and pulled him toward her.

This time there was no smile, no hesitation. His mouth covered hers in a searing kiss that sent heat shooting out along untried nerve endings. Desire coiled low in her. Her hands curled into fists, his hair imprisoned in her fingers. His mouth slanted back and forth, greedy, hungry and she matched him, her hunger as great as his.

The world around them vanished. The night, like a cloak, surrounded them, dark and safe and magical. There was nothing but Josh Colter, the feel of his mouth on hers, the power of his arms crushing her to him.

His tongue pushed at her lips, demanding entrance, and she surrendered to his demand. Her body tensed, poised, anticipating. The instant his tongue touched hers, the desire that was coiled so tight within her spiraled up and out, wild, frantic, engulfing her. It was passion, pure and carnal in all its delight.

She moved in his arms, her body refusing to remain still. She clung to him; held him to her and made small animal sounds in her throat.

Josh felt, as much as heard, the purring sound she made. Pleasure turned to lust. His hands splayed across her back, then dropped lower, seeking the curve of her hip. She arched into him and he pulled her up closer, wanting to feel her body against him, wanting to surrender to the blood pounding in his brain and between his legs.

All reason was lost. She met him fully, her hands touching his hair, his face, his neck. Everywhere she touched, his skin was heated. He ate at her lip, laved at the tender flesh of her mouth. She tasted sweet, like coffee. When she moved, her hair smelled like wood smoke, but she felt like fire in his hands.

Every muscle in his body tensed, straining with ardent need. Erotic fantasies, the ones he'd been struggling to keep at bay, paraded, bright and clear, through his mind. Every one of them had to do with her, naked and sprawled beneath him, her hair spilled out across the blanket, her soft breasts rubbing his bare chest as he moved on her.

Desire went off in him like a gunshot. He wanted her. Here. Now. This minute. And if he could only get through all these damn clothes she was wearing, he was going to have her.

His hand drifted around, fumbling with her buttons, while he kissed her mouth and jaw and neck. He laved at her ear, then blew warm moist air over the damp spot, delighting when she shivered. He wanted to make her shiver. He wanted to make her moan with the joy of what they would share.

He finished the buttons, found the edge of the coat and, pulling back, he slid it from her shoulders.

Maybe it was the absence of her mouth on his or the cold air that fell between them, chilling his overheated skin. Whatever it was, his throbbing nerves stilled. The world filled in around him, the sky, the stars, the fire. The woman.

What the hell are you doing, Colter?

With shaking hands, he grabbed her shoulders and held her away from him. "Alex, I didn't..." Passion clouded his vision, surged through his body like a living force. Demand drummed in his brain, nearly drowning out the voice of reality. But reality was not to be denied.

What was he thinking? This was the very thing he'd feared, the thing he'd warred against and now, now he'd been a willing participant.

She looked at him, her face so beautiful, so delicate in the light. Her hair was tousled where he had run his hands through the silken stands. Her mouth was red and swollen where moments ago he'd kissed her with more greed, more lust than he'd ever known. Oh, Lord, how he wanted her.

Alex blinked several times, clearing the fog, the passion haze from her mind. "What's wrong?" she asked, realizing she'd savored the kiss, had initiated it, in fact.

"I can't do this." He set her at arm's length, but the chasm between their worlds was so much greater.

Unrequited desire humming inside her, she reached to touch his cheek, but he jerked away as though stung.

"Why?" she asked in a husky voice tinged with confusion.

Why? he groaned inwardly. Was she so innocent that she didn't know what was about to happen—might still happen—if she kept looking at him like that.

"Josh?"

"Don't. Don't even ask." He surged to his feet, needing distance, a great deal of distance, or this could still end up in disaster. Towering over her, he said, "Go back to sleep!"

Humiliation replaced her desire. What a fool she'd made of herself, and with this man of all men, a stranger, a man whom only this morning she had worried about being alone with. Now it appeared *he* had more self-control than she.

"I . . ." she stammered, not knowing what to say.

Josh circled the fire, grabbed up his saddlebags and started away.

"Where are you going?" she asked, fearful he might be leaving.

"I'm going to take a bath. A cold bath."

"Josh, I—"

"Just go to sleep!"

Alex threw herself down on the blanket with bone-rattling force. They'd kissed. It had been a great kiss. The best she'd ever had. Had it been so awful for him?

She knew she wasn't skilled, but he'd seemed to be enjoying it, then he'd stopped. Why?

She was still awake when he returned to their camp. She didn't speak to him, out of embarrassment and temper.

But just because she didn't speak didn't mean she wasn't keenly aware of him.

Surreptitiously, through her lashes, she watched him. She'd have been better off not to have been so curious.

She watched him hang his towel on the wagon and his saddlebags beside it. He turned then, and she squinted her eyes smaller but not so small that she couldn't see he was looking straight at her. Did he know she was awake, watching him? Was he thinking about their kiss? Was he half as affected as she was? Probably not. It probably didn't mean a thing to him.

He walked past her, toward his bedroll. The warmth that had coiled inside her when he kissed her was still there, tight and uncomfortable down low, at the juncture of her legs. She drew her knees up in an effort to ease the discomfort. It didn't help. Knowing he was so close didn't help, either. She closed her eyes, trying to shut out the man and the longing.

She heard him moving around, then silence. After another few minutes she decided he must be asleep. She rolled onto her back and stared up at the sky, the blackness littered with tens of thousands of sparkling stars.

Josh.

Chapter Thirteen

"Coffee's ready!"

Josh winced, rubbed his face and rolled over on his side. His eyes hurt and his back was stiff. What the hell was she doing up?

He squinted at the horizon and knew it was late, somewhere between seven and eight. He'd overslept. He never overslept. Oh, now he remembered, he'd lain awake half the night trying not to think about her, trying to pretend he didn't know she was awake and watching him.

He sat up and rubbed the sleep from his eyes. She was there, a black skirt and green-and-white striped shirtwaist. The skirt was full, the shirtwaist fitted, long sleeves, high collar. She had her hair pinned up. She looked young and fresh and . . . breathtaking.

"Coffee's ready," she prompted again, pointing, with no little amount of pride, to the pot that was boiling away at the edge of the fire. "I can get the bacon and—"

"No." He tore his gaze away before he made a fool of himself again. He rubbed his eyes, then flexed his shoulders, trying to ease the stiffness there.

"Look, Mr. Colter," she started, her balled fists shoved into her narrow waist, "I don't have to do this, you know. I don't even like coffee and I never eat breakfast. But I was up and I remembered you said you had to have coffee in the morning and—"

He held up both hands in surrender. "Sorry." He was mean. A man gets like that when he's had to take a cold bath when what he really wanted was a hot woman. She had kissed him as if she were going up in flames, as if they both were.

Josh took a steadying lungful of cool Wyoming morning air, raked his hands through his hair and stood. "The coffee smells good," he said by way of apology. He knew she didn't understand what had happened between them. He couldn't tell her.

Her look was cautious when she handed him a cup.

He took a sip of the steaming liquid. It was brown and murky, sort of like coffee, but one tongue-curling sip told him it wasn't even close. He drank the whole cup and never grimaced. "Thanks."

"More?"

"Huh? Oh, no more. It's late and we have to get going." He didn't want to linger, didn't want to talk about last night.

She started to clean up, pouring the remains of the coffee on the camp fire, putting the utensils away, gathering the blankets.

"I'll take care of mine," he called to her as he hitched up the team to the wagon.

Alex tried not to pay any attention to him, but every time she looked around he was there, so it wasn't her fault that she noticed the way he moved in a long-legged powerful stride, or the way his black shirt pulled tight over his back as he reached.

His raven black hair fell across his cheek but he never tucked it behind his ears, and she had the strangest impulse to brush it back from his face. It was soft. She remembered that all too well from last night. How on earth could a woman forget being kissed like that? She didn't know kissing could feel so luscious, so exquisite. And there, in the early hours this morning, just as the first light was illuminating the eastern horizon, she had wondered what it would be like to make love with someone like Josh Colter.

"Lady, how long are you going to stand there staring at the cold fire?"

Alex jumped, the pot falling from her hand, and she had to do a juggling act to catch it. She spun around, a sharp retort on her lips, but he was standing there, by the horses, looking all dark and powerful and more handsome than any one man had a right to be.

"I was thinking," she stammered.

"Glad to hear it," he said flatly, turning to saddle his horse.

Her temper was back instantly. For all her daydreaming, Josh Colter was an unpredictable man, harsh, indifferent. He was not her kind of man, not the stuff dreams were made of.

Three days later they reached what was called Elkhorn Cutoff. Finally. They'd been at this every day from dawn to dusk, and she was tired from the bones out.

The darned wagon seat was hard as marble and she thought she couldn't wear enough petticoats or sit on enough blankets to soften the ride. At least the weather was holding.

Overhead, the sky was pale blue with the barest hint of clouds. The wagon creaked and groaned and rattled, more, it seemed, since they'd covered some rough country along the edge of the Sweetwater Mountains. The only good part was that she had found time to make a few sketches, nothing that she thought would be "the one," but some pretty good ones she might make into paintings later.

For now she still had her heart set on Yellowstone, and she knew if the place was this difficult to reach, no one else would have made the effort. She was sure to get the very unique painting she needed. She was going to win this contest and Yellowstone was going to make the difference.

Shifting the reins to one hand, she adjusted her hat back a little, enjoying the warmth of the sun on her face and trying to not breathe in too much of the dust kicked up by the horses. As it was, the front of her white blouse and her brown skirt were both covered in enough dust to write her name in, or it felt like that anyway. Why the devil she'd worn white was beyond her.

It was a good thing there were no mirrors out here. She had the feeling she was berry brown and her hair was permanently pushed into the shape of her hat. If the ladies of Nob Hill could only see her now, she chuckled to herself.

Well, one good thing, the days had been cool, cooler than when they'd left Gunlock, not coat weather, but if she stood in the shade there was a definite chill.

Of course, nothing was as cold as Josh. No matter what she did or didn't do, *he* never seemed to do anything but scowl at her. Since what she'd come to think of as "that night," he'd never approached her, and while she couldn't fault him for his extremely appropriate behavior, she did miss him. It was strange to say, since he was right there, but it was as though he weren't there, except in body.

Well, a few more days, maybe a week, and she hoped they'd be in Yellowstone. She hoped it wouldn't be longer. Josh hadn't said and she hadn't asked. They had this sort of speak-when-necessary understanding.

The road they were on dead-ended and clearly she either had to turn right or left. She reined in, and the horses stood with their heads up, waiting for the go-ahead. She glanced around at the valley floor, flat and covered in sage and tufts of buffalo grass. There were no buffalo to be seen, she noted sadly, remembering the stacks of hides she'd seen one day by the docks in San Francisco. She had wondered then how so many could be killed. Now, looking at the barren plain, she knew the answer.

A pair of red-tailed hawks circled above her and she shaded her eyes to watch the two glide effortlessly on the air currents. But even the altitude of the beautiful birds was dwarfed by peaks whose names she didn't know. Whatever they were, she was impressed. No matter which way she looked, spires rose thousands of feet above her. Pine trees, so thick and dense they looked black instead of green, dotted the sides of the mountains, and where the rock was exposed, the stone was gray and white and black and red, a rainbow of sorts.

Words like *magnificent* and *breathtaking* seemed the closest she could come to a description, and she wondered if she could do justice to the imposing quality on paper or canvas?

She felt compelled to try, so sketch pad in hand, she perched on the seat and tried to capture the majesty that was Wyoming's mountains.

Thirty minutes and she had finished the second sketch, noting colors for future reference. With a sigh, she felt daunted by the task.

Be that as it may, for now she needed to get moving.

She picked up the thick leather reins, the ones that seemed to weigh about a hundred pounds by the end of the day, then studied the road, two ruts cut deep in the soil, devoid of any grass. Clearly a road that was well used, though there was no one around now.

In fact, there was nothing—no signs pointing the way and no trail of bread crumbs to follow, but she knew she didn't have to be Kit Carson to know that Yellowstone was west and west was left.

The elusive Josh was nowhere to be seen. Oh, he'd trotted up awhile ago to tell her he was going ahead to scout the trail, for what, she didn't have a clue—a campsite, most likely. Well, whatever he was doing she'd probably meet him on the road.

Adjusting her feet to a more comfortable position on the wagon box, she hollered to the horses, "Git!" She was getting pretty good at this driving business, she thought with no small amount of pride. One thing was for sure: when this trip was over, if she never saw another horse's rump or felt another wagon's stiff springs, it would be fine with her.

She leaned into her task, back muscles stretching, pulling the cotton of her blouse tight over her shoulders. She knew that by afternoon she'd be staring straight into the setting sun. She was getting a headache just thinking about it. Well, the price of success.

She hadn't gone a quarter of a mile when Josh rode up fast, his horse skidding to a walk and kicking up enough dust to choke a mule or, in this case, her.

She gave him a hostile stare. Her temper flared. "Thanks," she said, and coughed, fanning the dust away with one hand.

"What the hell are you doing?" His expression was bulldog fierce.

It didn't take two seconds for her temper to explode. She yanked back on the reins with all her strength, fingers cramping. The horses stopped so fast they reared and pranced dangerously in the harness.

She stood, fury overcoming control. "Mr. Colter, I've about had it with this attitude of yours."

Horses danced and pawed the ground. Dust billowed in cough-causing brown clouds.

He swung down and held the horses. His angry gaze found her. "Dammit, woman, are you trying to cripple these animals? Don't you know what you're doing?"

Furious, she threw down the reins, the leather hitting the wood with a clatter and falling by her feet. He was holding the horses, let him be the damn brake.

"I know exactly what I'm doing, Mr. Colter."

"Then where the hell are you going? We need to go east to go north."

"Why would I want to go north?" she retaliated.

"Montana is north. You know—" he pointed as though he were talking to some child "—north."

"Yes. I know very well which way is north." She pointed. "And east." She pointed again. "And west." She pointed one more time. "I also know that I'm going west. That *is* where Yellowstone is, unless they've moved it in the last few days." She spat out the words punctuated with a withering glare.

"What the hell do you mean you're going to Yellowstone? *Who the hell* said anything about Yellowstone?"

"I did! I'm going to Yellowstone to do my painting."

He let go of the team and charged around to confront her.

"And just when, pray tell, did you make this decision?"

"When I left San Francisco, I believe." Clenching her teeth, she was furious at his autocratic behavior. "What *is* the problem?"

He paced back and forth by the wheel as though tethered to the darned thing. The man fairly shook with rage. She could see his fists curl and uncurl as he walked, marched, really. All the while those damned spurs of his kept jingling.

Finally he said, "Look, no one ever said Yellowstone. *You* said north. *You* said Montana." He whirled to face her, barely controlled anger bright in his eyes.

"I never said Montana," she countered icily. "Well, yes, I said Montana to pick up Davy, but—"

"Exactly. Find your brother. So what the hell is all this Yellowstone business?"

Exasperated, she said, "I'm going to Yellowstone first to do my painting for the contest. You remember me telling you about the contest...don't you?" Her voice had an edge to it.

"Yeah. I remember the damn contest." His voice was low and too quiet, the kind of quiet that made the hair bristle on the back of her neck. "I don't remember anything about Yellowstone. It's out of the way. It's too far. It's too hard to get there. We're *going* to Montana."

Another minute of this Mexican standoff and she railed, "Mr. Colter, you can go any *damned* place you want. Go to blazes for all I care. I'm—" she thumbed her chest with her gloved hand ''—going to Yellowstone. I've got a deadline and I don't have time or inclination to argue with you about destinations.''

With a flounce, she slammed down on the seat, snatched up the reins and slapped them hard on the horses' sweat-darkened rumps. ''Git-up!''

The horses took off in a canter, leaving him standing in the dust. Josh was furious. Feet braced, he stood there watching her drive away. Yellowstone! Son of a bitch. No way was he going to Yellowstone. Why, for two cents he'd ride after her, drag her off the wagon and shake some sense into her!

Well, that was it. Done. Finished. Let her go the hell to Yellowstone. Let the damned woman go wherever she pleased. *He* wasn't going. He was going to Montana to find that damn murderer.

He swung up into the saddle, and the sun-warmed leather creaked under his body weight. A gentle breeze skimmed the tops of the grass, making it bend southward then straighten.

''Yellowstone,'' he grumbled out loud to no one but himself. ''She's going to Yellowstone.'' Did she know how long that was going to take? A week at the minimum, more like two, he amended, still seething. If he'd known that, he would have gone another way, swung south more. Ah, hell, if he'd known that, he wouldn't have gone at all.

The wagon was no longer visible, only the cloud of dust.

So there she went, as though she could make it on her own. As though she'd find the Lander cutoff, which was the only choice now. Then there was the desert to cross, fifty miles of nothing. She'd have to do it at night if she was going to make it and she'd *never* make it. She didn't know about pushing hard, about conserving water, about a hundred other things that could go wrong.

The dust cloud settled, and as far as he could see there was nothing. The wagon and the woman were gone.

Yeah, and that's exactly what's going to happen to her if you don't help her.

He sat there for another minute. He grimaced and shook his head. Dammit to hell!

He put his spurs to Sundown's side and rode west.

It was late afternoon when the wind picked up out of the north. Josh was riding alongside of her. He'd caught up about fifteen minutes after they'd had that little tête-à-tête in the roadway. That had been several hours ago.

She'd given him a curt nod by way of acknowledgment. She'd been angry. She was still angry.

Two seconds after she'd given him that I-don't-need-you speech of hers, she realized she'd be in big trouble if the man took it into his head to ride off and leave her. That dependent feeling rankled her simmering temper even more.

Yes, for a few minutes there, she'd told herself it didn't matter if he'd left. She had a map, for the fat lot of good a few lines scrawled on a piece of brown paper would do.

It was just like Josh to do this to her, put her in this position. It wasn't as though she could pull into the nearest town and hire someone, for heaven's sakes. And assuming she did, how would she know she could trust a man for hire to get her there, on time, without robbing her or worse?

Looking around, there was nothing and no one as far as she could see, and that darned map didn't indicate a single town. She knew, she'd checked that right away.

Darn the man! And darn this wind. Dust swirled and spiraled and seemed to be determined to get into her eyes and mouth and nose. She coughed and wiped her face and eyes on the curve of her arm, for all the good it did, which was none.

The wind swirled a dust devil in the road, the horses balked and shied. "Whoa!" She strained, tugging on the reins to keep them in check, in tandem.

She shot a questioning glance over at Josh, riding grim faced alongside. He was looking straight ahead, as though he were riding along all alone. Well, fine, she thought, she'd be damned if she'd speak first.

The wind blew harder, yanking her hat off. She made a grab for it too late. It landed in the back of the wagon, lost in the jumble of boxes and crates. Her hair fell loose and lashed around her face. Annoyed, she shoved it behind her ears.

"Git-up!" she hollered to the team again, urging them forward, a direction they seemed determined not to go in.

When had the sky turned such a foreboding shade of gray? The wind came in threatening swirls, lifting dust and grass to blow across the road, worrying the horses who nodded and pawed the ground. There was a storm coming. Perfect, she thought, her anger building as fast as the billowing white thunderheads over the mountains. Just perfect. What else could go wrong?

"Git going! Curly! Sunshine!" she shouted, thinking perhaps they could outrun the rain. She didn't relish the idea of being stuck in a drippy wagon for hours, maybe days with *him*.

But the horses hesitated, twisting in the harness. "No! Get going!" If those dumb horses got tangled in the harness, they'd go down, possibly get hurt.

The unmistakable crash of thunder ended any hope that they were going to outdistance this storm.

Josh rode in close to the wagon, stood in the stirrups, and before she realized what he was about, he leapt up onto the wagon seat beside her. Arrogant as always, he just took the reins right out of her hands, as though she'd suddenly become incompetent.

"Hey—"

"We're gonna get wet if we don't move," he shouted over the clap of thunder. The constant slapping of the canvas only added to the noise. He grabbed the whip and cracked it smartly over the horse's heads. "Get going, you mangy critters!" He cracked the whip again.

The horses took off, whether scared by the whip or the equally threatening crack of thunder, she didn't know. Whatever it was, he'd gotten the horses moving. Out of the corner of her eye, she noticed Josh's horse racing along beside them, evidently eager to stay with his master.

The usual scent of sage was replaced by the moist, heavy scent of rain. Gray streaks fell from the distant clouds like fraying threads from a piece of cloth. The rain seemed to be coming from all directions at once, and they were surrounded with nowhere to hide.

"There's lightning in those clouds!" he shouted above the roar of the wind, the crash and rattle of canvas and wagon.

The horses were moving in a wild gallop, the wagon banging and slamming over the rough terrain. Breathing fast, she hung on for dear life. "Slow down or we'll all be killed!"

Lightning flashed like the devil's own pitchfork across the near-black sky. Thunder followed like the roll of an executioner's drum.

Josh tugged his hat lower on his forehead. The wind bent the front brim back, revealing his face, set in hard lines. He sat up straight, both reins in one hand, the whip in the other. "We need cover!" he shouted at her. "It's too open here. We're too vulnerable!" He slapped the reins again, hard, and lashed out with the whip once more.

"Slow down!" she ordered, as the wagon hit a rut and seemed to be airborne for one heart-stopping second, coming down with a teeth-rattling slam. "It's only rain!"

"It's lightning!" he hollered back at her.

"It's rain!" she repeated, not understanding the difference. She'd always liked storms, thunder, lightning, had always watched them from her window, exhilarated by the power.

He spared her a questioning glance. "It's open prairie. Flat ground!" He whipped the horses again and reined over so that they were headed for a rocky outcropping that jutted out of the plains like the smallest of mountains.

"So what if it's lightning?"

The wagon hit another bone-jarring rut. She clung to the seat, her fingers digging into the soft pine.

The rocky spire was close. The rain, the lightning, was closer.

"Lightning strikes the highest point!" he told her, leaning forward, whipping the horses who were running full-out. "We're the highest point unless we get to that rock formation!"

Overhead the sky lit up like a thousand rockets had gone off at once. Static electricity made the hair on her arms stand up. Her skin seemed to sizzle with the energy. Now she was scared. Now she understood his fear, and it became hers, too.

"We need cover!" he yelled.

Up ahead, she could see the rocks. Her body leaned forward as though to propel them in that direction.

Lightning cut through the sky again, hitting the earth like an arrow. Thunder raced to catch up.

The horses skidded to a halt, the wagon swinging wildly to the side.

Another blinding flash and a deafening crash of thunder. Alex covered her ears against the sound. She'd never known a storm could be so wild, so violent.

The horses reared, neighing and pawing the air and each other as though in protest. The harness strained and pulled. A strap broke under the tension and the horses were helplessly tangled in the web of leather.

The rain was upon them. The first drops of water— as big as tablespoons, hit them. The water splashed onto the seat and the ground and them, leaving dark stains on Alex's skirt and blouse. There was no time to get her coat.

Shoving the reins into her hands, Josh jumped down. "I'll untangle the team. I'll yell when I'm ready."

Lightning arched over them from horizon to horizon. It was as though the whole world were caught up in this storm.

Alex shook, her body vibrating with the power of it. Thunder exploded all around them like the slamming of some giant door.

Leaning into the wind, she managed to stay on her feet, frantic to keep Josh in sight, listening for his voice. The rain came down harder, the drops smaller, clinging to them like confetti.

She angled back and forth, trying to see in the rain-blurred darkness, holding tight to the reins, while he worked to free the horses. When he had, he grabbed hold of the lead lines. "I'll lead, you drive. Okay?" he called up to her.

Cupping her hand to her mouth, she hollered, "Yes!" Rain spattered into her mouth. More trickled through her wet hair, down her face and neck, pooling in her ears and eyes.

They hadn't gone fifty yards when lightning zig-zagged down and hit the ground only a few feet from them in a heart-stopping explosion. The air crackled. The horses screamed in terror.

So did Alex. "Josh!"

All the oxygen seemed to disappear from the universe. Alex gasped for breath. Her hands shook uncontrollably.

Terrified, she screamed again, "Josh!"

"I'm here!" He was busy hanging on to the lead lines, trying to control the horses, which were rearing, nearly lifting him in the air with them. Quickly he dodged flying hooves. "Easy, boys!" He tugged on the rope line. "Easy."

Lightning flashed again, thunder answered and the horses' panic increased. They tried to run. Alex pulled back on the reins, shoulder muscles strained with the effort. The horses kept twisting and prancing, and suddenly she saw one rear back again, saw his feet slip on the water-soaked ground.

Wild-eyed, the horse went down.

"Josh!" She strained to look, to see in the torrential downpour. "Josh! Are you all right?"

No answer.

Nothing but the downed horse, the other one pawing the ground, trying to sidestep away from its companion.

Lightning flashed again and her eyes beheld a ghastly sight.

"Josh!" she screamed.

Chapter Fourteen

She flung herself down off the wagon and ran to where she'd last seen him. He was there—pinned under the fallen horse.

She dropped to her knees beside him, mud oozing through her skirt, freezing her legs. "Josh. Josh!" She took his face in her hands. "Are you all right?"

"Hell no!"

"I'll get you out!" Frantic, she grabbed his shoulder, her fingers clutching the cotton of his shirt. Straining, she tried to pull him free. The shirt tore and she fell back, both hands sliding in the mud as she caught herself. "I can't. Josh. What are we going to do?"

Josh gasped for air and wished he hadn't. Lord, it hurt; two thousand pounds of horse flesh was crushing down on top of him.

"Josh, are you all right?"

"Do I look all right?" He was mad, damn mad, and if he could get his gun he'd be tempted to shoot the stupid creature, never mind that would make it worse.

Pinned from the chest down, he lifted his head, neck muscles aching from the effort, and managed to get both hands and arms free. He tried to move, to see if his legs were broken. He couldn't feel a thing except this horse.

Rain soaked the ground and him. "Don't just sit there. Get him the hell off me!"

"Okay!" Alex started to push on the horse's neck, back, anything she could. Her feet kept sliding away from her in the mud, making traction impossible. She kept trying, refusing to give up.

Josh braced both hands on the horse's spine in an effort to help. He pushed. Muscles strained along his shoulders and arms and back. Pain cut through him faster than a hot knife through butter. The horse's feet flailed around but nothing else.

"Good Lord." Releasing his hold, he needed a breath—as though he could actually get more than a mouthful of air into his lungs without the pain threatening to send him into near unconsciousness. Sweat beaded on his forehead and was lost in the downpour.

Gone were the big clumsy drops, replaced with tiny ones that pelted his face like thousands of needles. Water ran down his nose and into his ears. He had to keep blinking to keep it out of his eyes. Oh, God, he hurt.

His head fell back. Mud soaked into his hair and around his neck. He was cold and wet and the shivers had started about a minute ago. The only warmth was the poker-hot pain that kept slicing through him with every breath.

Rain fell like the second coming of the flood. Too bad they didn't have an ark. Lightning crackled and sizzled in a sky that was black as a witch's cauldron. They were in trouble, he knew, and he had to get them out of here.

He sucked in a breath, trying to still the pain, and shoved on the horse again. "Get off me...." His mouth pulled to a thin white line and his eyes slammed shut.

Don't pass out now. She needs you.

Desperate to free Josh, Alex rushed around to the other side of the team to survey the damage, the trouble. The horse was not dead, and as best she could tell, uninjured. At least nothing was obvious, no bones sticking out, no legs at odd angles.

She shoved the wet hair out of her face. Okay, so then the horse should be able to stand. All she had to do was get it up.

Josh braced both hands against the animal's back once more in a futile effort to get it up, moving, anything. That's when he realized Alex wasn't there.

"Alex. Where are you?"

"Here," came her voice.

"What the hell are you doing?" he hollered at her.

"The horse looks okay. I can't see any broken bones."

Josh wiped the water out of his face. "I'm happy for him. In case you haven't noticed... I'm the one in trouble here!" He couldn't remember when he'd hurt so much.

"Yes, I noticed!" Lightning dove into the ground about three hundred feet away. The hair on her head stood up straight. The other horse, Sunshine, whined and danced sideways, pulling at the harness. That's when Alex saw what the problem was.

"The harness is holding Curly down! It's wrapped around his front legs!"

"Then cut the damn thing!"

Cut the harness. Yes! Alex raced to the wagon to find something to use, a knife, an ax, anything to cut the leather. It was so dark. Damn. She couldn't tell one box from another. She tore into them—boxes, crates— tossing clothes and blankets left and right until she found the one with the utensils. Her hand curled around a butcher knife.

She scampered out of the wagon, the wind slapping the canvas against the bows, the rain soaked through her clothes and underclothes. Her skin ached from the wet and the cold.

"I've got the knife." She ran to cut the leather straps that held the horse down. "I'll holler, then you push. Okay?"

Josh was consumed by pain, but he was aware enough to know that he had to do something, do what she ordered him to do. "Yes."

She sawed at the thick leather, working back and forth. "Done! Now push."

With all his remaining strength, he pushed on the horse's back, his fingers curling into the animal's wet skin.

Alex pulled on the bridle. She leaned her full weight into the task, rearing back like a kid in a tug-of-war.

"Come on!" she commanded through gritted teeth. The wind swirled water in the air, the rain seemed to come from everywhere. She yanked hard on the bridle. "Come on. Get up! Get up!"

Miraculously the horse moved, rolling up, trying to get his feet under his large body. Another flash of lightning illuminated the night like a million candles. Thunder, like the boom of a cannon, careened along the valley.

This time the lightning helped. The spooked horse surged to its feet, eager to run, to get away from the storm.

Without a moment to spare, Alex ran to Josh.

"Help me...up," Josh commanded. She looped his arm around her shoulder and helped him stand. He leaned into her and she sagged under his weight, but she braced her feet and held on to him. His hand gripped her shoulder so hard she nearly cried out with the pain. Josh was up, moving, alive, and no way was she letting go.

Pain threatened to overwhelm Josh. He could barely breathe. Moving triggered a blinding white haze of hurt. He clamped his jaw down to trap the scream that erupted from his throat.

Rain cascaded down his face. His clothes, mud-caked and soaked, clung to his frigid skin. He shivered. Gasping for each precious breath, he said, "We've got to...get...out of here."

"Where?" She glanced up at him.

"The rocks," he said. "There's a cave I've used... before."

Wrapping her arm around his waist, she said, "Lean on me. Let's get you in the wagon."

He took an unsteady step. Her hand slipped upward and she squeezed his ribs. Agony consumed him.

"Not too hard," he said when he could manage.

"Sorry." She shoved the hair out of her face and his. They made it the ten or so steps to the tailgate. She made sure he was braced against the wheel while she tugged the bolts free and let the tailgate fall with a slam and a bounce.

"Can you make it?" She held out her hands, but they both knew he'd have to climb up there himself if he was going to do it at all.

Josh half fell, half climbed onto the platform. He wrapped his arms around his middle in a protective gesture, not that it did a damn bit of good.

Exhausted, he sagged down, feet dangling over the side, nearly touching the muddy ground.

"Don't move," she ordered, then ran to get them going. The storm showed no signs of letting up and they were still a likely target.

She checked to make sure there was enough harness to hold the team. Satisfied, she gathered up the lead lines of both horses. "Come on. Let's go!"

Blessedly the horses complied, evidently as eager as she to get under cover. She saw Josh's horse a few hundred yards away, too far to get. He'd have to come or stay on his own.

Rain fell in torrents. She didn't know so much rain could fall so hard, so fast. Puddles filled every little pothole, every rut.

Inside she was shaking harder than an earthquake. Josh was hurt bad, judging by the look of him. How bad?

The wagon rolled slowly, the horses shied and faltered. She coaxed and pleaded and demanded, and step by step they moved ever closer to the rocks and sanctuary. Fear pounded in her chest and curled noose hard in her stomach.

Please God, don't let him die.

She kept her sights focused on those rocks and refused to think about anything beyond getting there.

Josh tried to fight his way up from the dark recesses that called to him, offering blessed relief from the fiery pain that wrapped around his middle like the jaws of some enormous trap.

Occasionally he could hear Alex's voice coaxing the horses. He tried to focus on her voice, on the movement of the wagon, anything to stay conscious. The pain inside him swirled wider and wider until it consumed him. *I can't die. Don't let me die now.*

Alex steadfastly ignored the lightning crashing around her, the thunder that seemed to reverberate over the very ground, the rain that blurred her vision.

The rocks were close, only a few yards. Josh was right. They were huge. In a flash of lightning she could see a large cavelike opening that was shallow but deep enough to cover them and the horses and wagon.

"Hurry!" she cried, as though the horses understood. "Hurry!" She stumbled and fell to her knees. Breathing hard, she dragged herself up. Wiping her mud-caked hands on her skirt, she led them the last few feet to safety.

Gasping for breath, she took a moment to rest against the hard surface of the rock wall, grateful to be out of the rain, protected from the storm, grateful that Josh knew what to do. Josh!

Gathering up her drenched skirt, she rushed to the back of the wagon. He was sprawled awkwardly on the tailgate. His clothes soaked through, and clung to his skin. His face was grim, his breathing seemed to be coming in fast, shallow gulps.

She touched his arm. "Josh?"

No answer.

Panicked, she shook him. "Josh? Can you hear me? Josh, please!" She shook him again. He groaned in response. "Thank, God."

His eyes opened.

"Josh, we made it," she told him triumphantly. "How are you?"

He didn't speak, just reached out and grabbed hold of the edge of the tailgate. Slowly he pulled himself up into a sitting position.

Questioningly he glanced around as though uncertain where they were. His gaze returned to her. "Good, honey." He sucked in a breath, clutching his midsection as he did. "You did good."

"Thanks. But what about you? How bad is it?"

"I think my ribs are broken." He paused, waiting for the pain to ease, and when it did, he said, "Now...can you unhitch the horses and tie them to the wheel." He steadied himself. "If they bolt...they won't take the wagon with 'em."

Alex did as he'd told her, then rushed back to him. "I'm going to make a bed for you over there." She pointed to a spot near the back wall. She found the blankets she needed in the wagon, and when the pallet was set, she went to get him.

"Okay. Now you're going to have to walk over there."

He looked at her as though she'd gone daft. Alex was tired and wet and generally miserable, but she was determined to take care of Josh the best she could and that meant she had to get him out of the wagon and into bed. Then she could take a look at whatever was wrong.

"Come on, Josh. You can't sit up all night and unless I unload the wagon, which I'm not strong enough to do, then this is the only choice."

Josh knew she was right. He steeled himself and just did it, just slid down off the wagon, then stood there for a minute, maybe two, willing himself not to cry out at the pain that was ricochetting from one end of his body to the other.

Muscles quivered down his back and across his chest. He eyed the pallet she'd made. It looked soft and comfy and about a million miles away. He wanted to lie down but why the hell did she make it so far?

Alex moved in close, her body pressed hip to hip against his. She slipped her arm carefully around his waist, her fingers resting on his hipbone at the top of his gun belt. "Ready?" It was a marching order, if ever he heard one.

"Okay."

She gave him a small smile, one of those you-can-do-it smiles, then took a step.

The distance between him and the damn bedroll seemed to be growing larger with every step.

He groaned once and Alex glanced up to see him clamp his teeth down hard, a muscle flexing rapidly in his cheek. "Four more steps," she coaxed, afraid he might not make it, might pass out on her right here, and then what would she do?

But Josh wasn't about to pass out. That would be the same as giving up, and it wasn't something he did.

"Three more," she said gently. "Now two."

Josh kept going, one foot in front of the other, fighting to ignore the sharp pain that was slicing through him with each step, each breath.

"We're there. Okay, let's get you down."

"Easier said . . . than done, I think."

Alex swung around in front of him. "Put your arms around my neck."

He did as she ordered.

"Now, hang on to me and lower yourself slowly to the ground. I'd grab you but—"

"No."

Josh pressed one hand against the wall, and with the other he hung on to her and guided himself to the pallet. When his knees hit the ground, he groaned out loud then collapsed onto the bedroll.

Outside, the storm carried on full force, putting on quite a show. The thunder was bass drum loud. At least the lightning gave her enough light to move around. As it was, Alex was grateful they were alive. That was Josh's quick thinking. Once more, it seemed, he'd saved her . . . at the risk of his own life. This time *he'd* gotten hurt in the process. This time she'd take care of him!

She brought a lantern from the wagon and a box containing what few medical supplies she had—bandages, some alcohol and iodine. She lit the lamp and turned up the wick high.

"We need a fire," she called over to him.

"Yeah," he said.

Okay. Dry wood. Dry wood. She worried her bottom lip as she scanned the cave. Nothing. Not even a twig. Of course! She dumped the utensils out of the kitchen crate and dragged it to the edge of the tailgate, letting it fall onto the rock floor surface, hoping that . . . yes! The crate split and a few whacks with a hatchet and the wood was small enough to use.

"Dry wood," she called to him again, pleased with her ingenuity.

"So I . . . see."

She made the fire close to him, wanting to keep him warm. Once the flames were dancing over the wood, she turned back to him.

"Now let's have a look at those ribs." She tried to keep her tone bright and cheerful and confident and not let him know how scared she was.

His eyes were closed. His legs were stretched out in front of him and he was hugging his midsection protectively. His hair was raked back from his face, deep furrows in the inky darkness from where he'd run his fingers through it.

A sudden clatter startled her and she turned in time to see Josh's horse trot into the opening. Gear intact, he hesitated, then walked over to where the other horses were tied.

Josh's mouth turned up in the barest trace of a smile. "He's with me," he said softly, the tiniest bit of teasing in his voice.

She chuckled. "So I see." It was good to see Josh smile, even if it was tenuous.

A short distance away the rain cascaded over the outcropping like a waterfall, blurring the outside, leaving them isolated in their own private world.

"How are you feeling? Anything else hurt—arms, legs?"

He shook his head. "Not as far as I can tell."

She sat back on her haunches, her wet skirt bunched against his equally wet wool trousers. "Okay, I'm going to check. All right?" She covered his hand with hers but he wasn't moving, wasn't letting go of those hurt ribs.

"Since when . . . are you a doctor?"

"Well, Davy was always breaking something when he was a kid." She tried to make a joke of it, keep things light. "When it wasn't furniture or lamps, it was an arm or a shoulder." She pried at his hand once more.

Something hard flashed in his eyes, then was quickly gone. His expression turned gentle, his gaze questioning.

"Please," she added so very quietly, "I won't hurt you." She gave him her best bedside smile.

His gaze never leaving hers, he released his hold and allowed her to move his hand aside.

She started at his shoulders, running her hands carefully but firmly along the tops then down his well-muscled arms. The wet cotton of his shirt clung to him, outlining every tendon, every well-honed muscle. It was provocative, seductive, touching him like this. Her pulse reacted in a sudden flutter. "Move your fingers," she said when her hands reached his, hers tracing the backs of his hand and along his slender fingers.

He obeyed.

"Good." Still seated, she inched over enough to reach his legs, just above his boot tops. "Can you move your feet?"

Again he did as she asked.

She touched his legs, letting her hands travel up them slowly, skimming the wool, intimately touching the muscles, feeling them flex and tense beneath her fingers. When she got to his hips, she stopped and her gaze flew to his. He was watching her intently.

"Well, everything appears to be in working order."

His mouth turned up a lazy one-sided grin. "Glad you approve."

A faltering smile pulled up the corners of her mouth.

There was a suggestive quality to his voice, and his nearness sent familiar shivers up the backs of her legs. The teasing Josh was back. Hurting and exhausted, he was still more roguishly charming than any man on the planet, and even now she was not immune to him.

Like tearing flesh, she looked away. "Josh, how can we tell, for sure, if your ribs are broken?"

She touched his injured side lightly. Josh sucked in a sudden breath and got a stabbing jolt for his trouble. "They're not sticking out of the skin, so I can't...know for sure. But it hurts like hell...and they've gotta be wrapped."

With resignation, she straightened. "Okay, tell me what to do."

"Help me sit up."

She moved in closer and slid her hands under his shoulders. Her hair brushed his cheek and Josh knew if he turned his head, if he moved at all, her face would be there. It would be so easy to touch his lips to her cheek, to turn her face, to take her sweet mouth with his.

He didn't do any of those things. He didn't move one bit. He was afraid, too. Oh, not of the pain this time— it was her he was afraid of. Because even staved-in as he was, he wanted her. It was pathetic, but true. The one woman he shouldn't want, shouldn't even know, he wanted like he'd never wanted any woman before.

He didn't have long to think about his rampaging lust. She pulled him forward, and pain worse than the kick of a Missouri mule doubled him over. "Son of a bitch!"

He needed some relief and he needed it now. Fortunately Sundown had trotted in awhile ago. "Check my saddlebags." He paused and gulped in a couple of breaths. "Bottle of whiskey."

He was reaching for her before she got back.

Alex handed him the half-full bottle. Clutching his ribs with one hand, he pulled the cork with his teeth and spit it onto the blanket. He took a long swallow, holding it in his mouth a second before letting it slide down his throat. He waited for the whiskey to take the edge off the pain. He took another swallow.

She stood there staring down at him, one of those disapproving stares that women do so well. "This is *not* the time to get drunk." She shoved one fist into her narrow waist for emphasis.

"Woman, if ever there was a time to get drunk, this..." He gestured around the cave, took one more swallow and, gasping, continued, "This is it."

She frowned when she reached for the bottle and he decided not to put up a fight. He didn't want to fight, not with her, not anymore.

"I don't think this—" she waggled the bottle in front of him like the pendulum of a clock "—is the cure for broken ribs."

No, probably not, he thought, but it was the cure for what ailed him—namely a certain blue-eyed temptress.

"I'm going to get some bandages."

He noticed that she took the bottle with her and when she returned, she had towels but no bottle.

She dropped down beside him again. His gaze instinctively sought hers. She was wet and muddy and generally a mess. She looked like a drowned kitten. She looked beautiful. He prayed to God she hadn't poured that whiskey out.

"Have you treated broken ribs before?" she questioned.

"For someone else." Gritting his teeth, he sat up. "Help me out of my shirt." He worked the buttons but his hands were shaking, from cold and pain and most likely from desire. Why the hell did this have to happen? Why the hell did it have to happen with her?

"Let me do that," she said.

She tugged his shirt free of his waistband. His lips tightened, his fingers curled into fists. "Gimme another drink," he said after a moment.

"You don't need it. If you get drunk and pass out who will tell me what to do?"

She tugged one sleeve down.

"Son of a bitch," he swore. Lifting his arms was out of the question.

Alex stopped. "I'm sorry."

"Never mind, just finish the damn thing!"

He sat straighter as she hurried to slide the other sleeve free. She came around to look at him, and her fingers lightly touched his ribs. She saw the muscles flinch beneath her touch. "Does that hurt?"

"No," he said simply.

It scared her, the way his ribs were already turning blue. The flesh was swollen. "If I touch them, can you tell how many are broken?"

He flinched. "No," he said again. "Where's the cloth you brought?"

"Here." She held it up for his inspection.

"Tear it into strips about so wide." He gestured with his hand.

She did as he instructed. "Now what?"

"Give me one end. Okay, now I'll hold it here." He put it against his chest. "You wrap the cloth, as tight as you can around me, from waist . . . to armpit."

"Won't that hurt?"

"Yes!"

Wedged between him and the wall of the cave, she started. He held up his other arm as best he could while she leaned in close, reaching around him.

His heart raced frantically with every touch, every movement. He could feel her breasts pressed against the back of his shoulders, could feel her warm breath on the side of his neck. It was torture worse than any broken ribs.

"Holy hell, woman, are you trying to kill me?" He snapped when she touched a particularly sore rib.

"I didn't mean—"

Softer he said, "I know. Finish, will you."

More circles with the cloth, more touch and taste and smell of Alex until his senses were spinning with pain and with wanting her.

He tried to focus on the rock wall opposite, trying to trace the different veins of color as they emerged and blended with the rock around it.

When she finished, she tore the cloth with her teeth and made a nice neat knot to hold the bandage in place.

She looked up at him so expectantly he couldn't help smiling. Without thinking, he reached out and touched her cheek, her skin cool beneath his fingers. "Alex," he said huskily, his hand dropping down to cup her chin. "I'm sorry." He meant more than just his temper. He meant so many things, things he'd done and things yet to come.

Their gazes held. He'd expected her to turn away, but she didn't.

She smiled back at him, and it was forgiveness ... or perhaps an invitation?

It was self-defense that made him say, "I think I'll have another drink now and, no, I won't get drunk."

Alex hesitated.

"Go on, honey. I need that drink."

Yes, Alex thought, he probably did need that drink. She needed one herself.

"I don't think it's raining as hard." She spoke as she walked, bringing him the whiskey. "Not much left." She held up the bottle for his inspection, the brown liquid sloshing in the lighter brown bottle.

"Enough." He took a long swallow, then handed her the bottle. "You look like you need some."

"You read my mind." She had a mischievous spark in her eye when she tipped the bottle up to her lips and took a long swallow herself, leaving just a little for him to finish, which he did.

Josh eased himself down on the blanket, shifting until he found a comfortable position. Breathing slowly, he waited for the whiskey to do its work. He lay there for a long minute, thinking of her, of him, of the them that could never be.

"You get some rest," she told him, and started to get up.

He stopped her with a touch. "Alex."

"Yes?"

He didn't want her to go, to leave his side. "Thank you . . . for what you did, back there . . . and here." He touched his bandaged ribs.

She made a sound in the back of her throat that could have been a chuckle. "You're welcome, Mr. Colter."

"It was Josh awhile ago."

She regarded him seriously. "Every time we get to 'Josh' . . . something happens and we end up fighting. I'm too tired to fight."

He knew the "something" she was referring to was that kiss, a couple of near kisses, aw, hell, his generally bad temper. He had a right, all things considered, but she didn't know that.

"I don't want to fight. I promise. I'm sorry. It's just that I . . . well, all my life, I've been a loner, I guess. I'm not used to getting close to people." Or letting people get close to him—until now. She'd overrun his defenses faster than Sitting Bull overran the Seventh cavalry.

Nearby the fire crackled and hissed, the wood sending into the air gray-white smoke that disappeared before it reached the ceiling of the cave.

Josh kept talking. "I guess it's growing up the way I did. My mother left my father when I was young."

She arched one finely shaped brow. "Oh, I'm sorry, you never said."

"No. It wasn't like that. My parents loved each other very much, it was just that, well, they were from two different worlds." *Sort of like you and me,* he thought to say, but didn't.

"And you stayed with your father?"

"Most of the time. I loved him a lot. He was tough, but fair and the most honorable man I've ever known."

"Then, I'd say he'd be proud of you, of the man you are," she told him sincerely. Josh Colter was nothing if not honorable, she knew that. It was why she trusted him, had all along, she realized.

"Thanks."

She settled down next to him, her muddy skirt stiffening as it dried. "My father is a banker, not an occupation that's always connected with fair dealings, but my father is a good man. I've seen him go out on a limb more than once for someone, take a chance, extend a loan or expand it, all on a handshake and promise."

"I think I'd like your father."

"I think he'd like you." She felt a tenderness well up in her looking at this man who'd saved her life, who'd risked his own for her more than once. Feeling strangely awkward, familiar, she made to stand again. "You really ought to get some rest." She fussed with her skirt, her shirtwaist, which was prickling her skin.

"Don't go."

Chapter Fifteen

It was such a simple request. He looked so pitiful—a first for the usually formidable Josh Colter. It tugged at her heart and overwhelmed her better judgment.

"I wasn't leaving. I was just going to change—" she glanced down at her mud-stained clothes "—and let you get some sleep."

She emphasized the last phrase in one of those you're-not-fooling-me tones. He was being selfish as hell, but he didn't care. All he knew was that, for the first time in days, they were talking, really talking, and he liked it, liked listening to her, hearing the sound of her voice.

"Tell me about painting."

"Tell you what?"

"Why do you paint?" He was genuinely interested, intrigued. "It's not the usual, you'll have to admit. Most women get married, raise families . . ."

Her chin came up defensively. "I'm not most women."

"So I've noticed."

She blushed.

He continued. "So tell me."

She gave him a sigh, one of resignation. "I paint, I

guess, because it's what I have to do. Did you ever feel consumed by something, driven to do something?''

"Yes," he confirmed, thinking of his oath.

"I've painted since I was about twelve. My mother hired teachers . . . Mother was a bit of a free spirit."

He chuckled. "Like her daughter."

"Like her daughter. It's inherited." She laughed again. "Anyway, after the academy in Pennsylvania I, she and I, convinced Papa to let me go to Paris."

"All alone?"

"I shared a studio."

"With that friend you mentioned."

"Yes, Marie Elaine and I. She's a wonderful writer."

"Ah," he murmured. So the friend was not male. He liked that. "What else?"

"About Marie Elaine?"

"No, about you. Was it difficult being away from home? I went away to school for several years and it just about killed me, but I did it . . . for the family, you know."

"Yes, I know. And, yes, it was difficult, but I couldn't not try."

"Then what?"

She continued, "Then about a year ago, I met some artists who were working in a new style. They called themselves Independents."

"And the name appealed to you?" There was a teasing glint in his eyes.

"Yes. But also, once I saw what they were doing, I knew that was what I wanted to do. It was like starting over in some ways. More work, more study...more trial and error." She laughed. "I went through a lot of canvas that year."

"But you did it, didn't you?" It was a statement of fact, not a question.

"Yes," she confirmed with unmistakable pride. "I did. I had two paintings in a show just before I left." Excitement flashed bright in her eyes. "Do you know how difficult it is to get a painting in a show, a good show?"

"Tell me." He was enjoying her excitement, enjoying watching the way her eyes lit up.

"It's very difficult, but I did. No special favors, you understand." Her jaw set. "Someone saw my work at a smaller show and invited me."

"And did it go well?"

"The top art critic in Paris, Monsieur Beauchamps, said I was 'promising'!"

"And that's good?"

"That's terrific. To say an unknown *woman* artist is promising, in a city where there are hundreds of struggling *male* artists . . . yes, that's good."

"I'm glad. Really glad." He was glad for her, for her success, and mostly glad that she'd shared it with him.

"What about your family? They must be happy for you."

"Well, Papa still thinks I should give up this 'foolish notion,' as he calls it, and settle down. But Davy..." She grinned. "He's my number-one fan and number-one nemesis." She shook her head forlornly. "I love my family, but Davy especially, I guess. He's the one who's always in trouble, the needy one. Fortunately, I've usually managed to get him out of trouble, or at least pacify my father."

"Isn't your... he a little old for a nursemaid?" He didn't try to keep the contempt out of his voice.

"Not nursemaid," Alex replied, totally unaware of his change of mood. "He's my brother, my baby brother. I've always looked out for him, I guess. Don't you...look out for your brother?"

"I don't have a brother."

"Sister, then?"

His expression fixed, he said, "My sister was murdered."

"Murdered?" She went quite still. "Oh, Josh. No. How awful." She touched him lightly on the arm. "When?"

"A couple of months ago."

"Oh, no," she repeated, concern apparent in her face and voice. "What happened? I mean, was it a robbery, an accident?"

"No. It was deliberate rape and murder." He was treading on dangerous ground here. Unable to reveal all, still he wanted her to know the grief, the torment that drove him.

"Oh, Josh. I'm so sorry." Instantly Alex flashed on her own nightmare. She shuddered in the wake of the mind-numbing terror that had consumed her that awful night.

"Rape and murder," she repeated on the thready whisper.

Alone and helpless.

Her blood turned to ice. She could see the ugly leering faces of her tormentors, hear their crude remarks, feel their power over her. The helplessness of that night brought back her fury, her need to hurt them as they'd hurt her.

If Josh hadn't arrived...

Then she realized how unendurable this must be for him. He'd saved her. He'd been unable to save his sister. The thought of it tore at her heart.

"It must be horrendous for you, that you couldn't...didn't..." Her gaze sought his.

"Yes. It is." He knew what she'd been thinking, remembering, had seen the slight quiver in her chin. This time he did not try to protect her.

"Do you know who did it?"

"Unfortunately for them, I found out."

Her expression was grim, her mouth drawn down. "Were they arrested?"

"No."

She looked at him through narrowed eyes. "Why not?"

Should he tell her the truth, tell about his Indian sister that no white court would deem worthy of trying a white man for killing? Should he tell her it was her brother who did the killing? Should he risk losing her and the man he sought?

"Out here there's very little law. Out here a man takes care of his own." *If he can,* he thought to say, still not able to get past the guilt.

Her eyes widened slowly with understanding. "You mean that you are—"

"Hunting those men."

"And you've found them."

"Two. There's one more."

"And did you..." Her gaze flicked to the gun tied at his side then back to his face again.

"Yes."

She understood his pain, his quest for revenge. But the thought of him hunting men, risking himself was frightening. "Couldn't you let someone else, the law, take care of it?"

"No. I couldn't. That was *my* sister. Do you understand. My *sister.*"

"I do understand. If you hadn't taken that gun away from me that night..." She touched him again, her hand soothing to his skin and his nerves.

He let out a long, slow breath. *Please remember this later, Alex. Remember the anger.*

"So that's why you were in Gunlock?" she asked.

"Yes.

"Did you find him? The last man?"

"He was gone."

She was thoughtful for a long time. He thought perhaps she'd made the connection, figured out that it was David Gibson who Josh was trailing. If she did, if she asked him, would he confirm her guess? He didn't have to find out.

"I hope you do find him." Her voice had taken on a fierce tone. "I hope he gets what he deserves so that he can *never* do this to another woman."

"No matter what else, he will pay."

They sat together for several minutes, lost in their own thoughts, memories. Behind them the fire flickered, the wood nearly gone. Outside, the thunder was a distant rumble on the mountaintops. The rain trickled down the mouth of the cave like a delicate curtain that blurs but does not obliterate the world beyond.

As though coming back from another place, her vision cleared then sought his. She smiled and was glad when he returned the smile. "You really should try to rest."

His expression was so intent, so preoccupied, she touched him again just to make sure there was no fever. "Please," she said, soothing him the way one would a child. "Get some sleep, I'll be right here."

Sadly Josh watched her walk away. Maybe she did understand? Sure she did. She understood everything except that it was her brother, her darling baby brother, the one she'd obviously spent most of her life protecting.

She didn't have a clue what kind of murdering scum he was, and that was, perhaps, the toughest thing of all to take. For Josh would be the one not only to kill her brother, but in doing so he would reveal the man for what he was. He would leave her with nothing—no brother, no illusions.

Chapter Sixteen

Alex did a good job of keeping the fire going. Josh was impressed and told her so. The rain was still coming down, though lighter now, and the lightning and thunder were more distant.

They were both exhausted, and it wasn't long before Josh dozed. Alex changed her clothes and spread her wet ones out to dry. She sat up for a while in case he needed her, but when she was certain he was asleep for the night, she got out her blankets, put them near him and settled in.

The last of the wooden crate slowly disappeared in the flames. Alex slept in snatches. Ten minutes here, a half hour there. There were no more nightmares. Throughout the night, she checked on Josh. Each time, he seemed to be fine, to be resting comfortably.

Sometime in the small hours of the morning, she drifted off into a deep sleep, only to awake with a start. The cave was strangely quiet and she realized that the rain had stopped. The rhythmic plick-plop of water falling from the rock ledge to the earth below reminded her of the storm that had driven them into this place.

Josh!

Heart racing, she twisted around to look at him. She met a pair of sable black eyes, dulled with exhaustion to be sure, but dark and questioning and soft, oh, so very soft.

Her mind surged with relief. "You're awake?"

"Yes," he said on a husky tone.

She shoved at her hair as though to fix it. "How long have you been awake?"

"Awhile."

She fussed with her hair some more. "Why didn't you say something? Do you need something? I would have gotten up."

"I liked watching you sleep."

A warmth spread through her body that had nothing to do with the wool blanket she was partially covered with. There was a nervous excitement being here with him, looking at him. She was keenly aware of his bare chest where it peeked out above the bandage. She remembered the feel of his skin on hers when she'd put that bandage on him, remembered the feel of his body as her arms went around him. Just thinking of it made her fingers tremble.

She surged to her feet, alarm pounding in her blood. He must have felt it, too, for his expression seemed to clear, harden. His mouth curved down in a frown. "That fire's nearly out. Is there any more wood?"

"Not really. Looks like the rain has stopped though. Maybe I can find some wood."

"It'll be too wet."

"You're right." She looked over toward the wagon. "Well, then another crate is about to meet its demise."

All day Josh sat and lay around the camp. He was uncomfortable—miserable actually. He dozed often but every time he moved, his ribs jolted him awake, usually with a curse on his lips for rain and horses and just about anything else he could think of.

Alex cooked and made the camp as comfortable as possible. She took the horses outside and tethered them to a tree with a long enough lead to let them graze a bit.

She found some rice in one of the boxes and some dried apples. She thought about making biscuits but figured she'd be better at bacon and rice. The apples she boiled for dessert, making sure to save the thick sweet juice.

She waited on Josh, bringing him water and food, always asking if he needed anything else. Every time she got close to him, every time his hand touched hers, like when she handed him the drinking cup, anxiety fluttered and swirled inside her.

Soon she found that she was going out of her way *not* to get too close to him. She avoided him like quicksand, skirting the edges, hoping to get past without being pulled in.

She had things to do, none of which included a soft-eyed cowboy, no matter how tempting, and Lord, the man was tempting.

No! She was going to find her brother, make her sketches, win the contest and go back to Paris. It was that simple. Or it had been simple until Josh Colter had walked into her life.

Josh. It always came back to Josh. But she couldn't let him stand in her way. She knew her mind, she had her career. This . . . this attraction was merely a fleeting thing, a passing fancy, a phase. It came from being alone with him in intimate ways that would never have happened under different circumstances. Yes, that was it.

The trouble was, when she let herself acknowledge the feelings he stirred in her, it didn't feel like a passing fancy, and that worried her most of all.

Nothing had been the same since the first time he'd looked at her—and never mind the kiss. The kiss had nearly been her undoing. For a long time she'd had fantasies about him, erotic fantasies, lush and heated, that played in her mind until her body ached and throbbed with delicious need.

She had to stop this. The man was dangerous, more dangerous than she'd ever thought, and she was alone with him in the middle of nowhere. There was no escape.

Josh couldn't believe he'd slept straight through the night. The sun was at least an hour in the sky when he yawned and started to stretch. He got about as far as his shoulder when the pain whipped across his midsection. "Damn."

Every muscle in his body hurt, from shoulders to ankles. Cautiously he moved, testing one muscle after another. Not too bad, he told himself. Lord knows he'd been battered worse. A man can't work a ranch and not get kicked around a bit. Over the years he'd been bruised and stitched . . . he'd even broken his arm once. That was the result of an argument with a certain cantankerous bronc. That bronc won, too, he thought, rubbing his arm. The break still hurt sometimes in the winter.

There was nothing he hated worse than being sick or helpless. He'd given in a bit last night and it stuck in his gut that she'd had to take care of him. It was supposed to be the other way around. Now, more than ever, he needed to be up and able. She needed someone, needed him, he amended, to get her out of this trouble.

Alex. He levered up on one elbow and gritted his teeth until the pain eased to a manageable level. He glanced around the small cave for her and saw her asleep only a couple of feet away. Her delicate features were relaxed, her mouth slightly open, her hair tangled and messy, curled ribbonlike on her cheek. He thought she was beautiful. Her lips moved slightly in her sleep and the fingers of one hand twitched.

She was dreaming. Was it something good, of the contest perhaps, of going back to Paris? He resented that she was going, that she wanted to go. But he also knew how much that contest meant to her, how much her art meant to her. Knowing what was to come, he said, too softly for her to hear, "Don't worry. I'll get us out of this. You'll win that contest yet."

He rolled over and shoved himself upright. Another pause and he made it slowly to his feet. So far, so good. First things first. Get a fire going, get some coffee boiling. Yeah, coffee sounded really good. Check on the horses.

Pulling on his trousers was nearly an acrobatic feat. Shoving his feet into his well-worn boots was easier. The chill air sent goose bumps over his bare shoulders. His shirt was a mud-caked mess. He'd get another out of his saddlebag.

Outside, the rain had stopped and the sky was clear and lake blue. He retrieved the last of the crate to use as firewood and made the fire small, to conserve what wood was left. A few minutes later he had the coffee going and went to check on the horses. Blessedly, both the wagon horses and Sundown appeared uninjured. That was something anyway.

When he turned back, Alex was standing there, not four feet away, a worried look on her face. "Does it hurt much?"

"No, not much," he lied, thinking that what hurt had nothing to do with his injury. "There's coffee." He moved past her. "Want some?" He was already helping himself and gestured with his cup.

"Yes, please."

She joined him at the fire and accepted the offered cup.

He wrapped both hands around the cup, as much for warmth as to keep from touching her.

Her gaze was calm. "I could make breakfast."

"Not yet." He settled onto the ground. So did she.

After a few moments, he said, "Thanks."

She looked up, questioning. "For what?"

"For taking care of everything." More softly he added, "For taking care of me."

"You already said that, but you're welcome—again."

She had changed clothes sometime, he wasn't sure when. Her dress was blue, the sleeves long, the collar high, wrinkled where she'd slept in it. There were dark circles of fatigue under her eyes.

Rifling one hand through his hair, he felt the dried mud there. "I must be quite a sight." He rubbed his face, feeling the whiskers.

"Oh, not so bad. Certainly no worse than me, I'm sure."

He chuckled and made a show of appraising her appearance. What started as teasing turned quickly to something else, something more intimate. His voice went husky. "You are...more beautiful than any woman I've ever known."

She looked uncertain, then chuckled and pushed at her hair. "I'll just bet."

He chuckled, too, glad for the chance to change the subject. He rubbed his chin again. "You know, I think I could stand a bath and most certainly a shave."

"Do you think you're up to it?"

He wrinkled his nose in disgust. "I think it's a matter of self-defense." He stood. "There's a creek down there." He motioned with his head. "Just beyond that rocky ledge."

She followed the line of his vision with her own. "How do you know?"

"Oh, I know this area. I come through here a lot." After tossing down his coffee, he started slowly for the wagon. "How about it?"

"I'd love to, but what about your bandage?"

He rubbed a hand across his ribs. "I'll have to settle for washing up, but we'll see if we can't find a pool for you. How's that sound?"

"Sounds perfect."

They got a couple of towels from the wagon and went in search of that pool. Josh was moving slower than usual. Going down the small embankment hurt like a hot poker in the side, but he gritted his teeth and didn't make a sound.

They walked along the rain-swollen creek in silence until they found just the right spot, a little bend protected by several large boulders.

A gentle breeze rustled the tops of the trees. The air was fresh from the rain and the pungent scent of sage. In the distance the mountains were framed by the sky.

"It's beautiful, isn't it?" she said, handing him a towel. She paced off a bit. "The dark green of the trees against the bright blue of the sky, the way the mountains become dark shadows even in the sunlight.''

"You see everything from an artist's perspective, don't you?"

"Yes," she said, and chuckled. "I guess I do." She turned back to the scenery. "Just look at it." There was a wonder in her voice. "It doesn't take an artist to appreciate this." She made a sweeping gesture with her hand.

"Would it be enough for your contest?"

"I don't know." She frowned in thought. "Honestly, I don't think so."

"Why? You said yourself it was beautiful."

"I need something extraordinary, something so unique that it can't help but catch the judges' attention. There'll be, oh, maybe, a hundred entries. I've got to get them to pause and look at *mine*, then I've got a really good chance of winning."

"Ah, I see. No modesty here."

She turned, ready to defend herself, only to see the amusement in his ebony eyes. Her temper eased. "I'm good, Mr. Colter."

"I believe you are."

His voice interrupted her musing. "So when's the deadline for this contest you're going to win?"

"September first."

"That's only a couple of months."

"I know. That's why I'm in a hurry to get to Yellowstone."

Meadowlarks chirped in the grass nearby. Two chipmunks scampered along the opposite stream bank.

"You still have to allow for travel time. Where's the painting going?"

"Washington. The finalists will be shown at the National Gallery. The winner will be chosen by a panel of critics and artists."

"I was just thinking."

"About what?" she prompted.

"How proud I'll be to walk into a gallery someday and see your paintings there and say, 'One of our greatest artists. I knew her well.'"

"I think we'll be able to travel tomorrow," Josh said.

"Really?"

"Really," he confirmed.

Josh was leaning against one wheel of the wagon. His ribs still hurt, but he didn't have time, correction, *she* didn't have time to sit around here waiting a week or two while they healed. Now that he'd had a chance to move around, he was pretty certain they weren't broken.

"How long before we get to Yellowstone?"

He screwed up his face. "If we take the Lander Cutoff, then turn north, we'll go through Mcdougall's Gap in the Tetons in ten days, then up through Jackson's Hole. That'll take another four days and we should be there."

"That's wonderful. I can't wait!"

"Are you sure you couldn't find something around here to draw?"

This time it was Alex who frowned.

"It's a hard trip. Rough country. Desert. By rights we should have gone farther west then come up from the south. If there was something around here that interested you ... we'd ... you'd save time."

"Mr. Colter, after all that's happened, all I've gone through, I can't give up now. Please, I want to go to Yellowstone."

He was tempted to argue with her, to tell her it was out of the question, to tell her that she should forget about the whole thing. He couldn't, wouldn't. She wanted this, dammit, she'd earned it. He owed her.

"Yellowstone, it is."

Chapter Seventeen

A week later they crossed the Green River and turned due north. The worst of the trip was over. They had survived crossing the desert and had had no trouble as they skirted the Shoshone Indian Reservation.

They reached the Yellowstone Valley, late in the day on Tuesday. Alex was riding Josh's horse and he was driving the wagon.

Alex flexed in the stirrups and tried to take it all in. The mountains towered above her on all sides, the valley floor appeared flat and groves of trees ringed grassy meadows. The sky was blue and cloudless and reflected in the still surface of Yellowstone Lake. If she hadn't already been breathless from the altitude, seeing this lake would have done it.

"It's enormous." She spoke in a reverent tone. "It's as big as an ocean." It wasn't, of course, but from this perspective it appeared that way.

As if that weren't wonder enough, the edge of the lake was dotted with bubbling pots of water, the bottoms streaked in bright yellow and blue and crimson. Steam wafted up from the gently boiling water. As pretty as the boiling pots were, they smelled as bad, and she crinkled her nose against the rotten-egg smell of sulfur.

Josh laughed. "Come on, you. Let's get settled."

He drove on until he found a secluded spot in a grove of lodgepole pines. Not that they needed seclusion, for as far as she could see there wasn't another living soul. It was a place so foreign, so removed from anywhere she'd ever been, it was as though she'd been dropped down on the moon.

Josh practically shouted with relief. "This place never looked so good." He meant every word. He'd been here dozens of times over the years, but after that horrendous trip, he was thinking about kissing the ground, except that he'd probably get poisoned for his trouble. "We'll camp here. We can head out tomorrow. I'll give you the grand tour."

Alex slid from the saddle and looped the reins over a tree branch. Her eyes were bright with excitement, not only because they'd made it, but because she knew if the rest of Yellowstone was anything like this, she was bound to find the perfect scene, bound to win that contest.

Alex was too anxious to wait around. She scrambled up a rocky knoll and looked out across the lake. Sunlight reflected on the calm surface. Brown mallards swam near the edge closest to her and beyond, four gray-white gulls, their wings outstretched, skimmed the water. Everywhere, there were steam vents. Some single, some in clusters, all sending spiraling plumes of nose-crinkling steam into the hot, moist air.

Heart racing with excitement and disbelief, she just stood there trying to take it all in. After everything they'd been through, she'd made it. Now she knew how

Columbus must have felt when he'd finally reached the New World.

"Hey, you!" Josh's voice carried up to her. "No play until we get this camp set up. Then I'll give you the nickel tour."

"Okay, slave driver." Laughing, she came to help him.

Josh made a shelter out of pine branches and used canvas for a floor. He unpacked the utensils and water and foodstuffs for the night. Alex made a fire pit and gathered wood. It seemed to have become her official job and she didn't mind. After all they'd been through, all he'd done to get her here—it was nothing less than heroic. Mostly she was glad to see Josh moving around so well. His ribs seemed to have healed. At least he'd stopped complaining, though she had the feeling that more than once, there was some teeth-gritting going on.

They'd taken the bandages off yesterday. His midsection was still bruised but more yellow and light blue than the deep blue of that awful night.

"Hey, are you daydreaming again?"

"Not me," she replied, amusement sparkling in her eyes. "I never daydream."

"Right," he muttered, his tone light, teasing.

They hobbled the team horses, left Josh's horse on his own.

"Okay," he said with a showy sigh. "I can tell I'm not going to get any sleep unless I show you around a bit...right?"

"Right," she confirmed with great seriousness.

He made another showy sigh, but his eyes, gorgeous black eyes, were warm and smiling. "Then let's go. But we're not covering it all in an hour!"

"I promise. Just a little. I just want to see a little."

They set off on foot, skirting the lake, walking near the edge where the water lapped against the shore as though it were a small ocean. Whenever they came to a boiling pot, they paused to look.

"Don't get too close," Josh admonished. "It really is boiling."

The water bubbled and churned like a cauldron. Sometimes the water was clear, the bottom lined with beautiful colors, vermilion and sapphire and canary. Sometimes the pots were milky, grayish, concealing the bottom altogether. Everywhere, she saw another perfect landscape, another perfect scene, the unique colors lending themselves magnificently to the artist's palette.

"This is...I'm speechless." She grinned and he grinned right back.

Josh took her hand and they ran ahead, as though they could outrun the wind. They ran and ran, their feet cushioned by the pumice soil, their footsteps kicking up small clouds of dust that clung to his pant legs and her skirt hem.

"Wait!" she gasped, a stitch in her side making her surrender first. Laughing, she slipped her hand from his. Hands on knees, she bent, trying to catch her breath. Finally she craned her neck up to him. "That's it. From now on, no more corset. I don't care what Godey's says." She was still laughing.

"I promise I won't turn you in to the Lady's Society." He held up one hand in a pledge.

Another minute or two and she could breathe again. "Okay, lead on."

He did. But this time, they strolled. The day was perfect. The sunlight was warm, the air warmer. Ground squirrels played on the dirt and ran in and out

of the rocks, chattering at them, their tails flicking back
and forth like a railroad man's warning flag.

"This is wonderful. Thank you for bringing me." She
turned closely around, taking it all in, or trying to,
anyway.

"I'm glad you like it," he said, as though it were his
personal property. He wished it was. He'd gift wrap the
whole place and give it to her if he was guaranteed it
would keep her smiling like that.

"Oh, I have to see the geysers. I can see the geysers,
can't I? I mean, they aren't too far?"

"A little north of here." He took off his hat, raked
one hand through his hair then settled his hat more
comfortably on his head. "Some of the geysers shoot a
hundred feet in the air."

Her eyes widened in wonder. "Really?"

"Really."

"You've seen them?"

"I've seen them."

"Oh!" She did a little turn again. "When? When can
we—I—see them? Today?"

"Tomorrow, honey." Her face was flushed, her eyes
bright, and he wrapped his hand around hers, his fingers slipping seductively between her fingers. It seemed
it was becoming an obsession with him, this need to
touch her, to be close to her.

You're getting in trouble here, Colter.

He didn't care. That was the scariest part of all. He
damn well didn't care. This need to be with her overwhelmed all thought and reason.

He wanted to show her everything—Yellowstone, his
Yellowstone, their Yellowstone.

"Come on, it's getting late. I want to see if I can scare
up some meat for dinner before it gets dark."

* * *

The first pink rays of sunlight were brightening the horizon. The moon was still visible overhead. He raked both hands through his hair, shoving it back from his face. He blinked the sleep from his eyes.

She was there, up and dressed and, if his nose wasn't mistaken, that was coffee he smelled. "You're up early."

"Couldn't sleep."

"Why not?"

"Why not?" Her tone was incredulous. "We're here. *I'm* here. Come on, lazy. Hurry up. Morning light's the best."

"Morning light," he mumbled, tossing back the blanket and reaching for his boots. "If I'm not mistaken that oughta be in about an hour." He was nothing if not grouchy in the mornings. He took time to get his shirt on, splash water on his skin and run a razor over his face.

Evidently it was too long for her. The woman paced back and forth about three feet behind him, like an expectant father in a hospital waiting room.

"Okay. I give up." He tossed out the wash water and tucked his shirttail into his waistband. "I hope you realize I'm giving up my coffee for you. I wouldn't do that for just anyone." Although he was joking when he said it, he realized it was true. There were a great many things he'd do for her, and giving up coffee was the least of them.

He let her ride Sundown, and he rode bareback on one of the wagon horses, which he figured he could manage better. He carried her art supplies with him— easel, paint box, sketch pad, canvas stretched on a frame. This artist business took a lot of paraphernalia.

He'd thought cowboying was bad, but no more. He headed for the geyser basin. She followed.

Yellowstone wasn't anything new to Josh. He came here often to hunt. There was elk and moose and bear, among others. He preferred elk, though it wasn't quite the same without his mother's wild plum sauce.

"This way," he told her, angling the horses through a grove of lodgepoles, their thin straight trunks reaching toward the azure blue sky. The rich, clean scent of pine was a pleasant relief from the sulfur.

Alex gripped the reins and kept leaning this way and that trying to see through trees that were so dense they blocked her view almost completely. They finally broke out of the forest into a large clearing. There before her was the famed geyser basin.

It was incredible. No wonder that, for years, when mountain men had told of the valley, no one had believed them. She was looking at it and she wasn't certain *she* believed it.

Stretched out before her was an open area that was nearly round, ringed by forest so dense and dark it seemed black instead of green. In the center though, the soil was gray, light pumice, that was lifted and swirled by the wind. The entire area was dissected with wide rivulets of water overflowing from the dozens of boiling pots and geyser cones. Each rivulet was streaked with the truest of colors, red and yellow and blue, and even white.

The horses snorted and shook their heads at the unpleasant smell. Alex sucked in a breath and coughed.

"Can we get closer?" she inquired.

"Sure, but let's leave the horses here."

Dismounting, she took her sketchbook from him and they started out. Up ahead was a mound with scalding water spouting out, stopping, spouting again. He took her hand to lead her around the edges, knowing that the soil was not to be trusted.

"The colors?"

"From the minerals."

Suddenly a low rumble seemed to come from nowhere and everywhere at once. "Earthquake!" she shouted.

Josh's grip tightened on her hand, holding her. "There!" He pointed as a geyser spouted gray-white water tall as a sequoia, the sound louder than the rumble of an avalanche.

Alex was enthralled. Water roared into the sky. "I've never seen anything like this."

She flipped open her sketch pad, braced it on her hip and made a sketch, moving a couple of steps to the left to get the correct shadow, the perfect framing of trees in the background, boiling pots to one side.

Josh stood close by, watching with awe and respect as she displayed her skill. When she was done, she'd captured the scene as truly as any photograph.

When she finished, she smiled up at him. "What else?"

He grinned. "Greedy, aren't you?"

"Yes, yes I am."

They spent the next hour strolling around and among the geysers and paint pots. She had eventually wandered away, making one sketch after another. He kept a close watch on her. Couldn't let her get too close and mistakenly step onto the thin crust.

"Don't you want to see the rest?"

"I hate to leave."

He laughed. "Come on. This has been here a couple of million years, I think it'll be here tomorrow."

"Okay...if you're sure," she quipped.

"Yeah, I'm sure."

The ride was easy. There was little underbrush to block their path. She heard the noise before they got there.

"Is it another geyser?"

"No."

But the roar was getting louder and louder.

"What is it?" she spoke loudly. A pair of blackbirds squawked an answer.

"You'll see." With that, he reined up and helped her down.

He led her through a narrow strip of woods to a high ledge. "There," he shouted over the thundering rush of water. "This is my favorite place."

It was, in a word, spectacular. There, hundreds of feet below her was a narrow canyon. Water, like a frothy white torrent, poured over the precipice and into the canyon hundreds of feet below.

And where the sun shone on the rocky walls of the canyon, they gleamed the most glorious golden. "A golden canyon—yellow stone," she shouted above the noise.

"I guess that's where the name came from. I don't know for sure. Since Lewis and Clark, it's been Yellowstone." He shrugged.

Josh was right. This was the perfect spot. Everything was perfect, especially the man standing at hip-rubbing closeness to her.

"Aren't you going to make a drawing?" he prompted when she didn't move.

"I'm not sure I'm up to *this*." She made a sweeping gesture that took in the enormous area.

"Alex, I've been watching you all day, for weeks. Honey, you're good. Don't ever doubt that." It wasn't the first time he'd called her by some affectionate name. It wasn't the first time he'd stood so near. It wasn't the first time his smile had been so lush that her stomach did funny flip-flops.

One minute they were standing there and the next, she was lifting up on her toes toward him.

Desire sparked like a tangible force around them. Memories merged with dreams. Fantasy melted into longing.

As her lips brushed his, Josh's hand naturally lifted to her shoulder. She was looking at him, her dark blue eyes filled with sudden longing. He could not resist.

There were no words spoken, they simply came together in mutual consent. Her pad fell to the ground near his foot. He pulled her closer, wanting to feel her pressed against him.

It was wrong, so very wrong, he knew, and still he couldn't stop. Her lips were warm and soft and pliant under his in a way that sent desire pounding in his blood.

His fingers tightened on her upper arms, but wanting more, needing more, he slid his arms around her and his hands splayed out over her back. Her hands glided up to his shoulders then curled around the base of his neck.

His kiss was filled with invitation and promise. Her body came to life with excitement and newly found desire. Her nerves pulsed close to the surface of her skin, and heat stirred inside her in ways she'd never known before.

He lifted his mouth from hers, his breathing hard. "I want you. Do you understand? I want you."

For Alex there was no thought, no hesitation. His mouth slanted back and forth over hers, greedy, hungry, coaxing her response. Lost in each other they sank to the ground. Their bodies surged and moved to the rhythm they were creating.

Alex trembled, every fiber of her being suddenly aching with a wanting her mind didn't recognize but her body did. She clung to him. The more she touched, the more she wanted. Her nerves were on fire; lust, hot and insistent, pounded wildly in her body.

His mouth caressed hers, gentle then more demanding. She arched up against him, wanting to feel him, all of him, length to length. Josh. Her Josh. *Her Josh.*

Moving, flexing, unable to remain still, she wove her fingers into his hair, soft and warm from sunshine and his own body heat.

Josh was lost in her. There'd be no turning back, no walking away. He had to have her.

Deftly he unfastened the eight buttons of her blouse and pushed it aside, giving his hands access to her smooth flesh beneath. Blood racing, he let his hands glide across her slender shoulders, down her chest to the edge of her camisole. She felt so good, so damn good.

His ribs ached and breathing hurt. He didn't care if he ever breathed again. Alex was in his arms and that was all he needed, would ever need.

He reached for the thin straps of her camisole, surprised to find that she wore no corset. Good. He hated corsets. All those laces, like some trap to keep a man from getting what he most wanted. What Josh most wanted was to see her lush, ripe breasts.

Reason, faint but insistent, filtered through to him. *This is a mistake.*

The words were quickly silenced by the blood pounding in his temples and his brain. How she set him on fire. He slid her straps down.

"You're beautiful," he murmured, undoing the ribbons of her camisole, allowing the cotton to fall open.

She *was* magnificent, like some glorious wood nymph sent to ease his rage. Her hair splayed out over the pine needles in a golden halo.

He saw uncertainty flash in her eyes, and he feared that she was having second thoughts. If she asked him to stop, would he? Could he?

You won't die without her.

But desire coursed through his body and he wasn't so sure he would survive.

"I have to have you," he said in a voice thick with urgent passion. Ignoring the ache in his ribs, he rolled over, pulling her on top of him, discarding her camisole as he did. Her hands braced on either side of his head and he lifted them away, wanting to feel the weight of her body on his. He brought her hands together, kissing first one palm, then the other.

Alex was mesmerized, caught in the black fire of his eyes. He was promise and temptation and everything she'd ever imagined.

His hands drifted up her bare rib cage, then under her breasts, lifting them to him. His thumbs caressed each nipple again and again in a sweet rapture. Shock waves of delight careened through her body. Her nipples puckered and hardened into aching nubs, and a spiraling heat started deep inside her, burning, building with each delicious stroke of his hand.

"It feels . . ." she said, not sure what she felt, except wonderful.

"I know," he agreed, thinking this was only the beginning.

His mouth took her nipple in a gentle suckling kiss that turned her insides the consistency of sweet jam. He nipped at the overly sensitized skin of her breast, then laved away the hurt.

Alex lowered her head, her arms slid around his neck and she returned his kiss. Passion exploded in her and she moved against him, her body unable to control the longing that coiled and surged within her. She murmured his name.

He rolled them over, pinning her beneath him. He kissed the top of her breast and the luscious valley in between. Excitement built in him faster than storm clouds over the Rockies. He wanted every part of him touching every part of her.

An intense and urgent demand centered between Alex's legs. "Josh, I need..." She moaned against his lips, the longing so great, fulfillment too long in coming. She rifled her hands through his hair and held him close. Her nipples rubbed against the cotton of his shirt, making them hard.

In what seemed like one motion, he stood and lifted her to her feet. "No," she cried out, not certain how she would endure this pleasurable pain much longer. She grabbed hold of his shirtfront and hung on, knowing that her legs would never support her. "Don't leave."

"Honey, you'd have to kill me to get me to leave you." He kissed her long and hard, his mouth eating at hers. His tongue laved the tender flesh inside her cheek and at the corners of her lips. He sucked on her chin and nipped at her ears. All the while, his hands played up her bare back, tracing each vertebra there.

She swayed into him, clutching, clawing, desperate for him to end the torture, desperate for the release her body sought.

Josh unfastened the buttons of her skirt, then the tie on her petticoat. In one motion, he pushed them down. Another tie and her pantalets followed. He leaned back, anxious to see the woman he had dreamed about for so many endless days and nights.

His gaze traveled downward, skimming past her slender shoulders and high, firm breasts, over her flat belly and along the curve of her hips, then down the length of her long legs. How he loved long-legged women.

She stood before him, stiff, unsure, but proud.

He smiled then, a gentle smile, filled with wonder at this woman who was to be his. "No woman was ever as magnificent as you." He dragged in a steadying breath. "I've wanted you from the first time I saw you. I want you now."

Snatching up her skirt to use as a blanket, he carried her the few yards to the base of a fir tree in the small grove. He dropped to his knees, then lowered her to the ground. She sprawled on the cloth like the temptress that she was, pale flesh against green muslin. The air was rich with the fragrance of pine.

He made quick work of removing his clothes, then went to her, covering her with his body, heated flesh against heated flesh, the hard evidence of his arousal pressed against her abdomen.

Alex was consumed by a desire so strong she was helpless against it. Her breath came in shallow gulps, that is, when she remembered to breathe at all.

Josh's hand stroked her from hip to shoulder and back again, searing delicate nerves in the surface of her skin. His body, strong and sleek, moved on her, his muscular leg slipped between hers, his thigh pressed intimately against her core. She flexed and pressed hard into his thigh, eager to relieve the sensual ache.

"More," he whispered, wanting her touch, wanting her hands on him.

His mouth sought her nipples, sucking and licking, letting his teeth tease the rosy peaks until she moaned with the pleasure of it.

"Again," she pleaded.

Ruthlessly he repeated the process, coaxing, urging her on. She moaned and growled and arched under him, her nails leaving long furrows in his back. Still he would not relent.

"That's it, honey," he whispered against her ear. "Don't think, just feel the wonder."

Josh had known his share of women but none like her. She was wildfire and he was fast going up in flames. He knew it wouldn't take much to send her—or him—over the edge.

He drew two fingers across the warm, heated entrance to her, feeling the slickness there, knowing she was ready for him. Alex gasped and bucked at his touch. "You can't," she murmured, even as she pushed against his fingers in lush invitation.

"I can," he countered, caressing her again.

It excited him to watch her, to see her shudder and tremble with the ecstasy. With every movement, his own body tensed; blood pounded in his chest and throbbed in his loins.

He kept his hand between her legs. His fingers stroked her sweet core then plunged inside. She groaned.

"Josh, please...what's happening?" Her body convulsed with every stroke.

"That's it, Alex, don't stop."

She obeyed, her hips undulating while her hands clawed at the soft earth she lay on.

Carnal desire drove her. She kept moving, up and down. His fingers kept stroking, in and out. Her pleasure built, as though she were racing full speed toward some high precipice.

Josh felt the ripples of her orgasm start. Passion clouded his mind and body. He willed himself to wait, to do this for her.

"That's it, Alex. Let me please you. Let me love you."

He took her nipple in his mouth, sucking hard, while his fingers stroked her slick center. He was relentless. She was coming apart in his hand.

"Josh! Yes!" she screamed as bliss, like a blinding light, exploded inside her. Waves of glorious pleasure coursed through her, as though her body had simply liquefied and pooled in his hand. Heart pounding, she gasped for breath, her mind trying to understand what her body had given her.

Her eyes fluttered open to see him alongside her, his face so close, his smile so tantalizing.

"Oh, Josh. I never knew it could be like that," she whispered, stroking his face with trembling fingers.

"That was for you." He kissed her lips lightly, tenderly. "This is for you."

He moved to cover her, his knee gently spreading her legs apart.

She felt his manhood poised at the wet, hot core of her, where only moments ago his fingers had worked such magic.

Excitement rose in her, realizing what was to come. With word and touch, he aroused her desire. He spoke of erotic pleasures, lush and carnal. He spoke in English and another exotic language. Her body came to life and slowly the ancient rhythm pulsed inside her, strong and fierce.

"I want you," he said, his legs spreading hers more fully, giving him better access.

"Yes," she breathed, her hands threading through his hair.

She was wet and ready and Josh eased into her body. In one strong thrust, he buried himself deep inside her.

He felt her go rigid beneath him. "It won't hurt again. I'll never hurt you again," he promised. Now that he was where he most wanted to be, he stilled and waited for her to relax, to accept him.

When he felt her relax, he began to move, fully, deliberately. He took his time. He wanted to please her again, wanted to bring her to climax with him.

She was hot and tight and wrapped around him like fire-heated velvet. Slowly he withdrew almost completely, then slid inside again, letting her lush warmth engulf him. Nerves throbbed and ached. Muscles tensed and flexed, and he felt her convulse around him with every stroke, driving him to the brink. He hoped she peaked soon, because he was fast losing control.

Alex was not afraid. This was Josh and it was right. She met him fully, eagerly. She clung to him, writhed under him, took all that he offered and demanded more. Within minutes, she felt the tremors start. Her body raced to embrace the bliss.

"Josh. Yes," she groaned, her body arching up, reaching for the release. Alex was in a sweet agony all her own. Josh offered relief. Josh offered a rapture she must have.

Suddenly the world dissolved in a glorious white haze. There was no sound, no thought, only Josh and paradise, pure and sweet.

He pulled her close, crushing her to him, his fingers curling hard into her shoulders. Breathing labored, Josh reached his own climax and poured himself into her luscious body. He collapsed against her. Nothing and no one had ever made him feel this complete.

She was incredible, unique. She'd met him with a passion that took all that he offered and gave as fully. In a heartbeat, he knew he'd found what had been missing from his life.

Alex Gibson. The woman he loved.

Chapter Eighteen

The night at their camp had seemed interminably long. They had gone through their routine tasks making dinner, bedding down. Alex had welcomed the sleep, welcomed the chance to stop thinking about what had gone on today with Josh. Oh, yes, Josh.

She rolled over, pulling the soft red blanket tight under her chin. The night was still, an owl hooted in a nearby pine and in the moonlight she could see the columns of steam rising from the edge of the lake.

It seemed so unreal she might actually have convinced herself that she'd imagined it, that nothing had happened. But it had. Oh, yes, it certainly had. The soreness of her body, the wondrous pounding of her heart were proof enough of that. If she closed her eyes, she could imagine him kissing her, imagine his tongue licking the aching tip of her breast, imagine his hand...

Heart pounding, she sucked in a deep breath, trying to still the vivid memories. It had been heaven, purest bliss. He'd shown her what it meant to be a woman, and as she'd curled in his arms, she'd felt a peace, a rightness that she had instinctively known could only be one thing. Love. She was in love with Josh Colter.

She'd told herself it was lust, and it surely was that. Every time she looked at him, it was lust. But it was more. She was no child. She knew the difference. Yes, she was in love all right. She was startled. She was thrilled.

She was terrified.

Josh was awake long before the first light of dawn. Aw, hell, he'd been awake all night. Silently he rolled over to look at her sleeping a few feet away. Her hair curled down beside her face, her eyes closed, her lips drawn up in a sensuous pout.

Guilt twisted in his gut. This was never meant to happen. He'd gone with her in an effort to find her brother, the man who'd murdered Mourning Dove.

Instead he'd deceived her, then he used her in the worst way possible. Now it was too late. He *couldn't* tell her the truth. She'd *never* understand, never believe that making love to her was anything more than another attempt to get the information he so desperately needed.

Alex slowly opened her eyes. Her gaze immediately fixed on his.

Across the smoldering embers of the fire, he said, "I'm sorry."

She sat up slowly. Raking her hair back with one hand, the other held the blanket to her chest. She stared at him as the implication of his words, his tone, sank into her mind and her heart. Josh did not want her.

Tears, unwanted, began to cloud her vision and she turned her face, unwilling to share her hurt.

Josh, too, sat up. He saw the tears, saw the pain flash in her eyes. The last thing he'd wanted was to hurt her, but it appeared he was hurting her even more.

"Alex, please..."

She glanced around at him.

"I should never have done..." He lowered his eyes. More cautiously, he said, "I took advantage of you. You trusted me and I..." He surged to his feet and walked past her to where the horses were tethered, the pine needles soft against his bare feet. The morning chill prickled gooseflesh across his bare shoulders, his wool trousers protected his legs.

"I can't begin to explain...to tell you..."

He tried to think of David Gibson, of the man he sought, but all he could think of was Alex.

Dammit, he shouldn't have done this to her. She deserved better, much better, and she sure as hell deserved better than him. Yet, he knew that if he lived to be a thousand, he'd never regret the hour he'd spent loving her.

Alex stood, her underclothes no barrier against the cold. The first light of dawn cast the world in gray-white light. She watched Josh, his back to her as he spoke. Head down, he shoved his hands into his trouser pockets.

Alex had heard his words but she knew how she felt. "You haven't *done* anything to me. Nothing I didn't want you to do."

Despair clogged his throat. He slammed his eyes shut against the feeling. "I never meant for this to happen."

She wrapped her arms around herself to stop the shaking. Her voice was ripe with emotion, too raw, too intense to deny. "Josh. You made love to me. I wanted you to make love to me."

"No! You don't know what you're saying."

"I know exactly what I'm saying. I love you. It comes as a surprise to me, too, but it's the truth and there's no sense denying it."

"You can't love me. *You can't!*"

She gave a wry laugh. "Seems as though it's too late."

"No, it's not too late."

"Are..." Her voice caught. "Are you sorry?"

He turned sharply to face her. "Oh, no." He couldn't lie and he couldn't excuse himself. "It's all *my* fault. Everything." He faltered, trying to find the words to explain, to avoid telling her the truth of what he'd done...to both of them. He dragged in a deep breath, but it did little to stop the pounding of his heart or soothe the guilt that was tearing at him.

He was pledged to kill her brother. He was destined to lose her. His hands curled into hard fists, his fingers digging into his palms. "It was wrong. *I* was wrong. We can't change it." He turned away again.

Tears burned in her throat. All her joy was drowning in his regret and sorrow and apologies. "I will not forget what we shared, Josh Colter. I will *not* forget the joy. I love you, whether you like it or not, whether *I* like it or not." On a breathy whisper, she added, "I think I've waited my whole life, just for you."

He didn't move, didn't speak. Then he turned slowly. The look in his eyes was almost painful to see. "Alex, do you know what you're saying?"

"Yes."

"God help us both." He took a step in her direction. "I love you, too."

Having spoken the unspeakable, he went to her. His hands curved over her slender shoulders, feeling the delicate bones there. His gaze scanned her face, questioning. "Are you sure, Alex? Think what you're saying...what we're doing."

"I'm sure." As though to prove her conviction, she lifted up to touch his lips with hers.

For Josh, joy overcame desperation. *Don't think about tomorrow or the day after, only today, only now.*

Alex savored the feeling of being in his strong embrace again. It was as though all life began and ended here, with him. Her hands looped around his neck, and her cheek pressed against the smooth skin of his chest. The steady beating of his heart soothed and excited her all at once. Josh.

When she looked up again, he kissed her, long and slow, kindling the fire that burned bright, burned for him. Her fingers trembled with the joy of touching him.

His hands cupped her face then slid along her cheekbones and into her hair. He looked at her as though memorizing her features. His smile, like a soft caress, sent delicious shivers coursing down her spine. She knew what was about to happen.

Reaching up, she covered his hands with hers. His gaze turned dark, heated. She felt his body tense. "Alex, I never thought..."

With the barest of smiles, she said all that needed to be said. "I love you, Josh."

He didn't speak, just stood there looking at her, at the happiness that she was. He lowered his head and kissed her luscious mouth, coaxing, inviting, promising. He scooped her up and carried her to the blankets where he'd slept. The morning sun was warm and bright and the songs of robins and finches floated on the air.

She lounged temptingly on the navy blanket, her thin undergarments the most delicate of veils. Like the lover of his dreams, she reached for him. He didn't hesitate.

"I'll always love you," he said. "Say you'll remember." The fear of tomorrows haunted his delight.

She touched his face, her fingers trailing along his jaw, pausing at his mouth to trace his bottom lip. "I'll remember," she promised.

"Say it," he demanded.

"You'll always love me." She laughed, a rich warm sound that brushed across his skin like a flame.

Languidly she gazed up at the sky through the canopy of the trees. Time seemed to stop, she was so caught up in the moment and the happiness.

He moved partially over her, blocking out all but his handsome face. Images of desert sheikhs, of harems, of exotic perfumed nights, assailed her mind and her body. She smiled, a lush, come-hither smile, full of seduction and reckless desire.

"I dreamed about you last night." He undid the silk ties on her camisole, until his trembling fingers refused to work.

"I'm glad."

With a wanton's ease, she sat up and helped him, slipping the delicate cotton off her shoulder, revealing her breasts to him. Her nipples hardened beneath his heated gaze. "Touch me, Josh. I want you to touch me." She took his hand and brushed his palm over her tender nipples, sighing in delight. It was as though her entire body sighed, assured of the pleasure to come.

For Josh, desire was not slow or languid but a fast-moving energy that raced through him at the speed of a tidal wave. He rose to his knees and pulled her up to him.

"Woman, you drive me insane with wanting you."

"Good." She was as eager as he.

He removed her pantalets. She unfastened the button at his waist. Slowly they undressed each other until, at last, they were completely naked.

Passion flared. His body, tense as a caged lion, strained and flexed, anxious to be with her, in her. His hands glided up and down the length of her arms, over her bare back and down her spine. Her flesh was soft as buckskin, warmed by the sun and by the mindless need that was driving them both.

Knee to knee, thigh to thigh, he held her to him, the mounds of her breasts pressed against the plane of his chest like an exotic dream. He moved, twisted, needing to feel the exquisite delight of her nipples on his skin, letting her feel his hardness pressed against her belly.

He cupped one breast, his fingers closing over the nipple. He rubbed the hardened tip, she shuddered and groaned in response. He wanted to do that for her, ignite the passion, watch her succumb.

"Please, Josh. I want—"

"I know what you want," he whispered against her ear. "I want it, too."

He stroked her, his hands caressing every mound and valley, watching, learning what pleased her, what made her moan.

He kissed her knees and the insides of her thighs, and he laved at the tender underside of her breasts. He wanted her to know, to remember the pleasure that he alone could give her. When she began to moan, her body moving to a lover's song, he stroked the slick core of her.

"Again," she murmured, opening her legs to him.

He obeyed. "You like it when I touch you...there?"

She flinched. "Yes," she answered. "Again."

Her wetness was like the most expensive aphrodisiac, enhancing and magnifying the slightest sensation.

He couldn't wait to have her. In one motion, he moved over her and slid his heated length into her lush center. She bucked and moaned, and he thought perhaps he'd moved too quickly. But she lifted her legs, giving him better access, taking more of him into her sweet, lithe body. She wrapped tightly around him, cushioning him in her hot enchantment.

"Alex." He whispered her name like a prayer. "You belong to me." He withdrew then thrust in again.

She lifted up to him, taking all of him inside her. "Yours," she murmured, her fingers curled and clawing at his back. After that there was no thought, only need and longing and Josh. Always Josh.

His control was slipping fast. He whispered words of encouragement and need. He told her in explicit detail all that he wanted, all that he would do to her. All the while, he drove into her, the words, her body, urging him onward. Again and again he drove into her, gliding over the sweet flesh that made her writhe, made her head roll back and forth.

"Josh, I can't..."

"Relax, honey. Let it happen."

Breathing hard, he shifted, withdrawing completely each time, gliding over her sensitive flesh.

"Oh, yes! There."

He drove down again.

"Yes! There! Yes!" She clawed at the blanket, and her body arched upward. He felt her convulse around him, sending his mind spinning.

"Alex. I have to have you." Frenzied, beyond reason or conscious thought, he drove into her.

"Yes," she ordered, her mind hazy, her body reaching, stretching toward the promised enchantment that was so close. One more breath, one more heartbeat and...

When her climax came, it was more wonderful than ever. The world dissolved, the ground slipped away from beneath her and she was floating, clinging only to Josh. She felt him shudder, heard his moan as he poured himself into her.

Bodies melded into one, sweat glistened on overheated flesh. She held him close, her forehead nestled in the curve of his shoulder. Breathless, she drifted back to earth, never letting go of Josh, of the man she loved.

It was near sundown when Josh awoke. The evening breeze brushed across his naked body and he turned, looking with wonder at the woman sleeping peacefully in his arms. It was then that he realized he, too, had been asleep, peacefully asleep, for the first time in months. He felt blissfully content. They'd made love several times since morning. Each time more splendid, more erotic than before, erasing any doubt. He loved her, all right, with a fury that frightened him in its intensity.

He would not regret this time. He wouldn't allow himself to regret. She was here. She was his. It was enough.

With the lightest of touches, so as not to wake her, he lifted a lock of hair from her face and smiled. Her cheeks were red from whisker burn and he touched the spot as if to wipe it away. She moved, shifting against him, her hair brushing along his arm. Beautiful, he thought, as he lowered his hand to her bare shoulder. He let his gaze slide down the rest of her naked body, smiling as he saw gooseflesh prickle her skin in the evening chill.

She moaned her complaint, turned and curled against him. His hand slipped around her narrow waist, feeling the softness of her skin against his work-roughened palm before he let his hand drift lower, caressing her abdomen, the curve of her hip and down her thigh. Even now, after all their lovemaking, he was not sated.

He thought perhaps he'd love her a lifetime and still never have enough of her. Alex, the artist, the rebel, the woman—his woman.

Oh, the guilt was there, circling in his brain like a predator outside the light of a camp fire. Fear was there, too, knowing what was to come once she learned the truth.

But their truths were different. Hers would make her look at him with anger, hate perhaps, when she learned his mission. His truth was that, in loving her, he'd never love another, that he'd give up his future to be with her now.

She turned in his arms, her breasts brushing against his bare chest.

"Shh," he crooned, and pulled a blanket up to cover her. "Go back to sleep." He brushed a kiss on her cheek.

She snuggled lower in the blanket, turned away from him and did just that. Josh smiled. Very slowly, he inched away from her and stood. He grabbed up his clothes but didn't put them on. He was headed for the warm-water pool, their pool, near the camp at the edge of the lake.

The water was clear and clean, and only a slight sulfur smell teased his nostrils. Easing into the water he relaxed his muscles, and he stretched, luxuriating in the water. His arms floated out to his side, and he lowered himself down, letting the water flow over him until he was completely submerged. After a few minutes, he stood, combing the hair back from his face, wiping the water from his eyes. When his vision cleared, Alex was standing there.

She had the blanket pulled around her shoulders in a way that was all too enticing. She took a step, revealing her bare legs. Her hair was tousled. He didn't move, just stood there absorbing the sight of her, thinking this memory would stay with him until he died.

Her head was cocked to one side. "When I woke up, you were gone."

"Did you think I left you?" His tone was incredulous.

She gave a small nod of confirmation.

"Never." He moved toward her, the water churning around him. "If anyone leaves, *akhiikshe...* it will be you."

Her smile was instantaneous, a sensuous delight. "Then we will always be together." She started toward the pool. As she walked, she released the blanket. The red wool pooled like a gypsy's shirt on the ground. Naked, she waded in to join him.

"Hmm," she breathed, her eyes drifting closed for a moment. He watched the water inch up her body, waist, hips, breasts. She was pure pleasure to watch, pure bliss to love. He would be content to watch her forever.

Magpies chirped in the pine tree. Overhead a few bright stars could barely be seen.

"Warm enough for you?" he asked, scooping up a handful of water and letting it trickle along her shoulder.

"And if it is not?" she returned coyly.

"I could *make* you warmer," he told her confidently.

"Could you?" she murmured with feigned thoughtfulness, taking a playful step back. "I don't know."

"Would you like me to prove it to you?" He advanced on her, the look in his eyes hotter than any geyser.

"I suppose I could let you try," she teased, taking another step back.

"Woman, come here to me and I'll make you so hot we'll both go up in flames."

"I think I'd like that," she purred.

Their warm, wet bodies slipped against each other in a tantalizing invitation. Her arms circled his neck. He circled her waist, then drifted lower to cup her buttocks. He pulled her against him.

She tilted her head back to look up at him. "I'm glad it was you."

He arched one brow in question.

"The first time. I'm glad it was you."

"Then you aren't sorry?" he asked, his playfulness forgotten.

"Are you?"

"Never." The future—the grim and certain future—had not changed. He held her to him tightly.

He kissed the top of her head. She leaned into him and kissed his bare chest. Her tongue licked at the water beaded there. "You are beautiful, Josh."

He gave a small laugh. "Not hardly. You're the one who's beautiful." His hands cupped her breasts as if to confirm his statement.

She closed her eyes, letting the warmth of the water and the exquisite touch of Josh's hands send her mind and body spinning. Her fingers slipped on his wet flesh, but his embrace was tight as steel.

She felt his arousal against her hip. His eyes were bright with the fire of passion, a fire she'd seen many times in the past day. A thrill went through her.

"Let me love you, Alex."

She let her hands drift lower, below the water line, first to cup his buttocks then to touch his swollen arousal. She heard his sharp intake of breath, felt him flinch.

She closed her hand around him. "Lightly," he murmured, his hand guiding hers along his hardened shaft.

Suddenly shy, she released him.

He cupped her buttocks, lifting her, so her legs naturally went around his waist.

She pressed her cheek hard against his chest, and she could hear the strong, steady beating of his heart. *I love you, Josh,* she thought.

Wrapped together, he walked from the water and carried her the few steps to the back where he laid her down. For the next hour, they made love in the glow of the sunset.

Chapter Nineteen

For five days, they camped by the side of the crystal pool. The sun warmed the days, and the nights were warmed by the pleasure they gave each other.

Alex sketched and painted. Josh sat for hours watching her, admiring the way she made something so one-dimensional take form and life until it had a soul of its own. She was a marvel in so many ways.

Josh cherished these times. He pointedly chose never to talk about the future. Oh, yes, he knew it was there, in the shadows. He was determined to keep it there, for as long as possible, anyway.

They argued politics and appraised the latest fashions. They discussed opera and folk music and art, oh yes, art. Occasionally Alex would make some mention of places she wanted him to see, people she wanted him to meet. He would agree, then change the subject, because he knew that their time together was short, heartbreakingly short.

There were moments when he would fantasize about things being different. If only they were two different people... if only *he* was a different person...

They would meet at a party, perhaps. They would dine together, take rides together and eventually he would ask for her hand. Yes, he thought, marriage. It was a startling realization for a man who'd prided himself on being a loner. But Alex had changed that, changed him.

They'd be endlessly in love and *nothing* would intervene.

At the moment, Alex loved him, she'd said so, she'd shown him in ways that were so erotic his blood sizzled just thinking about her. For all that, each night he'd hold her sleeping in his arms, and the fears would come.

When she learned the truth, would she hate him even more because he had not told her, because he'd dared to love her? Perhaps she loved him enough to understand. Perhaps he would convince her of his justification. It was a hope, faint, but the only hope he had.

Sooner than he wanted, they had to leave. Alex had her deadline. He'd seen her work, and while he was no art expert, he knew she was good, very good. He wanted her to win. He wanted to think of her in her studio on St. Germain.

He hoped that when she was there, at night, alone in the darkness, she'd remember this time they'd had together, remember the man who'd loved her then, who would always love her.

Josh made special crates to hold her oil paintings and when he could delay no longer, they headed for the nearest town, Sulfur Hill—a used-to-be mining town on the fast track to dying, since the ore had run out the year before.

Josh didn't have much to say most of the day-long trip. What could he say? Towns and people meant a certain end to their time together. He didn't have the heart to tell her it meant the end of them, as well. He hated this. Hated her brother doubly, for he'd taken

Mourning Dove, and now, in a way, he was taking Alex, too.

Alex, of course, was excited. She'd made the painting she thought would win her the prize. She was confident, and there was enough time to pick up Davy and get to Salt Lake to catch the train east.

In recent days, Josh had refrained from asking about her brother. He almost didn't want to know. But the time had come, and he decided, tonight, after dinner he'd ask. Guilt merged with regret. How could he have known that his debt of honor would be so difficult?

It was near sunset when they rode into Sulfur Hill. There was a mercantile, a blacksmith, a barbershop with a sign proclaiming hot baths, and next door the Gilded Garter saloon.

They stopped there, the wagon brake screeching as he slammed it home. He helped her down. His smile was forced and he hoped she didn't notice. "We'll get rooms here," he said, his hands lingering on her waist, his fingers pushing into the stiff corset material. "How come?" She hadn't worn one all the while they were together.

"We're in town," she said, as though it were obvious.

"Oh." It was the first sign of reality.

He glanced over his shoulder at the saloon then back to her. "I've stayed here before. It'll be all right."

Conversation stopped when they entered and all heads turned in their direction. Alex felt awkward and a more than a little intrigued. She'd never been in a *real* saloon. The place was dark—shadows of blue and charcoal merged to conceal the dingy walls. The floor was brown, streaked nearly white where spurs had gouged the surface. The bar was wood, turned black by too many coats of shellac.

There were six men seated in pairs at three different tables. Their overalls were faded to light blue, their work shirts equally worn. They looked rugged and work hardened, but she didn't feel threatened, at least, not with Josh by her side.

She stayed in the doorway while he went to the bar. "Two rooms. Clean."

The owner, she noted, was tall, with a day's dark stubble covering his pointed chin. His red plaid shirt was threadbare with two buttons missing in the center, so that when he breathed, his hairy chest was revealed.

She couldn't help thinking the scene would make an interesting painting, though maybe she'd add a few cards to the one table, maybe a satin-gowned woman.

"First two, top of the stairs," she heard the saloon keeper tell Josh. "Two dollars each."

"A little high, isn't it?" Josh responded.

The barman gave a shrug. "Take it or leave it."

Like so many things lately, Josh didn't have a choice. He tossed some coins onto the wood surface, the metal clinking together. "Keys?"

The owner scraped the coins into his hand. "In the doors."

Josh escorted her to the stairs then paused, turning partially back toward the owner. "How's chances of getting some hot water for the lady?"

"No problem. Take about an hour." The man motioned toward the skinny kid who was sweeping up the place.

"Right away," the kid replied, and disappeared through a door near the back.

Josh led Alex up the stairs.

As they paused at the door, she glanced over at him. "Why two rooms?" They had, after all, been sharing a bedroll for the past several days.

"I think it's better this way. You know, appearances, an all."

"Oh." She frowned. She wasn't concerned with appearances but thought perhaps he was trying to protect her reputation.

He unlocked the door and handed her the key. "You get settled. I'm going to take care of the horses and see about the supplies we'll need if we're traveling on. We are traveling on, aren't we?"

"Yes." She fumbled with the key, the brass cold against her fingers. "I want to pick up Davy."

"Ah, yes, Davy."

There was an edge to his voice that troubled her, but before she could ask more, he turned and disappeared down the stairs.

Inside the room, Alex hesitated. It had been so long since she'd had anything but stars for a ceiling, it felt odd. Hands behind her, she leaned back against the door, the wood smooth to the touch.

As Josh had promised, the room was small and clean. A bed, two feet inside the doorway, was covered in a quilt. The calico fabric that must have been bright blue and yellow was now faded from the sunlight pouring in the one and only window. There was a three-drawer walnut bureau, one side propped up with a block of wood, a pitcher and bowl for washing displayed there. A mismatched wardrobe faced the foot of the bed.

She sank down on the bed, testing its softness. It was going to feel strange sleeping in a bed. It was going to feel stranger sleeping alone, she added with a blush.

Josh. He'd seemed distant since they'd left the camp. He'd had little to say. Maybe he was feeling sad at their trip ending. Was he was wondering about the future? She was wondering about that, herself. They were in love, but was she prepared to give up her career and become a rancher's wife? Was he prepared to sell his ranch and go with her to Paris?

Life had just gotten so much more complicated.

It was ten past eight when Josh knocked on her door. He'd been stalling going up to her, so instead he'd seen to the horses, ordered supplies and spent a half hour downstairs having a couple of drinks—for courage.

When he couldn't put it off any longer, he gathered her belongings, the ones he'd brought in from the wagon, and headed up the stairs.

She opened the door carefully, peeking around the edge. It didn't take him a second to realize she was wearing only a blanket, a small blanket that didn't cover her legs from the knees down and barely covered her from the knees up. Not that he hadn't seen her, all of her, but that was the trouble. He *had* seen her, wanted to see her again, wanted to make love to her until the world and all its demands went away.

"I'm sorry..." He made himself step back. "I thought you'd be ready, well, done washing, well..." He snatched off his hat, realizing that she was probably waiting for him to bring her clothes and such. "Here's your things." He handed her the carpetbag. "I'll wait downstairs until you're dressed."

"You... you could come in... if you want."

"I... no. I'll... I think I'll clean up myself." He backed away. "You come over when you're ready and we'll go down for some dinner. Okay?"

"Okay," she said softly.

He was sitting on the edge of the bed when she knocked. "Ready?" she called.

"Ready." He opened the door.

He stood there, looking at her as though for the first time. She'd put her hair up, the way he liked so much. A few stray wisps fell enticingly around her face. She wore her black skirt, which she'd obviously brushed clean, and a blue blouse, a little wrinkled but hardly noticeable.

"You look lovely," he said, her image indelibly imprinted on his mind.

Alex blushed. The man had seen her naked and still she blushed. Josh had a way of doing that to her, making her feel unique and alluring and all those things she'd never cared about—until Josh. "Thank you."

They stayed like that, lost in each other's gaze until a loud peal of laughter and a ribald remark carried up from the saloon.

Alex chuckled. "You were saying something about dinner?"

"What? Oh, sure . . . dinner."

Josh spotted a table in the corner and, after seating her, he went to the bar to order dinner—no waitresses here. In fact there were no women at all, except Alex, who seemed to be attracting a lot of attention. "What's the matter with these men?" Josh said loud enough that everyone in the room could hear. "Haven't they ever seen a woman before?" He dragged out a chair and sat down.

Alex did feel a bit conspicuous, but she tried not to show it. She had eyes only for one man. She wished they were back by the lake. Being here was too much like reality. Everything seemed different, the sounds seemed sharp and irritating, the smells acrid and unpleasant.

Josh felt it, too, he had from the moment they'd left Yellowstone. With every mile his joy had dissolved, until by the time they reached town, there was nothing left of their perfect life.

Are you giving up this easily?

No, but—

Find a way.

The steak and potatoes arrived. Josh wasn't interested in dinner. He went to the bar and returned with a bottle of whiskey. It was a good night for a drink, a lot of drinks.

"Did you get the supplies?" she asked.

"Yes, most of what we'll need." He poured a hefty drink and tossed it back in one throat-searing gulp. Hand gripping the glass, he asked the question he'd come to dread. "Where is your brother?" He poured another drink and ignored her disapproving stare.

"I'm guessing he's at the XJ ranch near Devil's Elbow. Do you know it?" She cut into her meat.

"Devil's Elbow?" How appropriate. If it had been anyone else, he might have laughed at the irony. But now he knew, and the absurdity of it was the damn place was close, a day maybe, less if a man rode hard.

There has to be a way. Find it.

"Do you know the ranch?" she was asking.

He focused on what she was saying. "No. That doesn't mean anything. There's hundreds of tiny spreads scattered over Montana." Not like his Bar HC. Josh ran ten thousand head of mixed Hereford. Fortunately he had a good foreman who was looking out for the place while he was away.

"Josh?"

"Huh?"

"I was asking if you knew Abe, with both of you being cattle ranchers and all . . ."

"Abe?"

"Abe Hallman."

"Nope, haven't met the man."

She gave a one-shoulder shrug. "There's a railroad there, isn't there?"

He toyed with the glass in his hand. "No. There's the one I told you about in Salt Lake and there's a spur at Camas, in Idaho. It's a long day's stage ride."

"That'll have to do. I can pick up Davy, put him on the train. He can collect Eddie, and the two of them can go to San Francisco together. I've decided to take my paintings to Washington, personally. I don't want them ending up in a railroad storage room. First, of course, I'll wire Eddie, make sure he's okay."

"Good," he muttered, only half listening. He tossed back the whiskey and let it burn all the way down. So this was it. He had the information he'd been after for weeks. How come he wasn't happy? How come he wasn't headed out the door? One look at her and he knew why. Dammit to hell, this wasn't right! He'd be damned if he'd give her up without a fight. "About your brother, are you certain he's at the XJ?"

"Well, I don't know for certain, since I haven't heard from him."

Josh took a long swallow of whiskey. He was halfway through the bottle and edgy as hell. "You don't think he'd strike out on his own?" He almost wished it was true, wished Gibson had run out never to be seen again.

She shook her head, taking a bit of steak into her mouth. "My brother—" she swallowed "—bless his heart, for all his bravado, is a gentle soul. He's no more suited for the cowboy life than...well, I don't know anything more unsuitable for Davy." She laughed. Josh wasn't laughing. Gibson might not be suited for cowboying, but he was evidently well suited for murder.

"...not even a very good rider."

Josh realized she was talking.

"If he's decided to do this, I can't imagine anyone but Abe would consider giving him a chance. I mean, don't most ranchers want experienced help?"

"Usually."

Find a way.

She arched one brow and made a small palms-up gesture with her hands. "So it stands to reason that he's at Abe's, blistered and sore, and wishing he was back in his nice chair at the bank." She made a showy sigh. "I'll put the rascal on a train for San Francisco, I'll go East, and when the contest is over—" she looked at him intently "—I'll come back...that is if you want me to come back?"

His head came up with a start and he fixed her with a dark-eyed stare. "I want you," he told her. "Make no mistake about that."

The words were right, but there was something in his tone that bothered her, something vague and unsettling. Alex let the silence fall between them, unsure of the change that had come over Josh since they'd returned to civilization. Something was wrong.

Absently she watched his hand curl around the whiskey glass, watched him turning the glass in his fingers, those same fingers that had stroked her cheek, touched her breasts, made her body sing with delight. Instinctively she glanced up at him, but he was looking at the whiskey glass he kept filling and emptying.

A knot of anxiety formed in her stomach. Suddenly she wasn't hungry anymore.

After a while, he said, "If you're finished, I'll take you back to your room. I'll get the supplies loaded and, well, I'll see you in the morning."

Alex forced a shaky smile. He looked so handsome, sitting across from her, and he looked so sad. "Josh? What is it? What's wrong?"

He kept staring into the whiskey glass. "Nothing's wrong."

She touched his hand. He turned his head first, looking at her hand then at her. "I'm fine. Nothing's wrong, just tired."

It was a feeble excuse and they both knew it, but it was the best he could do on short notice. His brain was working overtime, searching for an idea, anything so he could keep her, so she'd never know what he'd done, what he'd had to do!

"All right," she said, but she knew things were far from all right. Was it her? Was he having second thoughts? Would he take her to Davy then leave her? He'd said he wanted her. He hadn't said for how long.

They sat there for a long time, neither speaking, each lost in their own thoughts. The world filled in around them—the rowdy talk, the sharp scent of stale tobacco and cheap whiskey, the argument over a hand of poker. They didn't have to speak to know their dreamworld was gone.

The next day they arrived in Devil's Elbow. It was a typical ranching community—livery stable, mercantile that was also a bank, a saloon, a stage depot and a boardinghouse that let rooms by the night.

They checked in, two rooms, same as before. Josh settled her in her room, then retreated to his.

All during the trip, he'd been thinking, going over a plan. It was simple really, so simple he didn't know why he hadn't thought of it before.

All he had to do was slip away without her knowing. A few hours was all he needed. The ranch couldn't be far. He'd find the brother, call him out and kill him. *She'd* never know what had happened. Should they find the body, and he intended to make certain no one did, what was there to connect him to the death? Nothing. Not a damned thing.

It was foolproof.

Can you look her in the eyes, knowing how she feels about her brother and knowing it was you who took his life?

Damn straight! He didn't owe the murderer anything. She didn't know what kind of a person her brother was.

And why don't you tell her?

He sagged back against the pine headboard. He felt certain she wouldn't believe him, after all the stories she'd told him about her perfect but confused baby brother. The sun rose and set in Davy, that was clear enough, though why that was the case beat the hell out of him.

A fair fight. Two men. Guns. Simple.

Chapter Twenty

They had dinner together, this time in the boarding-house kitchen. There was one other guest, a short, balding man selling notions. He was passing through on his way to Helena. They had a pleasant conversation over venison roast and wild onions. Josh was withdrawn all evening. He'd checked at the livery when he put the wagon up and gotten directions to the XJ ranch, about thirty minutes north. He could get there, do what he'd come for and get back. Shouldn't take more than an hour and a half, he figured.

Alex wanted to walk after dinner, so they took a stroll around the town, such as it was. When they got back, he took her to her room and said good-night. He purposely didn't kiss her. He was only human, and it was killing him to be this close to her and not touch her, have her. He knew she didn't understand, he wasn't completely sure he did, either. It was just that he had to distance himself from her to do what had to be done.

"I need some sleep." He braced one hand on the door frame and leaned into it. She was looking at him with her luminous blue eyes, her face was turned up to him and if he lowered his head just a bit . . .

He stepped back. He forced a smile he didn't feel. "What say we have a late breakfast then ride out to the ranch. Okay?" Late breakfast, yeah.

"Okay," she confirmed. "Josh, don't you want—"

"Good night, Alex."

There were still stars in the sky when Josh tossed back the covers and got up. In the darkness, he banged into the dry sink, the basin crashed to the floor and the white porcelain shattered into about a million pieces. Cold water splashed on his bare feet and soaked into the floorboards.

"Damn!"

Where the hell was the lamp? Right on cue, his hand slapped the glass and the shade rattled dangerously in its holder. "No, you don't," he ordered, steadying the glass with one hand while striking a match with the other. He glanced around. Hell, there was broken china everywhere. It was a miracle he hadn't sliced his feet.

Great. This was all he needed.

He grabbed a towel from the peg on the wall and scooped up enough pieces to clear a path so he could get dressed.

The wardrobe door banged closed when he got out his shirt and trousers. "Hell," he grumbled. He was moving fast. He wanted to get out of here, get going so he'd be back in time for that late breakfast.

He stamped on his boots, yanked his trouser legs over the tops and fastened on his spurs. He buckled his gun belt, the worn leather molded to his waist and hips. A quick spin of the cylinder made sure it was fully loaded. It was.

He slapped his Stetson on his head, collected his rifle, just in case, and headed for the door. China crunched under his boots. He'd square the mess with the boardinghouse later. Right now he was a man on a mission. His whole life depended on the outcome.

Two steps across the landing, spurs jingling, her voice stopped him.

"Why didn't you call me?"

She was standing there, fully dressed, her valise in her hand. Her expression was puzzled. "I didn't think you wanted to leave so early, but I heard you moving around and hurried."

Speechless, he stared at her. This couldn't be happening, but apparently it was. Damn that bowl and damn his clumsiness. Now what?

Now nothing! What could he say, *Go back to sleep, I'm on my way to kill your brother?*

"I changed my mind," he told her sharply, knowing that there was no way out. "Let's go."

Twenty minutes later Josh had the team hitched and they were riding out of town on their way to the XJ ranch.

It was hopeless.

At the ranch they were greeted by Abe Hallman. A tall man, thin and muscular for his fifty-plus years, Abe showed the hardship of a man working the land.

"Alexandria, I can't believe you're here." He hugged her affectionately, his grin as big as a Cheshire cat's. She returned the hug. "Why didn't you let me know you were coming? How was your trip? How long can you stay?"

"Abe, you handsome devil," she teased, "I'm glad to see you, too. It's been too long. What's it now, two years?"

He put her back from him, his mouth pulled down in a frown. "Two? Hell, closer to four."

Her brows drew down. "It can't be that long."

"Your party before you went to Paris that last time, remember?"

She shook her head in dismay. "You're right." She grinned again. "Well, I'm here now."

It was then she looked over at Josh, standing near the wagon. "I'm sorry," she said to both of them at the same time. "Abe Hallman, this is Josh Colter."

Abe fixed Josh with a fatherly stare that Josh recognized and met square on. He extended his hand. "Nice to meet you."

Abe's questioning gaze flicked from Josh to Alex and back again. "If you're a friend of Alex's then, mister, you're welcome." He smiled, not an all-out grin, mind you. The man knew something was going on, but he didn't ask questions.

"Come on inside," he told them. Arm protectively around Alex's shoulders, he started up the wooden walk toward a house that was dirty white clapboard with faded red trim. Josh wasn't so much interested in color schemes as schemers. Discreetly he let his gaze search the yard, the corral, the porch on the bunkhouse.

Of course, it was spring and so the men would be out working the herd. If Gibson was here...aw, hell, he wasn't sure what he'd do.

Whatever he did, could he do it in front of her?

He followed them into the house. Heart thundering in his chest, he was almost relieved to see that the room was empty. He took up a position by the door and glanced around the room.

It wasn't a bad room, he thought absently. Large and square, the walls needed a coat of paint. The furniture was walnut, carved, the burgundy upholstery faded. Half an inch of dust covered every surface. Sort of reminded him of home, in a abstract sort of way.

Home.

Now that gave him a tug. He missed home—a lot. He wondered if Alex would like his place, his house? He wondered if she'd ever see his home?

Alex was seated on the curved-back sofa close to the fireplace. Light poured in the front window and seemed to settle on her. Her hair glistened like spun gold. Instantly he remembered the feel of it slipping through his fingers.

Abe spoke up. "Now, how long can you stay?" He sat down beside her, his dark blue shirt lost against the burgundy upholstery.

She cocked her head to one side and gave a little sigh. "Not very long, I'm afraid." She spared Josh a glance. "I've got a deadline...for a painting." She twisted around to face him more directly. "I'm looking for Davy. Has he been here?"

Abe fell silent. His smile melted faster than ice cream in August. Josh straightened. It was put-up or shut-up time.

Finally Abe said, "Davy's here." He stood.

"Wonderful!" Alex exclaimed. "I was hoping he was." Alex surged to her feet, her black skirt twisting around her legs. She looked over the room as though she expected her brother to materialize in front of her. Josh was half expecting the same thing. If he did walk through the door right now, he wasn't exactly sure how he'd handle it. He didn't have to find out.

Abe's weathered face was drawn, serious. Something flashed in his brown eyes, sadness or anger, Josh wasn't sure.

"Abe, what's wrong?" Alex closed on him. "Is Davy sick? Is he hurt?" Worry creased her brow. "Where is he?"

Abe seemed to be lost in thought. He toyed with a silver picture frame on the mantel, the faded image of a man and woman on their wedding day held there. He shifted from one foot to the other. "Naw, honey, he isn't sick. Davy showed up here about a month ago, I guess it was. He looked like something the dogs dragged home, so o' course I took him in."

He put the frame back on the mantel with a small thud.

"Abe, you're scaring me. What's wrong with him? Where is he? I want to see him!"

Abe didn't budge from his place by the mantel.

"Abe?" she prompted.

"He was looking for work," Abe said on a sigh. "You and I both know he barely knows one end of a horse from the other, but like I said, I took him in."

She nodded.

"He slept for a couple of days straight and that was fine, I mean he looked like he needed it, but when he woke up, it wasn't food he wanted . . . it was whiskey."

Alex's hand fluttered to her chest. "Oh, no," she whispered.

"I'm sorry, honey. But that's the truth of it. Every time I'd turn around, he was riding into town buying more whiskey. If he'd been some stranger, I'd 'ave fired him and been done with it, but it being Davy, well . . ."

"Thank you, Abe, you've been a good friend."

"Well, I don't know about that." He shifted. His gaze flicked to Josh and back to Alex again.

"Where's Davy now?" she asked. "In the bunkhouse?"

"No." He moved away from her, as though not comfortable with what he was about to say. "Like I said, he kept getting whiskey, so yesterday I loaded him and some supplies—no whiskey—and took him out to the line shack on the west end. I figured he'd sober up and come to his senses."

"Won't he ride off?" Josh spoke up for the first time. He wasn't interested in Davy's rehabilitation. The more he heard, the more he didn't like this guy and the more he knew the world would be better off... she'd be better off without him. Josh, sure as hell, would!

"Can't ride off," Abe replied. "Didn't leave him a horse. It's ten miles to town. He wasn't in any condition to walk, if you know what I mean?"

Yeah, Josh knew what he meant. Gibson was booze-blind drunk.

"Poor Davy," Alex muttered. She dropped down onto the sofa, her skirt billowing out around her. "He's probably scared and lonely out there. Can you take me to him?"

Poor Davy? Josh couldn't believe his ears. From what she'd told him, he could tell the man was spoiled rotten, drinking, gambling, carousing, murder. What's this poor-Davy stuff?

"Sure, I can take you to him," Abe said with about as much enthusiasm as if he'd been offered a second dose of castor oil.

Josh stepped more fully into the room. "You're probably busy, this being spring and all. If you give me directions, I could take Alex out and save you a trip." The less people around the better, he figured. When you call a man out, you like to know you aren't going to be interrupted.

"That would be fine, Abe. We've caused you enough trouble."

Abe didn't put up an argument. He headed to the small writing desk and sketched a map for Josh, giving him brief instructions. Josh figured it looked pretty simple.

"Ready?" he asked Alex, who was already moving toward the door.

"We'll take Davy off your hands, Abe. As soon as he can travel, I'll put him on the train for home. I'll wire ahead so Papa will meet the train." She sighed visibly. "Papa." She gave Abe a parting hug and a kiss on the cheek.

It was about an hour ride to the line shack, an eight-by-ten weatherworn structure of wood and shingle. There was no one stirring when they approached and no smoke came from the chimney.

Josh dismounted and helped Alex down from the wagon.

"Davy?" She hurried past him but stopped in the doorway. "It's empty. There's no one here."

Josh followed close behind her. There were clothes scattered around and the remnants of some burned food on the stove, but no Gibson. The place was a mess. He'd seen pigpens better kept.

She scanned the area. "Davy?" she called. No answer. "Where could he be? Something has happened to him, I'm sure of it." She paced back and forth. "Maybe he went for a walk and got lost and he's out there somewhere—"

"More than likely he's trying to cover those ten miles for a bottle of whiskey." Josh couldn't keep the disdain from his voice, and was rewarded with a stare cold enough to freeze milk.

"I'm going to find him." Before he realized what she was up to, she charged off along the trail. She didn't know where she was going and in no time he'd have both of them to look for. Okay, just one of them—he didn't give a tinker's damn about "darling Davy."

He mounted his horse and caught up to her. "Look, stay here in case he comes back. I'll see if I can pick up his trail and find him, okay?"

She seemed to consider this for a moment. "All right, but if you don't find him in thirty minutes, come back. We'll have to go to the ranch and organize a search party." Her features were drawn, her mouth set. "Abe should never have left Davy here alone. Davy doesn't know how to survive in the wilderness."

Josh's temper went up faster than a geyser and twice as hot. "Dammit, Alex, Abe was doing the best he could with a drunk. What the hell did you expect him to do, sit here and hold Davy's hand?" With that, Josh reined over and rode out. He was mad enough to take on the devil and give him odds.

Zigzagging back and forth, it didn't take long to find Gibson's trail. Hell, a blind man could have spotted the trail. He rode along for about a mile. The sky was clear, the day warm. The trail turned east. Well, so much for being lost. Davy was making a beeline for town, ten miles or not.

Josh kept riding, rage and grief his companions. Around him, the land was bare, sprinkled with sage and clumps of buffalo grass. Cattle dotted the horizon. An eagle's scream caught his attention, and he glanced up to see the golden bird soaring overhead. Much like Josh, the eagle searched for its quarry, too.

It was quiet out here, peaceful. Normally Josh would have enjoyed the solitude but today—

Wait a minute. He stopped, his horse shifting and flexing under him. Josh looked around. He didn't see Gibson, but more importantly, he didn't see anyone else, either.

Get Davy Gibson alone, kill him, and no one will know.

A breeze fluttered his collar against his cheek and he pushed it down. He was alone. *They* would be alone. Maybe the spirits were finally with him.

Another quarter mile and the trail led behind a bluff of reddish tan rock.

Sure enough there was the man he'd sought all these long angry months, slumped against the rocky base like a scarecrow in a cornfield. Looking at his sister's killer, blinding rage flashed red in his mind.

"Son of a bitch." His hand went to his gun.

Chapter Twenty-One

Alex paced back and forth in front of the dilapidated shack. Josh had been gone too long. Every few seconds, she'd pause, shade her eyes and scan the treeless horizon. Where was he? Why didn't he come back? Something was wrong, she knew it, could feel it in her bones.

When she spotted a rider, she took off running.

Another second and she realized there was one rider, one man. Where was Davy? Panic spurred her and she closed the distance, her feet cushioned by the loamy soil. That was when she saw the terrifying sight—another man, slung over the saddle in front of Josh.

Her heart rose in her throat. "Davy!" she screamed. Without seeing his face, she knew it was her brother.

She came alongside the horse and turned tearful eyes up to Josh. Her hand touched his thigh. "How did he..." She couldn't bring herself to say the word.

Josh kept his gaze straight ahead, his jaw set, his back rigid. "He's not dead, if that's what you mean." As if to prove the fact, he jabbed Davy in the ribs and got a groan for an answer.

She let go the breath she'd been holding. "What happened?"

Yeah, good question, Colter.

About that time, Davy evidently decided that he didn't like riding belly down on a horse, because he threw up a half bottle of whiskey and whatever he'd had for breakfast.

"Dammit!" Josh's stomach rolled at the sound and the smell. Alex jumped out of the way just in time.

"You asked what happened," Josh repeated her question. "He's falling-down drunk is what happened."

The breeze flung her hair in her face and she had to turn aside to clear her eyes. "Let's get him to the wagon and we'll take him back to Abe's." She ran ahead. "He needs medical help."

"Are you kidding?" Josh called after her. "He's *drunk,* Alex. What he needs is to be tossed in a horse trough and held down for about an hour."

Alex glared at him. "Can't you see he's sick?"

"Well, I'm not hauling him back to Abe's."

She rushed into the house and straightened bed covers, which consisted of two army blankets.

"Bring him inside," she ordered with all the efficiency of a general as Josh reined to a stop by the door. "Put him on the bed."

"Yeah, I know. We have to take care of baby brother."

Josh slung David over his shoulder and dumped him unceremoniously on the bed with a frame-creaking thud. Alex glared at him then rushed to her brother's side. "Davy. It's Alex. I'm going to take care of you now." She started cleaning him up. Josh couldn't bear to watch. He stormed outside. He didn't know who he was more disgusted with, Gibson or himself. Himself!

He should have killed the man and been done with it. He could have brought the man in dead over that saddle.

But dammit to hell, he couldn't do it. It was one thing to kill a man in an equal fight, it was another to shoot an unarmed, unconscious man. Even revenge had its limits or, at least, Josh Colter did.

Yeah, for all the good your high-and-mighty principles did you.

Not one damned bit.

Over the next twenty-four hours, Alex ordered Josh around. Bring firewood, make a fire, get supplies from the wagon, all the while she crooned over the drunken sot.

"Davy, sweetheart, come on now. Eat something for Alex. You need your strength."

"No more." Davy swallowed hard and rubbed the back of his hand over his eyes a couple of times in a futile effort to clear the cobwebs away. It looked like his sister was here, but that was impossible. If he could only think. No. He didn't want to think. He sank down into the black abyss of the alcohol.

Josh took in the entire disgusting scene from his place by the stove. He had been hungry, but watching this had pretty much done in his appetite.

"Now you just lie back and rest," Alex told Davy. "I'll do everything. A couple of days and you'll feel fine."

She fluffed his pillow. Josh couldn't stand it. He wanted to hit something, someone. He didn't know how much more of this he could take.

He stalked outside. He needed fresh air, needed space. He needed Gibson squared off in front of him with a gun.

Alex stayed with Davy. He was her brother and she couldn't turn her back on him, especially when he was so helpless. He'd always been there for her and she could do no less for him.

All the next day, she fetched and cared for Davy. Josh watched stoically, complained occasionally and even hauled water himself. He'd be damned if he'd stand by and let her wear herself out on this bastard.

It was early Wednesday morning when "darling Davy" opened his baby blue eyes and actually saw out of them, actually knew where he was.

"Sis?" His voice was shaky but strong, definitely strong.

Alex raced to his side. Josh sat up in his bedroll. *So you're awake.* He flexed, feeling the reassuring tug of the leather gun belt around his waist.

Davy's questioning gaze flicked to Alex. He smiled and Josh could see the strong family resemblance between them—the same blond hair, the same fine features.

"Sis? Is that you?"

"Of course, it's me." She grinned.

Davy's head ached like someone had taken a sledge to his skull. "What...what are you doing here? How...?" He smacked his lips trying to figure what furry creature had curled up and died in his mouth.

Alex took this as her cue to fetch him water.

"Thanks." His hand shook so badly she had to hold the cup for him. Hell. He took a long drink. "How did you find me?"

"Good detective work," she teased, brushing his overly long hair back from his forehead like a mother would a child.

Davy was confused. The last he remembered was Abe yelling at him. "But how did you get *here?*"

"Mr. Colter brought me."

Davy shook his head. She helped him with another long swallow of water. "I mean here, Montana, West, or east of San Francisco. You were at home and—" Davy's eyes slammed shut against the dizziness that swirled in his head faster than a carousel. He grabbed the edge of the bed for support. His stomach lurched and he was sure he'd vomit, except he hadn't eaten anything in . . . how many days? He wasn't sure.

"...and now I'm here." She chuckled. "I came West to do some paintings for a contest I've entered and I was going to pick you up and bring you along but you—" she ruffled his hair playfully "—had taken off. If I hadn't found out you were with those other men—"

"What men?" he shouted. "Who said I was with someone?" God, his head hurt. His stomach churned, bile prickled the back of his throat. Every muscle in his body throbbed.

Alex regarded him through narrowed eyes. "The desk clerk in Gunlock said he'd overheard you talking about cowboy work and so I took a wild guess and got lucky."

"Oh." He took another look at this Josh person Alex had brought along. The man looked dark and danger- ous, hardly the type to be with his sister. For that mat- ter, what was she doing out here. Cotton clouded his brain. Contest. Something about a contest.

His head hurt so bad. If only those sledgehammers would stop pounding. "Could I have a drink?"

"Sure."

His eyes brightened, that was until he saw she was bringing more water. He didn't need water, he needed hair of the dog, alcohol.

He rubbed his aching temples. "I mean whiskey. Have you got any?"

"Davy!" She had that holier-than-thou look he hated so much. He winced.

"Absolutely not. Even if I wanted to, which I don't, I wouldn't give you any. Do you want to tell me what's going on?"

No, he most certainly did not. He was ashamed and disgusted with himself, but he didn't want to tell her about it. He didn't want to see the shame reflected back in her eyes.

Whiskey.

Davy's gaze shot past Alex to the man watching him so intently. If he worked for Alex, then maybe... "But you have horses and Mr. Colter could ride—"

"No, I couldn't and neither could your sister, so don't even ask."

Well, so much for that. Davy sagged down on the bed, staring at the raw wood of the ceiling. What the devil was the problem? All he wanted was a drink. All he wanted was to forget. How was he supposed to sleep without whiskey?

Alex fussed with straightening his blanket in a way that annoyed the hell out of him. He pushed her hand away.

"Davy, what's wrong with you? I've seen you drink before but never like this. Is it money trouble?"

He wished it were that easy. He slammed his eyes shut and rolled over, away from her.

"Davy?" Alex prompted.

"You don't understand," he mumbled, his stomach churning as much from the memories as the whiskey hangover.

"Maybe it's a guilty conscience," Josh supplied cryptically.

Davy rolled back so fast he thought his head would explode with the movement. "What have you heard?" he demanded, but got only a funeral-cold stare that sent shivers up his spine.

"Guilty conscience about what?" Alex questioned, her gaze going to Josh then back to her brother.

Josh's gaze never wavered from Davy's. "About—"

"Nothing!" Davy cut him off. "Nothing at all."

Colter couldn't know. No one knew.

Josh lounged back. "Maybe something will come to you after your head clears, after your nerves are steadier."

Alex didn't miss their exchange. "Well, whatever it was, it's all in the past. Don't you worry. I'm here now and I'll take care of you."

And she did just that. All she did was fret and fawn over him until Josh thought he'd go crazy watching. She cooked and cleaned for the ungrateful wretch. She bathed him and fed him. She changed his bed when he vomited all over the blankets. She did everything except sing him good-night. She acted as though Gibson were some knight injured in battle instead of the lying murderer he was.

Hell, she hadn't fussed over him like that, and he'd had busted ribs... almost busted ribs. They'd hurt enough to be busted, he added, feeling more than a little surly.

As if that weren't enough, now there she was, across the room, spoon-feeding the killer the broth she'd spent all day making. "Come on now, sweetie, try to eat something."

"I don't want broth, Alex. I hate broth."

He turned away like some petulant child.

Days, months of anger exploded in Josh. Without thinking, he grabbed the bowl and hurled it across the room. The china slammed into the wall with an explosive thud and shattered, pieces flying through the air before settling on the floor.

In one motion, Josh pushed her aside, grabbed the sot by the shirtfront and hauled him to his feet.

"Josh! No!" Alex screamed.

Josh ignored her. He'd had enough. More than enough. He rammed Davy against the wooden wall with a bone-jarring fury.

"You'll hurt him!"

"Good." Eye to eye with Gibson, his face inches from the man he hated, so only he could hear, Josh muttered, "I'm sick to death watching you whine and snivel. I'm sick to death being in the same room with you, you murdering son of a bitch!" He slammed the man against the wall again. The wood creaked, threatening to break under the force. Gibson groaned. "I've been looking for you."

"No!" Davy cried.

He grabbed Josh's hands, but Josh never loosened his grip. Davy's eyes were wild with fright. Good. Josh wanted him afraid. He wanted him to know what it felt like to know you were going to die.

Alex screamed. "Josh, let him go! What's the matter with you? Have you gone crazy?"

"Just about." Josh shoved his forearm up hard against Gibson's throat, his fingers clutching the smooth cotton of his shirt. "Tell her. Tell her what you did." He wanted that. Alex was going to know the truth, and it wasn't going to come from him.

Davy shook his head back and forth in frantic denial. "I didn't. You're wrong."

"The hell you didn't. Larson told me." He pressed in closer, his mouth almost touching Gibson's ear. "Larson told me before I slit his throat."

Davy went still. His blood turned to ice. His heart beat like a drum in his chest. "Let me go!" He pushed at the madman who was determined to kill him, but it was like pushing on a granite wall. "Please... I didn't..." He gasped for air.

"Not this time." Josh shoved his arm harder against Gibson's windpipe, another inch, a little tighter, and...

Frantic, Alex clawed at him. "Josh, stop it."

Josh's heart hammered in his chest, killer-cold determination flashed in his eyes. At last he had the man he'd sought. Just push a bit harder, hold him a minute longer...

Alex tore at his arms, his waist. Josh saw nothing, heard nothing. There was just him and Gibson, and Gibson was going to die.

He tightened his grip, his fingers digging into the soft flesh of the man's neck. Revenge pounded in his brain. Every muscle in his body strained to the task. He would not relent.

Josh could almost feel the life slipping away from Gibson, could feel his body cease to struggle and he relished the feeling. "This is for my sister."

Josh never saw the blow coming. Her fist blindsided him, and he staggered not so much from the force of the blow but from the reality of what had happened.

Startled, he released his hold, and Gibson sagged to the floor like the sack of garbage he was. Breathing hard, it took Josh a moment to focus, to let the red haze clear from his mind and his vision.

Davy clutched his neck, gasping for breath like a winded horse. He realized that somehow Josh knew the truth.

Alex rounded on Josh. "Are you insane! You almost killed him!"

"I wanted to kill him." His face was hard, his eyes like obsidian. "He raped and murdered my sister."

Chapter Twenty-Two

Alex couldn't move. The accusation hit her with the force of a locomotive. Her head reeled. It made no sense. Davy would never do such a thing. Never!

But one look and she knew that Josh believed it. She remembered the gruesome details of his sister's murder, how he had been hunting the men responsible, how he needed to find the one last man.

In the beat of a heart, she put it all together.

Josh had used her to find her brother.

She went cold deep, deep inside. It was as though some part of her simply ceased to exist. She took a step closer to her brother and away from Josh, away from this man she'd loved and who'd lied to her.

"He killed my sister. Murdered her in cold blood." Josh spat the words like a verdict.

Her gaze flicked to her brother's pale face, his blue eyes wild with fright. She dropped down beside Davy, still curled on the floor, still gasping for air. She took him protectively in her arms. "I don't believe you. I'll *never* believe you."

Their gazes locked. In that instant, Josh knew he'd lost her and lost the best part of himself. "Alex, I—"

"No!"

Her eyes never leaving Josh's, she helped Davy the couple of steps back to the bed. "Don't worry." She fluffed his pillow. "I know you didn't do it."

"I didn't," Davy pledged in a quivering voice. "I didn't do anything. I swear it."

She tucked him into bed and positioned herself between him and Josh, who was pacing back and forth in the small confines of the shack. "There," she told him. "You heard him. *He didn't do it.*"

Josh looked at her along the length of his shoulder. "You want me to take the word of a rapist and murderer. Dammit, woman!"

"Don't curse at me and—"

"I wasn't cursing at you!"

"I'm telling you...we are both telling you—" she touched Davy's arm "—that you've made a mistake. You wasted your time—and mine."

With every word, she inched closer to Davy, concealing him behind the flare of her black skirt. "Leave. Now."

One look and Josh knew she wouldn't believe him. He could talk from now until a week from Sunday and she wouldn't believe him. It hurt. Standing here so close to her and knowing that he couldn't have her, would never have her. Just like that she was gone from him.

This was Gibson's fault. If he'd stand up like a man and tell the truth, then maybe...

Like a wolf closing in for the kill, Josh circled around to get a better look at the cowering bastard. "You tell her the truth or so help me I will kill you, gun or no gun, you lying son of a bitch!"

Davy rubbed his throat, Josh's finger marks clearly visible. "You're wrong. You're mistaken. I never hurt anyone."

Rage and grief warred in him. "Tell her!" Josh shouted, and made a lunge at the liar, who scooted across the bed in escape.

"Stop it!" Alex hollered. "This isn't getting us anywhere. If you're so certain Davy was involved, then we'll go into Bozeman and talk to the sheriff or the judge." She looked over at Davy, who was staring at her, his shirt torn in the front from the struggle, his breathing hard.

She continued. "Let's have a court decide if he's done anything wrong."

Josh laughed, a harsh sound with no warmth. "There's no way in hell a white jury would—" He broke off and paced away to the open doorway. "You want a jury trial?"

"Yes."

"No!" Davy countered.

Josh wasn't listening to him, only to her. "A *fair* trial?"

"Of course." Alex was squared off a foot in front of him.

"Then I agree. You'll have a jury trial."

A shiver of dread coiled up her spine.

What the devil were they doing in an Indian camp? Until the minute they'd sighted the tepees nestled along the stream, she'd thought they were going to Bozeman. She didn't like this—not at all.

Dread churned in her stomach like acid as they drove between the dozen or so tepees. Their white hide coverings were nearly translucent in the sunlight.

The day was bright and clear, only a few puffy white clouds marred the blue of the sky. Three cottonwood trees formed a small grove by the stream.

The wagon creaked and rattled along and the noise evidently drew the residents' attention, because the next thing she knew, Indians were coming out to see who would dare to enter their camp. Bare-chested men, in buckskin leggings and breechcloths, carried rifles in an easy way that said they knew how to use them. Women and children, also in buckskin, stayed back. They all regarded her, Davy, the wagon, with grim-faced stares.

That dread was turning into all-out fright.

Josh, the man who was responsible for this—and she wasn't exactly certain what "this" was—rode up ahead. Since they'd left the shack, he had tried to talk to her once, but she'd put a stop to that. She wasn't interested, not in him, not in anything he had to say.

The instant the Indians saw Josh, all those fierce scowls turned to smiles and she took a certain amount of relief from that. At least now she didn't think they were about to be scalped—or were they?

Josh dismounted, people gathered around him. She watched as he greeted the men, smiled at several women, who returned his smile, she noted with a tinge of jealousy. No, she was not jealous. You'd have to care about someone to be jealous, and she didn't care about Josh Colter.

Annoyed with herself, she leaned closer to Davy, who was sitting next to her on the wagon seat. "Do you know what's going on?"

"How the hell should I know?"

He was pale as a corpse, perspiration beaded on his forehead and upper lip and it wasn't from the heat. Well, it was not every day you rode into an Indian camp, she supposed.

People surrounded the wagon, suntanned faces all peering up at her. She forced a smile. It wasn't returned. The former dread in her stomach returned. A few yards away, Josh was still talking to the men. She tried to listen, but he was too far and she only caught a couple of words.

The sun was heating her face and neck. Any other time she would have rolled up her sleeves and taken refuge in the back of the wagon. She didn't move. She thought this must be the way the mongoose felt when it was eye to eye with the snake.

Voices raised in argument, but she couldn't hear the words. Davy was being awfully quiet. She wished she had her gun, the one Josh had given her, the one locked away in the back. Their days in Yellowstone had ceased all thought of harm. How could she have known the danger was from Josh?

Oh, Josh, why? How could you use me so?

Josh was still talking. His dark clothes made him stand out in the crowd so she could watch him easily. Suddenly there was a great cry from the men surrounding him.

Without thinking, she sprang to her feet. "Josh! Are you all right?" Instantly she felt foolish. She could see all eyes on them. Word rippled through the crowd like rings in a pond, the volume growing louder as it spread.

In the blink of an eye, men converged on the wagon and dragged a kicking and screaming Davy down from the seat. Angry faces surrounded him, hands pushed and shoved and grabbed him.

"Stop it! Don't!"

The men glowered at him, the anger dark and raw as a living force. Fear and regret warred in him. "Look, you don't understand," he tried to say, but a fist in the stomach silenced him. Muscles aching, he gasped for breath. "Let me—"

Blows came at him from everywhere at once. Fists hit his back, his ribs, his face. Pain shot out in all directions at one time. He tried to fight back. Hands curled into fists, he swung out wildly, trying to hit while protecting himself.

Another fist to the face and he staggered back. Blood trickled from his nose. The pain was blinding, and he dropped to the ground. A moccasin-covered foot slammed into his chest. Air rushed from his lungs.

Helpless, all he could do was curl in a ball and pray this wasn't the end. "Please!"

Alex leapt from the wagon. Unconcerned for her own safety, she shouldered through the men. "Get back," she ordered. "Don't." She pushed and yelled. Anger overcame good judgment as she took on these battle-hardened warriors.

"Leave him alone!" She pushed one man in the chest. He pushed her back and she sprawled on her back in the dirt next to Davy. She fought her way up. Breathing hard, fists curled, she faced them down. "Davy, get up!" she ordered.

His heart pounding, scared for Alex, Josh shoved his way through the crowd. "*Oochia!* Stop! *Oochia!*" He pushed at the men. He didn't give a damn about her brother, but Alex was in trouble, and there was no way she was getting hurt.

It took a couple of tries before the men would listen.

Facing the men, he spoke in Absarokee, "You agreed to wait for Blue Crow."

There were mumbled threats, promises of retribution and for a second, Josh thought maybe they wouldn't listen. Reluctantly the men agreed and backed off—a little ways. But were still angry, and Josh was still worried. He had to break this up before it was too late.

In a protective gesture, Josh shoved Alex behind him, one hand holding her wrist. "Stay put," he commanded.

"I will not!"

"You will if you want your brother to stay alive." His grip tightened on her wrist, letting her know he meant business. She must have understood, because she didn't move, didn't make another sound.

He continued speaking, and the crowd grumbled and made threatening gestures. *"Dee ashe,"* he told them. "Go home and wait."

A few did, the others split off into small groups, which congregated nearby.

"Are you all right?" Josh asked Alex.

Alex was busy helping Davy up. "Yes, no thanks to you."

He ignored the barb. "You still don't believe me, do you?"

She faced him square on. "No."

He dragged in a calming breath. What he wanted to do was pull her off somewhere and make her listen, make her see. "Looks like I'm not the only one who thinks old Davy here is a murderer."

"They believe what you told them," she fired back. She shoved the hair out of her face. "Why the devil have you brought us here?"

Josh's gaze flicked to Gibson. His face dirty from the fall, he clung to Alex like a lifeline.

"*This* is where we're having that trial."

Stunned, she muttered, "What?"

"You can't do that!" Davy spoke up. He rubbed his bruised cheek with his hand. "I demand to be taken to Bozeman."

"I'll just bet you do." Josh inched in closer. He hated Gibson, and it had been all he could do not to let the crowd simply tear him limb from limb. Hell, he'd thought about it himself more than once. If Alex hadn't gotten in the middle he might have simply stood by.

"You said you wanted a fair trial, and you're going to have one, here, tomorrow."

She glanced around at the encampment, the tepees randomly scattered over several acres, the horse herd grazing in the meadow beyond. Ironically, it looked so peaceful.

"Why?" she demanded. "Why would *this* be a fair trial?"

"Because," Josh told her, "my sister was the one raped and murdered."

"I remember."

"My sister, Miss Gibson," he repeated with unmistakable pride in his voice, "was an Indian."

"What?" She actually took a step back. "No, that can't be."

"Why not, Miss Gibson?" He took his hat off, raked one hand through his shoulder-length black hair, letting her look more closely at his obvious heritage. He saw her gaze dart to the men standing nearby, then back to him.

"You said your father was a rancher and your mother was—"

He knew the instant understanding flashed in her mind.

"Then that would make you a half—"

She shook her head in denial even as she spoke.

"Half-breed," he supplied. "You can say the word, *Miss Gibson*."

"Stop saying that."

He straightened. "What? Half-breed?"

"No. I don't give a damn about who your parents were. Stop saying 'Miss Gibson.' You make it sound like a curse."

His voice softened—so did his eyes. "In a way, it is."

She knew what he meant, felt the regret keenly. If she were someone else... if he were someone else...

He continued. "My mother was Absarokee—you'd say Crow. Mountain Crow to be precise. These—" he gestured to those gathered "—are my family, my people. Your brother will be judged by those he hurt."

"No. This isn't right," Davy said. "They can't. I demand a *real* court." He swallowed hard, his Adam's apple bobbing up and down in his throat.

"You're the one who asked for a trial. What's the matter, Gibson, don't like the odds? You like riding in on unarmed women and children better?" The hell with waiting!

She blocked his path. "You call this justice?" she hissed, her voice dripping with disgust. She'd trusted him before and he'd lied and deceived her on every front. He'd lied, to find her brother, tricked her into leading him straight to Davy.

She knew her brother, obviously better than Josh Colter did. Davy would *never* harm anyone, especially a woman. "This is no trial. This is a farce."

"Woman, don't press me. They—" he jerked his head back toward the frowning crowd "—want to kill him—now."

"But—" Davy started, his voice weak and faltering.

"Never mind denying it." Josh was repulsed by his cowardly hiding behind Alex. He cursed himself a hundred times for not finishing the man when he'd had the chance.

"And so, what?" she demanded. "You've saved me ... again, Mr. Colter! From now on I'll do my own saving, thank you. I can take care of myself and my brother. In the meantime, we are leaving."

"I'd like to see you try," he challenged.

Anger and hurt merged inside her. She had to get away, not only to protect Davy but herself. She had to get away from Josh. She couldn't bear to look into his eyes, those same eyes that had entranced her so and now were so cold.

She grabbed Davy by the arm and marched toward the wagon as though she had the Seventh cavalry behind her. Josh grabbed her wrist and spun her around to face him.

"Don't." His expression was so hard she stopped dead in her tracks. "You won't make it, and I don't think I could save you."

She cast around at the crowd that not only outnumbered and outgunned them but who could outrun them. A team and wagon were no match for war ponies. She was trapped. Josh had trapped her once again. The hurt and anger folded and magnified.

Josh spoke up. "A council will be held when Blue Crow arrives."

"Who's this Blue Crow?" Alex demanded.

"He's my brother-in-law." His deathly cold stare fixed on Gibson. "The husband of the woman you killed. They're sending a rider, and he'll be here tomorrow. In the meantime, we're locking ole Davy up." He motioned with his hand, and two tall, fierce-looking Indians grabbed Davy. One pushed him, and he went sprawling in the dirt.

"*Oochia!*" Josh pronounced, and the men stopped.

Davy scrambled to his feet again and the Indians pointed in the direction of one of the tepees.

"They want you to go in there," Josh told him.

"Why? What's in there?"

"Don't worry," Josh assured him smugly. "Nothing's going to happen until the council meets." The implication was as clear as a funeral dirge.

The warriors grabbed Davy and forced him to go along. "Alex?" He dug his heels in and struggled to break free, but it was a wasted effort.

Alex tried to follow but Josh blocked her path.

The crowd dispersed, and Alex was left alone with Josh.

"Alex, please. I'm sorry, but it's true."

"I trusted you." The hurt in her eyes was so bright it pained him to look. "You used me and now...now you want me to believe you...again?"

He raked one hand through his hair in an agitated gesture. "I *wanted* to tell you." His eyes were gentle, soft, the way she remembered them in the mornings—those lush mornings lost in each other.

Stop it.

She sucked in a steadying breath and rallied the anger. "When? Just when was it you tried to tell me? I don't seem to remember." She clung to the anger. It was the only thing that kept her going. If she gave in to the hurt, the loss, she thought perhaps she would be crushed by the weight of it.

He said the only thing he could. "I'm sorry."

Their eyes met and, for the span of two heartbeats, longing flashed bright and hot, until Alex looked away. "It's not enough, Josh. It's not enough." She went to find her brother.

Alex spent the rest of the day with Davy in the tepee that was being used as a jail. True to their word, the Indians did not bother them, except to bring water, which they placed in a gourd near the back of the tepee.

"I didn't do it, sis," Davy said, for what surely must be the thousandth time. She was tired and mean and brokenhearted. Her nerves were raw and aching like an open wound, and she thought that if he denied his guilt one more time, she'd scream.

She handed him the water cup. "I believe you, Davy. It's just that..."

"What?" He looked at her over the rim of the metal cup.

"They seem certain. How can they all be wrong?" She turned her back and paced a couple of steps away, her footsteps cushioned on the buffalo-skin rug.

"They are." He tossed down the cup. It landed silently on the soft skin-covered floor. "People make mistakes." He knew that all right. He'd made his share over the years. He had wealth and, the ladies said, good looks. But he also had a father who was more successful than Davy could ever hope to be—he was always being compared to his father and coming up short.

Alex was watching him. "Josh said there were two other men who'd given him your name."

He shrugged. "I know a lot of people. Anyone could use my name. How would I know?"

Her mouth pulled down in a frown. "But Josh said—"

Davy's temper flared. "Josh said, Josh said." He mimicked her. "Who is Josh to you anyway? What is he doing with you?"

"He's..." *my lover,* she thought to say, but, of course, didn't, couldn't. "He's my guide. I came to the

West with Eddie, but there was trouble. Eddie got shot—''

"Shot!" Davy was stunned. "What do you mean shot? Why didn't you tell me before?"

"You haven't been in any shape for me to tell you."

"Tell me now."

"Some outlaws attacked our camp. Eddie got shot. He's all right, though." She punctuated her statement with a little smile.

"So where's Colter fit in?"

"Josh, Mr. Colter, saved us, helped me get Eddie to the doctor in Gunlock."

Davy sank down in obvious disbelief. "Eddie shot," he repeated, taking in the news. They'd been attacked by outlaws and this Colter had saved them—had saved Alex. Thank God, Colter had been there. If anything had happened to Alex... His head came up sharply. "Were you hurt?"

"No." She managed another little smile. "A few cuts and bruises but nothing permanent." Nothing like the heartbreak of being lied to and used by the man you're in love with.

"I guess I owe him, huh? Ironic, don't you think?" He made a sound in the back of his throat that could have been a laugh. He crossed his legs, Indian style. Absently he brushed at the dirt stains on the denim. After a minute, he said, "Well, looks like I'm in big trouble this time, huh?"

She shook her head and sighed. "Davy, what happened? Why did you leave the bank?"

He grimaced. Good question. He wished to hell he hadn't. "I got tired. You know how it is." He pulled at the nonexistent crease in his trousers.

"But you were drinking. Davy, you promised."

The tone of her voice set his already-frayed nerves on edge.

"I had a few drinks. So?"

"Abe said you were drunk and that you kept getting whiskey even after he asked you to stop. If Josh hadn't found you, out there where you passed out—"

"Abe said. Josh said." His temper flared. "What about what I say? I didn't rape anyone. I didn't murder anyone." That panic was a constant companion. Now that there was no whiskey, the specter was fearsome.

Alex gave him one of those questioning looks, the ones he'd hated since he was a kid, the ones that usually meant she wasn't so sure. He never should have gone with Larson and Cordell.

Chapter Twenty-Three

Davy was in it now, and there was no getting out. "Whoever said I was there is a liar." He couldn't quite look Alex in the eye when he said it.

"Why would someone say it was you when it wasn't?"

Didn't she ever give up? She was supposed to be on his side. "They did. All right?"

She reached out toward him as though to mollify him. "Calm down. We need to keep our wits about us if we're going to get out of this."

He sighed again. "Yeah, but how?" This Colter had tracked him down and now they were stuck here, surrounded by Indians. Oh, God, Indians. Visions of anthills and being skinned alive made him shudder with fear. He had to find a way out of this.

Please, God, if you get me out of this, I will never, ever, drink again. I'll do anything you want, only don't let me die here. It was amazing how many promises a man could make in the face of death.

"We'll figure something out." She gave him a reassuring pat on the hand.

For the next several hours, they talked and couldn't come up with any solution. They thought about escape, but they reluctantly ruled that out. Chances of slipping free, getting horses and leaving unnoticed were about a trillion to one. Besides, the Indians would probably welcome Davy's attempt as an excuse to end things sooner.

Finally Alex decided that the best thing to do was wait. Perhaps the Indians would listen to reason. Perhaps they would see that there were no witnesses to identify Davy.

What a dream that was, Davy thought when Alex told him her strategy. But he couldn't come up with anything better. He had to stick to his story. He had to! It was his word against theirs, and as long as he didn't change, then there was nothing they could do.

It was starting to get dark when Josh ducked through the tepee flap. He was followed by a woman carrying a small bowl of delicious-smelling food. Alex's heart surged at the sight of him. Tall and dark, he looked outlaw wild, dressed as he was in his ranch clothes. She had to remind herself that he was the enemy.

The woman spoke in Crow, handed the bowl to Davy and left. He eyed the food suspiciously, giving it a cautious sniff.

"They aren't going to poison you, if that's what you're thinking," Josh said, as though reading his mind. "It's elk cooked with sage and wild onions."

Personally Josh didn't give a damn whether the man ate or not. But he was going to live up to his part of the bargain he'd made with the others. Gibson would be cared for until the council met tomorrow. In the meantime, he'd decided to talk to Alex, or try to anyway.

"Come on." He took her firmly by the elbow.

She twisted free. "Where to?"

"Dinner."

Her chin came up. "I can stay here, thank you very much."

"No. You can't."

"Yes. I can."

Josh was angry and frustrated and not a man to give up easily, not when he wanted something, and right now he wanted her to listen to him. "Dammit, woman, you're coming with me."

"Hey!" Davy stepped forward. "Leave her alone." He grabbed for Josh, and lucky for him, Alex intervened. Josh wouldn't mind taking a swing at this guy, maybe he would anyway.

Alex tried to defuse the situation. "It's all right, Davy. I'll go with Mr. Colter."

Davy arched one brow in question. "You sure? Because if you don't want to go..."

"I'm sure," she confirmed.

Once outside, however, it was a different Alex who whirled to face him. "You keep your hands off me, you lying bastard. I wouldn't go to a dogfight with you."

Alex tried to charge past him. She didn't know where she was going, as long as it was away from him.

Josh wasn't letting her get away that easily. "We're *going* to talk." Before she knew what was happening, he tossed her over his shoulder and strode for the river. She screamed, and cursed and threatened him. She kicked her feet, and if they'd been a little lower she'd have gotten more than his damned belt buckle.

"Dammit." Suddenly she was sliding down the front of him in a way that would have been provocative any other time. Now it was infuriating. "We're *going* to talk and that's that."

They were by the stream, shaded under the cottonwoods. Magpies chirped in the tree branches.

"I don't want to talk to you." She paced three steps away, keeping her back to him, wishing she could shut him out of her heart as easily.

"Fine. Don't talk. Just listen." He snatched off his hat and slapped it nervously against his wool-clad thigh.

"I don't *believe* anything you have to say. I was a fool to believe you before and—"

"I love you."

That stopped her. "What?" Of all the things she expected, she'd never expected that. A breeze tugged at her hem and she pushed it down.

"I love you." His voice was husky, the way she remembered, the way that sent delicious shivers up the backs of her legs.

He looked so handsome, his face cast in shadow. Vivid memories assailed her mind and her body. Memories of his face so close to hers, his smile so wicked, like an invitation to sin, an invitation she hadn't refused.

Her heart took on a hard, steady beating. Her body actually tensed, seemed to lean toward him, drawn to him and the powerful enchantment that was him.

Stop it! Stop it! Are you insane?

Yes, perhaps she was, because she wanted him.

In a voice gentle as the rush of wind through the trees, he said, "I think I've loved you from the first minute I saw you. Of course, that was before I knew . . ."

The memories evaporated like mist in the harsh light of day. "That I was the *murderer*'s sister?"

His shoulders slumped. "Yes." He tossed his hat aside in a gesture of frustration.

Anger and hurt welled up in her. "Was that when you decided to use me?"

"I *never* decided to use you."

"Ha! That's a laugh. No, I guess you were the one laughing, weren't you? What a fool I made of myself." She practically spat out the words.

He could see tears pooling in the corners of her eyes. He'd done that. He'd done a lot, and she'd suffered for all of it. He went toward her, but she backed away.

"Don't."

He stopped. "I never lied about loving you. I never lied when I *made* love to you."

"Stop it!" She covered her ears with her hands. Why was he doing this? Was it some perverse form of torture? Didn't he know how much it hurt loving him? "Stop the lies. You don't have to do it anymore. You got what you wanted, my brother and . . . me."

Josh felt his world tip on its axis. He'd thought . . . hell, he didn't know what he'd thought. All he knew was that he wanted her, loved her. It ought to be enough. It wasn't. A lump clogged his throat and he had to swallow to get his voice to work. "I never wanted this to happen. Never wanted it to be like this, but I didn't have a choice."

"Of course, you had a choice!" she yelled. He could have asked her. Could have believed it was a mistake. He could have trusted her the way she'd trusted him!

His hands curled into tight fists against the loss that was consuming him. "Don't you understand, Mourning Dove was my sister. *My sister.* If you could have seen her that day—" He broke off, the grief still fresh in his mind. "Your brother was there. I *know* it. There are witnesses to verify it. You seem to think he's some child caught playing doctor behind the barn. He's not a child, and you need to stop treating him like one. You and I—"

"There is no you and I."

"I had to choose between love and honor. Choosing one, I . . . lost the other."

They faced each other, five feet apart, it might as well have been five thousand feet, their differences were so insurmountable.

A woman's gentle voice interrupted, and Josh turned. His expression softened, but he couldn't quite manage a smile. *Kahee."*

"*Kahee,"* she answered. They chatted for a bit, then he turned to Alex. "This is Finds The Meadow. She's my cousin and has extended her hospitality to us for dinner."

Alex was in no mood to be cordial. "I prefer to spend the evening with my brother."

"It isn't polite."

She raked her hair back with one hand. "I'm sure, under the circumstances, she'll understand."

His mouth drew down. "It's dinner, Alex. They're offering a little friendship. Don't you think that you could manage some common courtesy?" In truth, it was Josh who'd asked Finds The Meadow to invite Alex, and his cousin had willingly agreed. Josh thought perhaps, once she met his family, she'd come to realize that these were good people who deserved justice.

Alex stiffened at the rebuke.

"Don't worry, your brother is being looked after," he added, as though reading her mind.

The woman, Finds The Meadow, gave her a warm but uncertain smile. She was tall, Alex noted, dressed in buckskin that was the palest shade of brown, like coffee with a lot of milk. Her dress was fringed and decorated with beads and shells, though what kind Alex wasn't sure. Her hair was long and black, and hung loose down her back.

These people were the enemy, the ones who were holding Davy, and now they expected her to have dinner as though this were some social event.

Awkwardly the woman extended her hand. Her eyes met Alex's and she could see the uncertainty there.

"You are...welcome," she said haltingly, her hand still out to Alex.

Alex relented, though why she wasn't exactly sure. Maybe because she was curious. Maybe because she thought that if the situation was reversed she wouldn't be nearly so hospitable. Besides, she thought, she might be able to learn something about this accusation, perhaps help Davy in some way.

"All right." She shook hands. "Dinner. Thank you."

They returned to the camp. This time Alex was under her own steam. She was also careful to keep away from Josh. Inside, her heart and her mind were playing a terrible game of tug-of-war. Alex was determined that logic win this time.

A camp dog darted in front of them, another hot on his heels. Two little boys followed in close pursuit.

"Dee," Finds The Meadow admonished.

Little boys chasing a dog; it seemed so normal, so ordinary. How many times had she and Davy chased their neighbor's dog until the poor thing took to hiding whenever he saw them coming?

A smile threatened at the fond memory, until her gaze found the tepee where Davy, that same laughing Davy, was being held prisoner. Guards were still in place outside.

She followed along silently as they closed in on a tepee at the farthest edge of camp.

A man was standing outside, evidently waiting for them.

"Kahee," he called, and Josh and Finds The Meadow answered in kind. Alex didn't speak, didn't try to mimic the language.

The man extended his hand in greeting and surprised her when he said, "'ello."

"Hello," she said, quickly accepting his offer of a handshake.

In a blink, she took him in. He was old, in his eighties, she guessed. A little thick around the middle, a little bent at the shoulders, he was still nearly as tall as Josh. He wore buckskins, shirt and leggings, with the most exquisite beadwork she'd ever seen. What looked like a starburst design of blue and green and red must have taken weeks of tedious labor to accomplish.

"I Two Deers."

"Mr. Two Deers," she returned, feeling more intrigued than threatened, possibly because she had Josh there.

"You eat," Two Deers said, holding back the flap for her to enter.

Cautiously she ducked inside. The lodge was very similar to the one Davy was being kept in—large, clean, the floor covered with buffalo skins and a fire pit in the center. A small fire was going there. Food items she didn't recognize were displayed on plates ingeniously made of bone.

Josh introduced Alex to Little Fish, who appeared to be about seven and spoke no English, except "'ello," which the girl said with beaming pride.

"Hello," Alex returned, grinning. How could she resist an adorable face with enormous black eyes, eyes so much like Josh's. Would Josh have been as engaging a child? Yes.

They settled on the floor near the fire. Josh seated himself beside her. There was no way she could move without making a scene. It was devastating having him so close.

Finds The Meadow moved around, cooking.

"She's making antelope," he said, as though guessing what she was wondering. "Those are wild turnips and those are wild onions. Dessert is, well, I'll wait on that, but I have a good guess."

Alex didn't reply. She was trying to remain aloof. She looked around and spotted the drawings immediately. "What are those?" she asked, and gestured toward the primitive drawings that decorated the inside of the tepee.

"Those are the story of Two Deers' life."

She arched one brow. "Really. May I?"

"Sure."

She went for a closer inspection. Josh and Two Deers followed.

"What's this?" She pointed to some horses that appeared to be running.

Two Deers spoke up. "Many coups." He beamed. His weathered face transformed instantly, making him seem less the warrior and more the grandfather.

"Coups?" She didn't understand.

Josh explained. "It's the way we count bravery. A warrior rides up to his armed enemy and touches him with a coup stick. If he does it without getting hurt or killed, he's considered very brave and can show it by making a drawing."

Sounded foolhardy to her and, yes, brave. She couldn't help wonder if Josh had a tepee, a place with drawings.

Feeling annoyed by her line of thought, she forced herself to concentrate on the painting before her, tracing the outline with her fingers.

Two Deers spoke. "You like?"

"Yes, I like very much."

For the next fifteen minutes, Alex studied his primitive drawings, asked questions about paints and brushes and made comments. Slowly, a bond was formed between the two, artist to artist.

"I think you are a fine artist."

After that they returned to the circle. The three were friendly and Alex relaxed, feeling strangely at home in these very unlikely surroundings.

When at last dinner was over, Alex said, "Thank you, Finds The Meadow." She was sincere in her thanks and her enjoyment. These were nice people, nicer than they could have been, should have been. "Thank you for your hospitality. I have to get back to my brother."

"Wait." Josh stood. "I'll walk with you."

"It's not necessary."

"I think it is."

Outside, the night was cool. Stars glittered in the ink black sky. "Did you enjoy dinner?"

"I did."

They strolled along. "Did you like my family?"

"They're nice people."

"I'm glad you think so." They continued walking, the silence between awkward. They'd shared so many nights like this wrapped in each other's arms and now, now they were enemies. Yet, feelings, emotions, love as powerful as theirs was not easily discarded.

They stopped outside the lodge where Davy was being kept. Josh's gaze flicked to the two guards standing close by and they discreetly moved away.

"Alex," he said softly, touching her cheek as he did. "Can't we—"

"No," she said on a thready whisper. She covered his hand with hers, giving in to the gentleness of his touch, giving in to the longing that seeing him, being close to him, ignited in her. She knew, in that moment, that for the rest of her life, all men would be judged against this man and, she knew, all other men would never compare. "There is no way out. You've made your choice and I've made mine."

His hungry gaze scanned her face and he brushed a nonexistent lock of hair back from her face, letting his fingers linger on her hair—like sun-bleached gold.

"I understand," he said honestly, because he did understand the choice of family over love. It was his choice. "But I'm not mistaken, Alex. Two men gave me your brother's name. They could have said there was no one else, though I knew there were three. Your brother was there. I'm sorry, but it's the truth." He touched her cheek once more, for the last time. "No matter what happens tomorrow, I will always love you."

His words were nearly her undoing, for she knew that she would always love him. But the choice he was asking her to make was too difficult, too painful. To give in to him would be to turn her back on her brother.

They lingered there in the moonlight, reluctant to let go yet each knowing they must. There was no way out, no alternative. Each was pledged to family, to honor.

It was like tearing flesh for Alex to step out of his touch and duck inside the tepee.

Her heart fluttered in her chest like the flight of a hummingbird and she thought she could still feel the warmth of his touch on her cheek. The rest of her life was going to be long and lonely.

Davy was pacing the five long strides that the tepee allowed. "Where the devil were you?"

His demand brought her out of her sad musing. "Visiting."

"Visiting! They're going to lynch me or shoot me or tie me to an anthill, and you're off visiting." He folded his arms across his chest and scowled at her.

"Yes, visiting."

"With Colter, I suppose."

"Among others."

"Others? What others? There are no others except *them*. His eyes widened in understanding. "Alex, you've been with *them?*"

"Don't say it like they're from another universe. Josh took me to meet some of his family. They were nice."

"Nice? Nice!" He started pacing again.

"Yes. Nice." She thought about Two Deers and Finds The Meadow. She thought about how they'd seemed kind and giving and very much like her own family. She thought about what Josh had said, about the other men naming Davy when they didn't have to. She thought about how sincere he'd been. After a while she said very quietly, "You were there, weren't you?"

He spun around so fast his foot tangled in the buffalo skin and he nearly went down. "I told you I wasn't, and I wasn't."

"You were there. I don't know how, but I know it. I don't believe you raped anyone, and I'm praying to God you didn't shoot anyone."

"I didn't! I only fired in the air and—" Davy stopped dead still. He never meant to say that. All of the blood drained from his face. "Sis, I didn't mean any harm. They said they were just gonna have some fun is all and, to my regret, I followed them."

"It's fun to terrorize unarmed women and children?" She didn't try to keep the disgust out of her voice.

"No. No, of course not," he pleaded. "I told you I didn't do anything."

"For heaven's sakes *stop* saying that! You were there! Say it. Dammit, for once stand up to what you've done!" She realized it was true. Josh was right about Davy being there and he was right about the way she treated her brother. He wasn't a baby. He was a man and it was time he stood up to what he'd done. "Say it, Davy. Say you were there."

"I . . ." He swallowed hard. "I was there. Oh, God, sis, I never—"

She waved away his plea. "How, Davy? How did it happen?"

Davy sagged down in front of her. She looked so sad, so disappointed, it tore at him. "You know—" he made a sound in his throat that was a pathetic chuckle "—in a way, I'm relieved to have it out in the open." And it was true. The truth had haunted him day and night for months. Once he started, he wanted her to know it all. "I met these two cowboys in Gunlock. We had some drinks, played some cards. They said they were going north to look for work. The bank job was so boring." He sighed. "There was nothing to do, just sit at that damn desk all day. Yes, sir. No, sir. I couldn't stand it.

So when Larson and Cordell said I could come along
with them, well, I did.''

"Then what?" She almost didn't want to know.

His lips curved up in a faint attempt at a smile. "I
remembered about Abe and said that he might give us
work. They thought it was a good idea, so we came this
way.''

"The Indians, Davy. Get to the part about the Indians.''

"I'm trying.'' He shoved his hair back with his cold
fingers. "One day we saw this camp. It was small and
Cordell said we'd ride in and have some fun. I didn't
know what they were gonna do. I didn't!'' he im-
plored. "Truly, sis, I didn't know what they were up
to.'' His shoulders sagged.

"Once we rode in, Larson and Cordell started
shooting. The women ran screaming. I saw a little girl
get trampled and—'' He surged to his feet and started
pacing again, as though he could outrun the ghastly visions. He knew he couldn't. He knew that he'd see the
horror until the day he died.

"I got scared. People were shouting, the horse
bucked and reared.'' He stopped in front of her. "I was
so scared, sis. I've never been so scared.'' Bile prickled
the back of his throat. "I rode out as fast as I could.''
The horror was too much to stand, and he started fidgeting again. "God, I wish I had a drink.''

Alex shook her head sadly. "Davy. How could you?''

Oh, God, how could you is right. She wasn't asking
anything he hadn't asked himself a hundred times.

"You saw what was happening, but you didn't try to
help?''

The shock, the shame, the disbelief in her voice and eyes hurt him more than any blow.

He wheeled around. "I didn't try to help. I was scared and I ran! There. I've said it!"

"Oh, Davy, what have you done?"

Chapter Twenty-Four

There was no knock on the door, only the sudden opening of the flap, the eye-squinting flash of sunlight as Josh and several Indians entered the tepee.

Alex's gaze went to Josh. He was dressed in his usual dark colors—black trousers and blue shirt. His hair was finger-combed back, deep furrows in the inky blackness.

"The council is convening." Josh spoke to Davy, but he looked at Alex. His bottomless black eyes held her, seemed to look through her, seemed to touch her soul.

More softly, to her, he added, "I'm sorry." There was the slightest shaking of his head.

"I'm sorry, too," she answered, and she was sorry for so many things, most of all sorry that she would not be with him by the lake.

But their fate was sealed when he deceived her, used her, when he accused her brother of rape and murder. How could she get past that? She couldn't.

"Alex?" Davy's voice roused her from her musings. "What am I going to do?"

"Tell them what you told me." Another flash of sunlight, and she didn't have to turn to know Josh was gone.

"What!" Davy couldn't believe his ears. She was telling him to confess. They'd never believe him. Never.

Alex sighed. She was suddenly so tired. All she wanted was for this to go away. She wanted to find a small dark place and curl up until the heartbreak healed. "Tell them what you told me," she repeated, trying to be patient. "These are not unfeeling people." She knew that, too. Josh had shown her that, had let her meet his family. *His* family. Who would have thought Josh was part Indian? Yes, she knew the remarks that were made, half-breeds and such. She didn't care. He was a man who fought to claim his place in the world, she admired him.

She loved him.

They could never be together.

She looked up at her brother, tall and lean. Whiskers shadowed his square chin, and his shirt pulled tight over broad shoulders. For the first time she saw him not as her baby brother, but as a man, with a man's responsibilities.

"Davy, there is nothing else to do. The truth is that you were there, at least part of the time. You saw things go wrong. You could have—" She stopped short. She'd been stunned when she'd learned the truth. Josh had been right about that, too, it seemed. She'd never have truly believed it if Davy hadn't told her himself. As it was, she was incredibly disappointed. How could he have done that, how could he have left people in need?

Davy watched as she turned away from him. For the first time in his life, his sister, whom he adored, was turning away, and he knew why. Worst of all, he felt the same way, ashamed of what he'd done and what he'd failed to do. Hell, he'd tried to drink himself into oblivion rather than face it. It had almost worked, too, he thought wryly.

Resolutely he said, "I guess there's nothing else to do, is there?"

"I don't think so."

He sucked in a steadying breath. "Alex, I'm scared." Almost as scared as he'd been that day.

She grimaced. "I know. Me, too."

He reached out his hand and she took it. He was grateful for that, for her touch, for her sisterly love. People always talked about it being a curse to have an older sister. They were wrong. It was a joy.

"Friends?"

She hugged him, tears pooling in her eyes. "Forever."

They hugged tightly. She leaned away from him and said, "They have to believe you. If they have witnesses, then they'll know that you were not the one who shot people or the one who murdered Josh's sister. They'll know it was the other men."

"What makes you think it will matter to them?" Davy wanted to believe her. Desperately he wanted to believe her. He didn't want to die and he had the dreadful premonition that was about to be his fate.

"They're going to all the trouble of this council, that makes me think that they're trying to do the just thing."

He shook his head. "I hope you're right, sis. I hope you're right."

A male voice called through the lodge, and the Indians escorted Davy and Alex out. The day was cloudy, a hint of rain in the air since last night. Hand in hand, they walked solemnly to the designated tepee.

Inside, the lodge was like all the others in design. A small fire crackled in the center pit and a group of seven men sat cross-legged around the circle. Josh, she noticed, was there. He didn't join the circle but stood behind them. He faced the door and so faced Alex and Davy, much as he had all along, she thought, ruefully.

The faces of the men in the circle were solemn. Alex recognized Two Deers. Their eyes met, and she gave him an uncertain smile. She saw the flash of recognition in his eyes, but he didn't return the smile.

Among the others, she recognized two men she'd seen around the encampment, but not the rest.

One of the men spoke up. He spoke in the Crow language and others nodded. He spoke to Davy in English.

"I am Blue Crow. Our brother, *Pee-lat-che*, brings you as the last who murdered our people."

Davy glanced around at those gathered. They were dressed in buckskin trimmed in shells and foxtails. Their faces were painted garish colors—black, yellow, red. Feathers and beads decorated their long straight hair.

Every dime novel he'd read since the age of ten seemed to materialize in his brain. Images of war parties, scalpings, men being burned at the stake, all flashed with frightening clarity in his mind.

His courage faltered.

"No!" he shouted, loud even to his own ears. More quietly he said, "It's not true. You have *no right* to hold me. This is *not* a legal court and if you try to do anything my sister will see that you're all hanged!"

If the men in the circle were concerned by Davy's threats, they made no show of it. They seemed to listen with the stoic patience of a parent with an ill-tempered child. Blue Crow said, "There are those who would tell us of what happened."

Helplessly he watched as a woman entered the lodge.
She spared Davy a glance then went to the circle. They
asked questions and Josh translated. The woman told
of the horror of that day and even Davy was sickened
by it, disgraced by his cowardly behavior.

The final question was asked.

"Is this man one who was there?"

In a voice barely above a whisper, she said, "Yes."
Three more witnesses came forth, the last a boy of
about twelve. All told the same story. All identified
Davy as being one of the men.

This time Davy didn't object, didn't speak. He could
no longer deny what was true. His head dropped down
to his chest. He wished he hadn't been there. He loathed
and despised what Cordell and Larson had done, and
despised himself, the most, for turning his back. Until
that moment, he'd never known he was a coward, afraid
to stand up for right when it counted for something.

Alex put her hand over his and, in a calm steady
voice, said, "Tell them what you told me."

"What are you saying?" Davy hissed. *Knowing* it was
one thing, *confessing* was another. In his mind he knew
it was true, but old habits are hard to overcome.

As long as you don't say it out loud, then it's not real.

Gently she told him, "It's time to tell the truth."

No one in the lodge moved. The only sound was the
crackle of the fire in the small pit. Outside, the whinny
of a horse carried through the hide covering of the tepee.

"Tell them," Alex coaxed, her hand squeezing her
brother's. She loved him dearly, but she knew that with
eyewitnesses putting him there, with no possible escape, her only hope, *their* only hope, was that he could

convince these men that he was not a participant in the carnage. Something she believed absolutely.

She gave him an encouraging smile. "Tell them."

With more courage than he'd ever known, he did as she asked. Haltingly at first, his voice cracking from time to time, Davy stood there and told the truth. When he finished, no one spoke. It was done. It wouldn't change what had happened. God help him, nothing could change that, could bring those people back to life. But, at last, he'd done the right thing.

Blue Crow conferred with the others for several minutes. Josh appeared to be part of the discussion.

Alex watched Josh's face, trying to gauge what was happening. She couldn't. Did he believe Davy? If he did, then surely he'd try to help.

The talking stopped, the leader turned to Davy. "You spoke the truth, and for that you are respected."

Alex's heart soared. They believed him. Thank goodness, now maybe...

"The truth was known *before* you spoke. The truth is that you were there. Was it by your hand that Mourning Dove died? There's no one among us to say. Who can say if you murdered or not. You yourself have said you did not help those of our people who were unarmed. For that you are guilty and the penalty is death."

Death.

The word fell on Davy like an ax. His body went very cold. He couldn't seem to move. He just stood there as though frozen in time. He was going to die. Today. Now. He was only nineteen!

"You can't," he pleaded. "Yes, I was wrong. God knows I'd change it if I could. If I could go back, have another chance, don't you think I would!"

The men stood almost in unison, indicating the time for talk was over.

He was going to die!

Alex was paralyzed with shock. She'd never expected they'd go this far. Somehow, in the back of her mind, she expected some punishment, yes, but not death. Not that.

"I won't let you do this!" she shouted to the assembly. She clung to him. Two Indians grabbed him. She slapped one across the face, the sound reverberated across the tepee like a rifle shot.

The Indian reared back to return the blow.

"Don't touch her!" Davy snarled, hitting the man in the face with his fist. The man stumbled back, slamming into the side of the tepee, making the structure flutter.

Two others rushed forward, and then another appeared from somewhere, grabbing Davy by the arms and shoulders and shoving him toward the door.

Davy dug his heels in, fighting, refusing to go quietly. "Sis! Sis!"

Alex turned to Josh. "Please! You've got to help him! He didn't do it! He isn't the one who murdered your sister!"

The men were still pushing Davy, kicking and struggling through the door.

"How do I know that? It's only his word, the word of a self-confessed coward."

"I'll never forgive you for this. Never!"

She raced out after Davy, determined to stop them. She'd get a gun, a rifle, she'd—

She skidded to a halt. Indians were riding into camp, shouting. Eerie war cries drowned out Davy's protests. Close behind the Indians was a detachment of the U.S.

cavalry. Men in blue. They couldn't have been more welcome than Saint Nicholas on Christmas morning.

The officer, a young man dressed in what looked to be a new uniform, reined to a stop in front of Davy. "Is there some trouble?"

"Trouble!" Davy shook free of those holding him and rushed toward the cavalry patrol. "Thank God, you're here. They were going to kill me."

The officer stiffened. One of the soldiers spoke up. "Ain't no Indian killing a white man whilst I'm around." He glared at those present, spitting tobacco juice to punctuate his remark.

Horses shied and kicked up dust. The unique rattle of sabers mixed with the creak of saddle leather.

The officer twisted in the saddle. "That'll be enough of that, Dobbs." He glanced around. "I'm Captain Osborne. Okay, someone tell me what's going on."

The officer appeared calm, confident with the two dozen well-armed cavalry men backing him up.

"What's the army doing here?" It was Josh's voice that carried from the door of the lodge.

The officer lifted up in the stirrups. "Who are you?"

Josh edged through the group. "Name's Colter." He didn't extend his hand and neither did the officer.

"We're here to escort these people back to the reservation."

"And if they don't want to go?" Josh asked, though clearly, it wasn't a question but a statement of fact.

"That's fine with us," the same soldier smugly replied, "Ain't it, boys." The man patted his rifle. "Wish the army was still payin' for scalps."

Several men mumbled their agreement.

"Shut up, Dobbs," the officer ordered.

Davy stilled. His earlier joy was replaced with something closer to dread. He wanted to be rescued. He wanted to be taken away from here. What he didn't want, he realized with a start, was for any more people to get hurt.

"Captain," Davy interrupted. "Can we go now?"

He reached out a hand toward Alex. She made her way to Davy's side, her hem catching the dust of the soft soil.

"Yes, Captain, we'd like to leave now," she confirmed, as though she, too, sensed something was about to happen. "It'll take minute to hitch the wagon."

"Yes, ma'am." The captain's eyes were fixed on the twenty-five or so Indians. "You're welcome to join us, but first I have to make arrangements for these folks—"

"They don't want to go back to the reservation, Captain." There was a flinty edge to Josh's voice. Behind him, Indians mumbled their agreement. The three scouts, mounted on horseback, flexed and postured, making comments about honor and revenge.

Josh had had enough of revenge to last him a lifetime. The toll had been too high. No, he didn't want any more trouble. He didn't want any more family killed, though what he was going to do was unclear.

"I know it's difficult to believe, but they don't like starving or watching their children starve. They don't like being prisoners in a country that was once theirs."

You could have heard a pin drop, it was so quiet. Even the blackbirds were quiet.

The captain leaned forward, forearm resting on his knee. "Look. I understand, but the law—"

Josh waved a dismissive hand. "They don't recognize white man's law. The white man's law never helped them, never brought a man to trial for killing an Indian."

Someone in the ranks hollered, "Damn straight!"

The captain glared at his men. "Sergeant, get your men in order or you'll find yourself wearing private stripes when this patrol is over."

The sergeant wheeled his horse around and rode along the line of troopers, cursing and threatening as he did.

The captain continued speaking to Josh. "There is a treaty, one which says the Indians are supposed to be on a reservation. They've got to go, and *I've* got to see that they do."

There was a murmur that floated across the crowd of Indians like a chill wind in July. A camp dog growled and nipped at one of the soldiers' horses, making the animal buck and kick. Warriors laughed and made comments that it didn't take a linguist to get the gist of.

"Control that horse!" the captain commanded.

"Damn mongrel cur," the soldier muttered. "Just like them damn mongrel Indians."

The laughter stopped. The warriors' expressions turned hard. Women, clutching their children, started backing away from the group.

"Stop." The captain straightened in the saddle. "You are all ordered to return to the reservation!"

Men took off running, ducking into tepees, only to reappear with rifles at the ready.

A shrill war cry split the air like a lance. Alex felt as though it had gone right through her. "Davy? What's happening?"

Wind whipped up, swirling dust devils across the line of soldiers. Horses shied and danced. Men shouted, cursed.

"Stop!" The captain hollered again, his horse side-stepping wildly. Alex jumped aside to keep from being injured.

Another war cry answered the first. Another. Then another.

A shot rang out. Where it came from, she wasn't certain. In the next instant, the soldiers had rifles in their hands and were firing. The Indians returned fire. Bullets zinged through the air, tearing holes in tepees. Children screamed. Horses reared and pawed the air.

"Cease fire!" the officer commanded, but was drowned out by the shots and shouts.

Women raced through the encampment as warriors leapt onto painted war ponies.

Soldiers broke rank and took off at a gallop. Warriors charged at breakneck speed. Dust clouded the air. Alex coughed and wheezed, her eyes blinking and watering from the dust. "Davy!"

Someone grabbed her. "Come on!" It was Josh. "I've gotta get you out of here."

"No, Josh! We have to help! We have to find Davy!" But Josh wasn't waiting. He wasn't taking any chances with her. He scooped her up and ran for the closest lodge. "Stay in here. Stay down and don't come out for anything." With that, he bolted out the doorway.

As he did, he saw a cavalry man riding down on a woman and a child. In a terrifying heartbeat, he realized it was Finds The Meadow and Little Fish.

"Xalusshe!" he shouted as he took off running full out.

Davy Gibson darted in front of him. Davy grabbed Finds The Meadow and Little Fish and shoved them to the ground, shielding them with his body. Josh hurled himself at the soldier's horse, pulling hard on the reins.

Man and horse twisted to the ground with a teeth-rattling thud.

"Cease fire!" the officer shouted again, riding through the camp. "Bugler, sound recall!"

The soldier did as ordered.

The sharp, tinny sound cut through the noise, the shouts, the war whoops.

"Cease fire! Return to ranks!"

As quickly as it had started, it was over. Soldiers retreated. Josh waved off the warriors. *"Oole! Oochia!"*

When the dust cleared, it was a miracle no one was hurt or dead.

"You damn men get in line," the officer commanded. "Every damn one of you is going to face a court-martial when we get back to the fort. The next man who moves, I'll shoot myself. *Is that understood?*" He emphasized the last words as though to drive them into their heads.

The men nodded solemnly.

The warriors circled around the soldiers, flexing their bows, cursing.

The officer eyed the Indians cautiously, and when he seemed satisfied that no further trouble would erupt, he dismounted and walked toward where Josh and Davy were standing. "Are they all right?"

"I think so." Heart pounding, Davy helped the woman and child to stand. The woman was young, not much older than he. The child was breathing hard and clinging to her mother for all she was worth.

He dropped down on one knee to look the little girl in the eyes. "It's all right now, sweetheart," he crooned, wiping her tear-streaked face. He pushed the hair back from her face. "I'm sorry if I hurt you."

The mother said something he didn't understa
Then the little girl said, "'ello."

Davy laughed. "Hello, yourself." He brushed at
clothes, wiping the dirt from her delicate bucksl
dress. To the mother, he said, "What's her name?"

"Her name's Kaate Bua," Josh supplied. "It mea
Little Fish. She's my cousin," he added tersely.

Davy stood. "Oh." He brushed himself off. Then
the child, he added, "Take care of yourself, Ka
Bua." He tried and pronounced it badly, so badly
child laughed. He was glad, glad to see her laugh.

Josh wasn't totally buying into this nice-guy stu
After all, ten minutes ago he'd been sentenced to de
and now...nope, Josh was suspicious. Trouble was,
couldn't deny what he'd seen, and what he'd seen v
this sniveling coward risking his life to save an Indi
woman and child. It was hardly the act of a rapist
murderer. He remembered that no one had seen Da
do anything. He remembered Davy's account of tl
day. Josh felt his wall of rage crumble.

He spoke to Finds The Meadow, making certain s
was unhurt and she assured him of that. She also
sured him that they had Davy Gibson to thank for th

But Josh refused. He'd be damned if he'd thank hi

So Finds The Meadow did. "Thank you."

"You're welcome," Davy answered.

She picked up her child and went to where the ot
women were huddled.

The officer shook his head in disgust. "I've no
cuses. I'm glad no one was hurt."

Josh was really getting confused. First the bast
Davy turned into some kind of hero and then the da
army officer was acting as if he were really concerne

What the hell was going on? No one was who they were supposed to be.

"That was a brave thing you did, sir," the captain told Davy.

"Surprised the hell out of me." Josh said out loud what he'd been thinking.

"Me, too," Davy replied, just as frankly. He stepped up to Josh. "I'm sorry about your sister's death, Mr. Colter. The thought that I might have been able to help will haunt me all my life. I guess that's why, when I saw what was happening here, I couldn't turn away. I'm not a coward, Mr. Colter. At least, I don't want to be."

The captain adjusted his hat. "You're no coward, mister. Take my word for it."

Josh sucked in a deep breath. It looked like the captain was right, Davy was no coward. He'd said he wasn't there when Mourning Dove was raped and murdered and, judging by what had just happened, Josh believed him. He wasn't sure he forgave him for not helping, but then he hadn't forgiven himself completely, either.

"Josh!" It was Alex's voice and he turned in time to see her running in his direction. The breeze tugged at her skirt and shirtwaist, outlining her slender shape, and she rushed headlong into his welcoming embrace. "Are you all right?" Face flushed, eyes bright, she scanned his face, touched his arms, his shoulders.

"Yes." Naturally his arms closed around her, feeling soothed at touching her again.

Then, as though she realized what she was doing, she pushed out of his embrace. She turned quickly to Davy.

"Are you hurt?" She fussed with straightening her hair and shirtwaist.

"No, I'm not hurt." Davy's gaze flicked from h[
sister to Josh Colter and back again. So that was ho[
it was, huh?

"What happened?" she asked breathlessly. Aroun[
her, the Indian warriors still circled, their hors[
prancing, bucking in excitement. The soldiers sat ster[
faced, watching the Indians the way a cat watches [
bird, waiting for the chance to attack.

The officer spoke up. "Your brother here saved th[
woman from injury *and*—" he turned a cold look o[
the one called Dobbs "—a man from the stockad[
There was not supposed to be any shooting. We are o[
dered to take them back to the reservation. This is n[
Sand Creek and I'm not Chivington."

Several of the warriors, those who'd been in t[
council, rode up closer, their expressions guarded. T[
horses snorted and puffed from the earlier run.

"Now—" the officer continued craning his neck [
to look at those on horseback "—could we talk?"

Josh translated. The Indians looked skeptical, b[
after some more rationalizing from Josh, it was d[
cided that they were willing to talk...just talk, n[
surrender.

Alex and Davy stood in the center of the cam[
mounted warriors on one side, mounted cavalry on t[
other, Josh in the middle. The tepees like a circle of g[
ant sentinels.

The officer spoke first to Davy. "Sir, before we sta[
you said earlier that you were in some trouble. Is th[
correct?"

Davy's gaze darted to Alex then to the Indians. [
was—"

"There is no trouble. We were mistaken." Josh spo[
to his people again, explaining Davy's act of selfle[

heroism, how he'd saved Find The Meadow and Little Fish.

Josh and Blue Crow exchanged a knowing look, for it was up to them what Davy's fate would be. Blue Crow nodded, and Josh answered the nod with one of his own.

Speaking to the officer but looking at Davy, he said, "This is not the man they were looking for. That man was a coward. This man is not."

Davy stared openmouthed at Josh, his gaze flicking around the circle. They were letting him go. He was being given a second chance.

He offered Josh his hand. "Thank you, Mr. Colter." Josh accepted his handshake, knowing that his trail of revenge was ended, the murderers of his sister were dead.

Alex's heart leapt with joy. She grabbed Davy and hugged him. Laughing, he lifted her up and swung her around, he was so happy. He wasn't going to waste this chance he'd been given.

The officer arched one brow in question. "So then there is no problem, is that correct?"

"That's correct," Davy agreed, grinning.

The officer straightened a bit and shifted his weight to the other foot. His saber rattled. "As to returning to the reservation—"

"They will not go. I'm telling you. There'll be another fight."

"Don't you think you should discuss it with them?" the officer prompted.

"If they wanted to be on the reservation they'd be there now, wouldn't they?"

The officer made a derisive sound in the back of his throat. "I've got my orders, Mr. Colter. Under the treaty, they have to be on the reservation."

"Captain, you seem like a reasonable man, something they don't have many of in the cavalry."

The officer smiled a little but said nothing.

Josh continued, "These people have been on the reservation. They've lived without blankets or food. They've watched their children beg for scraps. They've been lied to and cheated. They aren't asking for anything from the government. They simply want to go to Canada. They want to live the only way they know how. They want to hunt and fish and raise their children proud and free. Is that so wrong?"

"No, Mr. Colter, it isn't." He looked up at the people watching him so intently. His gaze paused on Alex and Davy before returning to Josh. "Things have not been as good as the Congress promised. I'm sick to death of agents shorting supplies or trying to pass off seconds as the government issue." He paced two steps away, then back. "I hate it, Mr. Colter. I hate seeing what's happening, but I'm powerless to do anything." He gestured broadly. "I'm only a captain, and, believe me, that's not very important in the army."

He surveyed the group again. "I wish there was some way to make those damn politicians in Washington sit up and pay attention. I wish there was some way to make them see that these are *people* they're dealing with out here, not figures on some ledger."

There was some grumbling among the soldiers, who were silenced with a hard look.

Alex looked at Finds The Meadow, Little Fish, Two Deers and the others she'd met. For the first time she saw them as victims not victimizers. She understood that while Manifest Destiny had meant new beginnings for some, it had meant the end for others.

"Thank you for that, Captain," Josh said. "But until a miracle happens, you can bet that Indians will keep leaving the reservations."

"I know." His mouth drew down in a frown.

"They won't go back."

"I know that, too."

No one spoke. Then the officer swung up in the saddle. "Mr. Colter, I regret that I will have to inform my superiors that we found no Indians."

"But—" Dobbs spoke up.

"Dobbs," the captain snarled. "If there are no Indians, then you didn't disobey a direct order and nearly start an Indian war, now did you?"

Dobbs looked grim until the realization that he was being let off the hook sank in. He straightened. "No... sir."

"That doesn't mean, however, that *most* of this company won't be on stable detail for the next month."

The captain looked back at Josh. "Tell them, if it was my family, I'd do the same damn thing. Tell them that if it was my family, I'd make a run for the border and not stop for anything. We're not the only patrol out here."

Josh translated and the Indians regarded the captain with genuine surprise. Two Deers walked over and offered his hand, which the captain shook. Then looking at Davy and Alex, he said, "We're headed south, toward Virginia City. There's a stage line there that'll take you farther south to the train at Cheyenne. Would you folks like to come with us?"

Her eyes never leaving Josh's, she said, "Yes."

"Fine." The captain gave orders. Soldiers hitched the team and in minutes they were ready.

Josh went to her. "Is this how it ends, Alex?"

"I..." Tears threatened. She wanted to throw herself in his arms, to say everything would be all right, forgotten, but she couldn't. Josh had deceived her, refused to help her. "I have to go," she said softly.

"Remember your promise."

The officer barked an order, gave a smart salute to Josh, and the column turned and rode away. Davy, driving the wagon, followed.

Josh stood there for a long time, until he couldn't see them any longer. She was gone, and inside he died.

Chapter Twenty-Five

The suite at the Willard was luxurious. A far cry from the rough and rugged existence of those weeks on the trail with Josh.

Josh.

Why was it all thoughts led back to Josh? She knew why but couldn't bring herself to say it or even think it. So here she sat, alone in her room, surrounded by silk upholstery on fine mahogany furniture and found herself longing for a rough wooden wagon seat instead.

Davy had gone to the station to buy his ticket for San Francisco. He was leaving for home in the morning.

They'd telegraphed Gunlock from Casper and were relieved when Eddie wired back that he was well recovered and more than able to get home on his own.

Alex had booked passage on the *Alicia*, sailing from Annapolis in three days for France.

Somehow, going back to Paris didn't hold the same lure it had a few months ago.

A sharp knock interrupted her musings, and before she could answer, the door swung open and in strode Davy, his gray suit making him look as handsome as ever.

"Hi, sis." He grinned ear to ear. A newspaper tucked under his arm, he tossed his hat down on the table and crossed the room to her.

"Hi, yourself," she answered with all the enthusiasm she could muster, which wasn't much.

Davy's expression sobered like a drunk confronted by the sheriff. "Aw, come on, sis, you've been moping around this room for weeks. What's wrong? You should be happy. You won the contest and Father had to fork over the matching funds he promised you." He chuckled and plopped himself down on the sofa, crossing his long legs at the ankles. "Not only that, but the paintings you did of the cavalry attack on the Indians have caused such a stir that—" He snapped opened the newspaper and held it up for her to read the headline: Congress To Investigate Corruption At Bureau Of Indian Affairs.

She looked surprised. "You can't mean this is because of me?"

"Who else?" He grinned again. "People have been lining up to see those paintings plus the others you gave the exhibit... the ones of Yellowstone. I understand there's been an offer for the one of the Grand Canyon of the Yellowstone."

"Really?" She twisted in her chair, the pale green of her dress flowing over the burgundy of the carpet.

"I ran into MacFee at the restaurant. He told me the good news. He'll be by later to discuss it with you, once he has it in writing."

"Nice." She went back to staring out the window, watching the carriages go up and down the street.

"Nice? Is that all you can say? You're an overnight sensation. People are clamoring for more western art, making offers to buy your work, and all you can say is 'nice'? Your reputation is made. Your *career* is set. You oughta be skipping around the room.''

"I don't skip."

"True," he agreed. "Maybe that's the problem. Maybe you should try skipping a bit, running, dancing, whatever it takes just to feel good."

"Like you," she snapped, and instantly regretted the words. "Oh, Davy, I'm sorry it's just that—"

He sobered. "It's okay. I deserve it and more."

She reached for him. "No, you don't. Ever since, well, ever since we got back from Montana—"

"You don't have to pussyfoot around for me, sis. I know what I was, what I did. I was a drunk and a coward, and it nearly took dying to wake me up."

"But you're all right now." She said it like a statement, but she meant it as a question. Her brother hadn't had a drink in the three weeks since they'd left Montana, which wasn't all that long, but she was optimistic.

"Yes, sis. I'm all right." He patted her hand in reassurance. He studied her for a moment then said, "You know, I owe a lot to Josh Colter."

Her head came up with snap. "Oh, yes, you owe him all right. You owe him for almost getting you hanged or shot or whatever they were going to do." She surged to her feet and began to pace the length of the room.

"I owe him for giving me the chance to finally see what I was doing, for making me face up to my responsibilities. Did I tell you that Father's gotten me a job in Senator Hallaran's Sacramento office? I decided that if I'm going to make a difference it's time I got started."

She whirled on him, one steadying hand resting on the mahogany table, the lace covering rough against her fingertips. "Davy, that's wonderful. But I still don't see, how can you be so forgiving?"

He shrugged. "There's nothing to forgive. Josh Colter had eyewitnesses that put me and two other men at the scene of a rape and murder. He didn't do anything that a lawman wouldn't have done, assuming that a lawman would be interested in the murder of an Indian woman," he added solemnly.

"He killed those other men," she prompted, remembering that he'd also killed for her, to save her.

"Yes, I know." He sat up straighter. "Truth is, he didn't have much choice now, did he? He was trying to carry out justice, one-man justice."

"You're telling me you think he was right?" She couldn't keep the incredulity out of her voice.

"I'm telling you I've had a lot of time to think about it. I'd like to believe that under the same circumstances, I'd do the same thing...especially if it was *my* sister." He met her gaze directly. "I think he's a good man, sis. I think a woman would be lucky to have him in her life."

Alex didn't move. She stood there letting the truth of Davy's words filter into her brain. Was he right? Was it that simple?

Josh hadn't done anything a lawman, an honorable man, wouldn't have done.

He had sworn his love for her; through it all, he'd never wavered. He didn't have to do that. If he had been using her, once he had his information, once he had Davy, he could have turned his back on her, but he didn't. Even in the Indian camp, he'd told her he loved her.

A smile teased the corners of her mouth. Josh Colter loved her!

Davy reached into his pocket and pulled out several papers, fanning them in his hand like playing cards. "You know the train goes right through Cheyenne and I just happen to have an extra ticket."

That smile turned into an all-out grin. "But how? I mean why?"

He shook his head in mock disappointment. "You're my sister. I know you just as well as you know me, remember? I saw the way he looked at you when we left and the way you've brooded ever since. I'd have to be blind not to know something was happening between you two."

"Was it that obvious?"

"Afraid so. Now about that ticket?"

"I can be packed in ten minutes."

Josh was in a foul mood, had been since he'd gotten home from seeing his clan safely into Canada. That was the easy part. The hard part was trying to forget her. Lord knows he'd tried. He'd tried hard. Certainly as hard as he was trying to stay on this bronc, which was determined to throw him off.

"Rake 'em, boss!" one of the hands hollered from his place on the top rail of the corral.

Josh's spurs dug into the horse's sides. The critter arched his back and left the ground like he was shot out of a cannon. Just as fast, he hit the ground on all fours like a pile driver dropped from fifty feet.

"Hell!" Josh snarled, half surprised he could speak at all after that brain-rattling jolt.

He forced his gloved hand to tighten around the thin brown leather covering the saddle horn. His arms ached like they were coming out of the sockets. Muscles in his shoulders and neck screamed in protest. And the dun just kept moving, twisting, slamming and bucking.

"Ride 'im, boss!"

"That's gettin' her done!"

The men shouted from their places on the top rail.

Josh hit the ground with a rib-cracking thud that left him seeing stars.

"Son of a bitch." He shook his head to clear the fog. He scrambled to his feet and flexed his arms just to make sure everything still worked.

Josh retrieved his hat, slapped it on his chaps-covered thigh, then clamped it firmly on his head. Throat-clogging dust swirled around him, churned up by the horse's pawing.

Josh eyed the stallion, who seemed to be eyeing him right back. Josh was tired and dirty and feeling more than a little mean. He was trying to work off excess energy—he was trying to forget, and getting his brains rattled seemed as good a way as any.

Trouble was, he wasn't having much luck with either, the horse or the forgetting.

Spurs jingling, he walked over to the horse. Grabbing the reins in one hand, and without using the stirrups, he swung up in the saddle.

The horse screamed in defiance. He reared, and Josh promptly hit the ground again, this time slamming his shoulder into the corral fence in the process.

He rolled to his feet and glared at the horse. "I'll turn you into stew meat!"

With the hands' help, they cornered the horse. Josh grabbed a handful of mane and swung up once more. This time it was a fight to the finish. Josh dug in and hung on. He wasn't a man who liked losing—in anything.

The dun bucked and twirled. Josh gritted his teeth so hard the pain radiated down his neck, but he wouldn't give in, not this time.

After ten minutes that seemed like ten hours, he'd worn the stubborn animal down to a standstill.

The ranch hands were both wide-eyed at the sight.

Slowly, more than a little stiff, Josh dismounted and tossed the reins to Ralph. "Cool him down, then turn him in with the others."

"Okay, boss," Ralph confirmed.

Josh headed for the horse trough and the cool water that waited there. He stripped off his shirt and tried splashing water on his face, neck and chest. It was too little, too late. Ah, what the hell. He bent over and dunked his head and shoulders in the water.

Standing straight again, he wiped the water from his face with the palms of his hands and shook his head, sending water spraying in all directions.

As he wiped his face once more, he glanced up at the afternoon sky. Four, he figured. Where was she now? Was she still in Washington or had she returned to Paris?

No matter what he did or where he went, she was there, on his mind. He'd promised himself he wasn't going after her. He'd told her how he felt. He'd told her loved her. He'd never told any other woman that because he'd never been in love before.

He wasn't going after her. A man had his pride, didn't he? *Yeah, Colter, and what's pride gotten you, except sleepless nights and a grim future?*

Grabbing up his shirt, he used it like a towel on his neck while he headed for the house. As he walked, his spurs left furrows in the dirt, and with each step he got angrier.

She had no right to leave him. She was his. It was clear that destiny had brought them together. Lord knows there was no other way they could have fallen in love. They had everything going against them, and still he loved her and she, damn the stubborn woman, she loved him, too, he just knew. He knew women, and no woman gives herself to a man like that without loving him.

Maybe he should go tell her, demand that she listen to him, that she—oh, hell, who was he kidding?

He was halfway through the parlor when he heard the sounds of a buckboard pulling into the front yard. He tossed his wet shirt over the chair and headed for the door. He was in no mood for company.

He recognized Harry Lindon from the livery stable and next to Harry was a woman who looked like . . .

He stilled, one hand braced on the open screen door, and squinted against the afternoon sun. She turned toward him.

"Alex?" It was a breathy prayer.

She started up the walk.

"Alex?" he said again, afraid to move, afraid it was a dream and if it was, he didn't want to wake.

"Hello, Josh."

What she was doing here he didn't know, but he did know that, as happy as he was, he was also afraid, afraid he wouldn't survive the pain of watching her leave him again.

"This is a surprise." He kept his expression schooled, his voice flat. Inside, his heart was racing and his breathing came in awkward snatches.

"I came to see you."

Her voice brushed over him like a summer's caress. She strode right up to him, stopping so close he had to look down into her beautiful upturned face. Eyes like the bluest sky, he thought, steeling himself against the sudden surge of desire.

"Why?" he asked, then thought, *I want you so much it's killing me.*

"I was wrong," she said softly, then reached up to cup his face with her hand. "Wrong about you. Wrong about us."

He didn't move. His mouth pulled down in a frown. Muscles along his shoulders tensed and ached with wanting her. She was so close.

"Why the change? What about Davy?"

"I see that you were only doing what you thought was right, what no one else would do. Davy said he would have done no less for *his* sister."

"Davy, huh?"

She traced his frown with the pad of her thumb while she looked at him with warm, liquid eyes.

"I've missed you. I was hoping that you'd missed me."

His mouth went dry. His heart took on a hard, steady rhythm in his chest. "Miss you? I haven't thought about anything or anyone else since . . . well, since we met."

"I'm glad."

Then she did something he was totally unprepared for. She lifted up on her toes and kissed his lips.

He curled his hands into fists at his side. She wasn't doing this to him, not again. Not this time. He didn't know what her game was, what kind of perverse punishment this was supposed to be, but he'd be damned if he was going along.

When he didn't return the kiss, she hesitated. "Don't you want me?"

"Oh, I want you, make no mistake about that."

"And I want you."

"Just like that?"

"Just like that."

It took a full ten seconds for the words to sink into his brain. Another ten seconds for him to realize that she was serious. At least he thought she was serious. She'd better be serious.

So, by way of a warning, he said, "Woman, I'm in no mood to play games. If you touch me again...if I touch you, I want you to know, I'm never letting you go."

She smiled coyly up into his face. "I'm here, aren't I?"

"What about Paris? What about your art?"

"I don't need Paris," she answered, not telling him she'd won the contest. She knew the only prize she wanted was him. "I *need* you."

The breeze ruffled his hair and it fell along his cheek. She brushed it back and he turned his face more fully into her hand, kissing her palm, sending delicious shivers up her arm. Their eyes met and held. "You see," she said on a thready whisper, "I'm planning another trip to Yellowstone and...I might need some...inspiration. Are you available?"

What are you waiting for? The woman is standing here saying she needs you. What the hell are you waiting for?

Damned if he knew.

In one motion he pulled her to him, her body pressed to his, length to length. His hungry mouth claimed hers, tasting, testing, claiming. She returned the kiss fully, eagerly.

When, at last, he lifted his head, he smiled, grinned from ear to ear. "Honey, I'll take you to the dark side of the moon, if that's what you want, only never leave me again."

"I won't."

He imprisoned her face in his hands. "Marry me?" It wasn't a question, but an order. One she'd gladly obey. She loved Josh as she would no other man. Fleetingly, she thought her father had gotten what he wanted, after all. She didn't care. She had everything she wanted, right here in her arms.

Laughing, her arms around his neck, she said, "I love you, Josh."

"Is that a yes?"

"Yes." She beamed. "Yes!"

"I love you, Alex."

He smiled and kissed her again.

*   *   *   *   *

IT'S THAT TIME OF YEAR AGAIN!

launches its
1997 **March Madness** celebration
with **four** of the brightest new stars
in historical romance.

We proudly present:

THE PHOENIX OF LOVE by Susan Schonberg
A reformed rake strikes sparks with a ravishing Ice Queen

HEART OF THE DRAGON by Sharon Schulze
A fierce warrior forsakes his heritage for a noblewoman on the run

EMILY'S CAPTAIN by Shari Anton
A Southern belle is ensnared by a dashing Union spy

THE WICKED TRUTH by Lyn Stone
A dauntless physician falls victim to the charms
of a beautiful murder suspect

4 new books from 4 terrific new authors.
Look for them wherever
Harlequin Historicals are sold.

You are cordially invited to a

HOMETOWN REUNION

September 1996—August 1997

Bad boys, cowboys, babies. Feuding families,
arson, mistaken identity, a mom on the run...
Where can you find romance and adventure?
Tyler, Wisconsin, that's where!

So join us in this not-so-sleepy little town and
experience the love, the laughter and the
tears of those who call it home.

WELCOME TO A
HOMETOWN REUNION

Gabe Atwood has no sooner rescued his wife,
Raine, from a burning building when there's
more talk of fires. Rumor has it that Clint
Stanford suspects Jon Weiss, the new kid at
school, of burning down the Ingallses' factory.
And that Marina, Jon's mother, has kindled a fire
in Clint that may be affecting his judgment. Don't
miss Kristine Rolofson's *A Touch of Texas,*
the seventh in a series you won't want to end....

Available in March 1997
at your favorite retail store.

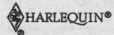

HARLEQUIN®

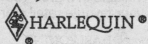

From the bestselling author of *Scandalous*

CANDACE CAMP

Cam Monroe vowed revenge when
Angela Stanhope's family accused him
of a crime he didn't commit.

Fifteen years later he returns from exile, wealthy
and powerful, to demand Angela's hand in marriage.
It is then that the strange "accidents" begin. Are the
Stanhopes trying to remove him from their lives
one last time, or is there a more insidious,
mysterious explanation?

Impulse

Available this March at your favorite retail outlet.

MIRA The brightest star in women's fiction   MCCI

Look us up on-line at: http://www.romance.net

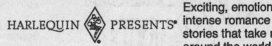

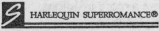